Julia James lives verdant countryside and the wild shores of Cornwall. She also loves the Mediterranean—so rich in myth and history, with its sunbaked landscapes and olive groves, ancient ruins and azure seas. 'The perfect setting for romance!' she says. 'Rivalled only by the lush tropical heat of the Caribbean—palms swaying by a silver sand beach lapped by turquoise water… What more could lovers want?'

USA TODAY bestselling author **Jennie Lucas**'s parents owned a bookstore, so she grew up surrounded by books, dreaming about faraway lands. A fourth-generation Westerner, she went east at sixteen to boarding school on a scholarship, wandered the world, got married, then finally worked her way through college before happily returning to her hometown. A 2010 RITA® Award finalist and 2005 Golden Heart® Award winner, she lives in Idaho with her husband and children.

THE GREEK'S DUTY-BOUND ROYAL BRIDE

JULIA JAMES

HER BOSS'S ONE-NIGHT BABY

JENNIE LUCAS

MILLS & BOON

First Published in Great Britain 2020
by Mills & Boon, an imprint of HarperCollins*Publishers*
1 London Bridge Street, London, SE1 9GF

The Greek's Duty-Bound Royal Bride © 2020 by Julia James

Her Boss's One-Night Baby © 2020 by Jennie Lucas

ISBN: 978-0-263-27807-1

MIX
Paper from
responsible sources
FSC® C007454

This book is produced from independently certified FSC™ paper
to ensure responsible forest management.
For more information visit www.harpercollins.co.uk/green.

Printed and bound in Spain
by CPI, Barcelona

THE GREEK'S DUTY-BOUND ROYAL BRIDE

JULIA JAMES

For Ilona—and the cultural heritage you gave me.

CHAPTER ONE

Leon Dukaris glanced at the invoice on his desk and then, with an indifferent shrug of one broad shoulder, initialled the hefty sum for payment.

The Viscari St James was one of London's most expensive and exclusive hotels, and the coup that had ejected Mikal of Karylya from his Grand Duchy in the heart of central Europe had happened with lightning speed less than two weeks ago, so it was not surprising that the Grand Duke was finding it difficult to adjust his royal lifestyle to that of impoverished former ruler, with none of the wealth of his small but highly prosperous fiefdom at his disposal any longer.

It was a difficulty that suited Leon—bankrolling the Grand Duke's exile was not largesse on his part in the slightest. He gave a tight smile, accentuating the strong planes of his face and indenting the deep lines around his well-shaped mouth, sharpening the gold flecks in his eyes. It was, rather, an investment.

One that he fully intended to pay out handsomely.

His eyes darkened. Suddenly he was not seeing the expensively furnished office, towering over the City of London far below, the private domain of a billionaire and his working environment. His vision went way beyond that— way back into the past. The bitter, impoverished past...

The line for the soup kitchen in the bleak Athens winter, holes in the soles of his shoes, shivering in the cold, queu-

*ing for hot food to take back to the cramped lodging where
he and his mother had to live now they'd been evicted from
their spacious apartment for non-payment of rent. He is all
his mother has now—the husband who professed to love
her for all eternity has run out on her, abandoning her and
him, their young teenage son, to the worst that the collapse
of the Greek economy in the great recession over a dozen
years ago can do to them...*

And the worst had been bad—*very* bad—leaving them
in an abject poverty that Leon had vowed he would escape,
however long it took him.

And he had escaped. His success, doggedly pursued,
his focus on nothing else, had lifted him rung by rung up
the ladder of financial success. He had taken risks that
had always paid off, even if he'd had to steel his nerves
with every speculative gamble he pulled off. It had been
a relentless pursuit of wealth that had seen him become a
financial speculator *extraordinaire*, spotting multi-mil-
lion-euro opportunities before others did and seizing them,
each one taking him further up into the stratosphere of bil-
lionairedom.

But now he wanted his money to achieve something else
for him. His smile widened into a tight line of satisfaction.
Something that had now come within his reach, thanks to
the coup in Karylya that had ousted its sovereign.

The gold glint in Leon's night-dark eyes came again at
the thought. A princess bride to set the seal on his dizzying ascent from the lines for the soup kitchen.

Grand Duke Mikal's daughter.

'Ellie! There is news about your father! Bad news!'

In her head, Ellie could hear the alarm in her mother's
voice, echoing still as she emerged from the tube station
at Piccadilly Circus, hurrying down St James's and into
the Hotel Viscari.

A stone's throw from St James's Palace, Clarence House and Buckingham Palace itself, it was often frequented by diplomats, foreign politicians and even visiting royalty.

Including deposed visiting royalty.

Deposed.

The word rang chill in Ellie's head and she felt her stomach clench. The coup causing her father and his family to flee their fairy-tale palace in Karylya had turned the Grand Duke into nothing more than a former sovereign in exile. Ellie's glance swept the Edwardian opulence of the Viscari's marbled lobby. Albeit a very luxurious exile...

She hastened up to the reception desk. 'Grand Duke Mikal's suite, please!' she exclaimed, breathless from hurrying and agitation.

'Whom shall I say?' asked the receptionist, lifting her phone.

She sounded doubtful, and Ellie could understand why. Her work-day outfit, crumpled from an overnight transatlantic flight, was more suited to the life she lived in rural Somerset with her mother and stepfather, where she had been since an infant, than to someone who had an entrée to a royal suite at a deluxe London hotel.

'Just say Lisi!' she replied, giving the Karylyan diminutive of her name.

Moments later the receptionist's attitude had changed and she was briskly summoning a bellhop. 'Escort Her Highness to the Royal Suite,' she instructed.

As she sped upwards in the elevator Ellie wished her identity had not been guessed—she never used her title anywhere outside Karylya, except on rare state occasions with her father. Instead she used the English diminutive and her British stepfather's surname—the name on her passport. Ellie Peters. It made life a lot simpler. And it was also considerably shorter than her patronym.

Elizsaveta Gisella Carolinya Augusta Feoderova Alexandreina Zsofia Turmburg-Malavic Karpardy.

She must have been named after every single aunt, grandmother and other female member of every European royal house her father claimed kin with!

From Hapsburgs to Romanovs, and any number of German royal houses, not to mention Polish, Hungarian and Lithuanian ones, and even an Ottoman or two thrown in somewhere for good measure, the nine-hundred-year-old dynasty had somehow, by luck, determination, shrewd alliances and even shrewder marriages, clung on to the mountain fastness that was the Grand Duchy of Karylya, with its high snow-capped peaks and deep verdant valleys, its dark pine forests and rushing rivers, glacial lakes and modern ski slopes.

Except now—Ellie felt her stomach clench in dismay and disbelief at the news her mother had announced—that nine-hundred-year possession had suddenly, devastatingly, come to an end…

The elevator's polished doors slid open as the car came to a halt and Ellie stepped out into the quiet, deserted lobby of this exclusive floor of suites and residences. One of the doors opposite was flung open and a figure came hurtling through, embracing her as she hurried forward.

'Oh, Lisi, thank heavens you are here!'

It was her younger sister, Marika—her half-sister, actually, one of her two half-siblings, offspring of her father and his second wife. Although Marika was here with her parents, Ellie knew from the fractured phone call she'd made from the airport that her younger brother, Niki, her father's heir—his *former* heir, she realised now, with a start of dismayed realisation—was still at school in Switzerland, in the throes of critically important university entrance exams.

How he had taken the grim news Ellie didn't know—

but Marika, as was clear from her heartfelt cry now, was not coping well.

'I can't believe this has happened!' she heard herself cry back, answering her sister in the Karylyan Marika had used.

'It's like a nightmare!' Marika said, drawing Ellie into the suite.

'How is Papa?' Ellie asked, her voice sombre.

'Shell-shocked. He can't take it in. No more can Mutti—' Marika gave a shuddering sigh. 'Come on…come in. Papa's been waiting and waiting for you.'

Ellie hurried forward into the spacious reception room beyond the suite's hallway. Absently, she took in the luxury of the place—though, of course, compared with the palace it was nothing at all…

Inside, she saw the room was crowded—her father, his wife the Grand Duchess, and several of the palace staff were there. Her father was standing immobile by the plate glass window that opened on to a private terrace, staring out over the rooftops. He turned as Ellie came in, and instinctively she rushed to hug him.

A sharp voice stilled her. '*Elizsaveta!* You forget yourself!'

It was the Grand Duchess, her stepmother, admonishing her. Realising what she was being called to do, she took a breath, dropping an awkward curtsy in her knee-length skirt. But as she did so she felt her stomach hollowing. Her father was no longer a reigning sovereign…

He came forward now, to take her hands and press them in his cold ones. 'You finally came,' he said. There was both relief and a tinge of criticism in his tone.

Ellie swallowed. 'I'm sorry, Papa—we were in Canada…far in the north. Filming with Malcolm. Communication was difficult, we were so remote, and then I had to get back here and—'

She stopped. In the disaster that had befallen him her father would hardly be concerned about her mother and her stepfather, a distinguished wildlife documentary film-maker, whose work took him all over the world and for whom her mother had left her royal husband when Ellie had been only a baby.

'Well, you are here now, thankfully,' her father said, his voice warmer. Then he turned to one of the nearby members of staff. 'Josef—refreshments!' he commanded.

Ellie bit her lip. She'd always believed her father's stiffly imperious manner had contributed to his growing unpopularity in Karylya. And her unspoken thoughts had been echoed in all the political analyses she had read since the news had broken, giving the reasons for the coup.

That and his intransigent refusal to entertain any degree of constitutional, fiscal or social reform in order to defuse the potentially toxic and historically fraught ethnic mix of the population, whose internecine rivalries had always required careful and constant balancing against each other to prevent any one minority feeling slighted and ignored.

Ellie sighed inwardly. The trouble was her father lacked the astute political management skills and charismatic, outgoing personality of his own father. Grand Duke Nikolai had successfully steered Karylya through the diplomatic minefield of the Iron Curtain decades, maintaining the duchy's precarious independence against huge foreign pressures and gaining the great prosperity the duchy now enjoyed. Her father's reserve and awkwardness had, in the ten years of his reign, only managed to alienate every faction—even those traditionally most supportive of him.

Which had left none to support him when the coup, led from the High Council by the leader of the ethnic faction with the strongest perceived grievances, had erupted.

Now her father and his Grand Duchess were harbouring a deep and, she allowed, understandable anger and resentment at their fate. It was evident in their condemnation of all who had contributed to their ignominious flight. For her part, Ellie merely murmured sympathetically—it was obvious her father and stepmother needed to vent their understandably strong emotions. More rational discussion could take place later—she hoped. And all the awkward questions could be asked later, too.

Finally taking refuge in Marika's bedroom, Ellie asked the question which was most concerning her, which she could not possibly have asked in front of any member of the remaining royal staff, however loyal they were.

'Marika, what's happening about Papa's finances? What has the new government agreed to? It must have been quite a generous settlement...' She glanced around her at the luxuriously appointed bedroom. 'This place doesn't come cheap, that's for sure!'

But her sister was looking at her with an expression that struck a chill through her. And her features were strained.

'Papa isn't paying for this hotel, Lisi! He can't afford it—oh, Lisi, he can't afford anything at all! We're completely penniless!'

The blood drained from Ellie's face. 'Penniless?' she echoed in a hollow voice.

Her sister nodded, her features still contorted. 'He's been told by the new head of government that he won't get any kind of financial settlement at all, and that all the royal assets have been frozen!'

'*Nothing?*' Ellie gasped disbelievingly. Then her eyes went around the luxuriously appointed bedroom again. 'But...but this place...? You've been here nearly a fortnight already...'

Consternation was flooding through her as Marika's expression changed. Now awkwardness was vivid in her pretty features.

'Like I said, Lisi… Papa isn't paying for this suite—someone else is.'

Ellie stared, dismay filling her like cold water. 'But *who*?' she demanded.

Marika's answer was fractured and disjointed. 'He's called Leon—Leon Dukaris—and he's a billionaire—Greek. He was in Karylya last summer, on business. He came to the summer opera gala that Mutti is patroness for. He was introduced to us—and Papa invited him to a garden party at the palace. Then he came to a reception and a dinner, too—I didn't really pay any attention. It was a business affair with some of the ministers and other foreign investors. He was mostly talking to them and Papa. I… I don't really know much more, except that when we arrived in London he got in touch with Papa and told him he would underwrite our expenses…'

Ellie was still staring. 'But *why*? Why should this…this Leon Dukaris care about Papa? Let alone fork out for this place! If he wants to do business in Karylya it's not Papa he should be making up to,' she finished bitterly.

A tide of colour washed up her sister's face, and something about Marika's expression curdled Ellie's blood.

'Marika, what is it?' she asked urgently.

Her sister was twisting her hands, a look of anguish in her face. 'Oh, God, Lisi—there's only one reason he's paying for everything! He wants…' She swallowed. 'He wants to marry me!'

Ellie's eyes widened in total disbelief. '*Marry* you? You can't be serious!'

'He's making it obvious!' Marika cried. 'He's been here several times, always very attentive to me. Way more than just being polite! I do my best to put him off, but I know Mutti is hoping I'll encourage him. She's worried sick about what's going to happen to us now, and if he really wants to marry me—'

She broke off, her voice choking. Ellie's dismay doubled. It was bad enough learning that her father was penniless, and that he was being bankrolled by some unknown Greek billionaire…but that her sister should believe the Greek billionaire wanted to *marry* her…?

Surely Marika was imagining it? Upset and overwrought as she so obviously was right now by the disaster that had befallen their family?

In a macabre attempt at humour, at a time when humour was absolutely impossible, Ellie heard herself blurt out, 'Just please don't tell me that this Leon Dukaris is some creepy, lecherous old man with a fat gut and piggy eyes!'

'No, not exactly,' Marika answered in a shaky voice. But then her eyes welled with tears. 'Oh, Lisi, it doesn't matter what he looks like or who he is!' Her tears spilled over into open weeping. 'I'm in love with someone else!' she cried. 'So I can't marry Leon Dukaris! I just *can't*!'

Leon vaulted from his limo, now drawn up in the entrance sweep of the Viscari St James, and strode into the lobby. It was time to visit the royal family again.

He had called upon the Grand Duke several times since his abrupt arrival in London two weeks ago—ostensibly to give him his assurance that all his expenses would be underwritten by himself for the duration of his stay, until such time as he had decided where to live out his exile and do whatever it was that former monarchs did when their countries no longer wanted them. But the real reason for his visits was quite different.

He was trying to decide whether he was truly going to go ahead with claiming a princess for his bride—the ultimate prize.

Thoughts played across his mind as the elevator doors to the penthouse floor slid shut. Was he simply being fanciful in even giving house room to the idea? It had come to him the previous summer, when he had been visiting Karylya on business, being invited to the palace, socialising with the royal family, meeting Princess Marika…

At the time he had given it no serious thought, but the idea had grown on him during the intervening months. The girl, though a brunette, and quiet in her manner, was very pretty, and if his own tastes actually ran to blondes—well, for the sake of a princess bride surely he could change his tastes…

Nor was she unintelligent, from what he could judge of her, and that was another key advantage. His features hardened momentarily. So was the crucial fact that, as a princess, she'd be perfectly open to the idea of marrying for practical reasons. Love—his mouth tightened—would not get to taint their marriage…

He snapped his mind away from his darkening thoughts. No, there was nothing to rule Princess Marika out of his consideration…and now that events had taken such a disastrous turn for the Karylyan royal family, from the princess's point of view—and her parents'—there was every incentive for her to consider his proposal seriously.

If he were to make one, of course…

But should I?

That his suit would be favoured by her parents was obvious—what could be more desirable than a very wealthy son-in-law to keep on bankrolling their exile indefinitely? As for the princess herself… He knew without vanity that he was highly attractive to women—his life, even while he had still been in the process of making his huge fortune, had been filled with eager females demonstrating that undeniable fact to him. Now, in his thirties, he was done playing the field. He would be perfectly happy to settle down with one agreeable female and he would make the princess a good husband.

And theirs would be an honest marriage. He wouldn't

delude and deceive his bride with hypocritical declarations of undying love and endless mouthing of romantic flummery that meant nothing when the chips were down.

Leon's dark eyes hardened with harsh memory. His father had made such endless declarations—Leon had grown up hearing him telling his mother how devoted he was to her, how much he loved her, how she meant the world to him, how she was the moon and the stars and all the other romantic verbiage he had lavished upon her.

It had counted for *nothing*.

When the Greek economy had crashed his father had taken off with another woman—conveniently wealthy—leaving his heartbroken wife and his teenage son to cope on their own. Abandoning them totally.

His mother had been devastated by the betrayal—Leon had been only angry. Deeply, bitterly angry. And contemptuous of the man who had abandoned them.

I will never be like him—never! I will never do to a woman what my father did to my mother! Because I will never tell a woman I love her. Because I will never fall in love. Because love doesn't exist—only meaningless words that lie...and destroy.

The elevator glided to a halt, the doors sliding open, and Leon shook his dark memories from him. The miseries of his teenage years were gone and he would not be haunted by them. He had made his life on his own terms—and those were the terms he would make any marriage on. Terms that would never include what did not exist—would never include love...

His wife, when he married—whoever she was, princess or not—would get respect, regard, friendship and companionship.

And, of course, desire. That went without saying...

It was a word he should not have admitted into his thoughts at that moment. Because as he strode out of the elevator the door to the royal suite opened and a woman emerged.

Instinctively his eyes took her in, in one comprehensive sweep.

Tall, blonde, slender, with grey-blue eyes and her hair caught back in a ponytail. Not wearing any make-up. Her clothes non-descript—certainly not couture or designer. Yet that didn't matter in the least. Because she was, without doubt, breathtakingly, stunningly beautiful... Instantly desirable.

He felt a rush of adrenaline quicken in his bloodstream. *Who is she?*

He had never seen her before—no woman that stunning would have escaped his eye.

He realised she was gazing at him, stopped in her tracks just as he was. For a moment—an enjoyably adrenaline-fuelled moment—Leon allowed himself the pleasure of meeting her gaze full-on, letting her see just how pleasurable it was for him to look at her...

Then, abruptly, her eyes peeled away from his and he saw colour flare across her high-cut cheekbones. Dipping her head, she hurried forward, veering around him to dive into the waiting elevator behind him. He gave a low laugh. Whoever she was, if she had joined the entourage of the Grand Duke, in whatever capacity, he would at some point see her again. And that would suit him very well...

His thoughts cut out. Realisation slammed into him. Hell, no, it would *not* suit him to see the breathtaking blonde again!

Taking an incised breath, he strode forward again, heading for the door of the royal suite. The breathtaking blonde, whoever she was, could be no concern of his. He had a princess to woo...

CHAPTER TWO

ELLIE SLUMPED BACK against the wall of the elevator car, feeling weak. Her heart was thumping like a sledgehammer. *Oh, sweet heaven, what had just happened?*

She had issued from her father's suite and, without the slightest warning that it was about to happen, had all but rushed right into the most devastating male she had ever set eyes on in her life…

Talk about tall, dark and handsome!

She felt weakness flush through her again, her heart-rate quicken. It had lasted only a handful of moments—a silent gasp from her, a sweep of night-dark eyes. That was all she'd needed to take in his Savile-Row-tailoring, his six-foot-plus height, broad shoulders and lean hips, his planed features… And those night-dark eyes, looking her over, liking what he was seeing, making no secret of it.

She shook her head angrily, as if to dissipate the afterburn on her retinas. Oh, what did it matter who that man had been? She had far more important things to think about.

Disbelief was still uppermost—surely her sister was just imagining what she'd told her? That some unknown Greek billionaire thought he could marry her? It was outrageous—just outrageous!

She's upset, that's all. Upset, shocked and distraught after what has happened.

And then she remembered what Marika had gone on to say.

'*I'm in love with someone else!*'

Ellie heard her sister's tearful voice as the elevator plummeted to ground level. And when she'd learned just who it was that Marika was in love with, her heart had sunk yet further.

A man Marika's parents would never allow her to marry…

Leon was bowing over the Grand Duchess's regally outstretched hand.

'Herr Dukaris.' She smiled with an air of stately graciousness, her Germanic accent courtesy of her long lineage of Austrian aristocracy.

'Highness…' Leon intoned dutifully, having already made a brief bow to the Grand Duke.

He himself did not stand on ceremony, but what was the point of paying the exorbitant bills of European royalty if he did not acknowledge royal protocol? After all, either they were royal, and marrying into their family would set the glittering seal on his worldly success, or they were simply penniless refugees in a turbulent world, seeking a new life in a less troubled spot.

His eyes went to the royal couple's daughter. She looked drawn and anxious, and Leon could understand why. Two weeks ago she'd been a princess in a fairy-tale castle in a fairy-tale realm—now she was just a penniless young woman with no prospects other than those an accident of birth had conferred upon her.

Well, if he did marry her, her fortunes would be restored and she would smile again.

He let his gaze rest on the princess with a warmth he hoped she might find encouraging. She was, he acknowledged, very attractive in her own way, with soft features and dark eyes, dark hair and a tender mouth. Yet before he could stop himself memory flashed in his head of that fleeting encounter just now in the penthouse lobby. Now, if that stunning blonde had been the woman now sitting beside the graciously smiling Grand Duchess…

He tore his inappropriate thoughts away again, warming his smile for Princess Marika. But she remained stubbornly woebegone, as if his smiling alarmed her. He gave an inward frown. But then the Grand Duke was relating, with understandable *schadenfreude*, how the new regime in his homeland was having difficulty getting endorsement from other governments.

'Perhaps when there has been an election, as promised?' Leon ventured.

It was the wrong thing to say.

A snort came from the Grand Duke. 'A stage-managed, propaganda-fuelled plebiscite in order to elect a dictator! That's all it will be!'

Leon made no reply. Like too many small countries in that highly volatile area of Europe, Karylya was a complicated cocktail of historic rivalries that still ran deep, despite the duchy's new prosperity as a financial hub for the emerging economies of the former Eastern Bloc. 'The Luxembourg of Central Europe'—that was the way the country was usually described, which was why he'd visited the place last summer.

And thereby made the personal acquaintance of the royal family and the princess…

His eyes rested on her now, their expression veiled, his thoughts inward. Was he seriously thinking of marrying Princess Marika?

Again the image of that breathtaking blonde out in the lobby fleeted across his consciousness. How could he be considering marriage to one woman if he was still capable of having his attention caught by another one?

Wariness filled him suddenly. Though he would never

declare love for a woman, he would never be disloyal to any woman he married. Not like his despised father.

Where his father was now, he had no idea—and he did not want to know. His boyish idealisation of his father, his wanting only to grow up like him, had crashed and burnt to ashes the day he'd deserted him and his mother. His father had put his own selfish interests first, abandoning his heartbroken wife, making a mockery of all those endless romantic declarations of eternal love—and abandoning his own son, betraying his paternal responsibility towards him. Thinking only of himself.

He dragged his thoughts back to the present. Whatever he decided to do now, he must not, out of decency, lead the princess or her parents to hope he would offer for her and then not.

I have to decide.

But to decide meant getting to know her better—and that, after all, was what he was doing here in the Grand Duke's suite.

'I was wondering, Highness,' he said now, addressing Princess Marika's mother, 'knowing your love of the opera, whether you might permit me to invite you to Covent Garden tonight? It is very short notice, and I apologise, but Torelli is to sing *Turandot*—and I recall from last summer that you hold her in some admiration.'

'Turandot!' exclaimed the Grand Duchess promptly. She bestowed her gracious smile upon Leon. 'How very kind. It will help to divert my daughter at this distressing time—will it not, Marika?'

The princess managed a smile, albeit a wan one.

'Then I will make the arrangements,' Leon said.

He would hardly get Princess Marika to himself, but it would be a start, and being seen conspicuously in public with the Karylyan royal family would begin the process of associating himself with them. And, of course, he added cynically, them with him.

Satisfied, he took his leave. Only as he headed back towards the elevator did he find himself wondering, yet again, just who that breathtaking blonde had been. And trying not to wonder whether he would ever see her again. Trying not to *want* to see her again…

Sternly he admonished himself.

I'm here to marry a princess—not have my head turned by another woman!

Like it or not, he had better remember that.

Ellie was hurrying again—this time into the foyer of Covent Garden's Royal Opera House. It was difficult in high heels and a full-length gown. Unlike her mother, who relished no longer having to meet the formal dress codes required of her when she had been Grand Duchess, Ellie's stepmother had insisted on evening dress tonight.

'It was quite bad enough you arriving the way you did, dressed like some sort of servant! It's out of the question that you should not remember your position from now on. Especially now.'

The Grand Duchess had said no more, but Ellie had got the message.

Especially now that her father had been deposed and sent into exile…

Well, she'd done her best this evening, but her couture wardrobe had not made it out of Karylya with her father, and all she'd had on hand at Malcolm's London flat was the outfit she'd worn to the last TV awards bash she'd attended with her mother and stepfather.

Much to Ellie's relief, her father had agreed she could stay there, since the suite at the Viscari was already crowded, and it would have required taking yet another room, running up yet another hefty bill.

The pale blue evening gown was perfectly respectable, but it was not couture, and since her Karylyan jewellery had also not made it out of the duchy and into exile, she was wearing only a pearl necklace of her mother's. She'd dressed her hair simply, applied her make-up likewise, and she knew perfectly well that no one would take her for a princess just by looking at her.

No more than that man did in the penthouse lobby.

She pushed the memory out of her head. Pointless to remember it—pointless to think about the man. Even more pointless to remember her inability to tear her eyes from him… No, it was far more important to focus on this evening.

Marika's text had elaborated on her stepmother's summons.

Lisi—you must come! Leon Dukaris will be there. Please, please, please try and keep him away from me!

Ellie's expression grew grimmer as she gained the almost deserted lobby. The performance was about to begin. She would do her very best to keep Marika's unwanted suitor from her, but her thoughts were troubled all the same as she was hurriedly shown up to the Dress Circle. For all that the man her sister had fallen in love with was someone utterly impossible for her to marry, Ellie had nothing but sympathy for Marika.

Of course Marika wanted only to marry for love!

Just as I do—and always have done!

In this day and age, after all, even a princess was allowed to believe in marrying for love…

Her face clouded. It was all very well believing that, and all very well trying to protect her sister from an unwanted suitor—but this unknown billionaire was all that stood between her father and penury. It was a sobering and unwelcome thought…

The house lights were already dimming as she was shown into the box reserved for them, and as they dimmed she made out the regal figures of her father and stepmother, already seated, another masculine figure silhouetted beside them, and beside him the slight figure of her sister.

Marika turned a grateful glance on Ellie as she hurriedly sketched a cursory curtsy to the Grand Duchess, who had thrown her an admonitory stare at her late arrival, before sitting down on the nearest chair, just behind her sister.

Busying herself with easing her skirts as she sat down, she dipped her head to smooth the fabric, missing the turning of the head of the masculine figure beside her sister until she raised her eyes, just as the conductor lifted his baton and the curtain rose on the opening scene of *Turandot*. But as she did so Ellie froze. The breath stilled in her lungs and her lips parted in shock.

The man who'd turned his head to see who was arriving so late was the same man who'd been crossing the penthouse suite lobby that afternoon. The man she had not been able to tear her eyes from.

She gave an audible gasp—she was sure of it—and for the slightest second it seemed she met that dark gaze again, head-on. Then, still in shock, she twisted her head so that her eyes were doggedly on the stage below. But she was sure that colour had run up into her cheeks and her heartbeat had grown ragged—and not just from the rush of getting here!

This was the unknown Greek—the nouveau riche billionaire bankrolling her father and setting his sights on her sister?

Her own words to Marika that morning replayed in her

head now, as the opening scene of the opera got underway
below her.

Old, fat and piggy-eyed...

She wanted to give a semi-hysterical choke—dear Lord,
she couldn't have been further from the truth!

What had Marika said? She racked her brain to recall
her sister's reply to her dismayed exclamation.

'Not exactly...'

The hysterical flutter came again—no, *definitely* 'not
exactly'!

In fact, he was whatever was the total and absolute opposite of her scathing description.

She felt a rush go through her that was nothing to do
with her hurried arrival and everything to do with the man
sitting just in front of her. Her heart thumping in her chest,
she thanked heaven she had the duration of the first act of
the opera to recover her composure. Time, more impor-
tantly, to dwell on what Marika had told her.

*It doesn't matter that he's like every woman's fantasy
male—he can't seriously think he can marry Marika just
like that! She must be imagining it—she must!*

But then why was Leon Dukaris bothering to pick up the
sky-high tab for her father's hotel bill? What did he think
was in it for him by doing so?

Cold chilled through her veins. Her eyes rested on him
now—on the broad back, the well-shaped head silhouetted
against the bright lights of the stage, where the main char-
acters were singing their hearts out, completely ignored by
her right now, for there was a drama going on right here
in this box that outweighed anything going on down there
on the stage...

She could see he'd crossed one long leg over the other,
in a kind of negligent pose, and from her angle behind him
she could make out half his profile. Apparently he was fo-

cused on the stage, but she fancied he was not particularly riveted by the scene or the singing.

She could see a square-palmed hand resting on one powerful thigh, the other laxly holding a programme. There was something about the way he was sitting that made her realise his body was very slightly inclined towards her sister, as if to indicate a nascent intimacy with her, making himself at ease in her body space.

An ease that was being entirely repudiated by her sister.

Marika was, Ellie could see, sitting ramrod-straight, tension in every line of her slight body. With a tightening of her mouth, she dragged her eyes away from her sister and the man beside her, back down on to the stage—where, she realised with a belated start of realisation, a princess was vowing never to marry and her unwanted suitor was determined she should do just that...

It mustn't happen—it just mustn't!

The words formed in Ellie's head and it was not the drama on the stage that she meant.

Leon let his gaze rest on the stage below, but all he was aware of was the woman sitting behind him. He still could not believe it. She was the breathtaking female who'd stopped him in his tracks that afternoon.

Who is she?

The question burned for an answer, but the best he could come up with, having taken her in at a single brief glance, was that she was some kind of lady-in-waiting. She'd dropped a curtsy to the Grand Duchess, who'd frowned at her, and the gown she was wearing was no couture number, like the duchess's and the princess's. So, yes... lady-in-waiting would be the most likely role, wouldn't it?

He could feel emotions conflicting within him—his overpowering visceral reaction to her clashing totally with his purpose to make Princess Marika his bride. This blonde might be a fatal distraction. He was feeling that distraction even now, fighting the urge to turn and look at her.

It seemed to take for ever before the curtain finally fell on the first act, to tumultuous applause, but suddenly the Grand Duchess was addressing him as the house lights came up.

'Torelli is in perfect voice!' she exclaimed approvingly.

'Outstanding!' Leon heard himself agree politely.

Then, forcing himself, he smiled at the princess beside him, who was still looking as stiff as she had all through the first act. Leon wished she would relax a little more.

'What did you think?' he asked in a kindly tone that he hoped was encouraging.

'She was very good,' Princess Marika said faintly.

Grand Duke Mikal was getting to his feet. 'It was a damned long first act!' he exclaimed.

Leon, who privately agreed, only gave a light laugh, getting to his feet as well. No sitting when royalty stood, he made himself remember. The Duchess was remaining seated, as was her daughter, but behind him Leon could hear the blonde lady-in-waiting standing up, with a slight rustle of her skirts.

Taking it as a signal, Leon finally allowed himself to turn, feeling it like the release of a bowstring drawn too tight to bear the tension much longer.

And there she was.

He felt his blood surge again as his eyes latched on to her. She was not looking at him, but he did not care. Was content just to drink her in.

She was as breathtakingly, stunningly beautiful as she'd been that first moment—even more so. She was wearing make-up now, enough to accentuate her eyes and mouth, to sculpt her cheekbones, and her hair was in a simple but elegant pleat. Her only jewellery was a single row of pearls, which added to the translucence of her fair skin. The style of the pale blue gown, albeit non-couture, complemented her slender beauty with its plissé bodice, cap sleeves and narrow skirt.

He felt desire, raw and insistent, spike through him. He tried to fight it back, knowing he should not indulge it—not if he was seriously considering marriage to Princess Marika.

But how can I think of such a thing when I'm reacting to another woman like this? Impossible! Just impossible!

As impossible, he recognised with a plunging realisation, as seeking to have anything to do with this unknown lady-in-waiting—even if he were to abandon the whole idea of marrying the Grand Duke's daughter. Any such liaison would be out of the question for Their Highnesses...

Frustration bit at him from every side, but still he could not tear his eyes from her. Not yet—and not when, even though she was still not looking at him, he could tell with every masculine instinct that she was acutely aware of him, responding to him as strongly as he was to her, just as she had in their initial brief encounter in the penthouse lobby.

He wanted her to look at him, but behind him he heard the Grand Duke step forward, and the blonde dropped him a slight curtsy, murmuring something in Karylyan that Leon took to be an apology for her late arrival.

The Grand Duke said something admonitory, then turned to Leon. 'You must allow me, Dukaris,' the Grand Duke announced in English, in his heavy, formal manner, 'to make another introduction to you.'

He paused, and Leon could not deny himself the veiled pleasure of letting his eyes go back to the blonde, because that was the only place he wanted his gaze to go. Back to feast on her pale, fine-sculpted beauty, her slender, full-breasted form. He wanted to breathe in the elusive, haunting scent of her perfume...even if she could never be his...

She was standing very stiffly, still not looking his way, but a tell-tale pulse was beating at her throat.

Then the Grand Duke was speaking again, the formality of his style even more pronounced. 'My elder daughter,' he was saying now, 'the Princess Elizsaveta.'

CHAPTER THREE

LEON FELT HIS expression freeze. Felt everything in him freeze. Then, like a sudden thaw across a frozen lake, he felt everything *un*-freeze—melt into the wash of sheer, gratifying release of every last fragment of the frustration he'd felt just a few moments ago.

He felt his features lighten—everything inside him lighten. Because everything now was just *perfect*.

As perfect as she is!

His eyes rested on her, his gaze brilliant.

'Princess…'

He heard his voice husky on her title. Without conscious awareness he reached for one of her hands, saw her eyes flare as he did so, and her lips part as if she was taking in an urgent breath of air.

Then, with absolute deliberation, Leon raised her hand to his mouth and gave the slightest bow of his head. With the same absolute deliberation he let his lips brush the back of her hand, infinitely lightly. He felt it tremble in his.

He relinquished her hand, letting his glance linger on her. He heard her murmur his name—a low 'Mr Dukaris…' that was even fainter than her sister's voice. But Leon could see the colour flaring out along those delicate cheekbones, and that was enough for him. And he saw the speed with which she had clasped the hand he'd just kissed, as if to stop it trembling.

Satisfaction filled him. And something much, much more than satisfaction.

He turned his head now to his guests, the Duke and Duchess. His smile flashed broadly. 'Champagne?' he invited.

Expansively he gestured towards the back of the box, where the requisite bottles were nestling in their ice buckets by a little table holding flutes on a silvered tray.

Champagne was exactly what was needed now. He'd never been more sure of that in his life.

Ellie was trying to hold on to the shreds of her composure—but it was impossible, just impossible! She should be used to hand-kissing—it was nothing out of the ordinary in Karylya for a female royal. Old-fashioned, perhaps, and somewhat formal as a deferential greeting. But nothing to set her fighting for composure the way she was now.

But then, never had a man as outrageously attractive as Leon Dukaris kissed her hand.

She gave a silent gulp, hoping her colour had returned to normal.

'Princess…?'

Their host for the evening, who was paying for the champagne he was now offering her with a polite smile, who was paying for this box at the opera—she dreaded to think how expensive that was—who was paying for the astronomically expensive suite at the Viscari St James, and paying for Ellie dared not think how much more, was standing in front of her, holding a flute brimming with gently beading champagne.

She took it, murmuring her thanks and adopting an expression of extreme graciousness that would have befitted her ultra-gracious regal stepmother. It gave her the protection she urgently needed. She took a sip from the flute, hearing Leon Dukaris speak again, asking her if she was enjoying the opera. His English was accented, she noted, but not much—less so than her father's.

There was a slight smile on his mouth—beautifully sculpted, with deep lines incised around it—and she felt another silent hollowing of her stomach. The planes of his face were strong, his nose bladed, his jaw edged. There was a toughness, a determination, underlying the relaxed slanting smile that invited her to respond to his conversational gambit.

'Torelli is as outstanding as ever,' she replied, echoing her stepmother's viewpoint readily enough, 'but the role is hardly endearing. *Turandot* can't be anyone's favourite heroine.'

She was making small talk, nothing more, and had done so a thousand times in Karylya when in princess mode.

She saw a faint frown on Leon Dukaris's face.

'No? But she's a very strong woman,' he replied. 'Insisting on not marrying just because that's what everyone expects her to do.'

Ellie felt her face harden. 'Strong? She's brutal! She has her suitors murdered and her rival tortured!' she bit out.

His rejoinder was immediate. 'The slave girl, Liu, could have avoided her fate any time she wanted, simply by telling Turandot the name of the unknown Prince.' There was a sardonic note in his voice.

'Whom Turandot would then have had killed!' Ellie shot back. 'Liu refuses to betray him—she *loves* him!'

Leon Dukaris lifted his flute to his mouth, taking a mouthful of champagne before he answered her. 'Much good it does her—he rejects her for another woman who's a better proposition than a mere slave girl!'

That sardonic note was more pronounced—harder. With something underlying it that for a moment Ellie wondered at. Then she realised that she suddenly had an opening to move the conversation away from a fictitious drama to the reality that she and her family were facing—a reality she must confront, for there was no other option but to do so if she were to protect Marika from an unwanted suitor.

'Well, yes,' she murmured, taking a sip of her champagne, pitching her voice carefully, 'Turandot is a princess—and there are, indeed, men who would like to marry a princess…'

She let her eyes rest on Leon Dukaris, mindful of her expression, nervous after her impetuosity in making so pointed an observation. Would it draw him out—make him say something that could give her any indication at all as to whether Marika's fears were justified or not?

Almost immediately, his expression was veiled. She saw his long lashes—ridiculously long lashes, inky dark and lush, she found herself noting with complete irrelevance—dipping down over those amazing dark eyes of his, tautening the muscles of her stomach.

'Well, that depends…' he replied.

And now there was no trace of any sardonic note in his voice—rather, she realised, with another pull on her heightened awareness of him, a trace of amusement…and, more than amusement, a sensual drawl that did things to her they should not…*must* not.

'On the princess in question…'

'Indeed,' she returned. 'And therefore perhaps you should be aware, Mr Dukaris, that my sister is in love with another man.'

She spoke in a low voice, for only him to hear. But even as she spoke she feared she had said too much—assumed too much.

What if Marika's fears were entirely groundless, the product of fear and distress? Well, it was too late now. She'd all but warned off Leon Dukaris from getting any ideas about her sister—ideas he might never have entertained in the first place.

It took all her training to keep her expression composed, as if she had said nothing out of the ordinary at all.

For a moment nothing changed in his expression. Then, as tension clawed in her, she saw his stance ease, a wash of relaxation go through him, and in his dark, dark eyes glints of sheer gold suddenly gleamed like buried treasure.

He raised his flute and quite deliberately tilted it to touch hers with a crystalline click of glass.

'I wish her as well as can be expected,' he said.

There was a carelessness in his voice, and again that underlying sardonic note that Ellie had heard before but had no time now to pay any attention to. For now all she had attention for was the way his eyes were holding hers, the expression in them, the way she could not move in the slightest.

'But I fear you have misunderstood the situation, Princess. I have not the slightest interest in your sister.'

He paused, and in that pause she could not breathe, for Leon Dukaris was dominating her body space, dominating her consciousness, smiling down at her with that smile that was not a smile, that smile that had nothing to do with humour in the least and everything to do with the complete lack of breath in her lungs and the bonelessness of her limbs, the hot rush of blood to her body.

'I would far prefer,' he said, and there was a sudden intimacy in the way he spoke to her, a sudden huskiness in his voice that weakened her boneless limbs, '*you* to be my bride...'

He touched his glass once more to hers. Raised it to his mouth and, smiling still, drank from it. Then, as if he had said nothing more to her than that he hoped she would enjoy the evening, despite disliking the heroine of the opera, he turned and strolled towards his other guests.

Behind him, Ellie felt her cheeks burst into flame, and the hand holding her champagne flute shook.

He couldn't have just said what he had.

He couldn't!

But he had.

She waited to feel the outrage she surely must feel—but it did not come. And she could only stare after him, motionless, hearing his outrageous words echoing in her head.

Leon stood by the plate glass picture window of the apartment above his offices. It was his London pied-à-terre, and furnished in ultra-modern, ultra-expensive style by top interior designers. He did not care for it, but it was prestigious enough for the business entertaining he did—and from time to time for the personal entertaining of those women he selected for the interludes in his life which had punctuated the years of his adulthood.

He made it crystal-clear to each and every woman that their affair would be brief, would be a passing mutual, sensual pleasure—nothing more. Never would he deceive any woman and pretend that he was offering any more than that.

His thoughts flickered as he took a meditative mouthful of cognac, staring out unseeing over the City skyline, glittering like jewels in the night at this late hour.

He was done with this lifestyle. Of that he was sure. It had served its purpose over the years of accumulating his vast wealth, but it had run its course. He wanted something different now.

Some*one* different.

His expression changed. How had it happened? That extraordinary confluence of two quite separate desires? The fanciful notion that had beguiled him last year in the fairy-tale Grand Duchy of Karylya, that he could crown his achievements with the most glittering prize of all—a royal bride… Then encountering a woman who, in his very first glimpse of her, had set his senses afire in an indelible instant—and then, in a veritable gift from the gods, to discover that she might be the royal bride he sought…

The woman I desire and the princess I aspire to marry—one and the same… The alluringly beautiful Princess Elizsaveta.

Dismissing the lovelorn Princess Marika from his thoughts for ever, he let the syllables of her older sister's name linger in his head, let memory replay every moment of their encounter, their conversation. He did not mind that he had declared his hand—he welcomed the opportunity she'd given him to do so. It cut to the chase—made things crystal-clear.

She was the princess bride he wanted.

Now all that remained was for her to agree…

And why should she not?

A slow, sensual smile pulled at his mouth, and his eyes glinted gold with reminiscence. The breathtaking blonde who had so incredibly fortuitously turned out to be a princess had not been able to hide from him the fact that she returned his attraction—her responsiveness to him had blazed in every glance, in her shimmering awareness of him as a man.

She desires me even as I desire her.

And added to that desire, which curled even now, seductive and sensual through his bloodstream, all the worldly advantages that would accrue with their marriage, for both of them—how could there be any argument against it?

It was the perfect match.

And, best of all, both of us will know the reasons we are marrying—and that the meaningless charade of 'love' has nothing to do with it!

And never would.

He lifted his cognac glass, toasting the one and only royal bride he wanted—the beautiful, the breathtaking Princess Elizsaveta.

* * *

The week that followed was the most tormented of Ellie's life. Her head ached with it. Had Leon Dukaris really meant what he'd so outrageously declared at the opera? Or had it been only a flippant remark in riposte to her warning him off Marika? *If* he'd actually needed warning off?

But if he wasn't entertaining such ambitions, then why was he forking out a fortune on keeping her family in horrendously expensive luxury?

His intentions remained impossible to determine.

When he invited the royal family to luncheon, two days after the evening at Covent Garden, to be taken in a *salon privé* at the hotel, she could detect nothing in his manner beyond formal civility. For herself, though she called on her training in royal etiquette to remain outwardly composed, it was a quite different matter.

The visceral impact Leon Dukaris made on her the moment he entered the room had strengthened, not lessened—she was even more hopelessly aware of him than ever—and it was the same yet again when, the day after, he took herself and Marika to afternoon tea at Meredon, her stepmother having graciously approved the outing for her confined daughter.

As they sat on the terrace of the ultra-prestigious country house hotel just outside London, overlooking the green sward stretching down to the River Thames, Ellie was burningly conscious of their host. Doggedly, she pursued safe conversational topics—from the history of the politically powerful Georgian family who had once owned Meredon to the flood protection measures needed for the River Thames in a warming world.

Marika was little help, merely picking at the delicious teatime fancies while staring off forlornly into the distance.

For his part Leon Dukaris, sporting a pair of ultra-fashionable designer shades that made him look even more devastatingly attractive than ever, kept the conversation going by asking lazily pertinent questions and giving the impression that his heavy-lidded gaze, screened by his dark glasses, was resting steadily on her...

As if, she thought wildly, he were assessing her...

For what? For my role as his royal bride?

A bead of hysteria formed in her throat, but she suppressed it. Suppressed all her emotions until finally, after a stroll through the manicured grounds, and a short excursion along the river in the hotel's private launch, she and Marika were finally returned to the Viscari St James.

She thanked Leon with what semblance of composure she could muster, only to have him glance a slanting smile at her, his long lashes dipping in a way that brought a flush of colour to her cheek.

'The pleasure was all mine, Princess,' he murmured.

He helped himself to her hand, bowing over it, and Ellie was sure he was doing so to remind her of how he had kissed her hand that night at the opera. There was something about the glint in his eyes that told her so...

Colour ran into her cheeks again and she turned away, glad that her stepmother was making some remark to him. Whatever it was, Ellie caught only his reply.

'Alas, Highness, I am scheduled to be out of the country for several days on business, but when I return I would be delighted if you would permit me to invite you to dine with me—and the princesses, too, of course.'

He swept a benign smile over Ellie and Marika—who was busying herself with her phone, frantically texting in a way that sank Ellie's heart. The distant beloved, no doubt. Distant and utterly ineligible...

She dragged her mind away from her sister's hopeless predicament, her eyes going to her father and his wife. With their visitor gone, she could see that they were allowing the front they'd put on for him to collapse. Her father looked old and tired—her stepmother tense and strained. They might not say anything to her or Marika, but it was evident that the stress of their precarious situation was eating into them. They knew, even if they did not say it, how grave their predicament was.

If Leon Dukaris pulls the plug on them what will happen to them?

Impossible to imagine—just impossible! A penurious exile? But where? Where would they go? What would they live on?

Fear bit at her, and she could feel it resonating in the room. Could hear, leaping into life yet again, that other question circling in her head.

A princess bride—is that what Leon Dukaris expects for the money he's spending on us? Can he truly be thinking that?

And what if he were? She felt emotion clutch at her. What answer could she possibly give?

What on earth do I tell him if he really, truly wants to marry me?

The only sane answer was no—no, no and *no*! How could she possibly contemplate even entertaining such an idea? To marry a stranger…a man she barely knew…

Everything in her revolted. All her life she had vowed to marry only for love. Hadn't her own parents' sad example shown how vital that was? Her mother was very open about how she'd felt so pressured by her father—flattered that his daughter was being wooed by a prince, he'd pressed her into a marriage that her royal husband had wanted only to please *his* own father and beget an heir to the throne.

It was a marriage that had never worked for either of them, and they'd parted from each other with relief, each of them glad to find love and happiness in their second marriages.

'Never do what I did, darling,' Ellie's mother had warned her all her life. *'Only marry for love—nothing else!'*

She felt her emotions twist inside her, tearing her to pieces, making sleep impossible as she lay tensely staring up at the ceiling in Malcolm's flat that night. For herself, it would be easy to reject Leon Dukaris's ambitions for a royal bride. As Ellie Peters her own situation was perfectly secure—a home in Somerset with her mother, a modest salary working for her stepfather's production company. The freedom to marry for love and only for love…

But she was more than just her mother's daughter—more than just Ellie Peters.

I am also Princess Elizsaveta, daughter of the Grand Duke of the House of Karpardy, and I have duties and obligations and responsibilities that are not mine to evade.

And the difference was everything.

She took a deep, decisive breath. Resolution filled her. No more endless circling, no more questioning, no more confusion. She must embrace the responsibilities of her royal heritage. Her face tautened. And if that meant setting aside her own personal desires and marrying a man she barely knew—well, so be it.

Decision made, she felt a kind of peace—a feeling of resignation and resolve—come over her. Sleep, long delayed, made her eyelids flutter shut. And as it did, it brought dreams with it—dreams of a strong-featured face, of heavy-lidded, night-dark eyes resting on her. Desiring her… Impatient to make her his bride. His princess bride.

CHAPTER FOUR

LEON WATCHED THE PRINCESS being ushered to his table across the restaurant and felt the familiar kick go through his system at the sight of her. The days he'd spent away from London had only increased his desire to see her again—and now here she was, walking towards him in all her breathtaking beauty.

She was wearing, he discerned, an outfit by a designer much favoured by the young British royals—a tailored suit in pale green, adorned with very correct pearls, yet again. But there was something about the air with which she carried herself that marked her out as different from just another wealthy young woman.

His expression altered slightly. Except, of course, the Princess Elizsaveta was not a wealthy young woman at all... She was, in fact, penniless. As penniless as the rest of her family.

Unless she marries me.

And she would—he was sure of it. After all, why else inform his PA that she wished to meet him for lunch today?

He got to his feet, murmuring a greeting, and she took her place opposite him. She had an air of calm composure about her, but Leon could sense that she was very far from being either calm or composed. Her every sense was on alert.

As the attentive waiter poured iced mineral water for her, then retreated, Leon sat back, his gaze openly appreciative of her blonde beauty, the soft grey-blue of her eyes, the curve of her mouth, the sculpted line of her high cheek-bones, the glorious pale gold of her hair, caught now into a chignon with low-set combs.

He was enjoying the elegance of her poise, the sweet swell of her breasts… She really was so very, very beautiful… He felt his senses stir, warming in his veins. Confirming everything he'd made his decision on. She was, without a shadow of a doubt, the ideal royal bride for him.

She is everything I want—everything!

She was speaking, and he made himself pay attention. She had leant forward slightly, her pose straight-backed, her manner very different from the subdued restraint she adopted when she was with her father and stepmother, or her determinedly polite, impersonal demeanour that afternoon at Meredon. Now her tone of voice was brisk.

'Thank you for agreeing to meet me, Mr Dukaris,' she opened. 'I have, as you may suppose, a particular reason for wanting you to do so.'

Leon veiled his gaze. He said nothing, merely gave a faint smile, waiting for her to continue.

For a moment she seemed unnerved, then she rallied, her tone still brisk. 'I need to be clear,' she went on, her voice deliberately cool, 'about a very important matter.'

Ellie paused, resting her eyes on his. It was taking her considerable resolve to do so. From the moment she'd set eyes on him across the restaurant, his relaxed but powerful frame had drawn her gaze immediately, and the familiar rush to her blood had sent heat flushing through her. She had had to fight hard to subdue it as she took her place. This was no time for any such reaction to him. She was here for one reason, and one reason only.

'Mr Dukaris, why are you paying for my father's suite at the Viscari St James?'

* * *

Leon stilled. He had not anticipated quite so blunt a question. But then, after all, he recollected, she had been just as blunt that night at *Turandot*, when she had, out of nowhere, warned him off her sister.

He heard her continue.

'Since my father now has neither power nor influence in Karylya, you have no obvious need for his favour. So...' she took a breath '...there must be some other reason.'

He saw her lips press together, as if she were steeling herself to go on.

'Tell me,' she said, and her voice was cool, yet Leon could sense the tension in it all the same, 'were you serious, at the opera, in your remark to me? Or was it some clumsy attempt at humour?'

There—she had said it—had finally put into words what had been preying on her mind all week and more. She had finally nerved herself to say what *had* to be said.

A faint smile flickered at his mouth, curving his sensuous lips, but Ellie refused to be distracted by it. She could not afford to be—not now. Far too much depended on his answer.

'It would be humour in a very poor taste, would you not agree?' A slight lift of one dark arched eyebrow accompanied his laconic reply.

'Indeed,' she said tightly. She took a breath, forced herself on. 'And I have to allow that my sister may be quite mistaken in her...her interpretation of just why you are being so generous to my father at this difficult time for him.'

She watched him reach for his glass again, take another leisurely mouthful. He appeared to be infuriatingly relaxed, that long-lashed gaze from his night-dark eyes still veiled, his expression unreadable, yet she could sense there was a sudden tension in him. She held her breath, waiting for his reply on which so much would depend.

Enough to change my life for ever—

The enormity of the moment pressed upon her, and she could hear the slug of her own heartbeat in her chest.

After an age, his answer came. His eyes held hers, still veiled, but it was impossible not to be held by them.

'No, she was not mistaken,' he said. He started to lower his glass to the table. 'Only,' he went on, 'mistaken as to my preference. As I told you, it is not your sister I have an interest in marrying…'

She heard him say it as clear as a bell, and not in any sardonic manner, or with any possible humorous twist, but with a sudden unveiling of his gaze upon her that stilled the breath in her lungs.

'Why?'

The word burst from Ellie—she could not stop it. She realised she had leant forward, giving vehement emphasis to her blunt question.

He paused in the act of lowering his glass. His expression changed minutely.

'Why…?' he echoed.

Then his expression changed again. Ellie could see it—could see his eyes veiling again, a slight smile deliberately forming around that well-shaped mouth of his.

'Why would any man *not* wish to marry a princess?'

The riposte was light, designed to deflect her, she knew. But this was no game, no joke, no humorous light-hearted situation. This was real—brutally, starkly real. Nothing to do with any fairy story…

'Why do *you* want to marry a princess?' Her question was like a scalpel. She wanted an answer and she would have one—a good one, a real one!—or she would walk away from the table right now.

She saw his expression change yet again. She gave a

start as she realised that she recognised what she was now seeing in those incredible, long-lashed, gold-glinting night-dark eyes, whose gaze resting on her seemed able to turn her to liquid mush. But they were not doing so now—they were resting on her with something quite different in them. Something she had not seen before but was seeing now.

Honesty.

'I have no idea how much you know about me, Princess,' he said now, his voice as clear-sounding as hers had been, 'but you will have been told, I am sure, that I am nothing more than a jumped-up, *nouveau riche* billionaire who has made a fortune speculating in the global markets. That is quite true, and a moment's search on the Internet will confirm that. There is no secret about that. And nor, by the same token, do I make any secret of the fact that I have more money than I know what to do with.'

He gave the slightest shrug of his shoulder—as if, Ellie thought, all those billions were just toy money.

'I want something else now,' he said.

He set his glass back on the damask tablecloth with a click. Levelled his eyes straight at her.

'I can buy anything I want—anything. But there are some things that are harder to buy. Without help.' He gave a smile now—a tight, knowing smile. 'The help of a princess. A princess as a glittering prize to crown my achievements in life.'

He sat back, his long, strong fingers still curved around his glass, eyes still resting on her with that same startling revelation that what he was doing now was telling her, bluntly and openly, just how it was.

Ellie kept her face still. 'A princess?' she echoed flatly. '*Any* princess?' It was a taunt, a challenge.

That negligent shrug came again. 'More or less,' he admitted. 'Of course the number of available princesses of marriageable age is highly limited, and even those who might be willing to marry someone like me would want to get something for themselves out of it.'

For my family, Ellie told herself. *Only for them.*

Yet even as she thought it she felt a flush go through her. And a thought that was utterly and totally irrelevant to the moment. Any woman who married Leon Dukaris would be getting *him*—all six-foot-plus of devastating male…

She dragged her thoughts away. They weren't relevant to the brutal discussion she was having…*had* to have…with this man keeping her father from ignominious penury… Who was only doing so in the expectation of a royal bride.

That much was obvious now.

She sat back. She felt as if she was doing a workout with weights too heavy for her. Yet she had to continue. This had to play out to the end.

I have to know exactly what it is I'm letting myself in for. Marrying a man who only wants to marry me for my royal blood—no other reason.

She felt something twist inside her and suppressed it. There was no point in feeling it. No point lamenting that her life-long dream of marrying only for love had become impossible. No point in anything except doggedly continuing.

She took a breath, saying the thing she *had* to say. 'Do you accept, Mr Dukaris, that my sister Marika is *not* "available", as you so charmingly express it?' Ellie could not stop a waspish note stinging her voice. 'Because she is in love with someone else?'

A faintly bored look crossed his face. 'I made that clear the other night, I believe,' he answered. One arched eyebrow lifted. 'With that established, shall we move on?' he invited.

This time the taunt was his, not hers. He was taking control of the agenda, and making it clear to her that he was doing so.

'So, having disposed of the subject of your sister,' his

tone of voice was bland now, 'I assume you are about to set out the terms and conditions of our marriage.'

Leon saw her eyes flash, impartially observing how it lent a dramatic aspect to her pale beauty.

'You take it for granted that I will accept your offer?' she asked.

He gave a shake of his head. 'No, I take it for granted that you do not wish to see your father destitute. And that as a loyal daughter you will do whatever is necessary to prevent that. And, of course…' there was a sardonic note to his voice now '…to enable your sister to remain free to pine after another man.' He frowned for a moment. 'Who *is* she pining for, by the way?'

Ellie's expression changed. 'Someone she'll never be allowed to marry. Antal Horvath.'

Leon's frown deepened. 'Antal Horvath? But isn't that—?'

Ellie's lips pressed together tightly. 'Yes, precisely. Antal is the son of Matyas Horvath—the man who led the coup deposing my father and who aims to be voted President of Karylya in his place!'

Leon's eyebrows rose. 'Well, that unpalatable fact will certainly test her youthful ardour!' he commented sardonically. 'However…' his voice changed '…the woes of your sister are irrelevant to ourselves,' he said dismissively, reaching for the leather-bound menu.

He looked across at the princess he infinitely preferred to her hopelessly lovelorn sister. Satisfaction was rising through him—he was achieving exactly what he wanted, and that always felt good. Very good.

'Shall we get on with ordering lunch?' he invited. He was hungry and he wanted to eat.

He made to flick open the menu, but the princess's voice stayed him.

'Not yet.'

Her tone was commanding, as befitting a princess, and Leon paused, setting down the menu with an air of patience. He lifted an enquiring eyebrow.

Ellie felt her jaw tighten, felt turbid emotions, clashing and turbulent, sloshing inside her. If she really, truly were to do the unthinkable—agree to marry a man she barely knew—she had to be rock-solid sure she would get the protection for her family they needed.

'There are, as you say, terms and conditions.'

She had got her brisk, businesslike tone back, and was relieved she could still adopt it. She took a breath, marshalling her strength to make things crystal-clear to him.

'The first of which is that I want a time limit on this marriage. Two years—no more. That gives you ample time to take all the social advantages you want out of marrying a princess.'

His face was closed. For a second—just a second—Ellie felt a thrill of apprehension go through her. Then, abruptly, his expression changed and he gave a slight assenting shrug of his shoulder, as if the stipulation meant nothing to him.

That stipulation means nothing to me! Of course it doesn't. Why should two years not give me everything I want from her? Why would I care if she leaves me then?

He felt his mind shift away, as if from a place it refused to go. Where it would always refuse to go.

'Good,' Ellie said decisively, relief filling her.

I have to know that I can eventually be free of this marriage—free to find the love I seek.

She forged on, knowing she had to put everything down on the table in one go.

A hefty capital sum settled on her father, yielding an income sufficient to maintain his dignity in exile, and a suitable property for him and his wife to live in *gratis* for their lifetime.

'Oh, and you must guarantee the university fees for my brother Niki—and a dowry for my sister. So that she, at least, will have freedom of choice when it comes to her marriage. Sufficient, if necessary, to defy her parents—' She broke off.

Was there a trace of bitterness in her voice? She hoped not—what was the point of bitterness in the face of brute reality?

Disbelief was possessing her—an air of absolute unreality that she was actually doing what she was doing… marrying a stranger in order to protect her father and his family. To ensure a future for them all.

At the price of mine.

She felt her stomach hollow. That was the truth of it, wasn't it? Everyone got what they wanted except her. She was going to have to hand herself over to a complete stranger, have her own life hijacked by making a marriage to this man she barely knew.

A cry came from deep inside her.

This isn't the marriage I wanted to make! I wanted to marry for love—only for love! Even princesses can marry for love.

But not this one. Like so many of her ancestors, she was going to marry for royal duty—because she was the only one in the family who could protect her father now, protect her stepmother, her siblings.

She felt a wash of misery flush through her and her eyes dropped away, her throat tightening.

She heard Leon Dukaris—the vastly rich billionaire who was going to ensure her family's future at the price she had agreed to pay for it—agreeing to all she demanded. And for a second—just a second—panic flared in her eyes. This marriage was going to happen…it really was going to happen! She was going to marry this man—this complete stranger—whose disturbing gaze on her could quicken her pulse and confuse her utterly…

The rush of panic beat up inside her again. And then suddenly she felt her hand being taken. His strong fingers closed around hers. His eyes held her troubled gaze.

Something seemed to run between them. As if, she thought, for the very first time she was seeing the man and not the billionaire. Not the devastatingly masculine male that her feminine senses were continually so perpetually aware of but the person—the individual, with a character and personality of his own.

A quiver seemed to go through her she could make no sense of.

'It will be all right, this marriage of ours,' he said quietly, his eyes still holding hers. 'I will make sure of it.'

Then, before she could realise his intent, he was lifting her hand to his lips. It was the briefest of hand-kisses, but as he lowered her hand back to the table and released it Ellie felt, for the very first time since her mother had given her the dreadful news about her father, the agitation inside her and the tumult of her emotions start to subside.

The man she had just agreed to marry smiled. An open, reassuring smile. And somehow—she did not know why or how—all her panic was gone…quite gone.

'Good girl,' she heard Leon Dukaris say approvingly, and he patted the back of her hand.

He looked about, summoning the maître d'.

'Now, let's toast our engagement in champagne! It deserves no less!'

CHAPTER FIVE

ELLIE WAS BUSY. Very busy. Not only was she assembling an extensive couture wardrobe suitable for her role as Leon Dukaris's fiancée and thereafter as his bride, but the wedding itself was to be lavish in the extreme, staggeringly expensive, and, it seemed, with a vast amount for her to do—even with the help of the wedding team at the Viscari.

They were to be married at the hotel, where her family would continue to live until her father and her stepmother and sister moved into a château in the Loire that Leon had purchased for that purpose.

The tabloids and the glossy magazines were in raptures. Ellie might be grimly aware of the real reason for her marriage, but to the world it was a fairy-tale romance.

The Princess and the Greek Tycoon!
Love in Exile!
Royal Bride for Billionaire!

Any number of permutations blazed in the headlines, accompanied by pictures from the carefully staged photo shoots set up by the PR machine activated by Leon Dukaris to show the world he was marrying a princess.

She'd let her father believe the same as the press, for the look of relief in his eyes when she'd told him her news had been painful to behold. If he wanted to keep the comforting illusion that his financial benefactor had taken one look at Elizsaveta and experienced a *coup de foudre* Ellie would not disabuse him.

It was not something she had tried with her mother, however. She and Malcolm were back from Canada, and Ellie had gone down to Somerset to tell her.

It had not been an easy conversation so far. Her mother was protesting strongly, but Ellie defended her decision.

'I can't abandon my father after what's happened to him—'

'Darling—he has *no* right to demand this of you!' her mother began.

But Ellie cut across her. 'He isn't demanding it!' she'd said. 'I'm doing this because I love him—and I want to protect him.'

She took a step back from her mother's anxious embrace, and felt something change in her face. She was no longer Ellie Peters, but Princess Elizsaveta of the Royal House of Karpardy.

'I am my father's daughter,' she said, 'and I have obligations to my birth. It's as simple as that.'

Her mother looked at her, her gaze troubled. 'And what of love?' she said.

Ellie's expression was wry. 'I must hope that I will be like you and Papa—each of you finding love in a second marriage.'

It was the thought she clung to as the wedding preparations swept her up. Of her fiancé himself she saw not a great deal, and mostly in public or in company. He seemed to be flying about the world a lot, and had told her that he was putting his business affairs in order so that they would not make demands on him after their wedding.

She knew that in a cowardly way she was relieved at his absence. It just seemed easier for her to cope with.

She was relieved, too—though she did not want to spell it out to herself—that when they *were* together he did not take advantage of their engagement to get up close and personal…

Her mind sheered away, blocking such thoughts—she would deal with them later, but not now, she thought hectically. Instead, whenever she was with him, she would take refuge in adopting the same brisk attitude she had at that fateful lunch, when she had committed herself to a man she barely knew.

This time, though, it was endless wedding details that needed agreement—anything and everything, from the music during the ceremony to who the huge guest list should include.

'Both my mother and stepmother are summoning all the relatives they can round up,' she told Leon frankly over dinner, during one of his intermittent stop-overs in London. 'And they're pressing for as many royals—British and European—as we can muster in the time available.'

She ran through a number of the names of people who had RSVP'd already.

'Very impressive,' acknowledged Leon dryly.

Had that been a sardonic note in his voice? Ellie lifted her chin.

'Well, that's what this is all about, isn't it?' she riposted, in the same openly frank manner. 'Making as big a social splash with our wedding and our marriage as we can?'

Leon sat back in his chair—they were at the same restaurant they had been for lunch all those weeks ago, when she had sealed her fate. Perhaps that was why she was speaking so frankly now, making herself face the reason she was marrying Leon Dukaris. To give him a princess bride to crown his achievements and give her beleaguered father the financial security he so desperately needed.

And it's for no other reason—none.

Leon had made that clear—he had spoken no soft, seductive words to the contrary, cast no lingering glances at her, made no pretence that he felt anything for her. So, however much she might find her heart rate starting to quicken when she was with him, however heavy-lidded that dark, gold-flecked gaze of his could be, resting on her with that veiled expression she could not make out, she had to set all that aside.

His expression now, though, was not veiled at all. His eyes had narrowed as she'd spoken.

'Tell me,' he said, and there was a silky note to his voice that she had not heard before, for usually he gave quick, good-humoured answers to her questions, 'do you intend always to be this blunt about our marriage?'

Ellie felt colour flush her cheeks, but fought it back. Lifted her chin again. Met that narrowed gaze full-on. Th world might be cooing over them, lavishing them with a romantic gloss that sold magazines by the truckload, but she would not collude with it. She would not pretend there was anything between them but what there was.

There was a spark in her eyes as she answered him. 'Leon, you're marrying me because I'm a princess, and I'm marrying you because you're rich enough to bankroll my father and his family. My title for your wealth. It's a pretty blunt situation,' she said unrepentantly.

She held his gaze, which all of a sudden was like coruscating black diamonds. She reeled from the impact of it— but she would not flinch. Then, abruptly, that coruscating gaze was gone—veiled by the long dark lashes sweeping down over those gold-flecked eyes. She saw him lift his wineglass and tilt it lazily towards her. The sudden tension in him relaxed. He smiled his familiar half-sardonic, half-open smile.

'Well, then, let us drink to our marriage all the same,' said Leon equably. 'An honest marriage…'

As most marriages are not—with the couple deluding

each other with the belief that eternal love will bind them, when the first misfortune to befall them will make a mockery of all their vows!

So why should he care if his beautiful royal bride was being so blunt about why they were marrying? It was only the truth.

Except that it is not the only *truth... It is not simply because I want a princess bride to show off on my arm and she wants a dignified exile for her father.*

There was another truth to their marriage. As potent a truth as those.

He veiled his expression as she touched her glass to his with a faint answering smile, concealing his thoughts, knowing that she was not yet ready for anything more from him.

But perhaps it's time...

Perhaps it was time that Princess Elizsaveta realised that he was marrying her for a great deal more than her title...

As he took another ruminative sip of his wine, watching with pleasure the way her delicate features caught the soft light pooling over their table as she skimmed her gaze over the next item on the wedding list, he knew exactly the occasion for her to do so.

The glittering opulence of their betrothal ball.

It would be ideal...

Ellie took a steadying breath, gathering her skirts. There were a lot of them—a cloud of palest blush-pink organza and chiffon—and her boned bodice was encrusted with crystal, another billowing swathe of chiffon framing her bare shoulders and arms. At her throat an ornate pink diamond necklace matched the long drop earrings of the parure, as did the twin bracelets encircling her wrists and the combs holding her elaborate upswept hair.

The very image of a princess.

At least I'm not wearing a coronet! she thought wryly to herself.

She'd drawn the line at that, explaining to Leon that tiaras were only worn by married women—indeed, her mother, sitting beside her in the huge limo now drawing up at the Viscari, was so doing.

'Heaven knows when I last wore this!' her mother had exclaimed when her jewellery case had arrived from its safety deposit box at her bank.

Her voice had been light, but her expression troubled. And Ellie knew why—tonight would be the first time her mother would meet Leon, the man who was bailing out her ex-husband at the price of her daughter's hand in marriage.

'I won't say a word, darling, I promise you—this is your choice and you have made it in good conscience. I will stand by you,' her mother had said, and Ellie had been deeply grateful. Grateful, too, to have her mother and stepfather with her tonight.

The doorman was stepping forward, opening the limo door, and with a final intake of breath Ellie got out, taking the greatest care with her voluminous ball gown. As she did she heard a scatter of applause from the gathered on-lookers, saw the flash of cameras, and realised that Leon's PR machine was ensuring that a quiet entrance was going to be impossible.

Then her mother and stepfather were beside her and they were all walking into the hotel. And in the marble-floored, mahogany-furnished atrium Leon was crossing the space towards them.

As it always did, Ellie felt her breath catch. Of all the men in the world, in evening dress Leon Dukaris beat them hands-down. He just looked...*superb*! And in white tie—for this was a fully formal evening—the effect was tripled.

'Princess...'

He was taking her hand, bowing over it but not kissing

it. His eyes were fastened on her, and in them was an expression that was like a blaze.

'You look *incredible*!' he breathed.

His gaze washed over her, taking in every detail of her sumptuous attire. She wanted to say something—anything! To make some light-hearted remark—something about Cinderella arriving for the ball, maybe, or something about a fairy-tale—whatever she could think of to say with a smile.

But she couldn't. She couldn't say a word as his blazing eyes devoured her. The breath had gone from her lungs, her head had emptied of anything at all except his gaze feasting upon her.

And then, dimly, she became aware that her mother and stepfather were waiting to be introduced to the man she was going to marry.

She had to make a huge effort but she drew back her hand, wishing it weren't quivering like a leaf in autumn. 'Leon, may I present you to my mother?' she murmured, trying to stop her voice quivering helplessly.

As if he were also coming to himself, Leon's expression changed, becoming formal. He turned towards her mother. 'Lady Constance,' he said, 'I'm delighted to meet you at last,' he said.

'And I you, Mr Dukaris,' Ellie heard her mother reply, with an assessing note in her voice.

'Leon, please…' he replied immediately.

'Then you had better call me Connie,' she invited.

There seemed, Ellie thought, to be a warmer note in her mother's voice now, and wondered at it, but was grateful, too.

'Lady Connie,' Leon compromised, his smile coming again as he turned to Ellie's stepfather.

Ellie performed the requisite introduction, and was glad that Leon's demeanour acknowledged that her stepfather was a man of some renown in his field.

As Leon made graceful reference to his work, and Malcolm made a jovial reply in his usual bluff and forthright manner, Ellie glanced around her. She frowned. The only people in the huge Edwardian-style atrium apart from some senior hotel staff were, she realised from their black-suited, discreetly tough-looking appearance, Security.

Leon had clearly seen her glance at them, and he took her arm and ushered them all towards the grand staircase sweeping up to the first-floor ballroom.

'The hotel is in lockdown until we are in the ballroom,' he said. 'Just a precaution, given both your family and the people on the guest list.'

Ellie just nodded. It wasn't just a precaution—she knew that. But she did not say so, for what would be the point? It was so the world could see and know that Leon Dukaris was marrying royalty, and that royalty were not like other mere mortals on this earth.

It was why, too, he went on addressing her mother as Lady Connie—highlighting that even on her mother's side, there was ancient nobility—albeit not royal. Her uncle, the Earl of Holmsworth, would be at the wedding, and his two young daughters were to be her flower girls, his ten-year-old son her page boy.

But before the wedding there was tonight's ball to get through.

Leaning on Leon's arm slightly more heavily than she'd thought she would need to, because of the sudden weakness in her limbs caused by his presence at her side, she processed with him up the sweeping staircase, then entered the vast, ornate ballroom, festooned with flowers and ablaze with light from a dozen crystal chandeliers, to receive another smattering of applause from the assembled guests.

Ellie smiled about her, but Leon was heading towards the far end, where her father and stepmother were. Two large gilded chairs had been procured, and the Grand Duke and Duchess were presiding over the whole affair.

Dutifully, Ellie curtsied when she reached them, her skirts billowing out in a cloud of blush-pink. Her father, splendid in white tie and tails, stood up and came forward to kiss her, then shook Leon's hand as he bowed. Behind him the Grand Duchess dipped her head in regal acknowledgement of their arrival, and beside her Marika—looking enchantingly pretty in pale blue—gave her a little wave.

The Grand Duke held up his hand, then announced to the assembled company that he was welcoming them all to the betrothal ball of his daughter and her chosen husband-to-be.

'The first dance is theirs!' he declared, and resumed his seat as the orchestra, placed on a raised platform to one side of the room, struck up.

It was a Strauss waltz, and with a strange little catch in her throat, finding it impossible to resist such familiar and lilting music, Ellie went into Leon's arms. She raised her left hand to his shoulder, had her right clasped in his firm grip. For a moment, as his arm came about her waist and he drew her closer to him, she felt her legs weaken further, felt heady at his closeness, and then, as the music sounded, he whirled her across the polished floor.

She gave a little gasp, her eyes darting to his. She held his gaze, unable to break the hold of it—for it was the fulcrum around which she was turning, around which the whole world seemed to be turning. Everything was becoming a blur but not the deep, dark eyes holding hers. And in them—not in their depths, but at the blazing forefront of his gaze—was molten gold. Pure molten gold...

And she melted into it. Just melted...

Suddenly, out of nowhere, the significance of the evening became clear—here she was, in this utterly over-the-top concoction of a ball gown, bedecked with jewellery, her satin slippers twirling her body around, caught in the arms of this impossibly devastating man, whose dark looks and planed face and sable hair were so ludicrously flattered by the white tie and tails that moulded his powerful body like a glove.

It's like a fairy-tale! A fairy-tale of mythical princesses and handsome heroes!

But it wasn't a fairy-tale!

It was true—all of it!

She was waltzing to the music of Strauss, the Waltz King, and she was Princess Elizsaveta of Karylya, and Leon Dukaris was— Oh, he was the most handsome man who had ever walked the earth!

She was enchanted, beguiled and enthralled, spinning around and around to music that no soul on earth could resist, to the music that whirled in her blood, carrying her slippered feet across the ballroom…

And she could not take her eyes from Leon. Not for anything in heaven and earth. Not while the music played, and she danced and she danced in his arms…

With a crescendo of sound, the music stopped. The waltz was over and she was standing there, heart pounding, the blood singing in her veins, exhilaration, wonder and enchantment consuming her.

She was still gazing up at Leon, and he was still holding her in his dancer's hold, his hand at her waist. Then she felt her hand released, and hers fell to her side, nerveless with exhaustion. She could feel her heart beating so strongly—with the exertion of the dance, and with so much more than that.

She drank him in—the chiselled planes of his face, the sculpted mouth, the dark, drowning gaze of his eyes holding hers. She felt his other hand slip from her waist and she swayed, as if he alone had been holding her steady. And then, with a catch in her throat, she felt him cup her face with his long, strong fingers, tilting it up towards him, the

touch of his hands catching at her breath. Her lips parted...
helpless, breathless...

'My Princess...'

His voice was low, and warm, and for her and her alone.
And his lips, when they touched hers, were warm and for
her and her alone. And his kiss was warm and slow and
for her and her alone.

She felt her eyes flutter shut, felt the soft, sensuous glide
of his mouth on hers, felt a liquefying rush go through her
as if every cell in her body was dissolving. It seemed to go
on and on, that kiss...on and on and on...

When his mouth lifted from hers she could only stare,
dazed, helpless, her lips still parted. She kept on gazing
up at him as his hands slid from her face and he smiled
down at her.

'My Princess...' he said again, his voice husky.

Then he was tucking her limp hand that suddenly
seemed to weigh half a ton into the crook of his arm and
he was leading her off the dance floor. And she had to lean
into him because she had no strength left in her body...not
the slightest bit of strength.

Her mind was a daze, her thoughts a whirl, and the orchestra was striking up again. She was aware that other
couples were taking to the floor now, and that Leon was
leading her back to where her family sat, her mother and
stepfather beside the royal couple, though on less ornate
chairs. Marika was being led out onto the dance floor by
someone Ellie vaguely recognised as one of the junior
members of the British royal family, and seemingly very
happy.

But she had no thoughts to spare for her sister or her
parents, or for the throng of glittering guests here tonight
to see Leon Dukaris present his royal bride-to-be to the
world. She had no thoughts at all for anyone at all who was

not the man who had swept her onto the dance floor and kissed her like the Princess in a fairy-tale…

Who had taken her, with that waltz and that kiss, to an enchanted realm she never wanted to leave…

CHAPTER SIX

LEON STOOD UNDER the rose-decked silk canopy as the celebrant threw him an encouraging smile. Yet for all that he could feel tension netting him. This was the day, the moment, when he would marry. Would marry his princess bride.

From that original fancy over a year ago, when the idea of marrying a princess had first come to him, to this moment now, when it was actually about to happen, seemed a blur.

Was he mad to do this? To truly go ahead with it?

Marriage was not an affair—it was unknown territory…

Unease flickered in his consciousness. Even with all the safeguards he had placed around what he was doing, ensuring that no delusions of love could come anywhere near this marriage, and that he and the woman he was to wed were doing so for reasons that had nothing to do with any such illusory notions, still unease flickered within him.

Memories, toxic and cruel, plucked at his mind.

Almost he gave them admittance.

Then, with a sudden rustle of movement amongst the serried ranks of guests behind him, he heard the music, up to this moment low and forgettable, start to swell, switching into full volume to herald the arrival of his bride.

He turned.

He could not stop himself.

And as his eyes lit upon her all doubts fled…

* * *

Ellie took a breath, pressed her hand on her father's arm. The music was swelling—the Royal Anthem of Karylya, insisted on by her father. And who was she to deny him this small comfort, when he did not even have his royal regalia any longer, and had to walk his daughter down the aisle in nothing more than commonplace morning dress.

The guests were getting to their feet with a scraping of chairs on the paved ground of the Viscari roof terrace. The unreliable English weather was blessedly clement, so that recourse to the glass conservatory along one side of the rooftop would be unnecessary—except for the serving of the wedding breakfast to follow.

An arbour of roses arched across the aisle and their scent caught at her, adding to the scent from the thousands more blooms arranged to beautify the already stunning landscape architecture of this green oasis high above the city, enclosed and private, far above the masses on the streets below, where the London traffic was quite inaudible.

She could see the celebrant, waiting for them at the far end of the aisle. A civil ceremony was what she had stipulated to Leon—yet even so she still felt a hypocrite as she stepped towards the man waiting to marry her.

The words she'd so bluntly put to Leon echoed in her head.

'Leon, you're marrying me for my title, and I'm marrying you because you're rich enough to bankroll my father and his family.'

Everything—all this extravaganza of a wedding, the guest list crammed with aristocrats and royalty, leaked to the press and the media by Leon for maximum coverage—was for that reason alone.

Yet even though she knew it she felt again the magical brush of Leon's lips on hers, the enchantment of his kiss whispering of reasons that had nothing to do with her father's exile, her bridegroom's ambitions…reasons that fluttered like a butterfly seeking the sweetest nectar…

She felt her hand tremble on her father's arm, and he patted it reassuringly as they processed forward. Nerves plucked at her, but she knew she must not let them show. Must be as composed, as calm, as perfect a princess bride as she could be.

Do her family proud.

Do Leon proud by being the perfect princess bride for him.

Beneath her veil her eyes went to him, and she was glad of the veil to hide the sudden heating of her cheeks. An air of unreality pressed upon her, as if she could not believe this was truly happening. But all her training came to the fore—as it must.

They reached the celebrant, the anthem ended and the congregation resumed their seats. Leon stepped forward to stand beside her. Her father stepped back to join his wife. Her mother and stepfather flanked them. Behind her Marika, her bridesmaid, took her allotted place, ushering the little flower girls to theirs, their older brother bringing up the rear.

The celebrant began to speak…

She heard the words but did not hear them. Heard her own voice but did not hear it. Heard Leon's but did not hear it. Let Leon take her hand, slide the wedding band on her nerveless finger, his touch cool. She said more words, and so did he, and then the celebrant was speaking again, to them both.

Joining them in matrimony.

And she was Leon's princess bride.

'Where are we going?' Ellie asked her new husband with mild enquiry.

Leon moved into the London traffic, shifting gear in

the million-pound, brand-new supercar delivered that very morning—an enjoyable present to himself for his wedding day.

'Wait and see,' he answered.

He had told her nothing about his plans for a honeymoon, and wanted it to be a surprise. A pleasing one, he hoped...

They had been waved off amidst laughter and an easily foiled attempt by his new bride's brother—finished now with his schooldays—and some of the younger males among the wedding guests to attach rattling tin cans to the bumper. Instead they had contented themselves by spraying 'Just married!' in shaving foam on the gleaming rear end of the car.

His bride's flower girls—Ellie's cousins Lady Emily and Lady Rose—had excitedly festooned them, and the car bonnet, with flower blossoms, giggling madly as their brother, the young Viscount, had vigorously popped streamers into the car's interior.

Leon had tolerated it all with smiling equanimity. These harmless aristocratic antics were, after all, what he was paying for. Just as he was paying for his bride's father and his family to enjoy their exile in luxury at his expense.

And in exchange...

His eyes slid to his bride. No longer in her wedding finery, she had changed into an ivory silk couture number and five-inch heels—which, Leon noticed with wry amusement, she was now kicking off into the spacious footwell with a sigh of relief.

'That bad?' he said sympathetically, nodding at the discarded killer heels.

'Not my thing,' she answered feelingly.

'You looked fabulous in them, though,' Leon said, as he headed down Piccadilly towards Hyde Park Corner.

'Well, that was the idea,' Ellie answered easily.

* * *

The shoes were part of her brand-new couture wardrobe, wearing which she would grace the arm of her billionaire husband when he showed off his princess bride to the world. Already engagements had been set, and they had a crammed social diary that would take them to one upper-crust event after another across Europe and beyond. They would be doing the Season—*all* the Seasons—and being seen at the best places with the best people, a high-flying, jet-setting couple who combined royalty and riches in a dazzling display.

It wouldn't be the life Ellie was used to. As Ellie Peters her only international travel was to jungle and tundra with Malcolm and her mother. Even as Princess Elizsaveta of Karylya she had usually stayed only in her homeland, accompanying her stepmother and sister to whatever royal functions they were involved with.

But if her husband wanted them to jet around the world in a glittering swirl of royalty and aristocracy, then that was what they would do. It was what she had signed up to.

Was that what he was intending for their honeymoon? Some ultra-fashionable luxury location half the world away? she wondered as they headed out of London.

But when Leon told her the drive would be a couple of hours, Ellie started to relax. The day had been long, with an early start for all the preparations needed to turn her into a royal bride in all her finery, and the lavish wedding breakfast had seemed to go on for ever. Now, in the late afternoon, she felt tiredness wash over her, and the smooth motion of the powerful car began to cradle her into drowsiness...

At her side, Leon watched her translucent eyelids flutter shut, her breathing slow.

He let her sleep.

Who knew how long the night ahead would be? And all the nights to come thereafter…

Pleasurable anticipation started to fill him. At last this most breathtakingly beautiful woman was his—and their honeymoon awaited…

Ellie stirred, blinking. 'Where are we?' she asked, looking around. Then, as she took in her surroundings, she gave a little gasp of pleasure.

Beyond the small gravelled parking area the reed-edged waters of a lake beckoned, girdled by broad-leaved forest all around. It was totally private, totally remote.

Leon cut the engine, turning to her. 'Do you like it?' He smiled.

'Oh, *yes*!'

She was slipping her shoes on, opening her car door and stepping out, and Leon did likewise.

Satisfaction was filling him—her reaction was just what he wanted.

He led the way forward, through screening willows and alders, to gain the wooden boardwalk edging the lake that glittered darkly in the late sunshine. The only sign of habitation was a cottage set a little further on.

'It's like a gingerbread house!' Ellie exclaimed pleasurably as she spotted it.

A manservant was emerging from the cottage, and Leon exchanged a few words with him. He would fetch their luggage and then leave them entirely in peace unless summoned.

Inside the cottage, tea had been set out in a comfortably appointed sitting room, whose wide bi-fold doors opened directly on to a broad deck flooded with sunshine.

Ellie turned to him. 'Oh, Leon, this is absolutely *lovely*!' She smiled warmly, her eyes lighting up. 'Ah, tea!' she exclaimed gratefully, sinking down on one of the two sofas, easing her feet out of her killer shoes again before reaching for the teapot and pouring for them both.

'So, what do you think of it?' Leon asked, taking the cup she held out for him.

'It's delightful!' she said warmly. 'And quite a surprise. I thought—' She broke off, stirring milk into her tea.

'Yes?'

Leon's prompt was pointed. She made a slight face and looked up at him.

'Well, I thought you would want somewhere more… public. Glitzy. You know, to—' She broke off again.

An eyebrow rose quizzically. 'To show you off? My royal bride?'

Was there an edge in his voice? He hadn't intended it, but perhaps it was there all the same.

She was looking straight at him now. 'Well, yes,' she answered frankly. 'After all, there's no point marrying a princess and then hiding her away, is there?' She spoke lightly, as if determined not to make too big a deal of it but not to shirk from it either.

He sat back, crossing one long over the other. 'I'm not sure that I want to share you with anyone right now,' he murmured, and he let his eyelids half close as his eyes rested on her. 'I think I want you all to myself…'

He saw a gratifying flush of colour stain her cheeks—only a swift wash, but it was revealing, and that was what he wanted.

He gave a laugh, to lighten the moment. 'And anyway, we've been on show the whole day—I think we deserve some relaxing time "offstage", don't you? And…' his eyes went to the deck beyond the open bi-folds '…this certainly seems to fit the bill for that!'

'Oh, it *does*!' The warmth was back in her voice. 'I'm so looking forward to exploring! Can we do that?'

'We can do anything we want,' Leon returned. 'It's our honeymoon, and we get to choose.'

He saw her eyes flicker again and knew why. It was the H word that had done it.

Because ours is not the kind of honeymoon an ordinary couple would be having...

But a honeymoon it was, for all that. And it would bring all the pleasures every honeymoon should bring…

He would ensure it.

Ellie sat at the old-fashioned, chintz-skirted, kidney-shaped dressing table in her bedroom and stared at her reflection. The gingerbread cottage was far too homely for a couture outfit, so she'd donned one of her own well-worn favourites—a mauve knee-length dress in fine jersey, with a boat neck and three-quarter sleeves. She fastened her hair with a simple barrette, then slipped her feet into comfortable low-heeled sandals and headed downstairs.

Her mood was strange—uncertain. Up to this point all her energies—mental and physical—had been focussed exclusively on making her wedding happen. And now it had. And she was here with Leon.

Alone with Leon—

She felt her heart rate start to skip, conscious of her quickening pulse and an air of nervousness as she headed down the narrow flight of stairs to the small sitting room. She thought there was something she ought to be thinking about—that she ought to have thought about for quite some time, but she had been too swept up in all the wedding preparations.

She felt it hovering at the back of her mind…knew it was time to bring it to the forefront. Face the implications of it…

But not right now. Her mind skittered away from it, not wanting to confront it.

I'll think about it later.

For now she would simply deal with the evening immediately ahead.

Leon's words to her over tea floated across her mind.

I think we deserve some relaxing time...

It was a sentiment that appealed.

In the sitting room, Leon was already there. A table-lamp had been lit against the night gathering outside, giving it a cosy feel. He turned from the drinks trolley, and as his eyes fell on her Ellie felt again that quickening of her pulse, that consciousness of his looks and masculinity that she always felt.

'An aperitif before dinner?' he asked pleasantly.

'Please,' she answered, opting for a sweet martini.

As she took it from him she thought she saw his gaze flicker over her, and was suddenly conscious that perhaps the jersey dress was just a little too softly draped over her body. But then her eyes flickered to him in turn, and she was conscious of how comfortably informal Leon was looking, too, with an open-necked shirt, turned back cuffs and a cashmere sweater slung casually over his shoulders. He looked, as ever, effortlessly drop-dead gorgeous...

'It's a mild evening—shall we go out on the deck?' Leon suggested.

She smiled and let him usher her out. Night was gathering over the lake, and there was the low sound of water lapping beneath the decking and an owl calling from nearby in the woods, then another from further away. She wandered across to the wooden balustrade at the edge of the deck, leaning on it to look over the lake.

'A pair of tawnies,' Ellie announced. Then, listening again, 'And a barn owl, too!'

'How can you tell?' Leon asked, coming up beside her.

She was glad to tell him, for it was a safely innocuous subject, and would help to take her mind off the fact that Leon was standing right beside her, his sleeve brushing hers from time to time as he sipped at his own gin-based cocktail in a leisurely fashion.

She launched into a description of the different kinds of owl hooting, giving a good impression of each herself that made him laugh, and her as well. Their shared laughter made her feel more comfortable...companionable.

'How do you know all that?' he asked with a smile.

'I grew up with a naturalist, remember?' she replied. 'Malcolm was a wonderful teacher.'

There was a fond note in her voice and Leon did not miss it.

'You've been fortunate in your stepfather,' he heard himself say.

'*And* my father.' Her rejoinder was adamant. 'I may only have spent school holidays with him, but they were always happy times. He loves me dearly. And I him. It's why I—'

She broke off, but Leon could hear the unspoken ending of her declaration.

It's why I married you.

He shifted his stance, wanting to change the topic. Away from why she had married him. Away from fathers altogether.

His thoughts twisted inside him. His own father had thought of no one but himself, putting himself first, his own interests, and if that meant deserting the wife he'd professed to love, and their son, too, well, he'd done it without a second thought. Abandoned them to their fate. Thinking nothing of them.

And is her father any better? Happy to see his own daughter married off to a complete stranger just so he can have a luxurious exile?

He felt a flicker of contempt go through him, familiar to him from the contempt he'd always felt for his own father. He, too, had once believed his father loved him—loved the wife he'd kept telling how much he adored her. Until he'd walked out on her.

So much for love...

He would have none of it.

His eyes went to his bride. Well, love had nothing to do with *their* marriage, and he didn't want it to. They'd gone into it clear-eyed, the pair of them, for mutual advantage, and each was getting something out of it that they wanted. That was enough.

He veiled his eyes suddenly. And, of course, for one other essential reason. The reason he'd brought his bride here to this remote, secluded spot...entirely private.

To claim her as my bride—in every way.

CHAPTER SEVEN

WITH A GESTURE of reluctant refusal Ellie pushed back the plate of exquisite hand-made liqueur chocolate truffles Leon was proffering.

'I couldn't eat even one more!' She gave a mock groan.

'We'll save the rest for tomorrow.' Leon smiled.

Dinner had been provided by staff who'd arrived at the cottage and then left again once the main course had been served. Ellie had made the kind of anodyne conversation with Leon that strangers could overhear, but once they'd gone she'd become conscious of a different kind of constraint—that of being with Leon on her own.

She was grateful, therefore, that he had continued with the same mild and genial air he'd adopted since they'd left their wedding, telling her about the cottage and its original Victorian owner, of his enthusiasm for wildfowl. That had led to wildlife in general, and then they had moved on to her stepfather's work, with Leon drawing her out about her experiences travelling with him and her mother on filming expeditions.

Ellie had felt herself relaxing more, regaling him with anecdotes about her adventurous travels in remote locations, where physical comforts had been scarce, and that had taken them through the rest of the meal.

Now, after pushing away the plate of truffles, she finished a particularly hair-raising account of privation and Leon frowned.

'Your mother couldn't have a more different lifestyle now than the one she had with your father—a royal palace versus roughing it in the middle of nowhere!'

Ellie laughed. 'She never could stand all the palace protocol and ceremony! It was bad enough being the Crown Princess, but being Grand Duchess never suited her—it was good that she found the courage to leave a marriage she felt she'd been pressured into by her parents' ambitions for her. They were dazzled by her royal suitor. It never worked for either of them. She's so much happier with Malcolm. And I know my father is so happier with my stepmother. My parents were right to part. No one should stay in an unhappy marriage.'

She saw Leon's face tighten. Had it been tactless to talk about marriages ending when theirs had only just begun? However unlike a normal marriage theirs was?

But his words dispelled any noting that he'd been thinking about their own marriage.

'But what if the wish to part isn't mutual?' he said. 'If it suits only one of the parties?'

There was a harshness in his voice that made Ellie speak carefully. 'That's…difficult,' she allowed.

'Difficult...?' he echoed, as if the word were a derisory understatement.

She looked at him, concern in her eyes. 'That sounds personal,' she said carefully.

Dark eyes flashed across the table at her. His words were stark when he spoke. 'My father walked out on my mother at the height of the economic collapse in Greece. We'd gone from affluence to poverty. He was a well-paid civil servant, suddenly sacked when the government ran out of money to pay him. He didn't like it—and so he took off with another woman who had money stashed abroad. Left my mother and me to fend for ourselves.'

'Oh, Leon, I'm so sorry!'

Instinctively she reached her hand out to his, but he'd seized up his cognac glass and taken a heavy mouthful, as if he needed it. As he set it down she saw his features lighten again, as if he were making a deliberate effort. Blanking the past.

He pushed back his chair, getting to his feet. 'Shall we get some fresh air?' she heard him ask, and his tone of voice was deliberately lighter.

It was understandable that he wanted to change the subject, for who would want to dwell on such painful memories? So Ellie followed him out on to the deck, to lean, like him, against the wooden railing, gazing out over the dark surface of the lake.

The country air was fresh, and sweet, after so many weeks in London, and she gave a sigh of pleasure. She felt a wash of sympathy for him—for his blighted youth, his plunge into sudden poverty, his father's desertion.

How little I know about him—about the man he is.

But then, how could she know more? Theirs was an artificial marriage—they were still strangers essentially.

Yet as he glanced down at her now there was a familiarity about the way he was smiling at her. A growing sense of ease between them.

'It's good, isn't it, this place?' Leon said, indicating with a nod the quiet, dim vista around them.

The night was cloudy, with a faint mild breeze ruffling the waters of the lake quietly lapping below the deck. Another owl hooted softly, adding to the peaceful atmosphere.

'Yes,' she said, nodding in slow agreement, 'it's good.'

She looked up at him. Returned his smile. But as she did so she saw, even in the low light, his expression change. Become...*searching*. And as it changed she felt something change within herself, felt a sudden consciousness of the two of them, standing out here, all on their own, far from anywhere and anyone else, with the whole world, or so it seemed, to themselves.

It seemed a very private moment. Very…intimate.

She felt her breath tighten in her lungs, wanted to look away, suddenly supremely conscious of his presence at her side. A tendril of hair fluttered at her cheek in the faint breeze, the air soft on her face. Her senses seemed heightened, the pulse at her throat tangible. Out of nowhere came the memory of that first waltz at their betrothal ball…of the kiss that had ended it. She felt the memory bring its sweetness again…

At the back of her mind she felt the thought she did not wish to think stir once more, seeking admittance. She held it back, held it at bay. Instead she gave herself to what she wanted to do, what she always wanted to do…what she had wanted to do from the very first.

She gazed up at his face, drinking him in, watching those dark, heavy-lidded eyes that were looking down at her in return, half veiled by those long, inky lashes.

Once before he had looked into her eyes like that… As the music of the waltz had ended and his hands had cupped her face, tilting it to his…

They did it again now.

His touch was cool as he cradled her cheeks, his fingertips drifting over the delicate lobes of her ears, teasing at the wafting tendrils of her hair. His face bent to hers, lips catching hers. She felt weakness drum through her…felt her eyelids flutter shut. Felt his mouth—his skilled, silken mouth—move on hers slowly, softly, sensuously.

She opened her mouth to his…

She felt her pulse surge, her lips part under his, her pliant body leaning into him as if her body were taking control of her, yielding to its own impulses, its own needs, its own demands. As his kiss deepened she felt the arousal of her quickened senses, her hands slipping to his chest, feeling the strong, hard wall of muscle beneath her splaying fingers.

Her body quickened, blood surging in her veins, and a flame caught fire within her that was not of her conscious being. It came from a place far, far deeper inside her—a hunger that had come from nowhere, possessing her...

Her mouth clung to his and a low moan broke from her throat. The sense of being possessed by more than she was seared within her. Her kiss deepened, feeding the hunger that had leapt within her. A hunger for him...for Leon... for his mouth, his body...

And it was a hunger he shared, for now his hands were sliding down to her shoulders, around her waist, fastening over her hips, moving lower still...

The hunger leapt inside her again, possessing her, and she felt her breasts engorge and flower. Another low moan broke from her throat and her body pressed itself against his, seeking more...so much more...

There was nothing else in all the world except this... now...and nothing mattered except this...now...as their mouths moved together, seeking, finding...

With a sudden rasping breath he hauled her close against him, his kisses devouring her. They were hip to hip, their bodies melding together, moulding together...

And his body was reacting to that closeness.

With a shocked gasp she pulled away, rearing back from him even though his hands still anchored her at her hips. She stared at him, eyes distended, lips still bee-stung from his. Her heart was pounding. Dear God, what had she done? To go from that soft, sensuous kiss to...to...

Her mind sheered away and her body did, too. Now she was pulling herself free from him, clutching at the wooden railings, head bowed, fighting for composure...

'What is it? What's wrong?'

Leon spoke behind her, concern in his voice—and

alarm. She could hear his breathing, heavier than it had been during conversation, and knew hers was just as hectic. Her heart was still hammering as if she'd run a race. As if she'd been swept away on a flood tide that she had never before experienced. Had never before known the power of.

But she knew it now.

'Tell me! Tell me what is wrong!'

Leon's voice came again, still filled with concern and alarm.

'Leon— I...' She tried to speak, but could not. Tried to look at him, but could not.

Her head dropped again, shoulders hunched. Heat flushing through her. And dismay. Dismay that she had allowed what she should never have allowed to overwhelm her as it had!

Her grip on the railings spasmed.

I should have faced it sooner—not hidden it away, out of sight, while I was burying myself in all those wedding preparations, blanking it. And now...

She started. Leon's large, square hand had lowered over hers, lifting her fingers free of the rail. Gently but inexorably. She felt his presence behind her. He was turning her now, towards him, leading her away from the balustrade, lowering her down upon a wide rattan settee on legs that were suddenly too weak to hold her. Sitting down beside her.

'Tell me,' he said quietly. He did not let go of her hand. 'Tell me what's wrong.'

Her eyes flew to his. Then dropped away again. And still she could not speak. Her skin was burning...her lungs were bereft of air.

'Elizsaveta, look at me.'

Uncertainly, she lifted her eyes to him as he spoke again. His voice was quiet still, but filled with an intensity that accentuated his slight accent.

'Have I confused you?' he asked.

His gaze was searching hers in the dim light. Only the lamplight from the sitting room behind them spilled out onto the deck.

A faint smile tugged at his mouth, and there was a rueful tone in his voice as he spoke again. 'I have been a very... inattentive fiancé, I know—but there was a purpose to it. Yes, I had to settle my business affairs—but there was another reason, too. I could not trust myself to be with you too much. Do you not know why that was?'

He paused, and now his gaze on her was not rueful, nor the tone of his voice.

'Did you really think I was marrying you only for your royal blood?' he was saying now, in that same quiet voice, with the warmth of his hand over hers, stilling the trembling of her limbs. 'Did you really think there was no other reason?' And now there was something else in his voice—an edge, and yet it was an edge softened by wryness.

He paused, and she could feel his thumb brush across the back of her hand with a slow, sensuous touch that seemed to be both calming her and soothing her jangled nerves.

His eyes held hers, their expression changing, and in the stricken veins of her body she felt her pulse quicken... like a ghost of what it had been before she'd torn herself away from him.

'Did I not show you with every look I gave you?' His voice was husky, his eyes fixed on hers. 'Show you when I kissed you at our betrothal ball...?'

She felt colour flush into her cheeks and knew he could see it, even in this dim light.

He was speaking again, in the same husky voice, and the slow brush of his thumb on her hand was still soft and sensuous. 'And when I kissed you then do you think I could not tell how you felt about me in return? And when I kissed you just now do you think I could not tell how the same flame you light in me every time you look at me, caught fire in you as well?' The husk in his voice was yet more pronounced. 'And do you think,' he finished, 'I would have married you if I did not desire you—if I did not know that same flame burned in both of us?'

He paused, giving a wry half-smile that tugged at his mouth. She gazed at him, wishing with all her being that she had not tried to shut out what had been in her head all along, what she had pushed down and back and out of sight and thought. Now it was here—standing foursquare between them.

Leon was speaking again, still with that quiet, reassuring warmth in his voice, yet there was an underlying timbre to it that plucked at her senses.

'We are married, yes, and for reasons we have both been honest about. And that is *good*—never think otherwise.' The slightest edge crept into his voice. 'But we can be honest, too, about the flame that burns between us! That, too, is good and honest and true. And why should we not yield to that flame? We are consenting adults, my most beautiful and alluring bride...' His voice had a wry humour in it now. 'So why should we not consent to what we both clearly wish to do?'

She felt him turn her hand in his, lift it to his mouth. He moved his lips across it slowly, sensuously...arousingly... and she felt the flame that his kiss had fired in her flicker in her senses.

'Why should we not consent?' he said again, turning over her hand so that his mouth was moving on her open palm, her delicate, sensitive wrist...

Her blood started to beat up inside her again, her breathing quickening. But it was a breath she must use for a different purpose. To speak—to tell. Before his caresses turned her mind to mush and that urgent hunger leapt in her body again...that hunger she had never known before.

'Because…' Her voice was low, barely audible, and her eyes were barely able to meet his, even in the dim of the night. 'Because I have never—'

His mouth lifted from her wrist and she drew her hand from his slackened grip. He stared at her, not understanding. She had to make him understand. *Had* to…

'I never have, Leon,' she said, her voice lower still, though she forced it to be steady.

She dropped her eyes again, unable to look at him. Her hands twisted in her lap. Her stomach clenched and her whole body was tense, suddenly. Awaiting his response.

It came after a silence that seemed to stretch for ever. 'You are telling me,' she heard him say, his voice expressionless, 'that you are a virgin?'

The word seemed to toll like a bell in the night.

She could not speak. Could only nod.

The silence stretched again and she could bear it no longer. Her eyes lifted to him. His face was shadowed and she could not read it.

She swallowed. 'I'm sorry,' she said. It seemed inadequate, but it was the best she could manage. 'I should… I should have told you…made it clear before I—'

With a sudden movement she jerked to her feet, trying to rush past him, wanting only to get away from him.

But he caught at her hand, getting to his feet as well, taking her other hand, his clasp warm and strong.

He looked down into her face. There was something different in his eyes now—something that made her throat tighten and emotion well up in her. It was an emotion she could not name, but only feel.

Slowly, infinitely slowly, he lowered his head to drop a kiss upon her. Not on her mouth, but her forehead. There was a half-smile on his face that she could not understand.

'It's been a long, long day,' he said. 'And this has all been too much for you. Go to bed,' he said quietly. 'And sleep well. Sleep deeply—and alone.'

His light touch fell away, and he stepped aside to let her go indoors.

On stricken limbs, she did.

CHAPTER EIGHT

OVER BREAKFAST THE next morning, out on the sunny deck, she told him of the romances that had never happened. She tried to make her manner not brisk, but frank—though she'd had to steel herself to talk about such a personal subject, and there were two tell-tale flags of colour high on her cheeks.

'I've dated,' she said, with an air of self-consciousness about her as she helped herself to toast and marmalade, not looking directly at him. 'I've been to films, the theatre, the occasional gig or party, with men who work with my stepfather, who scarcely realise that I'm anything more than simply his stepdaughter, Ellie Peters. But I've never been only her, Leon. And I can never let myself forget that.'

She made herself go on, knowing she had to make him understand. 'Because, you see, when you're a princess you have to be…careful. Other girls my age can afford to be carefree—care*less*, even—but for me, and indeed for my sister…' her voice changed as she thought of Marika's doomed romance with the son of their father's enemy '…an unwise choice can be disastrous. It always seemed safer—wiser—never to get involved.' She took a breath, made herself look at him. 'So I didn't.'

Even as she spoke she was conscious of her evasion. Everything she was telling him was true—but it was not all the truth.

I wanted to wait—wait for 'the one'—the man I would

love for ever, who would love me in return. It would have made things...simpler.

But how could she say that to this man whom she had married without any love at all?

She lifted her buttered toast and marmalade and looked across at Leon. She gave a little shrug—almost a defiant one. 'So, there it is, Leon.'

She looked away again, lowering her toast to her plate, and suddenly sitting very still, as if she were fighting for composure.

What would he say? How would he reply to what she'd confided to him?

The man who was sitting opposite her was her husband but still so very much a stranger. A man about whom her thoughts—ever since that kiss at their betrothal ball, ever since she had first set eyes on him, ever since that kiss last night—had been so confused.

As they still were.

Her gaze went back to him, unconsciously anxious for his reaction.

Leon made no immediate reply, marshalling the thoughts in his head. What she had told him, and the reasons she had given, made sense. He had thought—assumed—that once they were married they would both yield, with mutual desire, to the flame that burned so strongly between them. Two consenting adults, just as he had told her, happy to consent.

I thought it would be very simple...

But it was far more complicated than that—far more... delicate. And he must get it right...make his reply to her now with utmost care.

'I appreciate completely what you have said, and I thank you, truly, for trusting me sufficiently to tell me.'

His voice was serious, respectful, acknowledging what

she'd confided in him, but he smiled across at her—a warm, reassuring smile—saw the tension in her face ease a fraction and was glad. He felt that strange emotion again—felt a resolve forming in him that, whatever it took, he would guide her forward in this journey they would be making together.

I will be her first—her very first!

A sense of wonder struck him and his eyes rested on her again, more warmly still. Then, wanting to banish the last of that tension in her eyes, with a deliberately relaxed movement he reached for his coffee cup, made his voice as relaxed, too.

'So, tell me, what would you like to do today? Do you want to go out on the water? The lake looks very calm—shall we give it a go?'

He saw her eyelashes flicker for a moment, and then she returned his smile, as if relieved that he was talking about ordinary matters now. And such enjoyable ones.

'Oh, yes—let's!'

There was enthusiasm in her voice, relief, too, he could hear, and Leon was glad.

'We'll order a picnic to take with us as well, shall we?' he went on.

There was equal enthusiasm for that notion, and he knew he had set the right tone for the day ahead. He would take the H from honeymoon and make it stand for holiday instead.

His eyes rested on her, though his gaze was veiled. How incredibly beautiful she was! Her face was lit by the morning sun, minimal make-up, and she wore an open-necked short-sleeved shirt over short-cropped cotton trousers. There was a string of colourful beads around her neck, no more adornment than that, and yet she took his breath away.

Resolve filled him once more, and that same unknown emotion came yet again.

I must not rush her—it must be in her own time—only when she is truly ready to accept what is between us.

It was going to be a self-denying abstinence, but he knew he absolutely had to let her be comfortable with him…take everything at the pace she could cope with.

'I'll row. You steer,' said Leon, offering his hand to help Ellie into the rowing boat by the jetty, then seating himself and pushing off with one of the oars. 'Here goes!' he said cheerfully.

Cheerfulness was going to be his watchword. Cheerfulness, friendliness and easy-going companionship. That was what was needed now, and he would give it willingly. And it seemed to be working, for his bride, who had fled from him the night before, was now matching his cheerful demeanour in equal measure, and that gave him satisfaction enough for now.

She has to get used to me. Has to become at ease with me.

That was essential. Right now it was obvious to him that she simply could not cope with the intense physical intimacy that had burst into flame between them the night before—it had been too much, too soon. And for a reason that he had never dreamt of…

He felt again the echo of the shock he'd felt when he'd realised what it was she had been telling him last night. It was not, he knew, something he'd ever have thought about her—or any woman her age. She was twenty-six, after all, and had led far less of a sheltered life than her sister, still cocooned in the royal palace in Karylya. It would have been natural to assume she'd had romances in her adult life, and with her incandescent beauty, her outgoing personality and confident experience of the real world, thanks to her upbringing, anything else would have been unusual in the extreme.

Yet those romances had never happened. She had told him as much And it was to that end that he was now being so cheerful and easy-going, pulling strongly at the oars, heading across the lake.

Though he gave no sign that he had noticed, he had seen with satisfaction how her gaze flickered over his torso as he rowed, his muscles visibly flexing under the T-shirt he was sporting. It was a regard he returned in spades, drinking in the way her long bare legs were slanting across the hollow of the boat, her elbows resting on the gunwale, the sun kissing her face as he longed to do...

He speeded up his rowing. Vigorous exercise would be a sensible diversion from such longings.

Ellie settled herself on one of the rattan chairs on the sunny deck with a pleasurable sigh. It had been, she thought, a lovely day—just lovely! They had reached a tiny islet, dragged the rowing boat ashore, and made a mini-camp to enjoy their hearty picnic. She had fed the left-over pastry crumbs from their raised game pies to a suddenly attentive family of wild ducks—'Malcolm would disapprove, but I can't resist...and besides, it's to say thank you for invading their haven here!' she'd laughed—and then it had been her turn to take the oars, weaving a meandering course towards a jetty on the far side of the lake.

They'd moored up there and had gone ashore to explore the woods, with Ellie telling Leon what she knew of forest ecology and the wildlife it sheltered. There had been a path of sorts, but Leon had helped her over fallen branches, his hand strong and firm, his clasp nothing more than helpful.

Relief was uppermost in her. How much easier it was to have him the way he was being now—cheerful and relaxed, interested in what she was telling him, a convivial and easy-going companion. Oh, she was still constantly aware of his magnetic physical appeal, but she would set that aside for now. It was easier that way...

I've married a man who was all but a stranger on our wedding day—but now I want to get used to being with him, get to know him...spend time with him that is simple, easy. Without any complications...

She felt her mind sheer away from just what such 'complications' might be—they were too much to cope with. Now she just wanted to go on being the way they'd been today. Uncomplicated. Enjoyable. Very pleasantly enjoyable. And for that she was grateful.

He's easy to be with.

It was a good thought to have about the man she had married to protect her father and his family. He was sitting down opposite her now, unfolding a map of the estate as she poured out their tea.

'It's not open to the public at the moment, so we can roam wherever we want,' he was saying. 'We can visit the big house, too, if you like. Plus, there are cycle trails everywhere, with bikes provided.' He paused, then quirked an eyebrow at her. 'Does that all sound very tame?' he asked.

Ellie shook her head firmly. 'No, it sounds totally relaxing—and that is just what I want.' She glanced at him. 'Are you sure *you* won't be bored?'

As she spoke she felt colour mount in her cheeks. She knew Leon had had very different intentions for their stay here.

If he saw her start to flush, he gave no sign of it. 'I haven't been on a bike since I was a kid,' he said ruminatively.

'Me neither!' Ellie laughed, glad her flush was subsiding.

They pored over the map together, working out the best trails, and apart from catching the heady scent of Leon's aftershave, and noticing that at this hour of the day his chiselled jawline was roughening with regrowth, she coped with it admirably. Leon seemed unaware of her covert observation of him, and she was grateful.

She was grateful, too, that he continued to be cheerful and easy-going all through dinner and beyond. It had started to drizzle, so they settled down by the fire in the sitting room, watching a history documentary on TV. Leon stretched his long legs out towards the fire as he nursed a cognac at the other end of the sofa from her, and Ellie sipped a glass of sweet dessert wine.

It was easy, it was comfortable, it was companionable. And the same comfortable, companionable ease continued over the leisurely days that followed.

They made their cycling expedition—top-brand bikes having been delivered to the cottage after breakfast—whizzing along leafy forest trails and ending up at a Victorian mansion designed by a notable Gothic Revival architect for an exhaustive tour.

'An acquired taste,' Ellie said tactfully, more used to the delicately gilded rococo style of her father's palace or the medieval north country fastness of her uncle's principal seat.

They also explored the area by car. There was a race circuit nearby, and Ellie insisted Leon indulge in a track session, watching him with a stab of alarm at the terrifying speeds he coaxed from his beloved supercar—an alarm he laughed off afterwards with airy unconcern and post-race exhilaration. And she also sensed an air of satisfaction that she should have felt alarmed for him in the first place.

They added in a visit to a ruined abbey in a nearby river valley, sad and atmospheric, where one of the Romantics had once penned an equally sad and atmospheric sonnet, which Ellie had had to learn by heart at school, and quoted verbatim as they walked around the ruins.

They'd headed for a nearby scenic market town, where they browsed in second-hand bookshops and indulged in a pub lunch of fish and chips—only bettered by a lavish cream tea the following day, at a quaint tea shop in a picture-postcard traditional English village thronged with tourists taking photos of rose-covered thatched cottages and the well-stocked duck pond.

As they sat at their tiny table in the bay window, overlooking the village green, Leon listened to Ellie chatting amiably to the family sitting at the next table about the picturesque village.

When the other family left, he spoke. 'Do you never worry you'll be recognised?' he asked curiously.

She shook her head. 'Not really. Even those people who've heard of Karylya won't think a daughter of the ex-sovereign would be having tea here!' She gave a laugh, and pointed to where his sleek, low-slung car was parked outside. 'That monster of yours is getting far more attention than me!' she said.

A group of young lads and their dads were clustered admiringly around Leon's car and Leon, adopting his bride's own friendly attitude, found himself chatting to them as he and Ellie prepared to leave.

Exchanging performance data with those whose knowledge of top-marque vehicles way exceeded any hope of ever being able to afford one themselves, he amiably let them take selfies with the car, then gunned the powerful engine with a satisfyingly loud roar just for them, before finally heading off with a casual wave of his hand.

Ellie strapped herself into the passenger seat, smiling at Leon for what he'd just done. Her thoughts were warm.

I scarcely knew him when I married him—but now that I am getting to know him, how much there is to like!

Emotion fluttered in her.

To be so devastatingly good-looking and yet to be so good-natured with it!

It was a rare combination.

That flutter of emotion came again…

'That was so nice of you!' said Ellie. 'You could see how thrilled those boys were!'

The warmth of her thoughts was in her voice, and Leon turned his head towards her.

'Just following your example,' he said, and smiled.

It warmed him to hear the warmth in her voice, to see it in her eyes on him.

And he felt his longing for her ache through him…

'Do you know, we've been here a week already?' Ellie mused.

They were taking their customary after-dinner liqueur out on the deck. The sky tonight was clear, and starlight glittered on the dark surface of the lake. Her thoughts were strange. The week had passed so swiftly, and as each day had passed she had felt more and more at ease with Leon. He was a stranger no longer—

But if not a stranger—then what?

The question hung in her head—but she could give herself no answer.

She was glad when he spoke. 'I think that calls for a toast!' he said, and smiled, raising his glass accordingly.

Behind his smile, he rested his eyes on her as they stood by the railing, breathing in the soft night air.

Was she a little closer to him than she usually stood?

The scent of her perfume caught at him and desire flared. How incredibly beautiful she was! How enchantingly so!

How I ache for her...

Had something of his longing for her shown in his eyes as their glasses touched? It must have, because there was a sudden answering flare in her eyes...

Then her eyes dropped and she turned her face away to look out over the water. There seemed to be a new tension in her stance.

Deliberately, he let the moment pass. And he made his voice nothing more than casual as he spoke again. 'So, has it been a good week?' he enquired.

She turned to look at him. Her expression was glowing. 'Wonderful!' she answered.

She seemed to hold his eyes for a moment, as if she wanted to say something else but was unsure. Leon waited. Every instinct on alert.

Her eyes searched his face. 'I want to thank you,' she said, her voice low. 'Not just for bringing me here—for knowing that this place is just what I needed! But...but for so much else, Leon. For being so understanding.'

There was an intensity in her voice he had never heard before, and he felt himself respond. He knew the meaning of what she was saying—knew there was only one answer he could give her.

'You must know,' he said, 'that whatever you choose— or do not choose—I will abide by it.'

Her eyes were searching his. Something was working in her face that he had never seen before.

'You're being very good about it, Leon,' she said. 'Many men would have—' She broke off, not sure what word to use.

Leon supplied one. 'Sulked?' he suggested, not hiding the tug of humour at his mouth.

She gave a lip-biting laugh. 'Oh, dear, yes—perhaps!' She glanced up at him. 'But somehow, you know, you're not the sulking type, I think!'

* * *

Ellie had said it humorously, conscious, with a strange little flurry of awareness, that she'd also said it teasingly…
almost flirtatiously…

She wanted to break her glance away, and yet, feeling
again that same little flurry, she didn't. She held his gaze
for a moment longer. Had something changed in his eyes,
too? She wasn't sure—could only feel that flurry stirring
inside her again, that same low vibration in her blood that
had started up the first time they'd stood here like this, at
the water's edge, under the night sky.

She dropped her eyes, finding it too disturbing, and
let her gaze go out over the darkling waters of the lake.
Thoughts stirred within her…feelings and emotions she
knew she must make sense of.

But how?

What certainties were hers?

One above all.

*He can arouse in me a response that no other man has
ever drawn from me. A single glance from him can make
me tremble…a single touch can set my every sense aflame…*

She had fled from that flame, confused and overwhelmed. Unable to cope with it. But in the week that had
passed he had given her time and space to think again.

She had married without love—but had she married
without passion, without desire? She could give no answer
but the truth. The truth that Leon had spelt out to her—the
same flame burned in both of them…

She turned her head, looking at him again. He was
standing very still, as if giving her time, letting her think
the thoughts that filled her head. She felt the familiar catch
in her throat that came every time she looked at him, drank
in the strong planed features of the face she could never
willingly tear her eyes from…

The strength of it shook her.

The strength of her desire for him.

More thoughts came—thoughts that she had to frame and answer.

Two years they would be together—no more than that. Then she would be free to leave, to find the true love she sought.

But until then, would desire suffice?

Perhaps I am safe because there will only ever be desire between us. Because that is all he wants. For is it not what I want, too?

She had never been free to indulge her senses, but Leon was no passing boyfriend who might simply prove an unwise choice if their relationship soured. Leon was her husband—and he had shown patience and understanding, shown himself to be someone she could be at ease with, find companionship with, enjoy the hours she spent with him.

And he was the man she desired.

The man I want to give myself to—and take in return—

Surely it would be safe to yield to her desire for such a man?

The knowledge filled her, removing all doubt, all confusion. Making all clear to her.

She spoke his name, low and soft.

She saw something change in his expression—as if, she realised, he had been holding himself on a tight leash—a leash he had now loosened.

He lifted his hand, then paused, and she could sense he was exerting absolute control in doing so.

His eyes searched hers in the dim starlight. 'I don't want to scare you away again.'

CHAPTER NINE

Leon's voice was low. Intensity filled him, but he fought against letting it show. Every instinct told him that it was happening—that what he had yearned for all this long, long week, yearned for since the moment he had first set eyes on her, was now happening.

But it must be at her pace—and hers alone. His desire must remain leashed until she was ready to release it.

He felt his heart start to beat in heavy, insistent slugs. Desire was building in him—filling him…

Slowly, very slowly, she turned her head.

'I could stay here all night,' she murmured. 'Watch the stars set and the sunrise…'

She looked out over the glimmering surface of the lake, relaxing against the railing, aware that the movement would bring her closer to him, brushing his shoulder with hers.

She felt his arm go around her, drawing her closer still. It was warm and she leaned into him, feeling his strength and solidity supporting her.

It felt good.

Right.

She breathed in the sweet night air, felt the waft of the light night wind winnowing the tendrils of her hair, teasing at her cheek, the sensitive nape of her neck.

She caught the musky, masculine scent of him, the potent maleness of him.

It felt good.

Right.

The fingers of his hand started to play lightly on her bare upper arm, idly. She gave a sigh at the languorous pleasure it aroused, leaning into him even more.

She felt the drift of his lips across the crown of her hair, heard him murmur something to her in Greek. Husky and low.

She lifted her face to his, searching the gaze fixed on her. Reached with her free hand to his jaw, roughened at this late hour. Let her fingertips move slowly along the hard edge of his jaw, across the sculpted outline of his mouth…

In her veins, a pulse started to beat. Warmth was filling her, and there was a quickening in her senses. She felt desire pool in her, gathering strength, deepening in intensity.

She turned her body into his, sliding her hand around the strong nape of his neck, into the feathered sable of his hair, and his hand dropped to her waist, wrapping around it.

She could feel the desire inside her strengthen, become a yearning, an ache she could not still or banish. She could only give herself to it, fully and freely…

She said his name again, raising her mouth to his, kissing him softly, with infinite care.

He did not kiss her back, he did not move in any way, but he let her lips touch his, as if daring her to take such liberties with him. As if testing what she was doing and why.

And as her mouth moved slowly, exploring his, as she felt that sweet, languorous arousal welling up within her, she knew and had never been more sure of anything in her life that it glowed within her like a bright flame of truth—that this moment now was right—that being here, with Leon, with this man she had married, the man she desired, was right…

Desire, warm and sweet and overwhelming, swept through her, deepening her kiss, and as it did so it seemed to light an answering flame in him. And all of a sudden it was not just her kissing him, but Leon catching her mouth, her lips, parting them with his with a sudden urgency that was like a match thrown onto tinder.

She drowned in it, the blood leaping in her, a smothered cry in her throat, and then her hand at his nape was shaping itself to him, her other hand sliding across the broad, muscled front of his torso, glorying in the strength she found there.

He crushed her to him and the cry in her throat came again, filled with wonder and longing.

Instantly his mouth released her and his hands cupped her face. In the dim night, his eyes burned gold.

'Are you *sure*, Ellie? You must be absolutely sure! If—if this isn't what you want, you must say so now...*now*.' His expression changed. 'It would be agony for me to let you go again. I long for you so much!'

His voice was hoarse, his eyes dark and strained.

'I have given you time—the time I knew you needed. But if it's not yet right, if it never will be right, then tell me now...'

His voice seemed to crack, and it drew from her an answering choke. Her eyes clung to his, her hands now closing around the strong muscles of his upper arm as if to steady herself with his strength.

Her face turned upwards to his. 'This *is* the time, Leon,' she said. 'I want this... I want *you*.' The catch came in her voice again. 'Oh, Leon, I want this, and you, and every-thing—*everything*!'

Her hands spasmed on his arms, clenching them tightly, glorying in their muscled strength, glorying in his close-ness, in the heady scent of him, the heat of his body so close to hers. Glorying in everything!

I'm glorying in him...in the man I want...desire...as I

have never wanted any other! This man that I have married. Leon—my husband.

And it seemed to her the most wonderful thing in all the world that he was her husband.

He needed no other answer. No other reassurance. Nothing else to stop him doing what he wanted with every fibre of his being to do now.

He lifted her into his arms. She was as light as a feather, drifting down to the darkened surface of the lake to float upon the water, and her arms wrapped around his neck.

He gazed down at her. 'And I will give you everything…'

That husk was in his voice, and the gold blaze of his eyes was molten.

He strode indoors and she let herself be carried by him. She could resist him no more. Could not resist the overpowering response to him that she had tried to ignore, and then deny, and then be fearful of. But he had overcome her fears.

His name was on her lips and he paused on the stairs to drop the swiftest kiss upon her, as if to answer her, and then he was taking her into his room, lowering her down upon the bed as gently as if she were fragile porcelain.

He stood back, and in the dim light she realised he was swiftly, urgently peeling his clothes from himself, exercising the most ruthless self-control as he did so. Then, gloriously, he was coming down beside her, and whilst her eyes widened instinctively as the lean, naked strength of his body was revealed to her—along with the evidence of his desire for her—suddenly she had to turn her head away, as if it were a sight too much for her. She could feel heat beating up in her, like a kindled furnace racing flames through her veins.

The weight of his body beside her dipped the mattress and her body rolled to his as his hand reached out to clasp hers, while the other hand gently, inexorably, turned her head towards him.

He was propped on one elbow, looking down at her. 'I can't hide my desire from you,' he said. His voice was low, intent. 'I want you so much... I ache for you...'

His strong fingers were warm on her cheek as she gazed up at him, the breath tight in her lungs, her heart thumping beneath her ripened breasts, which were straining at the material of her top. Her own evidence of her aching desire for him...

'And now, my most beautiful, beautiful bride, we can share all there is between us—all our desire.'

He paused, and she saw again the absolute self-control he was exerting. She said his name, and as she did so it was as if that iron self-control was released. With a rasp in his throat, he brought his mouth down on hers again, and this time there was no urgency, only slow, sensual desire designed to arouse, to draw from her with every silken glide the quickening of her own desire.

It melted through her, feeding the hunger that now rose in her—a hunger not just for his mouth, his lips and tongue, but for so much more of him. For all of him.

But to have all of him—all of that powerful, glorious body beside her—she must divest herself of what separated them. Restlessly, still beneath his silken mouth, she moved her legs, as if to free herself of the folds of her dress. Then his hand was on her thigh, performing that very office for her, and with a sudden movement, a low laugh, he had lifted himself from her, flipping her over with an effortless twist.

'You must allow me to do what it will be my exquisite pleasure to do,' he informed her, and his voice was nothing more than a husk, his eyes glinting in the dim light.

And allow him she did. She let his hand move to the zip at the back of her dress and slide it slowly, achingly, down, exposing the graceful curve of her spine. With the slightest movement of his hand he had also unfastened her bra, she realised, and now, as she gave a gasp, he was peeling both dress and bra from her supine body, casually lifting her hips to allow him to slide it from her completely.

She gave another gasp, for somehow her panties had disappeared with the other clothes, and with burning consciousness she realised that she was lying there, her body naked to his view and to the sensuous stroke of his fingertips…

A sigh went through her. A sigh of bliss and pleasure as slowly, making indulgent trails and whorls, he explored the contours of her back, from the delicate nape of her neck, down the long elegant sculpture of her spine, to the ripe roundness of her hips and the sweet mound below.

She felt her fingers sink into the bedding, heard herself give a long, languorous sigh, heard his low, husky laugh as she did so.

Yet even as she sighed at the sweet, sensuous pleasure of his touch, she knew it was not enough. A hunger was building in her, an ache, a longing… A restlessness… She felt her legs moving, scissoring, her hips flexing.

In instinctive answer to her need, Leon rolled her over again, and with another gasp she realised she was gazing up at him now, her body exposed to his. She heard him say something in Greek—a low growl whose words she did not know but whose meaning she did.

A kind of glory filled her as she lay there. For the very first time in her life a man was gazing upon her nakedness, and she knew that her nakedness was for him alone, only for him. Only for Leon…

She lifted her arms to loop them around his neck—but not to draw him down to her, only to raise her breasts to him, ripe and swollen, their peaks cresting. She was offering herself to him. And his mouth was lowering to them, his lips coming around one and then the other, and the pleasure of it consumed her, made her cry out.

Her spine was arching now, as his hands shaped the swell

of her breasts, feasting on them. There was an urgency now in his movements, in his mouth as its touch drew from her a quickening of her flesh. She moved again, that hunger, that restlessness consuming her. She wanted more…and yet more. She wanted everything—everything he could give her, bestow upon her.

She felt his body lower to hers—felt with yet another gasp how strong and powerful his manhood was, pressing upon her. Instinctively, with a knowledge as old as time itself, she slackened her thighs, opening her body to his. He was kissing her mouth now, feasting upon it as he had upon her ripened breasts. She felt her hips lifting to his in invitation, with a hunger that came from the very core of her being.

And yet he drew back, though with a little cry she tried to hold him.

'Not yet—' That rasp of absolute self-control was in his voice again. 'Not yet,' he urged again, his mouth against hers, 'or I will hurt you. And I would give all the world not to!' He brushed his mouth against hers. 'Trust me—trust me on this.' There was a smile in his voice now. 'Be patient…'

'I can't!' she cried, her voice breathless, infused with the urgency that was filling her body. 'I can't! I want you so much, Leon—I didn't know… I didn't realise how this would be!'

Her legs moved again, that restless hunger consuming her. Her hand grasped at his hip, seeking to draw him down on her again, to feel the hard pleasure of his body upon hers, to open herself to him, to his possession.

But her restless movement was stilled. His palm was on her abdomen, splayed out, holding her still.

'Wait,' he said. 'It will be better for you this way—trust me.'

There was a command in his voice, but somewhere deep

within herself she did not mind. She wanted to give herself to him, she ached to do so with all her being, but he had asked her to trust him and trust him she would.

And then, as his palm slid downwards into the vee of her thighs, she realised that everything up till this moment had been only the *hors d'oeuvre* before the banquet of the senses he was giving her.

Her hand spasmed on his shoulder and her head fell back, a gasp coming from her that silenced all that had come before. 'Oh, sweet heaven…'

Had she spoken aloud? Perhaps… For he had given that low, seductive laugh again, and dropped a soft, sensual kiss on her mouth.

'Sweet heaven,' he said huskily, 'is exactly where I am going to take you.'

Her eyes fluttered shut. Sensations so exquisite she could not believe the human body could experience them quivered through her as his skilled fingertips sought and found her tender folds. She felt her spine arch again, heard low, helpless gasps break from her as the pleasure he engendered mounted and mounted and mounted, until it was unbearable…just unbearable…

'Leon… I can't… I can't…'

The soft kiss came again. 'Then don't,' he said. 'Don't fight it, my most beautiful, beautiful one. This…*this* is for you…'

One last sweet touch, one last, sweet pressure, one last pang of unbearably exquisite hunger…and then flame sheeted through her. An inferno of flame, lifting and burning her, consuming her, turning her body to liquid fire. She was threshing her limbs, moving her head upon the pillow, her spine arching like a bow. She cried out in glory and in wonder, in an ecstasy whose existence she had never even glimpsed. Her body was pulsing, convulsing…

And then, with a sudden movement, Leon's body was

over hers, fusing with hers, and they were becoming one flesh, melded together, and he was surging within her, strongly and powerfully. A cry broke from him, deep and low, and her hands clawed over his shoulders. His hands snaked around her hips, lifting her to him, and her thighs locked around him. He threw his head back, the powerful sinews of his neck exposed, the pulse at his throat surging with the intensity of his release.

Time stopped. Eternity started. An eternity of ecstasy that brought sobs from her throat.

Her arms cradled him to her as ecstasy turned to weeping, emotion overpowering her, overwhelming her. He was rocking her in his arms, saying her name over and over again, and still she sobbed.

He drew back from her, though she tried to keep him with her.

'Ellie, have I hurt you? *Have I hurt you?*' Horror was in his voice.

She did not answer—could not. She only pulled him back to her, and he let her…let her pull his head onto her shoulder, let her arms hug him to her as if she would never let him go. And as her body slowly stilled he realised, with a flood of gratitude and relief, that her tears were not from pain…

His arms came around her, turning her so that it was now she who lay cradled in his arms. He hauled her to him, stroking his hand down the long, tangled tresses of her hair, his voice soothing her, calming her, quietening her as her trembling body eased and stilled.

And still he stroked her hair, murmuring the words that she needed to hear and he needed to speak. Until her body was quiet in his embrace and the sweet lassitude of passion spent swept over them both and sleep possessed them— as they had possessed each other in the glory and ecstasy of their union.

CHAPTER TEN

SLOWLY, ELLIE MOVED. Rousing herself from the depths of a slumber so profound it seemed to have taken her to a distant world. Slowly, she lifted heavy eyelids, blinking in the sunlight that streamed through the uncurtained window. The pillow her head was resting on seemed to be flexing, shifting position, and she realised with a rush of dawning consciousness that it was not a pillow, but a shoulder... Leon's shoulder.

He moved again, lifted his head now, and his lips brushed hers softly and tenderly. 'Good morning...'

There was a smile in the murmur, and a smile in the deep, dark eyes pouring into hers. And in the ordinary words of greeting there was the sweetness of intimacy that brought memory rushing in upon her.

She did not answer him—could not. Could only lie there, gazing up at him, quite helpless to do anything else. Not wanting to do anything else. Her heart was rich and full, and she was in the only place in the whole world she wanted to be! In Leon's arms.

How wonderful he'd made it for her—and how right, how absolutely *right* it had been, that it was Leon who had taken her on that journey she had never taken before. Her eyes glowed with all she felt.

'Now, that,' Leon murmured, 'is a look worth getting up for in the morning!' He made his voice light, with laughter in it—but there was a lot more than laughter.

No woman had ever gazed at him like that, with everything in her eyes…

He felt a warmth start to fill him—as if… A thought came to him, strange but powerful, as if something frozen deep inside him was thawing. He found himself wondering at it… It was as if something he had held on to for too long—so many years—was melting away from him. But what it was he did not know.

He had known it would be special between them—his desire for her had been so instant, so overpowering from the moment he'd first seen her—but more than that it had been special because of what she'd told him. That he would be the very first to show her all that could be between a man and woman.

But is it even more than that?

His eyes searched her face…so beautiful. Her eyes were gazing up at him, and he felt again that strange sense of something thawing deep inside him. It was disquieting, disturbing, and he was glad when a smile broke across her face, dispelling those thoughts he could give no name to, no reason for, and she gave an answering laugh to his, her eyes warm upon him.

He dropped a kiss on the tip of her delicate nose. 'Time for breakfast,' he told her.

For himself, he would have lingered all morning here in bed with her, but he knew he must not indulge himself—he had been as gentle as he could with her, and he must be considerate still.

'I could demolish—what is it you call it?—a full English!'

Which was exactly what he did some twenty minutes later—a whole pile of bacon and sausages and fried eggs and tomatoes and mushrooms, and a mountain of fried bread—out on the sunny deck, watched by Ellie with a smile of doting indulgence on her face as she delicately crunched toast and marmalade.

Replete, finally, Leon pushed his empty plate away. 'Right,' he said. 'I'm ready to start the day. What shall we do?'

He knew exactly what *he* wanted to do, but that was out of the question. Time, instead, for some more diversion. Energetic diversion, preferably.

'Shall we take the rowing boat out again?' he ventured.

'Oh, yes, please!' came her immediate answer, her face lighting up. 'And another picnic lunch on that little islet?'

'Whatever you want,' Leon promised her. 'Absolutely whatever you want…'

His gaze rested on her, warm and golden.

My princess bride—my very own princess bride! Made mine at last.

In the days that followed, in the same easy-going way of those days they'd spent together already, the intimacy of passion and desire that he had craved—as she, too, did now, he thought—they seemed to be bathed in a kind of perpetual golden light.

Which was odd, really, for the sunny weather they'd had since the wedding had broken, and rain swept in from the west, drumming on the lake, on the deck, on the windows of the cottage.

But Leon was glad of it—grateful for it.

For now, indoors, hunkered down by a roaring fire, toasting muffins on long forks or lolling on the sofa, drinking champagne, their arms around each other, watching rom-coms and thrillers and anything else that took their fancy on the TV, it really was as if the rest of the world simply no longer existed.

And that suited him fine—just fine.

Oh, soon he would be showing Ellie off to the world—his radiant princess bride!—but right now all he wanted was simply to revel in having her entirely to himself. This was new to him, he knew, being constantly with a single woman. And it felt good—very good indeed.

As he gazed down at her now, snuggled up to him on the sofa as the rain lashed down outside, he felt again that same strange feeling that had come to him as he'd woken that first morning with her in his arms, as if something were thawing deep inside him. And with it came that same feeling of disquiet…

Deliberately, to dispel that strange feeling, he bent his head to brush her mouth with his, letting his lips glide sensuously, arousingly, across hers. He felt her mouth respond, move against his, deepening the kiss. His hand closed over the sweet mound of her ripening breast and he felt his own body quicken…

Making love, he discovered, beside an open fire, on a soft deep hearthrug, was a blissfully pleasurable experience, sating him completely…banishing all disquieting thoughts.

He kept them banished—they had no place in his marriage. Not in the glittering marriage he had made to crown the achievements of his life, obtaining for himself a wife whose royal blood flowed in the veins of the most beautifully alluring woman he had ever known, whose embrace fired in him an intensity of desire that flared between them every time…

And it continued to do so, just as intensely, in the weeks that followed, even after they'd left the haven of their honeymoon cottage and set off into the wider world again. A world which welcomed them with open arms and showered invitations down upon them as they embarked upon an exhaustive round of every fashionable high-society event in the social calendar so that he could be seen with her.

He revelled in it all, and the radiantly beautiful Princess Elizsaveta—his wife, his bride!—made an entrance wherever she went, *en grande tenue*.

They were photographed and fêted, deluged with invitations to balls and dances, to house parties and yacht parties, beach parties and polo parties—every kind of glittering gathering of the highest of high society. They had become the most glamorous, fashionable newlyweds in Europe and beyond.

It was a world away from the life Ellie had lived with either of her parents, in very different ways—whether with her mother, accompanying her stepfather on location, or with her father at the royal palace in Karylya. But with Leon at her side she gave herself to it all—to the non-stop hectic whirl of endless socialising, dressed in couture gowns, adorned with jewellery and every chic accessory she possessed. To make herself beautiful for Leon. To dazzle the world for him…

Leon.

Her gaze went to him now, as they strolled companionably along the terrace above the marina in Monte Carlo. They'd just come from a lavish bash on one of the multi-million-pound yachts moored below, and the hour was late.

She felt desire quicken within her. How effortlessly fabulous he looked, as he always did, in a superbly fitting tuxedo, moulding his tall, muscled body, with his loosened tie giving him a raffish look, as did the edge of regrowth along his jawline.

Her stomach gave a little flip, anticipating what would come when they were back in their hotel suite.

The intensity of her desire—the desire his touch always unleashed in her—washed through her. It had swept her away—*he* had swept her away!—into a world she had never known, of physical desire and sensual bliss.

She slipped her hand into his, rejoicing in the strength of his clasp, the warmth of his fingers meshing with hers.

She was eager to get back to their suite. To have Leon all to herself, to take him into her arms and to feel that sweet, eager desire released in her…

But even as she felt the rush of desire flushing through her, something stayed her.

What they had, she and Leon, was a comfortable camaraderie in the day and a burning ecstasy in the night. By day, friends. By night…lovers. Lovers fuelled by an intensity of passion that burned between them without quenching.

A sense of restlessness possessed her suddenly. These weeks with Leon had been wonderful, an adventure she had embraced as they had travelled across Europe and beyond to wherever the jet set roamed and gathered, living it up by day and by night, dressed to the nines whatever the time of day, looking her very best for Leon. But it was a rootless existence, staying in hotels or other people's homes. Always with people all around them.

She felt a longing to be done with it—at least for a while. To have Leon to herself again, as she had on their honeymoon. Simple days…and searing nights.

Because if she did—if she had Leon entirely to herself—then perhaps…

Perhaps something more could grow between them—something more than friendship and desire…

Is that what I want? More than what I have now with Leon?

The question plucked at her, seeking an answer. An answer she could not give.

She broke off her thoughts. Leon had paused in their strolling, and was looking out over the marina. She welcomed the diversion from her sudden restlessness.

'So, what do you think—shall we hire a yacht for ourselves?' He turned to glance at her.

The idea beguiled her. She pointed to a yacht that was

considerably smaller than most of the others, but looked leaner and faster. It also looked as if it wouldn't need a crew.

We could be alone together on it and sail off into the sunset, she thought wistfully. *Away from all the crowds and the people and the parties. We could be alone together again, the way we were on our honeymoon...just Leon and me...*

A yearning filled her to have Leon all to herself again, but he was speaking.

'Sure you don't want that one?' he quizzed, pointing at a mega-yacht lit up like a Christmas tree, the size of a floating hotel, dwarfing the other yachts and sporting not one, but two helidecks and three underlit swimming pools.

She gave a gurgle of laughter, knowing he wasn't serious, and glad to have her unexpectedly pensive mood lifted by humour. She made some archly disparaging remark about 'vulgar oligarchs' and left it at that.

Leon chuckled and drew her away, strolling with her hand in hand back to their nearby hotel.

His mood was good—very good.

As ever, Ellie had been fêted today, as she always was, wherever he took her, and he'd loved seeing her the cynosure of all eyes, her beauty and natural charm radiant. His glance was warm as he looked upon her in her ivory evening gown, diamonds around her slender throat. How incredibly beautiful she was—and how absolutely and totally *his*!

The two months since their honeymoon had just flashed by, in a whirl of pleasure and travel and hedonistic enjoyment. His vast wealth was being managed by the highly paid professionals he'd appointed, and overseen by himself, so all he had to do now with his money was enjoy it.

With Ellie at his side. His perfect princess bride.

How right I was to marry her—how perfect she is for me!
It was a now-familiar refrain that came to him again, in

the small hours of that night, as she lay in his arms in the sensuous aftermath of their slaked desire. This marriage he had made so deliberately, to set the seal on his achievements, was proving even better than he'd anticipated! They were good together, he and his princess bride—comfortably companionable by day, and by night...

Oh, by night she exceeded all his hopes and intentions! He had known from that very first exchange of glances across the penthouse floor lobby, which had signalled their physical responsiveness to each other, that when the time came to claim his bride how good—how *very* good!—it would be. But the reality had been way, way better!

He eased his hand over the soft roundedness of her hip and felt sleep beckon, his thoughts faintly flickering. Was it because he had been the very first man to lead her into the pleasures of intimacy? Or because she was no passing affair but the woman who was his wife, his bride, his dazzling Princess, prized above all other women?

The questions drifted across his slowing thoughts but no answers came. There was only one certainty—the one he lived by and would always live by.

He would never deceive himself—deceive *her*—by calling it by a name that was nothing but a delusion, destructive and dangerous.

No, what drew him to her—and she to him—was desire. Honest and true, burning between them. He wrapped his arms around her more tightly. *This* was all he wanted—desire, and the slaking of it, with his beautiful, passionate bride. Nothing more.

In his close embrace, her body languorous and sated from the bliss and pleasure still throbbing through her, Ellie felt her hectic heart rate slow and sleep start to creep over her. As it did so, she felt memory start to play in her drowsy thoughts. The memory of how she'd stood on the terrace, overlooking the marina, wanting to sail off into the sunset with Leon…only with him…the man she desired so, so much…

That same sense of yearning filled her now as then, but for what, she didn't know.

Was it the sense of wanting something…*more*?

Ellie reached for the croissant nestling in a silver basket as they breakfasted on their balcony. Below, the yachts moored in the marina were crowded together, mirroring the built-up coastline of this ultra-expensive principality. They were due to attend a reception at the candy-box-pink stucco palace that evening, and Ellie was glad of the invitation for Leon's sake.

But her face shadowed. Being here in Monaco could only be a painful reminder to her of all that her own family had lost for ever.

For a second she was blind to the azure Mediterranean, dazzling beyond the marina—in her mind's eye she saw the snow-capped mountains of Karylya, its verdant forests and lush meadows, the graceful white and gold rococo palace she would never see again. Nor would any of her family…

Had her throat caught? Perhaps it had, for Leon was talking to her, concern in his voice.

'Ellie, what is it?'

She blinked, and the vision of her homeland was gone—but not her yearning for it.

'I'm sorry,' she said. 'I was thinking of Karylya…that I'll never see it again. Thinking of my father…'

She swallowed, her fingers tearing absently at the croissant. She had neglected her parents, she knew, in the months since her wedding, caught up in the hectic social whirl Leon had swept her into. Her mother she felt less bad about—Malcom had taken her to New Zealand and the South Seas, to mix filming with an extended holiday. But her father was having to face his unwelcome new life in exile, in a new home, a new country. And her stepmother and siblings, too—their lives changed just as radically.

On impulse, she spoke. 'Leon—do you think…? Could we visit him?'

Maybe it would do her good—not just to see her father and her half-siblings again, but to take a pause in the social whirl that she and Leon lived in. Take her mind away from that disquieting sense of yearning that hovered about her for the unknown 'more' she could give no name to.

Would give no name to.

She blinked, surfacing from her introspection, and realised that Leon had not answered immediately. That his expression had shuttered.

She swallowed, wishing she had not mentioned it. 'I'm sorry, I shouldn't have asked. You don't want to.'

He gave a shrug of one shoulder. 'Of course we can visit if you want,' he said, but there was a terseness in his voice that she did not miss.

Leon had heard it himself, but did not soften it. He had no wish to see her father again—a man who had been happy to see his daughter marry a complete stranger rather than face poverty for himself. His thoughts darkened. He knew all about fathers who put their own interests above their children's…

'Thank you,' she said awkwardly. 'It's just that I know from Marika's texts that my stepmother is expecting a formal visit from us at some point. And Marika—' She broke off, clearly thinking there was no point in telling Leon she was worried about her sister.

Her eyes were still on him, though.

He had been browsing through glossy yacht brochures, ready to consult the agent that morning about which to hire, but now he set them aside.

'We'll do this another time,' he said. 'Let's visit your father first.'

He did not add, *And get it over with*—that would have been too harsh, and she did not deserve it.

His gaze softened. No, his beautiful princess bride deserved only the best! The best he could bestow upon her!

For an instant, memory thrust at him. His father, presenting his mother with a top fashion label silk scarf, sapphire earrings, a pair of her favourite designer shoes... All with a flourish and a flurry of extravagant declarations of love and devotion. His mother had clapped her hands in excitement and pleasure, telling him he was the most wonderful man in the world, and how she adored him—how he was her whole life...

He slammed the door of memory shut.

He would not allow the past to poison the present.

The present was so very, very good.

His expression softened again. Desire started to rise within him as his gaze rested on Ellie's sunlit face, on a flake of her croissant caught on her lower lip. He reached across the table to brush it off with his thumb, then glided his thumb along the delicate inner surface of her mouth, his eyelids drooping.

He saw her pupils flare, and smiled. His voice was husky with growing arousal. 'Come back to bed...'

He drew her to her feet, and took her there...yielding to the flame of their desire.

All that he wanted...

CHAPTER ELEVEN

LEON'S FACE WAS set as he drove up the poplar-lined avenue leading to the elegant château in the heart of the Loire. He was not looking forward to this visit, and the moment the former Grand Duke and Duchess greeted them, with as much ceremony as if they were still on the throne of Karylya, his mood worsened.

Stilted conversation took place as the royal couple led the way out on to a shaded terrace, where they were served drinks.

'Marika and Niki are playing tennis,' the Grand Duchess informed them. She glanced at Leon. 'The court needed completely resurfacing, alas, and there has, of course, been a great deal of other work required to make everything...' she hesitated briefly '...suitable.'

There was the trace of a sigh in her voice, and Leon found himself bristling. No doubt she was thinking of the palace in Karylya, and all the other royal residences that she no longer possessed now she was reduced to a single château.

Paid for by me.

He cut the thought short. The money he'd spent on them—was still spending—had brought him Ellie. Was he going to complain about that? Of course not!

His eyes went to her as she said hurriedly, 'And you've made it all absolutely beautiful!'

Her stepmother smiled her gracious smile. 'We've worked extremely hard,' she murmured.

Leon said nothing. He doubted the Grand Duchess had done so much as lift a paint pot with her own fair hands...

'Indeed,' her husband was corroborating her story. 'For myself, I have been starting a library here.'

'Papa had a wonderful library at home—' Ellie said.

But she broke off, conscious that she had said what she should not have, for her father's face was stiffening at the mention of all that he had lost.

She felt her expression tighten. They should not have come here. From the moment of their arrival she had been conscious of it. Leon was clearly steeling himself, and as for herself...

She glanced up at the château. Her father's home in exile. Thanks to Leon. *Only* thanks to Leon.

She felt her stomach knotting. Without Leon her father and his family would be homeless, penniless.

He's paying for all this—paying for all of them!

Just as he'd agreed he would when she'd agreed to marry him...

She'd known it—of course she had—but somehow being here, seeing her father and stepmother here, living at Leon's expense, settled here for the rest of their lives on his largesse, made her...uncomfortable. Ultra-conscious of the reasons behind her marriage. To give her father a secure home in exile—to give Leon a princess bride.

It was what their marriage had always been about—yet somehow, in the dizzying rush of passion and desire for Leon that had consumed her since their honeymoon, it had been so easy to forget it...so temptingly easy to forget the blunt truth of her marriage.

My title for his wealth.

A heaviness filled her, weighing her down. She heard Leon's voice in her memory, when they'd discussed their wedding preparations.

'Do you intend always to be this blunt about our marriage?' he had demanded.

And her answer—*'It's a pretty blunt situation.'*

But in the months since then, even though she'd felt the heaviness press at her again, she had done her best to forget that. Ignore it.

Deny it.

Deny it because she *wanted* to deny it! Had wanted to deny it, she knew now, with bitter self-awareness, ever since Leon had swept her off to his bed…

Because the bluntness of the truth about their marriage did not sit well with the bliss she had found in Leon's arms. It made a mockery of it.

A shout from the gardens below the terrace pierced her sudden bleakness.

'Lisi! You're here! Brilliant!'

A moment later her brother vaulted over the balustrade, his tennis racket clattering on to the stone terrace. Then he was wrapping her in an exuberant bear hug before clapping Leon on the back.

'Great to see you both!' he exclaimed, grabbing a glass of orange juice and knocking it back as Marika made a more sedate entrance than her brother, coming up to hug Ellie.

The arrival of her half-siblings was a welcome release from the disquieting thoughts gripping her in such unwelcome fashion. But when Marika exclaimed expressively, her eyes speaking volumes, 'I'm *so* glad you're here!' Ellie had a different reason for disquiet.

There was a febrile quality to her sister she had not seen before—an air of suppressed excitement…of secretiveness…

But then Niki was targeting Leon, enthusiastically grill-

ing him on the performance characteristics of his car, blatantly asking to take it out for a spin, promising—with a
laugh—not to crash it. His exuberance lightened the atmosphere, and Ellie was glad. Gladder, too, when Niki
turned to her.

'I need to celebrate!' He grinned insouciantly. 'I got my
exam results through today, Lisi…'

Ellie's face lit and she was immediately diverted from
the bleak thoughts in her head, grateful to be so. 'Oh,
Niki—did you make your Oxford offer?'

He tilted his glass at her. 'Indeed I did,' he said.

'That's *wonderful*!' she exclaimed. 'Congratulations!'
She turned to Leon. 'Niki's the brains in this family,' she
said fondly.

'What are you going to be reading?' Leon asked.

And Ellie knew that, despite wishing he was not here, it
was impossible for Leon to dislike her brother—his cheerful exuberance was a world away from the Grand Duke's
chill formality.

'PPE,' he answered. 'Politics, Philosophy and Econom-
ics. Though it's the first and the last I'll be most focussed
on. I'll need to be if I'm to—'

He broke off, his expression changing. He looked Leon
in the eye.

'It's you I have to thank, and I am fully aware of it.'
Suddenly he wasn't an exuberant teenager any more, but
serious-faced, older than his years. 'The international stu-
dent fees at Oxford are sky-high, and there's no way I could
take up my place without your generosity.'

Ellie could see her father's expression stiffen at his son's
blunt reminder of their dependence on his daughter's husband, and she felt herself stiffen, too. But Leon was simply
nodding, telling Niki he could thank him by getting a first.

It was thanks to Niki that the evening was not the ordeal
it would have been otherwise. His good-humoured remarks

lightened the stolid conversation conducted by her father
and stepmother, which centred mostly on the history of
the château. Even so, it was heavy going, with Leon visibly unrelaxed, and Marika still with that distracted, febrile look about her.

Ellie was filled with unease. Her sister's parents seemed
oblivious to it—but not Niki. From time to time Ellie dis-
tinctly saw him glancing at her…almost conspiratorially.
She frowned inwardly. Something was going on, and she
wasn't sure what. Antal, she assumed, with another silent
sigh.

Her heart went out to her sister, pitying her. To love so
hopelessly…how agonising must that be…?

She pulled her thoughts away. She had her own issues
to deal with. She was wishing she had not come here. Yet
knew it was good that she had.

No, not good—necessary.

Her face set. Yes, necessary to remind herself of just
what her marriage was based on. Uncomfortable truth
though it was. And it was time—more than time—that
she acknowledged it…and not just to herself.

The long evening finally ended and, having drunk a du-
tiful *demi-tasse* of coffee from delicately translucent Sevres
porcelain, in the exquisitely redecorated drawing room—
all paid for by Leon—Ellie glanced at the antique ormolu
clock on the marble mantelpiece—also paid for by Leon.

Marika and Niki had retired to a distant sofa and were
absorbed in their phones—paid for by Leon—every now
and then showing each other something on the screens, but
saying nothing, which added to her unease.

Finally she felt she could get to her feet and bid her
father and stepmother goodnight. Leon immediately did
likewise, with barely disguised impatience, and she felt
her face set again.

As they gained their apartments—just as beautifully

decorated as the rest of the château, and all paid for by
Leon—she turned to him.

'Leon, I'm sorry I dragged you here—but thank you
for bringing me.' She swallowed, knowing she had to say
this, to acknowledge it openly. 'And thank you…thank you
for making all this possible.' Her arm swept around, encompassing the château and all that went with it. She took
a breath, looking him square in the eyes, 'I am extremely
appreciative of it.'

He was looking at her, a strange expression on his face.
Frowning slightly.

'What's brought this on?' he posed.

Ellie's chin lifted. 'Just being here, Leon. Seeing it all
for myself. What…what you've done for my family.' She
swallowed again. 'And I'm glad Niki thanked you, too, for
paying his uni fees.'

Leon started to shrug off his dinner jacket. 'He's OK,
your brother. Unlike—' He stopped.

Ellie bit her lip, but tacitly acknowledged what Leon
had not said. The ex-Grand Duke might be taking his
luxurious exile for granted, but at least his son was aware
of it.

'Niki is so different from my father,' she said awkwardly.
'He has a much more open nature—like our grandfather,
Grand Duke Nikolai.' Her expression changed. 'I think it
will help him, you know, now that he has to make his own
way in the world and will be forced to make a future for
himself outside Karylya, having had his life smashed to
pieces. Everything he thought was stable has gone. The
future he took for granted has simply…disappeared.'

She saw Leon's face tighten. Too late she remembered
what he had said about his own youth—how the safe, secure world he'd grown up in had been ripped from him in
the cataclysm of Greece's economic collapse. And how his
father had abandoned him…

Hurriedly, she went on, sounding awkward again. 'I'm sorry. I didn't mean to compare my brother's situation to yours—you were younger, even!—and I am truly, truly grateful to you for making it possible for him to go to Oxford. I'm incredibly grateful for *everything*, Leon—everything you're doing for my family!'

His expression changed, softened. He disposed of his jacket, walked up to her. He placed his hands on her shoulders. Warm through the thin silk of her gown. Holding her there.

'Stop,' he said. 'You don't have to say it. You don't have to thank me. It was what we agreed. Your father and his family get financial security and in exchange I...' his hands moulded her shoulders in a sensual gesture...possessive '... I get my princess bride.' His eyelids drooped. 'My incredibly beautiful, desirable, alluring and irresistible princess bride...'

With each word his voice grew more husky, his gaze washing over her.

'My irresistible princess bride,' he said again, his voice more husky still, 'whom I don't intend to resist a single moment longer after the most tediously long evening ever.'

Leon slid his hands languorously from her shoulders down her arms, to move around her pliant waist and draw her against him. He didn't like to see that troubled look in her eyes. He wanted to banish it. Banish it the swiftest way possible. The way he liked best—

He brushed Ellie's soft mouth with his, feeling his mood improve even as his desire quickened. His kiss deepened.

This—*this* was what he wanted! Ellie in his arms—his princess bride.

With effortless ease he swept her up to him, carrying her towards their waiting bed...

* * *

'Niki?'

Ellie's voice was tentative, but she knew she needed to speak to him before she and Leon left the château that morning, and she was glad to find him on his own.

'Mmm?'

Her brother did not look up from his phone and she realised he was looking at a Karylyan newsfeed. She frowned. She was aware that the much-vaunted presidential elections that the council which had ousted her father had promised the population were fast approaching, but she had done her best not to pay attention to it. What point would there be? No one was going to vote to recall her father. Karylya would become a republic, with a president and not a grand duke, and that would be that.

She sighed, before saying as much to her brother. 'Niki, it will only upset you to follow the elections. They don't want us back and that's all there is to it. History has moved on. We have to accept it.' She paused. '*You* have to accept it.'

Her brother's face closed. 'Of course I accept it,' he said, his voice offhand. He gave a nonchalant, teenage-style shrug. 'Morbid curiosity, that's all.'

He tossed his phone on to the cushion of the chair he'd been sitting in and got to his feet. His expression lightened.

'So, sis, how's it all going with you and Leon? The celebrity rags are *full* of you! Is that what you intend to do with the rest of your life now? Non-stop jollies? Wall-to-wall parties?'

His words were light-hearted, but Ellie coloured.

'It's what Leon wants,' she said. She looked her brother square in the face. 'And, considering everything he's doing for our family, Niki, it's the least I can do!'

Niki sighed. 'If you put it that way…' he allowed.

Ellie's face tightened. What other way *could* it be put?

Coming here to the château, seeing the reality of her father's situation, had made it impossible to hide from that.

Hadn't Leon spelt it out to her last night, before sweeping her up into his arms? Spelt it out as bluntly as she once had. He wanted a princess bride to show off—she wanted financial security for her penniless father.

Oh, Leon might tell her that he would never have married her without desiring her—or her desiring him—but that didn't take away the blunt underlying reason for their marriage.

He wouldn't have married me if I weren't a princess.

And she—she felt a hollowing inside her—she would not have married him had he not been rich enough to support her father and his family.

Her eyes shadowed. Before her marriage she had talked to her mother about her obligations and responsibilities as the princess she was—Princess Elizsaveta of Karylya—and she was still bound by them. Would always be bound by them. Whatever they cost her...

More than I dare allow.

Restlessly, she moved about the room, forcing aside her darkening thoughts. She could not pay them attention now. There would be time enough later... For now—right now—she had to seize this brief opportunity to speak to her brother about their sister. It would not easily come again.

'Niki, I'm worried about Marika,' she said roundly. 'Can't you help me convince her that she has to give up on Antal Horvath? Nothing can come of it! You know that as well as I do!'

Abruptly, her brother's expression changed. 'She'll be OK,' he said impatiently. 'Don't stress out over it!'

Ellie frowned. That had sounded like a typical off-hand remark any teenager might make, but she had heard an evasive note in it.

'Is she still in touch with him?' she pursued.

She saw that evasive blankness come over Niki's face again.

'How should I know?' He shrugged. He reached for his phone again, obviously wanting this interrogation to cease.

Ellie opened her mouth to challenge him, but her step-mother was coming into the room.

'Your father tells me you are leaving after lunch!' she announced, displeasure in her voice. 'This has been far too brief a visit, Elizsaveta!'

Ellie was apologetic—what else could she be?—and made mention of the social engagement she and Leon were committed to in Paris.

'Well, next time you must arrange to stay longer.' The Grand Duchess's tone was reprimanding. 'You have responsibilities to your father—do not forget that. You cannot spend your life perpetually flitting from one party to another!'

Ellie tensed. The fact that her stepmother had echoed her brother's criticism galled her. But she said nothing. For her father and stepmother, as for all the world, her marriage to Leon was a *coup de foudre* romance—how could she hurt them by slamming home the unvarnished truth?

But that unvarnished truth—the truth that she had become so dangerously neglectful of in the blissful weeks and months she'd spent with Leon—was something she must never let herself forget again.

She sighed inwardly as they drove off from the château later that day—Leon with a palpable air of relief—heading for that glittering social event in Paris where, yet again, she would arrive *en grande tenue*: Princess Elizsaveta of Karylya, dazzling Parisian high society with her beauty, her couture gown and the priceless jewels bestowed upon her by her impossibly handsome billionaire husband.

They would resume the endless social whirl he loved to enjoy with her at his side and she knew, with a sudden clenching of that emotion she would not name, that in such a marriage as theirs there could only be what they already had.

Friendship and desire.

What else could be between them?

However much she might long for there to be more— much, much more…

CHAPTER TWELVE

'WELL, I THINK that went off all right, don't you?'

There was a satisfied note in Leon's voice as he spoke, dropping his cufflinks on the vanity unit in their penthouse suite at the Viscari Roma, with its sweeping views over the ancient city.

'It was certainly a good turnout,' Ellie agreed, making her voice equable as she disengaged herself from her emerald necklace.

She felt a combination of being exhausted and strungout. But she didn't want to let it show—it would spoil Leon's ebullient good mood.

They had hosted a party that evening, to repay all the invitations they had accepted since their wedding. It had been held in the hotel's banqueting suite—a glittering, opulent affair, no expense spared, that Ellie had thrown herself into organising with a determination that had been almost a frenzy, as if she were proving something to herself, to Leon. She had spared no effort to make it as dazzlingly brilliant as he could want and they themselves had been at the heart of it—Leon Dukaris, billionaire, and Princess Elizsaveta of Karylya, his royal bride, adorned in yet another priceless gown and draped with yet more priceless jewels.

As they'd received their guests, memory had plucked at her—their spectacular betrothal ball, where Leon had first kissed her...

How far I have come since then!

To a destination she had never dreamt of.

I never imagined it was waiting for me...

She felt emotion twist within her, but silenced it. She must always silence it.

Her eyes went to Leon now. He was looking as impossibly handsome as he always did, loosening his tie and chucking it aside to slip the top button of his dress shirt. She felt her breath catch—as it always did—felt that emotion she would not admit twist within her and crushed it back, as she always must.

He started to remove the diamond studs on his shirt, adding them to the gold cufflinks.

'Yes, definitely a good bag. A dozen royals, three *principessas* at least, one archduke, a couple of marquesses and I lost count of the counts!' he joshed.

Was it crass of him to take satisfaction in just how many of Europe's royal and aristocratic elite had attended the glittering party that had finally drawn to a close as dawn approached over the seven hills of Rome? After all, it was a long, long time since he'd stood in that line for the soup kitchen...

Do I really need to prove to myself—let alone the world—how far I've come since then? Prove that I will never go back to that misery again?

He was in a good place now—a very good place.

His eyes rested on Ellie, removing the emerald drops from her delicate earlobes—his beautiful, very own princess bride!—and they warmed as they always did.

Memory came to him of what he'd said to her so laconically that lunchtime so long ago now, when she had come to find out whether he really intended to marry her. How he'd told her that 'any princess' would do for him for a royal bride. Even her sister.

How absurd the idea seemed now!

No other princess could compare with Ellie.

No other *woman* could compare.

The words were in his head before he realised it, and hung there like an echo.

No other woman? Was *that* how he felt about Ellie?

His eyes fastened on her. She was lifting her hands now, to remove her tiara and unpin the ornate hairdo created by one of the top stylists in Rome to go with her exquisite couture gown in layers of pale green ombre silk.

No other woman…

The words were still there, resonating in his consciousness. Demanding he pay attention to them. Take in their meaning.

But Ellie's lustrous golden tresses were cascading down over her bare shoulders, distracting him from any thought but one.

He closed the distance between them. 'I believe,' he murmured, in a voice that was husky, 'you will need some help with the hooks of your gown…'

It was an office he was only too ready to perform for her. And all that came after…

Urgency filled him—urgency, desire and an arousal so fierce he could only do what every instinct in his being impelled him to do. Yield to it.

But afterwards…long afterwards… Leon lay, his arms wrapped tight around her, their exhausted limbs still meshed, their hectic pulses slowly easing, yet again those words came to him that had entered his head unbidden…

No other woman.

Only Ellie. *His* Ellie. As he said her name in his head he felt once more—just as he had when she'd gazed up at him after their first incredible night together on their honeymoon—the strange sensation that something was thawing, deep inside him. What it was, he did not know— could not tell.

He would think about it later…

Right now the only priority was sleep—with this wondrous woman held tight in his possessing embrace. All that he wanted.

And in his arms—his in exchange for the security she sought for her father, her body sated with the passion of their union—she stared with sleepless eyes into the dark room, knowing with the clutching of emotion in her that was like a pain, that what she had now was all that she could ever have…

Ellie was sitting on the sofa in the sitting room of their suite at the Viscari, methodically working her way through the latest batch of gilt-edged invitations that had flooded in after their own lavish party, dutifully checking with Leon which ones to accept.

He gave a careless shrug, walking back to her from where he'd been standing by the doors opening on to their balcony, looking out over the roofs of Rome with a slight frown on his brow, hands thrust into his trouser pockets.

'Say no to all of them if you like,' he said. His expression changed. 'You know,' he mused, 'maybe we should call time on all this socialising. Maybe,' he said, 'after that mega-bash of our own, we'd like a break from it.'

Ellie looked across at him, her expression flickering. 'Only if you want to,' she said uncertainly.

He quirked an eyebrow. 'And what do *you* want?' he countered.

'I want to do what *you* want,' she answered.

It was the answer she would always give…must always give. And she must be scrupulous in doing so.

I can't forget—must not forget!—the reasons we are married.

Since their return from the château it had been her mantra. Diligently repeated to herself.

Leon frowned. 'That's not an answer,' he said.

Ellie bit her lip. 'What…what answer would you like from me, Leon?'

His expression darkened. 'Don't talk like that!' His frown deepened. 'Ellie, what's up?' He skewered her with his dark eyes.

She swallowed. 'Nothing—' she began.

His mouth tightened. 'Yes, there is.' He eyed her narrowly. 'Something's wrong, Ellie. Don't tell me otherwise. Ever since…' He paused, his mouth tightening again. 'Ever since we came back from visiting your father!'

He took a breath.

'Do you think I haven't noticed the difference in you? You got stuck into organising our party like there was no tomorrow and you haven't relaxed since. Something's eating you. At first I put it down to you being…well, upset… whatever…seeing your father again now that he's exiled and so on. And then…' He frowned again. 'And then while we were there you trotted out all that stuff about being grateful to me for paying for the damn château, for paying your brother's university fees—'

He stopped. Eyeballed her. This was important and he wanted it clear.

'You do *not*,' he said, 'have to thank me—*ever*!' His expression changed, and there was a rueful humour in it now. 'You were the one who spelt it out to me, remember? Set out just what the conditions were for your agreeing to marry me! So no thanks are due in either direction.'

She was looking at him, with an expression on her face he hadn't seen before. Heavy and tense. He didn't like to see it there.

'No, but there are obligations, Leon—and that is what

I am fully aware of.' Her voice was sombre, serious. Un-flinching. 'You've provided for my father and my recipro-cal obligation is to be, and do, what *you* want. You wanted a princess bride, and that...' she took a breath '...that is what I am. Your princess bride. And *you* get to choose where and when and how often to show me off—I don't.'

As she spoke, Ellie saw his face darken again. For a second a frisson of apprehension went through her, but she held her ground. Inside, she was conscious of a silent cry—but she must give no voice to it. She had silenced it for weeks now—ever since they'd driven away from the château.

Silenced it to him.

Silenced it to herself.

A word broke from him. Coarse, she could tell—but it was in Greek, and she was thankful not to understand it.

Tension racked through her suddenly. Had she been tactless, spelling it out like that? But that was what she'd done at that restaurant before their wedding, insisting on a bluntness about the reasons for their marriage that she would not try to disguise. Not then—and not now. Not any more.

I almost made myself forget—because I wanted to for-get! Because I was so swept away by him!

Swept away to a place she had never thought to go with him—a destination that had never been part of her reason for marrying him!

But it was a place she must not approach again.

I have to keep to the limits of our marriage. Anything else is...

Impossible.

The bleak word hung in the echo of his expletive.

She saw him take a breath. Saw something flash in his eyes like gold.

'To hell with showing you off! And to hell,' he said,

'with you being a princess! I want *you*, Ellie! *You!* The beautiful, irresistible *you*! *You* are the woman I want!'

He reached forward, hauled her to her feet, planted his hands on her hips and held her right in front of him.

'I couldn't care less about bankrolling your father—if it gets me *you*!'

He took another ragged breath, and another flash of gold seared across his eyes.

'So, do you get that?'

The expression in his flashing eyes softened. His hands lifted to her face, cupping her cheeks with a tenderness in his touch.

'Do you get it?' he asked again, and now his voice was thickening, the gold in his eyes turning molten. 'Because if you don't...' he said, and now there was a huskiness in his voice that was melting through her, making her limbs suddenly weak even as she felt as light as air, as if she were being lifted up with every word he said. 'If you don't I'm just going to have to kiss you senseless until you *do* get it...'

He lowered his mouth to hers. To Ellie—the woman he wanted...the woman no other could compare with.

His kiss was slow and lingering. The revelation that had come on him in the night possessed him—that there was no other woman for him but Ellie...his Ellie...princess or no princess. He couldn't care less...not any more.

He lifted his mouth away. There was a dazed look in her eyes and he smiled, well pleased.

'Let's get out of here,' he said. 'Out of the city—away from everyone! Get into the car and drive...' His eyes caressed her. 'I want you all to myself—I'm done with showing off to everyone. Let's head to where no one knows us. I want...' his voice grew husky, his eyes washing over her '...a second honeymoon...'

He saw her face light up—knew he had said exactly the right thing. He let her ago. If he kissed her again he knew they'd just end up back in bed, and he was filled now with a sudden impatience. He wanted to get out of Rome.

'Where shall we go?' he asked. 'Somewhere deserted that we can drive to—somewhere by the sea—it's too hot for anything else!—but not too far away. I want to get there today!'

'I don't think anywhere is completely deserted in Italy in the summer...' Ellie answered faintly.

Emotions were sweeping through her, lifting her off her feet. All the heaviness that had crushed her since visiting her father had evaporated. In its place a new emotion was soaring. One she dared not even name.

But for all that she knew what it was—and why.

Hope.

How could it be anything else, with Leon wanting to sweep her off on a second honeymoon...?

Oh, what if it's really true, what he is telling me? That he wants me—the woman I am! Not the Princess! Oh, if that's really, really true—

She broke off her thoughts, not daring to go further. Instead, gathering her soaring hopes, she pulled them into a semblance of sense.

'Um...maybe Puglia?' she ventured. 'Not as touristy as places like Amalfi or Portofino. And Puglia,' she added, with a sudden eagerness in her voice, 'has *trulli*! Oh, Leon, can we stay in a *trullo*? Please say we can!'

Her spirits were soaring still.

Leon laughed indulgently. 'We shall stay anywhere you like!' he promised expansively.

He'd said the right thing to her—said the right thing to himself! What did he care if the woman standing there in front of him, her eyes shining like stars, had a drop of royal blood in her?

Not a jot or an iota.

Then, abruptly, he frowned. 'What are *trulli*?' he demanded.

His answer was a laugh. 'Traditional stone houses in Puglia—they're round, with very pointy tiled cone-shaped roofs, and they are absolutely *adorable*!' Ellie exclaimed happily.

'Let's go for it,' Leon said decisively. 'We'll leave our fancy togs here and head off. Right now!'

Ellie needed no urging and whisked into the bedroom to start packing, her feet still not touching the floor.

Their *trulli*—for the secluded villa consisted of a linked cluster of several of the beautifully restored conical buildings, set in the grounds of a converted *masseria* farmstead—proved every bit as adorable as Ellie wanted. And their holiday in Puglia was as blissful as she could ever have dreamt. A second honeymoon indeed.

Leon had swapped his monster car for a far more practical and less eye-catching SUV, and in it they explored the ancient towns of Puglia, with their ornate basilicas and crumbling buildings, their air of sleepy isolation from the busy world in the somnolent heat of high summer.

There were tourists, true, but it still felt uncrowded, and she and Leon blended easily with them, both of them dressed down in shorts and T-shirts, with Ellie wearing nothing more fancy in the evenings than a floaty cotton skirt and lacy top—perfectly fine for eating out at harbourside *trattoria*, or cooking for themselves at their villa—simple pasta dishes or barbecued steak, grilled fish, freshly caught, anything that was easy—and drinking the local wines.

It was a universe away from their glitzy life as Leon the billionaire showing off his royal bride to the admiring world and Princess Elizsaveta of Karylya.

As the days passed in a leisurely parade they set no particular end-point to their sojourn here. Their meandering days sometimes took them inland, to discover almost deserted villages lapped by endless olive groves, sometimes down to the coast to swim off the rocks in the crystal-clear waters of the Adriatic, and they even ventured to Lecce, the Florence of the South, to admire its baroque extravagance—*barocco lecchese*, as she informed Leon from the guidebook as they strolled around the *centro storico*, the historic heart of the city.

Ellie knew she had never been happier in her life.

And knew why.

She had Leon all to herself! Just as she had yearned to have that night that seemed so long ago now, above the marina in Monte Carlo, with the sound of fashionable revelry coming up from the lavish yachts. That was something she missed not at all, she knew with absolute certainty. Nor all it stood for.

And nor, it seemed, did Leon.

After abandoning any plans for an expedition that day, content to enjoy their *trulli*'s charms, they were lying by their pool, shaded from the hot sun by a parasol, and he stroked her thigh idly to get her attention as she drowsed beside him, sleepy after their *al fresco* lunch of fresh-baked bread with cheese, dried meats and ripe tomatoes, drenched in olive oil from the groves nearby, with luscious peaches for dessert, washed down by the Puglian white wine Verdeca.

'When we leave here shall we change our ways?' he asked.

She looked across at him. There was something new in his voice—something she had not heard before.

'I told you in Rome I was done with non-stop socialising. I've had my fill of it—for good.'

Leon spoke decisively, knowing he meant what he'd just said. OK, so he'd got a massive kick out of it originally, revelling in having the world see him walk into a room with not just a royal bride, but the most breathtaking royal bride there had ever been! But, hey, he'd been there now—done that and got the T-shirt.

His expression tightened momentarily. And besides, there was no way he ever wanted Ellie saying to him again what she had said to him that morning in Rome. That she felt she had some kind of obligation to do whatever it was he wanted.

He pushed the memory aside roughly.

I don't want that having anything to do with our marriage! We've gone beyond that. Way beyond.

He turned his head to look at her, seeing her eyes on him, a question in them. A question he was going to answer.

His hand dropped from her thigh to pick up hers. He meshed his strong fingers with her delicate slender ones and raised it to his mouth, kissing it with something that was not homage or desire…

It was affection.

He felt something warm within him—that strange sense of thawing that he had felt before and didn't understand. But knew it was good to feel it, whatever it was.

He folded her hand in his and dropped it to his bared chest, taking a breath. This was important and he wanted to get it right.

Just as I had to get it right on our honeymoon, when I realised how much was at stake.

Just as much was at stake now.

Maybe more.

The thought was in his head and he held it there, seeking the words he needed to say.

'Ellie, I know we married to achieve our own particular aims—your title for my wealth, just as you've always said. But...' He paused, taking another breath, unable to read her expression, only knowing that there was an absolute stillness about her suddenly. 'We've achieved those aims, haven't we? Your father and his family are safely settled, and I...' He gave a rueful laugh. 'Well, I've showed you off to the entire world as my princess bride!'

His expression changed, and he felt the constraint in it suddenly.

'That soup kitchen in Athens was a long time ago and I can let it go now. I've nothing to prove to the world. Not any more.'

He saw something move in her eyes and knew it for what it was—compassion. But she said nothing, only perhaps tightened her fingers on his. He felt his throat constrict suddenly, as if that look of compassion were too much for him—as if he had to keep it out, away from him.

Because if he didn't—

He felt his muscles clench suddenly and knew he was fighting for control—a control it was absolutely essential he retained. As he had always done—had had to—all his adult life.

Even before his adult life.

No! He would not go there. He was not revisiting the past—he was escaping it!

He made himself breathe out slowly before speaking again. Knowing he must get it right.

'Ellie, what we have together is *good*. Both in bed and out! And...and we're happy together, aren't we? So...' He took another breath and then he said it. 'So why don't we just be ourselves? You and me—just...well, *us*.'

She wasn't saying anything, and he could feel the tension

mounting in him. Had he got it wrong? He'd got it wrong on their wedding night—read her wrong and nearly lost what he'd wanted so much.

'Ellie—say something…'

His hand tightened on hers as if he would not let her go. *Could* not let her go.

'Say we have a chance, at least a chance, of making ours a real marriage! Nothing to do with me being rich and you being royal! And not bound by any time limit.'

He took another breath, his eyes fixed on her, willing her to say something…anything…

Anything but no.

'What do you say?' he prompted.

He had to know—he *had* to!

There was a knot inside him and it was pulling tighter. He saw her face working, saw something in her eyes he could not read. And then she moistened her lips, as if they'd gone suddenly dry, and he heard her speak.

'I say yes,' she said.

For a moment there was silence, and then, a torrent of Greek breaking from him, he drew her bodily across him, hauling her to his chest.

His eyes burned gold, bright as the sun. 'This,' he said, and his voice was husky, 'calls for a celebration.'

He meshed his fingers in her golden hair, his mouth seeking hers, filled with an emotion he could not name. He only knew that it was good. It was very, *very* good…

CHAPTER THIRTEEN

'WE'RE GOING TO need a place of our own to live. We can't live out of hotels any longer.'

Leon's voice was decisive as he gazed around their suite at the Viscari Roma. The city had seemed noisy and crowded since their return from Puglia, and he wanted out. Wanted to be done with hotel living altogether.

'So, where do you fancy?' he asked. 'The world is our oyster!'

OK, so privately he hoped she wouldn't say *A château on the Loire next to my father*, but if that really was what she wanted he'd go along with it.

Hell, he'd go along with anything she wanted.

His gaze softened. How right he'd been to put it to the test that afternoon—to risk all and claim not his princess bride but his wife.

My wife.

His eyes swept over her. They were dining in their suite, neither of them wanting to go out or to face the hotel restaurant.

My wife.

He said it again to himself, hearing the words in his head.

Certainty was filling him—this was the woman he wanted to be with. Not because of her royal blood—and not even because of her extraordinary beauty. He knew that with a strange realisation. It was for more than that—much more.

And he knew with equal certainty that he wanted it for much longer than the mere two years she'd stipulated when they'd hammered out their marriage terms all those months ago.

Everything's changed since then!

Everything had changed and it was so much better than he had ever dreamt it could be.

'We don't just have to have just one place, of course,' he said now. 'We can have homes all over!' He gave a laugh. 'Let's pick a country we both like and start there. How about it?'

He was keen to get going on house-hunting. He wanted to make a home with Ellie. A home *life* with her.

He saw there was a considering look on Ellie's face.

'Would it seem very tame to pick England?' ventured Ellie. 'It's what I'm most used to. Now that Karylya—'

She stopped. No point stating the obvious. And definitely no point thinking of anything sad at all.

Not when happiness was soaring through her. Had been soaring through her ever since Leon had, in this very room, told her that he didn't care if she were royal or not. And then on that day in Puglia, lying by the pool at their enchanting *trulli*, he had said what she knew she had longed to hear.

I wanted more—oh, much more than what we had! So much more! But I didn't dare say it—didn't dare think it.

But now—oh, now she dared. Dared to do more still.

Now, finally, I dare to admit what I feel for him! Not just friendship—not just desire. But love.

Wonder filled her. She had married him out of duty and yet love had been waiting for her all along!

As she gazed at him, her heart full, she veiled her eyes

lest her love blaze out too brightly. She must take this gently—the revelation was still too new, too fresh.

Leon had said no word of love to her—but if *she* had only just realised the depths of her feelings for him she must allow that he, like her, might not yet think in those terms.

But surely he would one day? Surely she had every reason to hope that he would move to that same glorious realisation?

He has said he wants ours to be a real marriage—and what else is a real marriage but one based on love?

He needed time, that was all—she was sure of it. Time to discover, as she had done, just how deeply he felt about her. And she would be waiting for him when he did so—when he gave his love to her and she gave him hers.

A glow set about her, radiating her happiness.

'Not tame at all,' Leon was saying.

She brought her mind back to the subject in question, away from that golden image in her imagination of Leon clasping her to him and saying how infinitely he loved her!

'So, whereabouts in England should we start looking?' he went on. 'Your mother and stepfather live in Somerset—is that right? Would that be a good place to look first? All I know about it is that it's famous for cider. We could have a cider orchard of our own.'

Settling near Lady Connie and her bluff husband would be no problem for him, he mused. As for the ex-Grand Duke—well, he was welcome to sponge off him for the rest of his life with his compliments. It was of no account to him.

Only Ellie mattered. His wonderful, wonderful wife Ellie—with whom he was going to spend the rest of his life and be happy every single day of it! Nothing could stop that now.

Because our marriage is based on what is honest and true—not on deceit and delusion. So it will stand the test of time. Stand all tests.

'Somerset's beautiful!' Ellie replied enthusiastically.

Thinking of her mother made her long to visit her as soon as possible. To tell her how groundless her fears had proved—how much she loved the man she'd married for duty...

She felt her heart glow with warmth.

'Good,' Leon was saying in his decisive fashion, and they fell to discussing what kind of property they might like to live in.

'We'll need somewhere warmer for winter breaks, though,' he went on. 'How about a villa in the Caribbean? We'll explore the islands and pick the one we like best.'

Enthusiasm fired him. How right he'd been to want so much more from this marriage of theirs! His wonderful wife Ellie, their companionship together, the searing desire that flamed between them... And now to settle down together, make their lives together.

What better could there possibly be?

Gladness filled him.

I have everything I want—everything! I want for nothing more—nothing at all.

The next week passed in a happy blur. Because they did not wish to be uncivil, there were still some outstanding invitations they felt they should honour. But they were already in touch with estate agents, and had a list of potential properties to view the following week, when they would visit Ellie's mother on her return to the UK.

They had also agreed that Ellie would stop by her father en route to England, to tell him in person of their plans to settle in the UK, while Leon flew on to London to check up on his business affairs. Besides, the presidential elections were imminent in Karylya, and she wanted to support her father at such an inevitably upsetting time.

Her brother was due to go up to Oxford at the end of the month, to start his degree. He was visiting some school friends in Switzerland, and she hoped it would distract him from the news in Karylya.

As for Marika... Ellie sighed as she sent her a lengthy text, making it as cheerful as she could. Her mood would be particularly down at the prospect of Antal's father becoming President, setting the final seal on the impossibility of her sister ever finding her longed-for happy-ever-after with Antal.

A wave of pity for her sister swept through her. Loving without hope. How heartbreaking that must be, compared with her own wonderful, radiant happiness.

Her eyes glowed with it every time she looked at Leon, met his glance at her. She felt her hopes soar. Oh, surely soon Leon would realise he felt for her what she felt for him? Surely her hopes would be fulfilled! It was just a matter of time, that was all...

And until then she would wait patiently, loyally, bathing in the happiness she had, and in the wonderful future she was looking forward to. Making a home with Leon. Being his loving wife for ever!

How happy I am! How absolutely happy!

The thought ran in Ellie's head constantly, like a silent companion. Nothing could spoil it now—she was certain of it.

Ellie paused in packing her toiletries bag and glanced at her phone screen again, frowning. Anxiety nipped though she tried to dismiss it.

She and Leon were leaving Rome in the morning, by private jet. She would deplane at Angers, and Leon would fly on to London. She couldn't get to Angers soon enough. She wanted to see Marika…talk to her. Her assiduously encouraging text to her sister had brought a vehement response.

Lisi, you haven't the faintest idea! Not being with Antal is agony! Pure agony! I love him so, so much! I just want to be with him! I can't bear my life without him! And I'm not going to!

Ellie had texted back immediately, but there had been no further reply. She'd texted Niki, too—no reply from him either.

OK, so he was probably out, but she wanted him to phone Marika, make sure she was…

Was what?

She felt that stab of anxiety nip again. Marika had never sounded so openly fraught—or so despairing. She wanted to phone her, but she knew it would not go down well with Leon if she disappeared into the sitting room for half an hour of sisterly consolation, with Marika weeping over the ether.

She could see him from the en suite bathroom, lying on the bed in his bathrobe, idly flicking through printouts for the houses they were going to be viewing, a glass of cognac on his bedside table. She could see from his glances at her that he was impatient for her to be done with packing—and with texting. He had that look, that anticipatory gold-flecked glint in his eye that she knew well. And as they wouldn't be seeing each other for several days she wanted to make the most of tonight—just as he did.

She would try one final text. She didn't like the way Marika had ended her last one—she didn't like it at all. Extravagant hyperbole, probably, but all the same…

I can't bear my life without him! And I'm not going to!

* * *

'What's up?'

Leon tried to penetrate Ellie's clearly uneasy thoughts. He set aside the estate agents' print-outs he'd been whiling away the time with, reaching for his cognac, wanting Ellie to be done with fussing over her creams and cosmetics—she didn't need them to make her any more beautiful than she was.

His eyes washed over her slender form, enticingly outlined by her silk peignoir. Her lovely face was frowning as she tapped at her phone. He didn't want her texting and he didn't want her frowning—he wanted her to come to bed so he could make love to her...

'Marika's not answering my texts,' Ellie said, that frown still on her brow.

Leon reached for his cognac again, feeling irritated. Ellie's woebegone sister had always irritated him. 'Moping over her boyfriend, most like,' he said. 'As usual.'

Ellie bit her lip. 'She can't help being hopelessly in love—' she began.

Leon replaced his cognac glass with a sudden movement. He was more than fed up with the perpetually lovelorn Marika. Yet another example of how the pernicious delusion of love screwed up lives, ruined happiness...

'That's exactly what she *can* help!' he snapped. 'Your sister's a fool! Don't waste your sympathy on her—it won't help a thing!'

He jack-knifed to a sitting position.

'She needs to grow up—get real!'

Ellie stared—his voice had been so scathing.

She rushed to defend her sister. 'She *is* real, Leon! She's breaking her heart over Antal—'

A word broke from him.

Dimly, Ellie recognised it as the same Greek expletive

he'd come out with when she'd said it was her obligation to let him show her off endlessly as his princess bride…

His face darkened. 'No,' he said, and there was an implacable note in his voice she had never heard before, as if what he said could never be gainsaid. 'She just imagines she is! Like I said, she needs to grow up! Grow up and learn that nobody breaks their heart—*nobody*! That nobody is *worth* breaking your heart over!'

'But that's just what I'm afraid of!'

The words came out in a rush. Whether it was her reaction to Leon's out-of-the-blue vehemence she didn't know, but suddenly she was coming towards him with her phone, its screen illuminated, all the anxiety she'd felt and had tried to suppress leaping in her.

'Look!' She held the phone out, then realised that the texts were all in Karylyan. 'It's what she says, Leon: I can't bear my life without him. And I'm not going to.'

In front of her eyes she saw his face masked, as if a steel visor had come down over it. He got to his feet, coming around the bed to her. There was a fury in his eyes that made her step back. But he reached for her shoulders, pinioning her with a hard, immovable grip.

Blackness was in him—a dark, bitter tide. It had come from nowhere, suddenly unleashed by Ellie's unthinking words, her maudlin sentiments about her idiotic sister who was moping in endless self-inflicted misery—totally unnecessary and indefensible self-inflicted misery! Wallowing in a fantasy that hadn't existed in the first place! Ruining her life because of it.

And not just her own life.

Memory slashed at him of another time—another woman—and he tore it from him. No, he would not go there. He refused to go there. He would stay only in this place he had made for himself. Facing reality square-on.

'If you seriously believe that then phone your father, your stepmother, right now. Tell them to go and check on her!' he ground out. 'Otherwise listen to me—*listen* to me.'

He took a breath, a searing breath that razored his lungs. The darkness was still inside him, roiling in his vision. He had to make her see—*understand!* Understand the essential truth.

'I say your sister is a fool—and I mean it! A fool because she believes in something that doesn't exist! She only thinks it does—and look where that has got her? Where does it get anyone? It doesn't get them anywhere! It screws them up—that's all! Screws up lives, Ellie! Ruins them and destroys them! And all for something that doesn't even exist! Because it's garbage—all of it! All that hearts and flowers, all those vows and promises! Just garbage! Toxic garbage!'

Shock was naked in her face and it angered him. Angered him that she was shocked at what he was saying. He was telling her the truth.

The truth she has to believe—just as I do!

And she did believe it—of course she did! Why would she have married him otherwise? If she'd been like her sister—obsessed by some poisonous fantasy, believing in it—she would never have married him!

He felt the black tide that had swept over him like a tsunami out of nowhere beginning to recede. The pressure of his hands on her shoulders slackened, but he did not let her go. She was staring at him, and he could see a pulse beating at her throat. He didn't want her upset. He needed to calm her—calm himself.

'Ellie, it's OK—it's OK.'

His hands moulded her shoulders. He wanted to take her in his arms, but there were things he needed to say first. To reassure her—reassure himself.

'Look, why do you think we're so good together? Why do you think our marriage works so well?' His voice had lost the last of its vehemence—but not its emphasis. 'Why do you think it's going to go on working all our lives together?'

He took a breath, feeling his thumping heart-rate easing now, thankful that the black tide had left him, receded back into the past he never wanted to let it out from again. His eyes were pouring into hers now, making her see, making her understand, spelling it out to her.

'Right from the start we avoided any of that hearts and flowers, vows and promises rubbish! We never pretended anything to each other! Oh, the press might have drooled that we were some kind of sentimental fairy-tale romance—it sells papers! But we've known better right from the off! We've never deceived ourselves about why we married! We were honest with each other and we're honest with each other still. Our marriage has moved on and we're taking it forward together. Clear-eyed and honest. Neither of us is fooling ourselves or trying to fool each other.'

He took another breath, knowing he never wanted to have this conversation again—that he wanted it done with for ever.

His hands pressed on her shoulders, warm and reassuring. 'We both know that *love*—' he said the word with scathing, sarcastic inflection '—has got nothing to do with us! *That's* what makes our marriage so successful! Why it works so brilliantly! And it will go on working brilliantly! It's the same for every relationship that actually works—by keeping love well and truly out of it!'

He saw her swallow. The pulse at her throat was still beating strongly, but there was a pallor to her skin, a sharpening of her cheekbones.

Something shuttered in her eyes. 'Are you saying,' she asked slowly, 'that you don't think couples are ever in love with each other?'

Leon's lip curled. 'Oh, they may *think* they are,' he said derisively, 'but more fool them! Both of them are deluded!

Thinking themselves in love makes an unholy mess of things! Because when the chips go down they'll find out for themselves, too late, how much garbage it all is!' There was an edge in the way he was speaking now, sharp and serrated. 'That all their hearts and flowers, their vows and promises, mean nothing—just empty words!'

A chill was starting to spread inside Ellie—as if icy water were being poured into her veins. She could feel her heart thudding in her chest. Too much emotion was in her, poured upon her out of nowhere, without any warning. And it seemed to be draining into a vortex that was sucking everything out of her. Everything that was her...

'What about...?' She swallowed. 'What about when *you* fall in love, Leon?'

She saw the same dark expression flash across his face that she had seen when she had read out Marika's despairing text. Before he had shocked her with his furious outburst...

'I never will,' he retorted harshly. 'I told you—it doesn't exist.' He held her distended gaze, his dark eyes implacable. 'It doesn't exist,' he said again. 'So I will *never* tell a woman I love her. Will *never* tell her that lie.'

Something twisted along the tight line of his mouth. His eyes were boring into hers.

'And I never want to hear a woman tell me she loves me—*never*. I don't want *any* woman to say she loves me—and certainly not you!' he finished emphatically.

Finally his voice softened, and his hands started to caress her shoulders, kneading them, trying to draw her to him, hold her in his arms.

'Because you are too important to me, Ellie.' His voice was husky now, and his eyelids started to droop over his eyes. 'Who needs illusions, or delusions, or dangerous fantasies, when we have what *we* have—so much better, so much more real...'

* * *

Leon lowered his mouth to hers, moving over it sensually, arousingly. Desire pooled in him—honest and true. As honest and true as everything else that there was between them. What there would always be down all their years together…

Somewhere…dimly…way beyond the quickening of his desire, the quickening of his body as he drew this wonderful, beautiful, irresistible woman into his arms—his bride, his wife, his own most precious treasure—he became aware of two things.

Her phone was ringing.

And she was not kissing him back.

CHAPTER FOURTEEN

ELLIE HEARD HER PHONE. As if she were a sleepwalker she pulled herself free, staring at the number. Everything seemed distorted, as if the whole world had suddenly tilted—warped.

She thought it must be Marika, finally phoning her back. Or Niki.

It was her father.

And as she realised that the world suddenly shifted into terrifying focus. Fear knifed through her.

She answered the phone. Heard her father's voice. Answered in Karylyan.

Then she disengaged and stared at Leon. Who was staring at her, waiting to be told.

'That was my father. Marika has gone—left for Switzerland. She's…she's going to Karylya. And Niki—' she swallowed '—is taking her there.'

For a moment she just stood there, as if paralysed. All that was in her head, just for a second, was relief at the fact that she'd totally misinterpreted what her sister had meant by her vehement text. The next second the relief had vanished.

If Marika and Niki reached Karylya…

Urgently, she swung round, swinging open the door of the wardrobe, where her outfit for the flight tomorrow was hanging. But she would not be flying to Angers now.

Thank God I'm ready to travel—my hand luggage, my handbag, both sorted. My passport...

Her passport most of all.

Essential.

She felt her forearm seized as she moved to take out her clothes.

'Ellie—stop. What the hell are you doing?' Leon's voice was urgent.

She stared at him. There was a tempest in her head, but she could not pay it any attention right now.

'I'm going after them.'

'*What?* Are you mad? Ellie, the moment they reach the border they'll either be stopped or arrested! They're banned from entering the country! And so are you!'

She shook herself free. 'Princess Elizsaveta of Karylya is—but my passport is British. Ellie Peters. I'm a British citizen. They can't touch me!'

He swore. Not in Greek this time, but in an Anglo-Saxon vernacular that she understood only too well. She ignored it—just as she ignored what he was saying now, his eyes flashing angrily.

'Of course they damn well can! They can do anything they like! Matyas Horvath is a political hard man who is turning Karylya into a police state, and he will be president by the end of the week! Of *course* he'll jail you! Jail the lot of you! All you and your moronically irresponsible siblings will achieve is to feed his propaganda machine— he'll make huge political capital out of it! You'll be playing right into his hands if you go there!'

Her face contorted. 'I don't care! Leon! I have to *try*! I have to do *something*!'

'But *not* chase after them! I absolutely forbid it!'

She froze. Colour flared in her face.

'You can't stop me,' she said.

She said it coldly, deliberately. Biting out each word.

He took a step away from her, but still his height towered over hers. His face had hardened—just as it had when she had told him about her sister's text.

Anguish speared her. Oh, dear God, fool that she had been—unforgivable fool!

But she could not think about that now—could not think about the tempest raging in her head. She could only force her mind to do what it had to do now—make her body do what it had to.

To go after her sister, her brother—

And Leon would not stop her. *Could* not stop her.

'No,' he said, and his voice was as heavy as lead, as hard as iron, 'I can't stop you. But what I can do—and I will, be very, very sure of that, if you insist on this insanity—is pull the financial plug on your father. Totally. Right now.' He ground each word out, his features frozen and rigid.

A gasp broke from her, ragged and torn.

Leon plunged on. He had to make her understand—understand in what seemed to be the only way to penetrate the insane stupidity of what she was planning.

He felt emotions war within him. One was blinding fury at what she was trying to do—walk into a country that was days away from becoming a one-man dictatorship. But the other emotion was stronger still.

Gut-wrenching, convulsing fear.

Fear that he might lose her to years of incarceration—maybe for ever.

I can't lose her—I can't!

The horror of it leapt again. Making his voice harsh. Making him ruthless in preventing her madness by whatever means possible. He would exert the only leverage over her that he had. To keep her safe from herself. Safe for him.

Harsh lines incised around his mouth. 'If you go after

them I will evict your father and his wife, render them penniless. I can do it—and I *will*, Ellie.'

The words seemed carved into the space between them.

She was staring at him, her face as white as a sheet. Her hands were clenching and unclenching at her sides, her breathing laboured. It was like a knife in his guts to see her like that, but he had to do it. Had to do it for her sake—for his.

Then, abruptly, she slumped, her hands falling limply slack. She looked at him with weary, stricken, defeated eyes.

'You win, Leon. I can't do that to my father—not now.'

She turned away, half stumbling. He moved to catch her, but she evaded him.

He spoke again, his voice clipped, decisive.

'I'll rearrange our flight to take you straight to your father's tonight. It's late, but doable.'

Ellie heard him speak through a mind numbed with too much shock—too much fear for her sister and her brother.

It stayed numb—blessedly numb—all the way to the airport, long past the midnight hour, where she was escorted by Leon on to the private jet, to have him kiss her cheek, then stride down the steps, back to the car waiting on the Tarmac, while the cabin door was swung shut, the plane starting to taxi.

In her head she heard Leon's last words to her on their way here—the assurances he'd tried to give her.

'I'll start kicking up all the hell I can—the Karylyan embassy in Rome, human rights lawyers, press, governments—whatever it takes, Ellie. Whatever it damn well takes to get them back!'

Only as the plane soared off into the night sky did the numbness leave her.

And in its place only two emotions were left to her.

Fear for her siblings.
Despair for herself.

At the château, when she arrived in the early hours of the morning, her father swept her up into his arms, holding her tightly. Even her stepmother embraced her. They both looked haggard, as did Ellie.

'Leon persuaded me that I would only make things worse if I followed Marika and Niki,' she told them, as they made a sketchy breakfast for which none of them had any appetite. 'I thought my British passport would protect me, but—'

'Horvath will respect *nothing*!' her father burst out.

'Is there any news from them?' her stepmother asked frantically.

Ellie could only shake her head. She'd been texting constantly, ever since landing, but no reply had come. She had no idea where Marika and Niki were—or what had happened to them. Her eyes went to the television set, tuned to the Karylyan news channel for the breakfast news—all it was showing was the preparations for the election, and the presenter was fulsomely extolling Matyas Horvath as the best candidate for president. The only candidate…

'The media dare say nothing else,' Ellie's father said grimly. 'The clampdown on press freedom has been comprehensive.'

Ellie fished out her tablet. 'There is *some* real news coming out,' she said cautiously. 'Pretty clandestine, but it's hard for Horvath to silence the Internet entirely.'

She found the unofficial newsfeed that she had been following all the way from Angers. It was being broadcast from outside Karylya, and there was some criticism about the elections having been manipulated—criticism over Horvath being the sole candidate. It lamented the fact that no other candidate was brave enough to stand against him, to be a rallying point for all those who opposed the looming dictatorship.

She checked her phone again. Still nothing from Marika or Niki. Fear clutched at her. Had they been stopped at the border—were they already in detention? No one would know until the new regime was ready to make propaganda out of it.

Her eyes went back to the TV screen, and then again to her tablet, her heart heavy and fearful…

The morning passed, the hours leaden, and still there was no news. No contact.

Leon phoned her briefly, sounding strained and terse, asking for any news, saying he would be in touch again later, telling her to keep him informed. Then he rang off.

Hearing his voice had been…difficult.

She could hear her father in the library, talking to one of his small staff, preparing a press statement to be issued if it was discovered that his children were intercepted. He asked only for their safe return, said that they were young and misguided—innocent of all except youthful folly.

Would it be enough to secure their safety? Or would Matyas Horvath make political capital out of it, as Leon had warned—even subject them to a trial of some kind, sentence them to prison…

The very thought of it sent knives into her stomach. She knew Leon had been right to castigate Niki and Marika for being so insanely reckless—for going now, at the worst of times, into the lion's jaws.

Why now?

The anguished question stabbed at her.

She picked up her phone. She would text Leon to report that there was still no news. She could not face speaking to him.

Turbid emotion swelled within her, but she dared not let

it out. Later—later there would be time. Time to answer the voice that was going round and round in her head.

What happens now to Leon and me? What happens now?

She could not listen to it—yet nor could she silence it.

She stared at her phone screen, steeling herself to text him. Then, before she could do it, she halted. A text was arriving. Instantly everything else went out of her head.

'It's Marika!' she cried out loud.

Her stepmother turned, and her father hurried out of the library.

Ellie read out the text, voice breathless.

Ellie—we're here! We crossed the mountains on foot! Antal met us! Watch the newsfeed! It's amazing! It's why we came!

Frantically Ellie snatched up her tablet, holding it up so her father and stepmother could see. And there on the screen was a sight that told her exactly why her siblings had chosen to get back into Karylya now—a sight that absolutely froze her in disbelief.

It was a live feed from the main town in the southern region of Karylya—a part of the duchy that had always been monarchist. And apparently it still was—or at least pro-Karpardy.

For, there on the town hall balcony, live-streamed, was Marika, standing to one side of Niki. On the other side of her was Antal Horvath. All three were smiling and waving. And above their heads was a banner, held up by the other people now crowding out on to the balcony—a banner that declared the presidential candidacy of Nikolai Karpardy.

Ellie felt her eyes widen in disbelief, and amazement, and another emotion that made her cry out and crush her hand to her mouth.

And as the banner was unfurled, waving in the bright sunshine, a roar went up from the huge crowd the camera had panned round to show, filling the town square to bursting point. The deafening sound of cheering.

Leon stared, mesmerised, watching the same live feed a few moments after Ellie had urgently texted him to do so. Ellie's brother was talking now, addressing the crowd, his Karylyan being simultaneously displayed in English language subtitles.

'I was born and raised to serve my country,' he was saying, his youthful voice clear and ardent. 'That is still my purpose! The only purpose of my life!' His tone changed, his hands reaching out. 'Citizens—my fellow citizens, for I am one of you now!—Karylyans, be loyal to all that our country is and should be! Not a medieval monarchy—nor yet a new dictatorship! But a free democracy! A democracy that must resist tyranny—the fearsome tyranny of a police state—and must have truly free elections!'

With each passionately voiced declaration a roar of cheering went up. And then Antal Horvath, the son of the man who wanted to turn Karylya into a police state, was speaking, too, bewailing his father's ambitions for an uncontested presidency, pledging his support for democracy to Ellie's brother and then taking Marika's hand, telling the still cheering crowd that his heart was hers.

There was yet more deafening cheers and thunderous applause as Niki wrung Antal's other hand and swung it with his into a united triumphant wave, to even greater cheering.

It was masterly—even Leon, with all his cynical worldly wisdom could see that.

The boy's youth—he was barely a legal adult—and his passionate idealism… The young Antal Horvath, only a half a dozen years older than Niki, denouncing his tyrannous father... Mix all that with romantic love—Antal's for Princess Marika—and all of them young and good-looking... People would believe every heartfelt word they said.

Masterly indeed—and incredibly dangerous.

To themselves.

His expression set. Getting Ellie's siblings safely out of Karylya had just become infinitely less likely.

Ellie's brother had declared open defiance—thrown down his gauntlet to the man who had ousted his father. Leon's expression grew grimmer yet. And Matyas Horvath would do everything in his considerable power to crush him.

Ellie was trying to keep her father and stepmother's hopes alive, but the ex-Grand Duke and his Grand Duchess were morbidly fearful. The Karylyan regime had immediately denounced Niki's campaign as illegal, an incitement for monarchist rebellion, and the militia had been despatched to crush it.

As the next days passed the world's media watched with bated breath. This was a news story that had every element to catch the public's attention, from the three young, idealistic and highly photogenic protagonists, to the royal connection, the romantic connection, and Ellie knew with a sinking heart the fact that she herself, with Leon's courting of media coverage of their own wedding and glamorous social life since then, had already made Karylya far more famous than it had been previously.

Ellie cursed herself for more than just that at her sister's naively buoyant texts and obdurately optimistic phone calls, in which she persisted in denying the danger they were in, refusing all her pleas that they flee the country while they could...*if* they could...

Of course we're not running away! Ellie, we know exactly what we're doing! We're saving Karylya! We've been determined to do it ever since Papa was exiled!

Dismay and guilt smote Ellie at her sister's passionate words.

I was so busy with Leon I never noticed what Marika and Niki were planning!

Her heart wrung heavily. But then it seemed she wasn't very good at noticing a lot of things, was she?

Like the way Leon lived in a universe that was as remote from hers as outer space. Cold, lifeless outer space.

She sheered her mind away from that. At least she didn't have to think about it now—didn't have to answer the question that circled endlessly in her head.

What happens now to Leon and me? What happens now? What could happen?

It was impossible—just impossible. Impossible, impossible…

At least she was spared Leon's presence…

Leon had left Rome immediately after Niki's declaration, heading for Washington to lobby as hard as he could for their rescue, blatantly leveraging his position as Niki's brother-in-law—if not for active support for Niki's candidacy, then for support for his democratic right to run against the man who thought the presidency was his for the taking. Support for Niki's right to safety and condemnation for Matyas Horvath, should he try to crush any opposition to himself.

Then he was back in Europe again, using every contact and acquaintance he'd accumulated in his rise to wealth, pulling every string he could with those bankers and investors to whom a stable and prosperous Karylya was far more valuable than one breaking down into civil strife, potentially even civil war.

The crowds that had initially rallied to Ellie's brother were swelling by the hour, and opposition to Antal's father was mounting daily, now that they had a focus for their protest.

Matyas Horvath had postponed the election and declared a state of emergency, creating sweeping new powers to crush all opposition.

A crisis was clearly looming, Leon thought grimly, emerging from yet another meeting with as many influential financiers as he had been able to muster, having asked them to freeze their investments in Karylya, withdraw all deposits from the Bank of Karylya, sell all their currency holdings and put collective financial pressure on the regime not to be punitive of their ardent new opponents at the risk of destabilising the economy. But what it would be, and when it would strike, he could not say.

He was haunting the Quai d'Orsay in Paris, home of the French foreign office, to garner what news he could from their sources, and had set up similar sources in Berlin, Moscow, Vienna and London's Whitehall. And he had contacts amongst the broadcast media and press, with all their sources of information, as well.

In part of his head he wondered why he was doing it. What was the rest of the Karylyan royal family to him? A sponging ex-Grand Duke and a couple of fecklessly irresponsible younger children...

He thrust the question from his head. He was doing it—that was all.

And when, less than ten days after he'd put Ellie on that plane to Angers, he threw himself into his car and sped out of Paris, he knew exactly why he was doing it.

He arrived at the château as night fell, and strode into

the salon, where Ellie and her father and stepmother leapt to their feet, fear instantly on their faces.

'They're safe!' he announced. 'Safer than I ever thought possible.' He took a heaving breath. His eyes wanted only to go to Ellie, but he knew he had to address her father first. 'There has been the most extraordinary development…'

His voice sounded disbelieving even to himself, and if he had not had confirmation of the facts from the French foreign minister himself, and promised to take the news immediately and in person to the ex-Grand Duke, he would not have believed it.

'There's been another coup—Matyas Horvath is under arrest.'

For a second there was complete silence. Then, with a rush, Ellie hurled herself into his arms, clinging to him and bursting into abject tears of relief.

Why was he doing it? Again Leon had his answer.

An answer that within forty-eight hours would turn to ash and bitter cinder in his mouth.

CHAPTER FIFTEEN

LEON STARED AT the television screen in his hotel room above the busy streets of Manhattan. In Karylya it was bright morning—here the dead of night. He took another mouthful of single malt, knowing he should not torment himself by watching, but he could not tear his eyes away.

The ancient medieval cathedral in Karylya's capital was packed, but his eyes were on the figures in the foreground. On one of them only.

Princess Elizsaveta—*his* Princess.

His face contorted, emotion stabbing him and bleakness filling the empty space inside him.

His Princess no longer.

Soon to be his wife no longer.

The bleak words drummed in his head, as they had done ever since he had received her letter, sent from the Karylyan Embassy in Paris, where the Grand Duke and his wife and older daughter had been driven in a chauffeured car flying the royal insignia the moment he'd informed them of the astonishing turn of events in their homeland.

Ellie's letter had arrived two days later.

Dear Leon,
This is to let you know that I am releasing you from our marriage. Thanks to the unexpected events in Karylya, there is no longer any necessity for it.
I wish you well in all your future endeavours, and

*remain so very grateful for all that you have done for
my family, and for our brief time together.*
With warmest wishes,
Ellie

He knew it by heart. Every line of it. Every damnable
line…

He heard music swelling—the Karylyan Royal Anthem,
now being played again in its own land.

The royal family were in exile no longer.

And as the anthem finished he watched the familiar male
figure seated on the throne in front of the altar reading out
the oath that had been presented to him by his archbishop,
his voice resolute.

Watched as the archbishop stepped away and another
figure stepped forward, dressed in full ceremonial uni-
form, ascended the two steps to halt before the throne. He
bowed his head and knelt, took the hand of the enthroned
man to bestow upon it a kiss of obeisance. He spoke the
words of fealty and homage. Straightened and stood aside.

And as he watched something inside Leon rose within
him and constricted his throat. An emotion he had thought
long destroyed.

The camera pulled back, and now he watched the Grand
Duchess and her stepdaughter and daughter walking forward slowly, with sweeping trains. The three of them were
curtsying deeply, the enthroned figure bowing his head regally in acknowledgement.

Leon could watch no more.

He jolted to his feet, snapping off the television set and
striding with rapid footsteps into his bedroom, to throw
himself down on the bed. His face stark, he stared at the
ceiling.

And that long-buried emotion—destroyed so long ago,
never to be permitted existence again—forced itself, syn-

apse by synapse, into his head. Widening and growing, strengthening and gaining power...

The power he had denied it for so long. The power he had felt it taking more and more since his marriage. The power that had made him want to unite his life with the woman he had married...the power that had savaged him with fear when she'd wanted to risk her freedom for the sake of her siblings. The power that had devastated him when she'd left him.

The power which now broke from its life-long chains to sear across his heart.

His hands clenched at his sides as it took him over, forcing itself upon him, making him face everything he had rejected and denied. Forcing its truth upon him.

He was crying out inside.

She's left me! She's left me and I cannot bear it—I cannot bear it!

And as the words cried out inside him a terrifying realisation swept through him, jolting him upright to his feet.

The blood drained from his face, bleaching his features. Then slowly, so very slowly, words took shape in his head. Words he clung to like a drowning man a raft.

It's not too late.

Not too late to go to her, to tell her—tell her what now blazed in him with a certainty that shook him to his very core.

Ellie sat herself down on the wooden bench in her stepfather's apple orchard. The mossed trees were heavy with fruit, and wasps were feasting on the windfalls in the long grass. She had come here seeking only solitude, knowing that her mother would take one look at her, when she arrived from Karylya to burst into tears on her bosom, and understand totally that all she could do now was seek refuge like a wounded animal.

She shut her eyes in misery.

At the very moment of her greatest happiness—Leon wanting to make his life with her, she discovering her glorious love for him and having faith that he would return that love—everything had turned to ash and bitter cinders. All she had hoped for, yearned for—thought she had been granted!—had been destroyed. Destroyed utterly…

Every word of the brief letter she had made herself write to Leon burned in her memory. She had said only what she *had* to say—nothing of what she longed to say, what she could never say.

She had set him free.

As she herself could never be.

Because I will love him all my life.

Anguish filled her face.

And it is because I love him that I have set him free! I must never impose on him what he told me he's never wanted!

A woman's love.

Her love.

She felt her hands move to her lap, clenching together. She had been over this again and again—was still at war with herself. Longing with every fibre of her being to rush to him—to be his wife on any terms, never telling of her love for him.

But how could I live with him, loving him as I do, knowing he will never—can never—love me in return? That he will never want my love at all! It would slay me, destroy me…

She had asked herself that question over and over again in those terrifying days of fearing she might never see her brother and sister again.

What happens now with Leon and me?

The answer had been impossible to face. But now she had. She had faced it—and given him the freedom from an unwanted love that he had never asked for, never sought. And never would.

So I can never see him again. Never will see him again.

Anguish and loss—tearing, unbearable loss—pierced her like a sword.

A sound came from the top of the orchard—the creaking iron gate opening. Her head twisted round and up. For a second—just a second—her vision was confused by the dappled sunlight under the trees. Then, with a sudden constriction of her throat, her vision resolved itself and she felt a leap in her heart that was boundless joy. And agonising pain.

It was Leon.

Leon paused, stilling as Ellie's head lifted jerkily and she saw him there. He saw something flare in her eyes—something that speared through him like a fire-tipped arrow. Then it was gone, and all that was in her face was wariness and withdrawal.

He felt emotion stab in him, and then, with determined resolve, he headed through the long grass towards her.

'I need to talk to you.'

Something moved in her face, but she did not speak.

Ellie was incapable of speech. Her senses were drumming with his presence, her heart leaping—but she crushed it back.

Her eyes clung to Leon's face. There was something different about it—his features were etched starkly, tension in every line of him. He sat himself down heavily on the end of the wooden bench, turning towards her. Emotion surged within her, yet still she leashed it back.

'Why?' The single word fell from her lips.

Something flashed in his face, his eyes.

'Why?' he echoed.

Something in Greek broke from him and then, as if getting control back over himself, he leant forward, his hands clasping each other on his thighs. Absently she noticed the muscled power beneath the smooth material of his trousers, noticed the way his knuckles were whitening with the strength of his grip.

'That is *my* question!' he shot at her. '*Why* are you divorcing me?'

He drew breath heavily, his chest rising and falling in a way that made her eyes cling to him. Faintness was washing through her...emotions were churning through her. To see him again like this, when she had thought never to see him again...

He was speaking again, more words bursting from him.

'Is it just because your father can now afford to repay everything I spent on him, including buying the château? I told you, Ellie!' There was vehemence in his voice. 'I couldn't care less about bankrolling him—or not bankrolling him! That *cannot* be the reason you're ending our marriage!'

His expression changed, became still, and now there was self-condemnation in his voice.

'Is it because I was such a brute when you were trying to go to your sister and brother in Karylya? Threatening to evict your father?' He took another breath. 'I said it only to force your hand! To protect you from yourself! I would never have gone through with it—'

She was shaking her head. Wishing, as she did so, that she could clutch at what he'd said and give him the reason he had come here to find.

The real reason she could never give him.

Because to explain why I have left him will be to place the burden of that reason upon him.

'Then *why*?'

His question came again. His dark eyes rested on her like weights she could not bear—but must.

'I have to know—' He broke off. Shut his eyes a moment.

Ellie's gaze went to his long, dark lashes, brushing the tanned skin of his cheeks. Emotion washed through her again, weakening her when she must stay strong.

'It is because…' she said slowly, knowing he wanted—needed—an answer, an explanation. 'Because I know I cannot be honest with you. And honesty…' Her voice changed, twisted. 'Honesty is what you value above everything. The only foundation for a marriage.'

A sound broke from him.

'Honesty?'

The derision in the word was infinite. Scathing.

Ellie felt her face blench, the blood draining from it. Dear God—did he know? Had he guessed? Please, no! *No!* She could not bear it—could not bear to place upon him the burden of her love…a burden he did not want—would never want.

But Leon's stark features were twisting again…

'There was nothing *honest* in what I said to you. Nothing!' His jaw set. He felt as if a vice was clamping his throat. 'There was only—' He forced the words out of the depths of his being into the light of day. 'Only fear.'

She stared at him, not understanding. He saw the blankness in her eyes—those beautiful, expressive eyes whose merest glance could stop the breath in his body. Longing filled him, and an ache for her that was a tearing hunger—a hunger for her that had driven him across the Atlantic, to seek and find her…to tell her what he was now telling her. What he must tell her—must face.

The truth he must face himself.

Whatever it cost him to tell her.

He tore his gaze from her, turned his head aside, unable to bear looking at her, longing for her.

He looked, instead, back down the years.

Unconsciously his shoulders hunched, as if he were protecting himself…

Protecting myself from the cold of the Athens winter. My hands thrust into my jeans pockets, my jacket too thin to keep me warm, the soles of my feet freezing as I stand for so long in the queue for the soup kitchen, to fetch the meal I need to take to my mother.

He felt his thoughts shear away, as if an insect had flown too near an open flame and would burn to a frazzle in the space of a second.

'Fear,' he said again.

His gaze lowered, dropped to the sun-dappled grass beneath his feet. The late summer warmth embraced him. A world away from that bitter Athens winter.

His voice, when he spoke, was stark.

'I've told you—have made no secret of it—how bad things were when I was a teenager. How I was left to look after my mother.' His voice hardened unconsciously, as it always did, when he thought of his father abandoning his wife, deserting his family, taking the selfish, uncaring, cowardly way out of a situation he had not wanted to face. 'I did the best I could—'

His voice broke off and for a moment he could not speak, and when he did he felt a bleakness that ripped the very soul from his body.

'I did the best I could,' he said again.

His eyes rested on the lush orchard grass, where a wasp was busy with a fallen apple, but it was not that he saw. It was himself, carrying the metal dish of thick soup, hugging the loaf of bread that had been doled out to him, hurrying up the dirty staircase to the dingy one-roomed flat where he and his mother had to live, their former spacious apartment long gone.

He saw himself opening the door, calling to his mother that he was back, that he'd brought hot food for her.

But she had not answered him.

Had not been able to answer him.

Not then. Nor ever again—

'But it wasn't enough,' he heard himself say now. *'It wasn't enough.'*

A noise came from his throat—a tearing sound. He lifted his gaze, bringing it up to meet the eyes that were resting on him. A light was beginning to form in them that seemed like a mirror of his own. Filling with dread...

'I came back one day from the soup kitchen and found her...found her...'

His fists spasmed, features contorting.

'She'd—she'd cut her wrists. There was blood soaking into the sheets of her bed...so much blood. *So much.* And her face was white—white like the corpse she was. My mother—'

The words were wrenched from him, from the depths of him. From the memory he would never, never allow into his life. The emotion that went with the memory. The emotion he could not bear to feel.

'She left me a note,' he said. 'She said she could not live without the man she loved—my father, who had left her. She could not bear to live without him. So she left me.'

He closed his eyes, screwing them shut so tightly that the sockets ached. His hands were an agony of clenching.

Pain and grief and loss—unbearable loss—were racking him, and the darkness that filled him, that had always filled him, waited to feed on him, enveloped him as it had that nightmare day.

There was no comfort. No consolation. No way to bear it except the way he had.

Denying love.

Protecting himself from it.

From what it could do.

Had he said the words aloud? He did not know.

But arms were coming around him, around his stricken body…arms were folding him against a body, arms so slight and so slender—so strong. Strong enough to hold him now, as his body shook. And she was cradling him, holding him, saying his name over and over again. He could feel tears on his cheeks, breaking not from the man he was now but from the boy he had once been, too young to bear what had been done to him by a woman who had pitied herself, loved herself more than she had her son, betraying him even as his own father had betrayed him, too.

The arms around him were fast about him now, not letting him go, drawing his head down to her shoulder. She was smoothing his hair as a mother might smooth the hair of her infant, comforting him in her arms. Until at last he felt the racking of his body ebb and was exhausted, spent.

He lifted his head from her shoulder, aware that her hand was enclosed in his, as if he would never let her go. *Could* never let her go.

Ellie was speaking to him. Very slowly, very clearly, her eyes holding his smeared gaze…

'Leon, you must understand me. Just as I now understand you.'

She heard something change in her voice as sudden realisation hollowed her—the realisation of just why he had lashed out so furiously—so condemningly—when she had told him of her sister's despair and her own fear of what it might lead to…

He was remembering his own mother, what her despair did to her, to him…

'Listen to me—*listen* to me.'

She took a breath, impelling him to hear her. To understand. It was the most important thing in the world for him to understand—the most vital thing to make him. Emotion was storming inside her but she could not let it show—horror and disbelief and a pity so profound it wrung her heart.

She spoke again, her voice steady, intent, for he *must* understand this.

'What your parents did to you between them was…' she took another breath '…unforgivable. Your father without a doubt is to be condemned without compunction! But your mother, however great her own misery and heartbreak—' She heard her voice catch, knowing these words were for herself as well as him. 'She should never, *never* have abandoned you the way she did! *No* parent should put their own feelings first!'

These were the words that would show Leon—show that abject, deserted teenager, so cruelly abandoned by the very people who should have been there for him—that it could be safe to love… That he need not fear love as he did. Need not deny it to protect himself.

Compassion filled her, along with pity and understanding. She lifted her free hand to his cheek, her eyes pouring into his with all that she felt. All that she must show him to make him believe and understand—and trust.

'Your parents failed you, Leon—but not all parents do. Mine have not, for all that they were not happy with each other. And the partners they now have they are truly devoted to. As is my sister to hers, and he to her. And although…' Her voice faltered, but she went on, knowing she must do it for him. 'Although we cannot choose who we fall in love with—or, indeed, out of love with, as your father did your mother, or my parents each other—it doesn't mean we must become slaves to that love, sacrificing our children's happiness to it. We can still make the right moral choices—even if it costs us heartache and heartbreak.'

Just as I, Leon, cannot tell you of my love for you lest it burden you with something unwanted.

And she still could not tell him.

Emotion twisted inside her. Her understanding of Leon now was infinitely greater. Pity and compassion for what he had suffered seared within her. But why should that change anything for her?

'Sometimes, Leon,' she said slowly, 'we have to be brave to love. And one day...' She made the words come, putting into practice what she had just said to him about courage, though it cost her to do it. 'One day you will meet a woman you can love without fear—on whom you can bestow the heart that you have protected so desperately since your parents abandoned you, each in their own disastrous, self-obsessed way, to make the choices they did. I wish that for you, Leon, with all my heart—'

She broke off. It was impossible to say more. Impossible.

Is this the one gift I can give him out of my love for him? To set him free not just from me but from the fear that has imprisoned him all his life? Free to find love.

He was looking at her and his expression was strange. Her hand dropped away from his cheek and suddenly she moved to stand up. She was too close to him—way too close. And for all her brave words she felt her heart contract within her. With love...with pain...

He was getting to his feet as well, still with that expression on his face she had never seen before. But suddenly it seemed to stop the beating of her heart. He stood in front of her but made no attempt to touch her, or close in on her.

His eyes were searching as he spoke. His voice low.

'And what if I told you that I have already found her?' he said, and there was something in his voice that she had never heard before. 'Found the woman I love.'

He paused, and something shifted in his eyes.

'The woman who is already my wife,' he said.

She heard him, but did not hear him. Her gaze could only hold his, uncomprehending. She did not dare to understand. To believe…

He was talking again—and now she heard him. Heard every word.

'It's why I came here,' he said, with that same low, intent tone in his voice. 'To tell you why I said such things to you that night in Rome. To tell you how great a lie they were—to tell you the truth of what I feel for you. What I will always feel. What I started to feel right from the moment of our first incredible night together, though I could not recognise it. A kind of…of *thawing*…as if something frozen deep within me was starting to melt. I felt it again and again—most of all in Puglia, when I knew I wanted to spend my life with you, to make a home with you.'

He took a breath and his voice changed, became edgy.

'I came to tell you of my fear for you—fear that knifed me in my guts—when you said you wanted to risk imprisonment by trying to rescue your brother and sister and I thought I might lose you for years. To tell you of the pain I've felt since you told me our marriage was over. My fear that I'd lost you for ever—just as I lost both my parents—showed me that truth. Showed me so strongly that I could deny it, flee from it, no longer.'

Leon paused, and then he said the words he had come to say.

'The truth is that I love you with all my heart and being—my most beautiful, wonderful Princess, my most beautiful, wonderful woman, my most beautiful, wonderful wife—the love of my heart and my soul.'

He stopped, felt his throat tightening so that he could hardly speak, yet still he knew he must. He could read nothing in her face—nothing in her eyes. But in his head he heard the words she had just spoken to him.

Sometimes we have to be brave to love.

He felt emotion twist in him. Well, he was being brave now—and he must be braver yet.

So he said the final words he must say.

'But if that love is something you do not want I will not burden you with it—'

A cry broke from her. A cry of anguish and heartache. And then tears were spilling from her eyes, from her beautiful, wonderful eyes, and suddenly she was in his arms and words were coming from her in a cry.

'Leon, I want your love with all my heart! For I love you with all my heart! Being without you has been agony—I've missed you so much! I left you, forced myself to leave you, because I didn't want to burden you—'

He did not let her finish her echo of his own words. Words that were cast to the wind now. He swooped his mouth upon hers and as he kissed her felt her cheeks wet with tears. Tears of joy—only of joy.

Ellie held his face in her hands as his mouth released hers, her eyes pouring into his. Joy and thankfulness filled her—not just for herself, but for him, the man she loved, so grievously wounded by the very people who should have protected him. He had found a way to pass beyond what had been done to him. To come to believe that love could be true—that he could risk loving another human being.

And this time—oh, *this* time that love would never be betrayed.

'I will love you always, Leon. Always!' she vowed.

His gaze poured into hers, burning with all that he felt. All that he was now free to feel. And to tell to the woman he loved who, miracle of miracles, returned that love…

His heart overflowed with it.

'And I you,' he said. 'I love you, my one and only love, my beloved wife, my beautiful, peerless princess bride—and I am your liegeman for all time.'

He took her hands, pressing them with his, leading her to sit down on the wooden bench again.

'Your liegeman,' he said again, and lifted each hand to his mouth in homage and in love.

Then he tucked them both into his, holding them fast. He smiled down at her.

So much was in his heart, soaring and swooping, but he had one more thing to say to her. One more wound to heal. For one day, God willing—and he felt his heart soar again even at the very thought that this most precious woman in the world, the woman he loved with all his heart and soul and being, might one day bear a child for him—he must be the father his own had not been to him. The father he could be—*would* be. For now he had proof that such a thing was possible.

'If you want to know,' he said, his voice half-wry, half-serious, 'when it was that I first brought myself to believe that I did not have to perpetually distrust the very concept of love, it was when I was watching the live broadcast from the cathedral. It was seeing your father—'

He broke off. A faint frown creased his brow and his gaze flickered out across the dappled orchard.

'I never liked your father,' he said abruptly. 'I despised him. Like my father, he put himself first. He was willing for his daughter to marry the man—a complete stranger to her—who was paying for his comfortable exile.'

Words of protest rose to Ellie's lips. 'Leon, he was ashamed of relying on you, and was doing so only for his wife and children's sake! That's why I let him think I'd fallen for you in a *coup de foudre*!' she exclaimed. 'It made it easier for him.'

'Conveniently so,' Leon said tightly. Then his expression changed. 'But all my contempt for him evaporated in that single moment when I saw him in the cathedral. It… it showed me how…how unselfish a father could be—as mine was not. Watching your father do what he did for the sake of someone more important to him than himself—'

'Paying homage to his own son—his sovereign now?' Ellie finished for him. She took a breath. 'He did so, Leon, with all his heart, and such pride in Niki! I promise you— as did we all. That coup which removed Matyas Horvath wanted to restore the monarchy—but not the monarch. And we welcomed it with absolute thankfulness. It was the best possible outcome once the Council had come to see Horvath as a liability. Although…' she looked straight at Leon '…they were helped in that regard by all the lobbying you did, both politically and financially, for which we are all deeply grateful.'

Her expression changed as she went on.

'If there was any concern it was that my father abdicating in favour of his own son would place a burden on Niki that he is very young to take on. But the Council has been incredibly supportive, as you know. Niki will study at Oxford, as was always planned, and get his degree, and as well as attending a monthly Council meeting he will spend his vacations in Karylya, learning the craft of sovereign politics.' She made a wry face. 'My only royal sisterly fear is that he might remember with too great a fondness those heady days when he ran as candidate for a republican presidency!

'But of course,' she went on musingly, 'it was the very fact that he had shown himself so courageous, so idealistic, in risking imprisonment or worse at Horvath's hands, by returning to Karylya at so dangerous a time for him, that so impressed not only the populace but the Council as well. Hence the compromise, which all Karylyans must hope will work for this generation and the future—that my father stands down, of his own free will, and lets his son ascend the throne, calling for fresh elections to a newly created national assembly and instituting a reformed constitution that promotes a more redistributive tax system and gives a fair and just representation to all ethnicities within Karylya.'

'And your sister? What will she do?' Leon raised an eyebrow.

'Well, with Antal's father having now taken himself off out of the country—with a generous pay-off insisted upon by Niki, I might add, who has already learned the wisdom of political clemency to neutralise opposition—Antal is starting his own career: standing as a pro-royalist but re-forming candidate in the elections. As for my sister—she and her mother are totally absorbed in planning Marika's wedding...'

She paused, looking at Leon. Her expression changed again. Lightened.

'Will you be my plus one?' she asked.

There was a glint of humour in her eye. And an answering glint in his.

'All your life,' he said. 'For everything. I am your own true liegeman for all time.'

She lifted her face to his. Lifted her heart to his. The heart that was singing with a rapture she had never dared to hope could be hers.

But it is—it is mine, all mine, for all time!

Joy streamed through her—and wonder and elation. She had always yearned to marry for love—and now she had.

And so had Leon. Free to love at last.

As his mouth lowered to hers one thought and one soaring emotion filled her.

So have we both.

And then all conscious thought was lost in the bliss of their embrace.

EPILOGUE

THE DRAWING ROOM in the château on the Loire was bathed in early summer sunshine as Ellie and Leon, newly arrived from their Elizabethan country house in Somerset, purchased just before Christmas, stood in front of the ornate fireplace, smiling at the assembled company.

'My whole family,' said Ellie happily.

They were all there—her parents and their spouses, her half-siblings and her new brother-in-law—and she beamed at all of them.

'We have, as you may well have guessed, an announcement to make,' Leon said.

His voice was warm, and he slipped Ellie's hand into his, throwing her a loving glance which she returned.

Then his gaze went out over the faces smiling back at him. *His* family, too. His mother-in-law, Lady Connie—who was, he knew, overjoyed at their loving happiness—had a fondly expectant look in her eyes that told Leon she had already guessed what he and Ellie's announcement was going to be, and couldn't wait to hear it.

Her husband was stooping to greet the handsome and usually irascible Pomeranian newly acquired by Ellie's stepmother, which under Malcolm's experienced approach was being far more friendly.

Leon made a mental note to consult his wife's stepfather after dinner—Ellie had recommended they ask Malcolm about the mountain nature reserve in Karylya that he was financing, one of the new young Grand Duke's enthusiastically promoted schemes for his country.

Another was the new national ballet school, of which the newly-wed Princess Marika was patroness along with the opera house, having taken over that role from her mother.

Her young husband, Antal, now an elected member of the National Assembly, was a junior minister for the arts, with a particular brief for the promotion of traditional crafts amongst the myriad ethnicities in the country, and he was organising an annual cultural festival to celebrate Karylya's diversity.

As for the young Grand Duke himself… Leon could not prevent his lips twitching in amusement at the memory of his arrival, flying in from Oxford for the weekend. Ellie had rushed forward to hug him, only to be brought up short by her stepmother's shocked exclamation.

'Elizsaveta, you forget yourself!'

Dutifully Ellie had halted, dipping down into the required curtsy before her sovereign.

'Not *nearly* deep enough, sis!' her brother had reprimanded pompously, in exaggeratedly lofty tones—which had promptly earned him a thump on his chest and the tart observation that he looked hungover after what had doubtless been a heavy session out clubbing with his university mates the night before.

Niki's parents, once Princess Elizsaveta had acknowledged her brother's sovereignty, had, to Leon's surprise, looked on indulgently—both at the irreverent sibling banter and at the thought of the Grand Duke of Karylya carousing with his fellow students.

But then, Leon thought, everything about the former Grand Duke and Duchess and their new, far more relaxed attitude to life was surprising to him.

Ellie had explained it to him. 'My father never *enjoyed* being Grand Duke,' she'd told Leon. 'To him it was his duty, but always a difficult one. Now that the baton has passed to Niki—who, as is already evident, looks set to make a highly successful go of his reign, for he's wildly popular as my father never was—my father and stepmother are actually much happier. They've genuinely come to love the château you installed them in, now that it's their own. My father's filling the library with his precious rare editions—and he's been invited to remain a patron of the national collection in Karylya, which has pleased him no end—while my stepmother is busy restoring the château's gardens, preparatory to launching an open-air summer opera season in the grounds next year. Oh, and be warned: now that Marika's left home she's got herself a dog! It yaps!'

Now, as Malcolm straightened up, said animal gave a yap of indignation at being deprived of attention and trotted across to his owner, who scooped him up with a doting, 'Up you come, Chou-Chou!', cooing to him fondly in German and urging him to be good because an important announcement was about to be made.

Leon caught her exchanging knowing glances with her predecessor, who nodded as if in confirmation of what both of them were pretty sure they were going to hear.

Well, he would keep them waiting no longer.

'Thank you all so much for coming here,' he opened, smiling at Lady Connie and Malcolm, then at Princess Marika and Antal, 'and, of course,' he went on, 'to my wife's sovereign, for dragging himself away from his studies...' He cast a conspiratorial grin at Niki, who returned it shamelessly, if a trifle blearily. 'Most of all, and it goes without saying...' he inclined his head to the Grand Duke Emeritus and the Grand Duchess Emerita '...to their Royal Highnesses for their hospitality this evening.'

He had married a princess and royalty was royalty.

'A pleasure,' his father-in-law assured him, his tone genial.

Leon drew breath. 'So, I shall hesitate no longer in telling you what I suspect is no secret for some of you…'

His gaze swept over Ellie's mother and stepmother, as well as encompassing Marika, who was whispering something in an excited fashion to her husband.

His gaze came back to Ellie. 'You tell them,' he invited.

Ellie's eyes gleamed and her hand squeezed Leon's. 'We're having a baby!' she exclaimed.

Her mother surged forward. 'Darling, I *knew* it!'

Her hug was tight, her delight warm. Then Marika was hugging her, too, and even her stately stepmother, after handing Chou-Chou to her husband, issued forward to bestow a careful but pleased kiss upon Ellie's cheek.

The former Grand Duke got a protesting yap for his pains, so that he hurriedly set the small dog down on the floor, where it skidded excitedly around on the parquet floor, yapping madly, picking up the excitement of the assembled company.

'My dear, I am so happy for you both!' Ellie's stepmother informed her smilingly.

Her father was shaking Leon's hand in congratulation, and then he was wrapping Ellie in a paternal embrace.

'My darling daughter—'

There was a choke in his voice and Ellie could hear it.

For her ears alone he spoke on. 'My gratitude to you, for what you did—'

She knew what he was referring to, and would let him say no more.

'Oh, Papa, it's all worked out so wonderfully, blissfully well! I love Leon so much! And he loves me! And now…' It was her voice's turn to choke with emotion. 'Now there'll be a baby as well. For all of us.'

'When's it due?' Marika was there now, eagerness in

her voice. 'And what are you going to call him or her? Can I be godmother?'

'Autumn… Don't know yet, but there are heaps of names to choose from on our side of the family! And, yes, of course, I'd love you to be godmother!' Ellie laughed.

'If you're having a baby…' Niki's interjection was speculative, his expression even more so '…you can't possibly fit a baby seat in that car of yours, Leon. So you might as well—'

'No way,' said Leon firmly. 'No way am I going to hand it over to you to smash up!'

'As if!' Niki was indignant.

'You can drive it over the weekend—*if* you stay sober!' Leon told him with a half-laugh that got an exclamation of thanks from his brother-in-law. 'By the way,' he prompted the young Grand Duke, 'you should talk some more to Malcolm while he's here…about the nature reserve you want to set up.'

Diverted, Niki sauntered off to intercept the renowned naturalist who was once more practising his dog-calming skills on an over-excited Chou-Chou.

Leon turned to Ellie. Staff were circulating now, serving the celebratory champagne that his father-in-law had summoned, and he took two glasses, drawing her aside a little now her family had let them be.

'One sip won't hurt,' he said, and smiled.

Ellie hoped he was right. It would be the last she could indulge in for quite some time.

She gave a sigh of pleasure at the prospect. Happiness filled her from top to toe, bathing the beloved baby she carried in its glow.

Leon raised his glass to hers. Memory plucked at him, of how he had called for champagne the day she'd come to him, telling him she would agree to marry him.

The most blessed day of his life—but he had not known it then.

He knew it now, though, with a thankfulness that shook him.

'To us,' he said to her, his most wonderful, precious princess bride.

'To all three of us,' Ellie answered, her hand sliding protectively over where their baby lay, so loved, so precious.

As Leon was to her, and she to him.

'And to our child we will be what your parents were not to you,' she said, her voice low and filled with a certainty, a reassurance, that she knew he needed to hear. 'And oh, Leon…' her voice changed '…who knows? Perhaps, just as it was for my own father, it was shame at his failure to provide for you that made yours do what he did?'

Her eyes searched his.

'Since both of us have experienced the heartbreak of thinking ourselves parted for ever from each other can that not make us a little kinder to your mother, in her despair?' Her expression changed. 'I do not—cannot—condone either of them for abandoning you, each in their separate, heartless way, but—'

'"To understand all is to forgive all"?' Leon finished for her.

His expression was sombre, and there was something in it that she had not seen before. It warmed her to see it there.

'We are so blessed, Leon, you and I—so blessed! Perhaps we should be generous…'

He kissed her softly. 'With you beside me, I can be,' he said. 'With you beside me I can be anything!'

Her eyes clung to his. 'Be the man I love,' she said. 'That is all I ask of you—all I will ever ask of you!'

She kissed him softly. Her strong, wonderful, beloved husband.

Then she clinked her glass to his, and he clinked his to hers, and they drank to the baby that awaited the most loving parents ever...

* * * * *

HER BOSS'S
ONE-NIGHT BABY

JENNIE LUCAS

CHAPTER ONE

SOFT PINK CLOUDS glowed between modern skyscrapers as the sun rose over Tokyo. It was early April, and white-and-pink cherry blossoms covered the trees like wedding confetti, as joyful and sweet as a first kiss.

But Hana Everly barely noticed. She stared out the window of the Rolls-Royce, her heart pounding, her skin in a cold sweat.

"And find a new housekeeper for my penthouse in New York, to replace Mrs. Stone…"

Her boss's low growl came beside her in the back seat as he tersely listed other tasks he needed her to handle immediately—if not sooner. Hana's pen moved listlessly, but his words barely registered. She took a shuddering breath.

She couldn't be pregnant.

Couldn't be.

They'd been careful. And her boss had been clear about the rules. Even as his hot, sensual lips had kissed her, his voice had murmured against her skin, "One night, nothing more. There will be no romance, no marriage. No consequences. Tomorrow you will be my assistant again, I your employer. Do you agree?"

Such a deal with the devil, and yet she'd whispered, "Yes."

Hana would have agreed to anything then, when he'd had her spread across his bed, experiencing such intoxicating sensuality for the first time. But even that hadn't been enough. He'd pulled back to look at her, his black eyes cold, even cruel.

"You will leave my bed before dawn, Hana, and neither of us will ever speak of this again. Even to each other."

Lost in a haze of pleasure, she'd nodded, and with a heavy-lidded smile, Antonio had lowered his head to plunder her lips with a sizzling kiss.

She'd thought she knew what she was doing. At the age of twenty-six, she'd told herself she could handle sex without commitment. Because Antonio Delacruz could never be her boyfriend. He was her boss, the ruthless billionaire CEO and largest shareholder of the world's fastest-growing airline. There was a reason that CrossWorld Airways was crushing its competitors. Antonio stopped at nothing to get what he wanted.

But he hadn't been the one to cross this line.

She'd been the one who'd kissed him first. She still couldn't believe she'd done it. But when he'd found her crying, late one night in his *palacio* in Madrid, he'd taken her into his arms to comfort her.

And at that, two years of repressed, pent-up desire had exploded inside Hana. Shocking even herself, she'd lifted on her tiptoes and kissed him through her tears. It had been the barest whisper of a kiss. Terrified at her own boldness, she'd started to pull away.

Then he'd stopped her, pulling her back swiftly into his arms...

For the last two months, Hana had tried not to remember that night in Madrid. She'd tried to be modern about it. She'd tried to forget, as Antonio obviously had.

But now it seemed her body would not let her. The single night of hot, raw, shocking pleasure between Hana and her handsome, arrogant, rich-beyond-imagination boss would be one she'd live with forever. Because she was going to have his baby.

As the sedan drove north through Tokyo in the cool morning, Hana put her clammy hand to her cheek, feeling dizzy with morning sickness and fear. Her baby would grow up with no father or worse—a bad father. Because Antonio Delacruz hadn't become rich by caring about other people. He'd won by being ruthless. He had no family and, in the two years she'd worked for him, his longest love affair had lasted six weeks. Not that she'd been paying attention.

A lump rose in her throat. This wasn't how she'd imagined having a baby. Her plan had been to get married, settle down and *then* get pregnant.

This was wrong, all wrong. She didn't even have a home. She couldn't raise a child like her parents had raised her, always on the move, never staying long enough to build roots, yanking Hana out of each place the moment she started to make real friends.

The lump in her throat turned to a razor blade. She never should have slept with Antonio, no matter how incredible it had felt in the moment. She should have waited for a real relationship, a committed one. She should never, ever have sought comfort in Antonio's arms, placing her whole future, and her unborn baby's future, in his careless hands—

"Hana?" her boss demanded acidly beside her in the back seat of the Rolls-Royce. "Hello?"

"Yes," she said. Numbly, she looked down at her notes. "You want the SWOT analysis for the expansion into Australia, the numbers from the Berlin office, hire a new housekeeper for New York and arrange the after-party in London."

He stared at her for a long moment with his deep black eyes, and she felt a shiver of fear. But not even Antonio Delacruz, the fearsome billionaire with the mysterious past who'd built a worldwide empire from nothing, had the ability to read minds.

At least she prayed he didn't. Otherwise, she was in big trouble.

"Good," he said grudgingly. He looked back at his laptop screen. "And contact the lead architect on the new first-class lounge design for Heathrow…"

As the chauffeur drove them north toward the Marunouchi district, she fought her despair as she looked out at the glittering skyscrapers. She had visited Tokyo many times since she was a child. She loved this city, the place where her grandmother had been born before she'd emigrated to America. Her best friend Ren lived here, and the *sakura* season, or cherry-blooming season, was the most beautiful of the year.

But for once, the sight of Tokyo Tower, which looked like a bright red Eiffel Tower overlooking the city, did not make her heart rise. Even the lushly blooming trees did not cheer her. She was lost in her own panic.

There will be no romance, no marriage. No consequences. Neither of us will ever speak of this again. Even to each other. Do you agree?

Yes.

She'd never imagined their one night together could lead to a child. What should she do? Should she tell him? Could she?

Hana had only found out about the pregnancy a few hours ago, when she'd taken the test on their private jet from Madrid. But already, this child felt real. She placed her hand wondrously over the curve of her belly. *A baby.*

"What's wrong, Hana?" Antonio demanded beside her. "Why are you so distracted?"

Looking up with an intake of breath at the handsome Spaniard sitting beside her, she choked out, "Antonio, there's something I need to tell you."

The local driver and Ramon Garcia, the bodyguard who usually traveled with him, glanced at each other in the front seat. None of Mr. Delacruz's employees would dream of calling him by his first name. Aside from their night in bed, Hana had never taken such a liberty before. At least not out loud.

He looked at her coldly. "Yes, Miss Everly?"

His husky, slightly accented voice put her firmly in her place, reminding her—if she needed reminding—that she was his employee, nothing more.

Hana's soul quailed. They were nearly to the Marunouchi district, where a critical business negotiation waited. She and Antonio, along with the rest of the Tokyo-based team, had been prepping for this for months. Antonio was obsessed with negotiating a codeshare with Iyokan Airways, an important regional airline that would gain them routes to Tokyo, Osaka and beyond.

Maybe she should put off telling him about the baby for now.

Maybe she should put it off forever.

She pushed the traitorous thought aside. Even if Antonio rejected her and the baby outright, didn't he have the right to know? Didn't her baby at least deserve the chance to have a father?

"I need to tell you something," she whispered. She glanced uneasily toward the two men sitting in the front seat, who were pretending not to listen. "About…that night."

Antonio looked at her, his dark eyes like ice. "Which night is that?"

Did he truly not remember? His handsome face was so arrogant and cold, she almost wondered if the night he'd taken her virginity had been a dream. But the pregnancy test had left no doubt.

Hana lifted her chin and said clearly, "Our night together in Madrid. Two months ago."

The eyes of the men in the front seat went wide. Antonio calmly pressed the button to close the privacy screen between the front and back of the luxury sedan. Once it was closed, he turned on her fiercely.

"You promised never to talk about it."

"I know, but—"

"There's no *but*. You gave me your word."

"I have good reason—"

"I can imagine." His jaw clenched as he turned away. "You will put that night from your mind, Miss Everly. It never happened."

As the Rolls-Royce Phantom turned up the sweeping curve in front of a gleaming skyscraper overlooking the wide green-and-pink vistas of the East Gardens of the Imperial Palace, her voice was a squeak. "But—"

The car stopped, and a waiting doorman reached to open his door.

"It never happened," Antonio repeated, and without bothering to look at her, he swept out, all masculine power and hard muscular angles in his dark suit and sharply tailored black cashmere coat.

Pulling her handbag over her shoulder, Hana climbed out behind him numbly. Her heart was pounding. She held her notebook and briefcase tightly against her chest, as if they could protect her.

"Welcome, Mr. Delacruz," Emika Ito, the Tokyo team lead, greeted them in English with a respectful bow of her head. She was pretty, black-haired and chic. She smiled at Hana, who tried to smile back. "All is ready, sir."

Standing on the sidewalk, Hana glanced at the building. Inside the glass and steel lobby, she saw the rest of the lead team already assembled, waiting for their arrival so they could go to their new office on the top three floors.

"Yes, of course," Antonio said. "Thank you, Miss Ito. Give me a moment." With a nod, the girl returned to the lobby, leaving Hana and Antonio alone, with his bodyguard at a discreet distance. He looked down at her.

"So you agree?" he said tersely. It was intimate, having them so close together on the sidewalk in the cool spring morning. "It's forgotten?"

Hana felt a breeze against her hot cheek, saw a single cherry blossom floating and twisting in a tumult on the wind, before disappearing into the traffic of Hibiya Dori.

She couldn't tell him. She just couldn't. She'd nod and quietly go into the building, and be the assistant he needed during this important meeting. Afterward, she would quit. She would disappear. She bowed her head.

"Good," he said. She saw the glint in his eyes as he turned toward the door. She tried to follow. To be silent.

But her heart wouldn't let her.

"I'm pregnant, Antonio," she heard herself blurt out.

Pregnant?

Antonio Delacruz froze, sure he'd heard her wrong. Above them, the sky was overcast as from a distance he heard ominous thunder.

Slowly, he turned to her on the sidewalk. "What?"

"You heard me."

His eyebrows lowered fiercely. "April Fool's Day was yesterday."

"It's not a joke. I'm pregnant."

Antonio told himself he felt nothing. He wouldn't, couldn't, feel the rush of emotion suddenly circling him like a predator, looking for any crack in his armor, so it could invade and destroy his heart.

She'd slept with another man.

He tapped the roof of the car harder than necessary, and the chauffeur drove away from the curb. Forcibly relaxing his shoulders, he said merely, "I thought you had more sense."

Hana's sweep of dark eyebrows lifted over her warm brown eyes in surprise. "What?"

He wondered who the baby's father might be. She'd been a virgin when—he cut that thought off immediately. But she must have found a new lover right after.

The same week?

The same night?

For Hana, it would be easy. Any man would desire her. Unwillingly, Antonio's gaze traced over her slender form. Hana Everly was the most beautiful woman he'd ever met, though he'd spent almost two years trying to pretend she wasn't, trying to think of her as only his secretary and nothing more.

Her beauty was elusive and indefinable. All the attributes of her melting-pot American heritage combined into exquisite grace. He'd asked her once about her ancestry, and she'd shrugged. "I'm American. My family came from everywhere. England, Ireland, Brazil, Japan. Other places. And you, Mr. Delacruz?"

"Spain," he'd said shortly. It was probably true, but he'd never know for sure.

Now, Hana looked at him, her brown eyes huge in her oval face, her lips pink and full, her dark hair pulled back into a long ponytail. Always the consummate professional, she wore an elegant, feminine white skirt suit that was simple and sleek as required for the executive assistant to a billionaire, without drawing undue attention.

And yet Hana always drew attention, whether she wished it or not. Even here on the Tokyo sidewalk, as men passed by, their eyes lingered on her. She looked untouchable as a star.

But Antonio had touched her. He was the only man who ever had.

At least so he'd believed—

"Is that all you have to say to me?" Hana said in a low,

harsh voice, her lovely face caught between anger and pain. "You thought I had more sense?"

"I'm disappointed," he said tightly.

"*Disappointed*," she repeated.

He'd relied on her. Believed in her. Now she was pregnant by another man. She was going to quit her job to be with him and raise their child. That had to be the reason he felt this crushing sense of emotion, like he couldn't breathe. Hana was the best damn secretary he'd ever had, and he was going to lose her.

How had she hidden her love affair from him? He and Hana had been working together day and night in Madrid and around the world, preparing to negotiate this deal. How had he not known she'd taken a lover?

Antonio had known Hana's value as his assistant. So in spite of his attraction to her, he'd never crossed the line of professionalism, not once. Not until that night in Madrid, when he'd found her crying for reasons she wouldn't explain. He'd been trying to comfort her—that was all, truly—when, like a miracle, she'd suddenly lifted up on her tiptoes and kissed him full on the lips.

That kiss…

Antonio pushed away the memory, closing down his feelings, burying them along with the other things he didn't want to remember.

All right, fine. She was leaving. He wouldn't be a jerk about it. Hana had been a good assistant. He'd try to be happy for her. After all, she'd made it all too clear she wanted the whole domestic fairy tale someday—husband, kids, house. Damn it, he'd send her off with a wedding check big enough to pay for the kid's college tuition. She'd been worth it.

He'd pay her off. He'd move on. And above all, he'd make damn sure he never let himself ask…

"Who's the father?" he heard himself say, as if his mouth was no longer controlled by his brain.

She drew back, her lovely face incredulous. "Are you kidding? You know who the father is!"

"Do I?" He frowned, searching his memory. "I'm amazed, actually. How did you manage to sneak away for an affair, in the midst of our working twenty-hour days? Does the man work for me? A gardener? A driver?"

Hana's face blazed with sudden fire. "Stop it, Antonio. Just stop."

He stared, astonished to see her so angry. Hana never showed anger. She was always patient, kind, understanding. She was the kindest person he knew. "Why are you upset?"

"Because it's you, you idiot! *You're* the father!"

Antonio's body felt the impact of the words before his mind comprehended them. He felt them like a blow. "What?"

"Of course it's you!"

Stumbling a step, he instinctively reached a hand out against the column of the building. He had to. His legs were shaking.

"Do you really think I would sleep with someone else, after we were together?" she demanded. "I can't jump in and out of affairs so quickly. Even if you can!"

If only. If only he'd been able to forget her. If only she meant nothing to him now. As the first raindrops fell from the gray sky, one fell against his cheek. Antonio stared at her, feeling sick and betrayed.

"I've been feeling out of sorts for the last month. I thought my cycle was messed up by too much work and stress and not enough sleep but…" She hesitated. "I bought a pregnancy test in Madrid. I took it on the plane, right before we landed. I'm pregnant."

When Antonio still didn't respond, Hana's forehead furrowed. Her expression became almost bewildered.

"Look," she said finally, "I know you've never been interested in anything like marriage or children. This was a surprise for me, too. We used a condom. It shouldn't have been possible. But I thought you at least had the right to—"

"Enough," he ground out. "Not another word."

"Was I wrong to tell you?" Her eyes were luminous with unshed tears that seemed utterly genuine. He despised them. And her. Most of all, he despised himself for ever letting his guard down. For thinking she was different. For believing he could trust her, as he'd trusted no one else on earth. For resisting his desire for her, day after day, so they could maintain that precious working relationship, the closest relationship of his life.

And all along, she'd been sleeping with another man. And now lying about it.

Assuming she was even pregnant at all. It was possible that, too, was a bald-faced lie.

But either way, she must have planned this all along, from the moment she'd started working for him. She'd set him up, hoping to take a nice juicy portion of his fortune. And Hana likely would have succeeded in her goal, except for a vital fact that she didn't know.

He couldn't have gotten her pregnant. It was physically impossible.

Antonio's body shook as he reached out to take the briefcase and files from her hands. He said abruptly, "Your services are no longer required, Miss Everly."

Her luscious pink lips fell open. "You're—you're firing me?"

"You'll get severance pay as your contract dictates. But I want you gone."

"But—but why?"

"You know why."

"Because I'm pregnant with your baby?" she cried.

"Because you lied to me," he said harshly. "You tried to

trap me. Tried, and failed." He narrowed his eyes. "Good-bye, Miss Everly."

Turning on his heel, Antonio went into the building, followed by his glowering bodyguard. He went through the swiveling door into the lobby where his team waited to help negotiate the Iyokan Airways deal. He left her standing alone on the sidewalk, shivering in the cold Tokyo morning. And he didn't look back.

CHAPTER TWO

SHOCKED, HANA WATCHED the father of her baby turn scornfully and leave her abandoned and alone on the Tokyo sidewalk.

Except Antonio hadn't just left her.

He'd *fired* her.

He'd taken her innocence. He'd changed her life forever. And now, to add insult to injury, he'd kicked her out of a job she loved.

Shivering, she heard another low rumble of thunder, rolling above the city, making the glass and steel and neon tremble. She felt a cool breeze against her overheated skin, and looked up at the lowering gray sky as the drizzle turned to rain.

Obviously, Hana had known that Antonio wouldn't react like the hero of a romantic movie, and kiss her joyfully at the news of her pregnancy. She'd known he didn't want children, or the slightest commitment.

But she'd never imagined he could be such an utter bastard as this.

Trembling, she wiped her eyes as she felt the cold splatter of raindrops against her face. Why was she so surprised? As his assistant, she of all people had seen how heartless Antonio Delacruz could be, especially to his lovers. She'd seen him relentlessly pursue a woman until the thrill of the conquest started to wane. It never took long—a few weeks, or perhaps even just a single night, until he was bored, finished.

Hana had always been amazed at those foolish women who let themselves care for him, each of whom apparently believed, incredibly, that she'd be the one to finally tame the untamable playboy. Hana had pitied them. Could they not see how he turned on his interest and charm like a switch? One moment, he was a passionate lover, with all the intensity of relentless desire; the next, he was gone.

Although it wasn't fair to say Antonio was just a plague to womankind. He treated everyone badly, men and women, though with men his ruthlessness was manifested by him taking their businesses if he wanted them—their businesses, and their girlfriends.

But Hana had thought she was special. For two years, she'd worked at his side, often twelve-hour days, seven days a week, and for the last few months, far more than that. She'd been inspired by him, challenged by him. His success was her success, and she'd given him every bit of her blood, sweat and tears to make CrossWorld Airways the global airline he wanted it to be.

She'd thought that they were partners of a sort, if not friends. But now she saw how truly unspecial she was.

You tried to trap me. Tried, and failed. Goodbye, Miss Everly.

The cold rain pattered the rhythm of his words against her, soaking through her dark hair and white suit. People stared at her as they passed by, all of them sensibly holding umbrellas to block the rain. She probably looked like a fool, standing there with her mouth still agape. She felt like one.

Antonio had made her one.

No, that wasn't fair. Hana took a deep breath. She'd done this to herself.

Closing her eyes, she lifted her face up to the sky. But she'd never imagined in a million years that he'd fire her for being pregnant. However the world saw him, she'd thought, at his core, Antonio Delacruz was an honorable man. She'd thought, however badly he'd treated his other mistresses, he would never act that way toward her.

Hana's eyes abruptly opened.

She, who'd always prided herself on being practical, clear-eyed and smart, had been the biggest fool of them all.

Traffic had increased on the busy street. Rain—only rain, not tears, definitely not tears—made her vision blurry as she looked down at her white suit, now plastered to her skin, gray as a dove in the wan light.

She'd devoted her life to him, been honest with him in spite of her fear, and this was how he repaid her?

He'd insulted her. He'd fired her. And worst of all: he'd coldly rejected his own child, now growing inside her.

A white-hot flame of anger burned through her. It grew inside Hana, grew and grew until it left room for nothing else in her heart.

She and the baby were on their own.

Hana lifted her chin. Fine. They didn't need him. They'd be better off without him—soulless, heartless, backstabbing jerk!

Her hands tightened on the strap of her purse. Her satchel of clothes was unfortunately still in the back of the Rolls-Royce that had brought them from Haneda Airport. All she had in the small black purse over her shoulder was her passport, credit cards and a little bit of cash, a mix of yen, dollars and euros. But she was also in Tokyo, which meant she had something more.

Ren.

Her best friend, whom she saw just a few times a year. Just thinking of his kindly face made her want to get to him as quickly as possible.

Blinking back hot, furious tears, she waved down a taxi. As one started to pull to the curb, she saw the driver hesitate, looking at her in the rain, obviously fearing she'd flood his upholstery given half a chance. But then he sighed and pulled his taxi over.

"*Sumimasen,*" she said over the lump in her throat, trying very hard to keep the wettest parts of her clothing off the seat. Holding her bag tightly against her chest, she gave him the address in Harajuku then stared out at the passing streets. Ren Tanaka. It was by sheerest luck that she'd had her heart broken in the same city where her best friend lived.

She and Ren had been friends since childhood, when they'd been pen pals as Hana traveled the world with her adventurous teacher parents. He was the only friend she'd kept in touch with, moving as often as she did, first with her restless parents and then later, working for an airline tycoon. Hana was an only child, an orphan now that her parents and grandparents had died, but somehow, in their frequent online conversations, Ren had become her family.

Although…

Unease went through her as she remembered the last time she'd seen him, on a brief business trip to Tokyo a few months earlier. He'd acted very strangely. It wasn't actually what he'd said, so much as the way he'd looked at her. It had made her nervous.

Was it possible that somehow, after all their years of friendship, Ren could have gotten some crazy idea that he was in love with her?

Absolutely not, Hana told herself. Why would Ren imagine himself in love with her, when he had so many girls interested in him, right here in Tokyo?

He was her dear friend, like always. And he'd help her figure out what to do now. Hana tried to imagine what he'd say when he heard about her unexpected pregnancy—and how her boss had abandoned and fired her. Ren already disliked Antonio intensely, though the two men had never actually met. Her boss didn't even know of Ren's existence. Why would he? Hana's childhood friendship had been entirely through letters, and even now it was mostly online.

As the taxi turned toward the hip, colorful street in Harajuku where Ren managed his family's boutique hotel, she took a deep breath. She was not going to cry over Antonio. No way, no how. He wasn't worth it. He'd proven himself totally unworthy of either Hana or their baby.

So she'd move on. Think only of the future. She'd put Antonio Delacruz behind her and never, ever think of him again.

But still, she heard the echo of Antonio's sensual voice spoken into the hot, dark Spanish night.

There will be no romance, no marriage. No consequences.

And in spite of her resolve to feel nothing, Hana gasped out a sob, hating him with fresh, hot tears.

Liar!

"Possible?" Antonio choked out, dumbfounded. "What do you mean, it's possible?"

"Just what I said." The doctor looked at him gravely over his thick glasses. "We did the test, as you requested. And the results are conclusive."

It was good Antonio was already sitting down. He felt sick and dizzy at the news. The minimalist decor and medical equipment in the examining room of the private clinic swam in front of his eyes.

"I don't understand," he stammered. "As I told you, I had a vasectomy eighteen years ago, at a reputable hospital—"

"Yes. It seems your body has healed itself."

Antonio stared at the doctor in shock.

All morning, he'd felt his insides churn, in spite of his best efforts not to think about the lies Hana had told him on the sidewalk: pretending to be pregnant with his baby, clearly in an attempt to extort money or a proposal of marriage. Going to the top floor of the skyscraper with his team, he'd pushed aside the feelings of betrayal and rage, and tried to focus on the details of the business negotiation.

But the meeting had been a disaster. He hadn't been able to find the right papers in the portfolio, or track down the points he'd previously marked to discuss with his lawyers before they formally presented the offer to Iyokan Airways. Hana had always been in charge of solving his problems, finding papers, sorting out details, arranging whatever he needed.

Now he was alone.

Abandoned.

Betrayed.

During the meeting, his lawyers and his Tokyo lead team had looked at each other worriedly as they were forced to repeat certain clauses in the contract multiple times to their normally razor-sharp boss. Emotion—rage and anger and, worst of all, hurt—had built inside him, until finally, it had exploded. He'd scattered the pile of papers in fury across the large glass table in his conference room on the top floor of the skyscraper, with its view of Tokyo.

"Reschedule," he'd growled, and stalked out, knowing they were probably wondering if he was drunk, or if he'd lost his mind—or his nerve. His business rivals would smell blood in the water. He himself had always enjoyed attacking the businesses of weaker opponents. He'd never experienced what it was like to be on the other side of it. Not since he was young, when he was helpless and alone—

He pushed the memory aside. This was Hana's fault. His secretary had betrayed him at every level. Personally. Professionally.

He never should have slept with her. The success of his company was far more important than any sexual desire. CrossWorld Airways was the only thing that mattered. Once he expanded routes into Asia, he would build to Africa and South America. He would have the first truly global low-cost airline. His company was his family, his lover, his religion and meaning. His company was his soul.

So why had he done it? Why, when she'd kissed him, that night in Madrid, hadn't he had the strength to push her away?

Yes, Hana was beautiful. But he'd ignored beautiful women before. It was something more. She'd been different. Pure fire. And when she'd kissed him, he could have no more pushed her away then he could have stopped breathing.

He'd wanted her then. He wanted her still.

But she'd been setting a trap for him, all along. Playing him for a fool, luring him in with her innocent beauty and apparent warm heart. All so she could seduce him and claim to be pregnant. He could hardly believe he'd been tricked so thoroughly.

But that was the problem.

The whole thing was hard to believe.

And the more Antonio had thought about it during the business meeting, the more distracted he'd become, obsessing over a single question.

How was it possible everything about Hana was a lie?

For two years, she'd worked at his side. She'd been hardworking, loyal, honest to a fault. How could anyone maintain an act like that so well, and for so long?

Antonio couldn't understand it. And every time he'd tried to focus during the business meeting, he'd seen the eviscerated look in her eyes. *You're firing me? Because I'm pregnant with your baby?*

And he'd felt his heart, his guts, every part of his body twist like a rag wrung dry.

Stalking angrily from the meeting, he'd grimly arranged to see the best fertility doctor in the city. Just to prove, once and for all, that Hana Everly was a liar. He hadn't done anything wrong. He was the victim here.

And now this.

He'd come to the clinic for reassurance, not to discover his worst fears were actually true. He'd never expected he'd be told it was possible that he'd fathered Hana's child!

"No," Antonio told the doctor hoarsely. "I had a vasectomy!"

The other man stroked his white beard thoughtfully. "You had the procedure when you were very young. Sometimes the body heals itself, as I said. It's rare, less than one percent of cases. But it happens." He paused. "We can book an appointment to redo the procedure…"

"What's the point of that now? It's already too late!" With a low snarl, Antonio rose to his feet and stormed out of the clinic. All he could think about was the stricken look on Hana's face when he'd left her standing alone on the sidewalk. The shock in her brown eyes.

If she was really pregnant with his child, and he'd treated her like that—

Antonio pushed the thought away ruthlessly. It wasn't his fault. How could he have possibly known the vasectomy he'd had as a teenager would fail nearly two decades later? Of course he'd assumed Hana was lying. How could he think otherwise? People had always proved themselves worthy of his worst assumptions.

Everyone except Hana. But he'd been all too ready to believe the worst even of her. Because it scared him, how much he'd come to trust her.

As he stepped out of the medical clinic, Antonio saw the rain had lightened to a drizzle, with flashes of sunlight like silver breaking through the clouds.

You're firing me? Because I'm pregnant with your baby?

He felt another twist in his gut.

"Mr. Delacruz, if I may speak freely…" His longtime

bodyguard Ramon Garcia, who'd been waiting in the lobby, followed him toward the waiting car. "*Señor*, I think you've made a mistake about Miss Everly. She's a good person. She didn't deserve to be treated like that."

Perfecto. This was just what he needed. One more person judging him. And now that Antonio knew he was indeed in the wrong, he *really* didn't want to hear it. "It's none of your business, Garcia."

The man's accusing eyes met his. "If you didn't intend to step up, you never should have slept with her—"

"Enough," he snapped, causing his bodyguard's jaw to set. Wonderful, another trusted employee enraged with him. Antonio's shoulders were tight as he climbed into the waiting Rolls-Royce. Garcia got into the front seat without a word.

"Where to, sir?" the driver asked him after a pause.

"Just drive," Antonio ground out.

Looking out at the soft drizzle in the spring afternoon, his eyes fell on the pink cherry trees. Hana had been so excited that the negotiations would be in Tokyo at the same time the trees were likely to bloom. *They bloom for such a short time,* she'd said. *It's precious and beautiful. You have to enjoy it while you can. Before it's gone.*

Just like their night together, he thought.

For years, almost from the day he'd hired her, he'd resisted seducing her only by an act of pure will, because of her importance to his company.

Then she'd kissed him, and all his self-control had exploded to dust, burned away by fire. For the first time in his adult life, he'd given in to the demands of his body, the demands of his heart, over the cold decision of his reason.

Antonio had tried to tell himself that bedding her could somehow be a good thing for their working relationship. That it could end his desire for her. He'd even extracted a promise from Hana that they'd both forget the night ever happened—a promise he knew he himself could not fulfill.

Useless, all useless. From the morning he'd woken up with her soft naked body in his arms, he'd discovered taking her virginity hadn't lessened his desire, only increased it. His need for her had been a constant torment for the next two months as they'd worked together round the clock on the Iyokan Airways deal. Every time he'd felt her brush against him innocently as they looked over documents together, he'd grasp the desk, remembering how he'd held her virgin body naked against his in the breathless heat of passion. As he heard her speak of business details, he'd hear, against his will, her cry as she'd gasped out with pleasure, gripping his back so tightly, he could still feel the marks of her fingernails—not against his skin, but against his heart.

It had terrified him.

Antonio had known, if he ever touched her again, it would destroy everything he cared about. His company would be hurt by her loss, and he would certainly lose her. Their working relationship could perhaps survive a one-night stand, but not a full-blown affair. He never kept a mistress for long. And how many times had Hana told him that her biggest dream was to someday have a real home, commitment, marriage, children? All things he could never give, not to her or anyone.

So he'd done the impossible. He'd pretended their night together had been forgettable. That it had, in fact, already been forgotten by him.

He'd been the one lying all this time. Not Hana.

Staring out the window blankly as his chauffeur drove him through Tokyo, Antonio looked down and realized his phone was somehow in his hands. Without letting himself think, he dialed Hana's number.

She didn't answer.

He tried again.

Same result.

No wonder, he thought grimly. He'd fired her, hadn't he? She was no longer obligated to pick up when he called.

"Find her," he barked at his bodyguard.

Turning in the front seat, Garcia's rough face lifted into a crooked smile. "Her best friend lives in Tokyo. If she's not answering the phone, she's probably with him."

"Who is he?" he demanded in a strained voice.

"His name is Ren Tanaka. His family owns a hotel in Harajuku."

A best friend? A man? Antonio didn't know which surprised him more. But as his driver changed route through the crowded streets, he told himself he wasn't jealous, just curious. Hana had been a virgin; of that, there could be no doubt. And it wasn't like Antonio had any claim on her.

Except that she was expecting his baby.

A baby.

After everything Antonio had done to prevent fatherhood, he was going to have a child.

A lump rose to his throat as he looked out at the passing streets of Tokyo in the soft spring mist.

Hana would be better off raising the child without him, obviously. What did he know of fatherhood? He'd never had parents. Better to stick with the choices he'd made long ago—to focus on his company and his fortune. They were the only things that mattered.

He'd gotten a vasectomy for a reason. He didn't have the capacity to commit to anyone for life. He wasn't fit to be a husband or father. Hana wouldn't be shocked by this. She knew him better than anyone. All he could offer was financial support. It shouldn't be hard for him to convince her.

As long as he didn't touch her. Damn it, he was only a man. If he touched her, he would take her. Not just for a one-night stand. His repressed desire for her had become a ferocious beast, which if unleashed, would be unstoppable.

He'd keep her as his mistress until his body was utterly satiated, whether that took days, weeks, or even months. For Antonio, sex was a physical thing, like eating or sleeping. But Hana's heart was warm, not frozen like his own. All those months in his bed might lure her into blindly loving him. Then, when their affair inevitably ended, her love would just as inevitably turn to hate.

And perhaps she'd teach the baby to hate him as well…

No. He could never touch Hana again.

"We're here, *señor*."

Getting out of car, Antonio remembered Hana's satchel in the trunk and got it out. He felt new shame as he remembered how he'd fired her, sending her off without even her bag of clothes. As he lifted it to his shoulder, a crack of sunlight burst through the clouds. Harajuku was very different from the financial district, crowded, lively and colorful. He looked up at the seven-story hotel silhouetted against the soft gray sky. Garcia started to follow, until he gestured sharply for his bodyguard to stay. He wanted to talk to Hana alone.

The last thing he wanted to do was hurt her, or the baby. But he was a selfish bastard, and that wasn't going to change.

And Hana would be an amazing mother. The baby would never even miss having him as a father. After all, what did Antonio have to offer a child, beyond his fortune? There was no question of Antonio being more involved than that. He'd give Hana an enormous financial settlement. They'd be set for life.

Now all he had to do was convince her of that.

Walking through the sleekly modern Japanese-style lobby of the hotel, he stopped a passing employee.

"Sir?" the man responded politely.

"Is an American girl staying here? A guest of Ren Tanaka?"

The employee looked Antonio over from his bespoke suit to his Italian leather shoes, then with a nod, motioned toward a quiet, darkened bar, separate from the lobby. "They're in there."

Glancing at the door, he set his jaw. Then he held out the satchel. "Make sure this is delivered to her room."

"Of course, sir."

Leaving the lobby, Antonio stood for a moment in the doorway of the darkened hotel bar. It took several seconds for his eyes to adjust. He blinked. Then blinked again.

Then he sucked in his breath when he saw Hana sitting alone at a table, across the empty bar. Her white skirt suit was edged with a sultry blue glow from the neon light on the ceiling. His body was instantly electrified. "Hana."

Turning, she saw him. "Antonio?" She rose unsteadily to her feet. "What are you doing here?"

"I had to see you," he said, searching her beautiful face.

She glanced uneasily at something on the other side of the bar. "Why?"

"I…uh…" Now that he was looking at her, all his carefully planned arguments flew from his mind. Against his will, his gaze fell to her trembling, deliciously full pink lips, and down farther still. Her breasts seemed bigger—yes—the top two buttons of her white fitted jacket were stretched about to burst. How had he not noticed that before today?

Because he hadn't wanted to notice.

But he wanted her. Suddenly. Savagely. So much his hands shook with it. He wanted to grab her, push her back against the wall. He didn't care what the cost might be to his company, to his peace of mind, to anything. He wanted to have her even if the cost was setting fire to the world.

"Delacruz. It's you, isn't it?"

Hearing a man's low growl, Antonio turned and saw a young Japanese man, tall and handsome in a sleek suit, perhaps ten years younger than Antonio's thirty-six years, approaching from behind the bar.

"Who are you?" he asked, though he'd already guessed.

The man's lip curled. "My name is Ren Tanaka."

Antonio's eyes narrowed as he sized up the younger man. "So you're her *best friend*."

He lifted his chin. "And you're her bastard boss who got her pregnant and abandoned her like a—"

He spoke a Japanese word that Antonio didn't understand, but the meaning was plain enough. Tanaka looked as if he'd like to strangle him with his bare hands.

The feeling was mutual. As Antonio saw the other man gently hand Hana a glass of water, then step protectively in front of her—as if he were trying to protect her from Antonio!—his own hands clenched into fists.

Then he saw Hana's face, her worry and fear as she looked between the two men. He saw the way her body, newly lush with his child, was trembling.

With almost superhuman restraint, Antonio forced his hands to relax. He'd already shown her enough bad behavior today. And he didn't give a damn about Tanaka. That wasn't why he'd come.

"Can we go and talk?" he asked Hana in a low voice.

"You don't have to go anywhere with him," Tanaka said to her. Setting his jaw, he scowled at Antonio. "Leave my hotel. You are not welcome here."

His eyes narrowed. "You'd do well to stay out of this, *friend*."

"You've hurt Hana enough. I'm not going to give you another chance."

"Why?" Antonio lifted his lip in a snarl. "You want her for yourself?"

The younger man lifted his chin. "What if I do?"

"Back off, or I'll knock you flat into the wall."

"I'd like to see you try."

"No!" Hana pushed anxiously between them, separating them before either could throw the first punch. She looked at them pleadingly. "No, please—don't!"

The two men glared at each other. Antonio itched to shove the other man aside. He was shocked by his own rage. He'd never felt so possessive about any woman before.

But Hana was different. And Antonio suddenly knew, with stunning clarity, that he'd never let Ren Tanaka—or any other man on earth—have her.

Because Hana Everly was his.

CHAPTER THREE

HOW HAD THINGS spiraled so far out of control, so fast?

"Stop it! Both of you!" Hana cried. "This isn't helping anything!"

"It would help if I punched his smug face," Ren muttered in Japanese.

Glancing swiftly at Antonio, she saw that even though he didn't speak the language, he'd understood Ren's meaning perfectly. He narrowed his dark eyes.

The last few hours had been exhausting. Going from that ghastly scene with Antonio on the sidewalk to coming here to talk to Ren had been a classic case of frying pan to fire. She'd never forget the look on Ren's face when she'd told him she was pregnant by her boss.

"I knew it," Ren had breathed, then his eyes had flashed fire. "I'm going to kill him."

It hadn't been easy to talk him out of immediately going to find Antonio and start a fight.

It was almost funny. Hana had come here looking for comfort. But instead, she'd spent the last few hours trying to make *Ren* feel better.

"Are you sure?" he'd kept asking incredulously. "Are you really sure you're pregnant?"

To shut him up, she'd finally let him take her to the hotel's on-call doctor, who had an office down the street. They'd just barely returned from the appointment, where

Hana had learned what she already knew: she was two and a half months pregnant.

But she'd heard the baby's heartbeat for the first time, which had been wondrous to her. And bittersweet. She'd kept thinking of her baby's father, and thinking Antonio should have been there, then remembering with fresh pain how he'd rejected them both.

Ren didn't exactly offer much solace. All the way back from the clinic, Ren had demanded over and over, "And you told Delacruz? But he abandoned you? He denied being the father? Then he *fired* you?"

None of it was very comforting.

Just a few minutes earlier, as they returned to his family's small hotel where he was manager, Ren had growled again that he was going to go look for Delacruz and make him regret treating her so badly. To distract him, Hana had asked for a glass of water, and a quiet place to sit down and catch her breath. He'd immediately become solicitous and led her to the darkened, empty bar while he went to fetch her water.

Then, like some apparition of a demon brought by the speaking of his name, Antonio himself had appeared in the doorway.

Now, the two men were bristling like full-grown stags ready to clash at each other with sharp, murderous antlers.

"Stay out of this, Tanaka." Then Antonio turned to her, and his voice became gentle. "Can we go somewhere to talk, Hana?"

"What more could you possibly say to me?" she said, at the same time Ren snarled, "She doesn't want to talk to you!"

"Please," Antonio said, looking only at her. She took a deep breath.

"Fine." She put a restraining hand on her friend's sleeve. "It's all right. I'll talk to him."

Ren's face was a glower. "He doesn't deserve it."

Hana gave a rueful smile. "He's my baby's father. I have to hear him out." She turned to Antonio. "Here?"

Antonio shook his head. He started to reach his hand toward her, then abruptly stopped himself. Turning away without touching her, he said gruffly, "Follow me."

Outside the hotel, the sky had turned blue and the sun was shining, in the bright changeability of early April.

But that was nothing compared to the unpredictability of her baby's father, Hana thought. As they stood in the small, crowded street, filled with pastel-colored shops, outrageously dressed mannequins, toy shops, fashionable high schoolers, so vibrant and young, Hana looked up at Antonio's darkly handsome face.

"All right, we're alone. What do you want?"

"Not yet," he said grimly, glancing behind them. Following his gaze, she saw Ren's face watching from the hotel lobby. A group of laughing girls walked by, wearing bold clothes and makeup, their eyes lingering on Antonio's handsome face and powerful frame. He said grimly, "Let's go where it's not so crowded."

Hana followed him down the small street to a larger avenue. Passing Harajuku Station, they crossed a bridge into a large, beautiful park. They walked some distance in silence, through a forest, past an impressive shrine.

Hana took a deep breath of the cool, fragrant air, feeling the dappled warmth of the spring sun on her face, beneath the pink-and-white flowering cherry trees. She realized she was trembling as she waited for him to speak. Why? What more could Antonio possibly say to hurt her?

Nothing. Whatever it was, she told herself she wouldn't care.

Finally stopping in a quiet clearing, he turned to face her. "What did you tell Tanaka about me?"

"The truth," she said.

Antonio tilted his head. His black eyes were glinting in the sun, the hard line of his jaw already growing dark with five o'clock shadow. "That I was a heartless monster who seduced you, got you pregnant and then abandoned you?"

"I didn't tell him you seduced me." She set her jaw. "Is that why you tracked me across Tokyo? To give me a hard time for sobbing on a friend's shoulder?"

His dark eyes flashed. "*Friend?*" he repeated incredulously. "The man's in love with you!"

She could hardly deny it, not when Ren had acted like she was his personal property. She looked away. "I... I don't know what that's all about. We've been friends since childhood."

"Is he your lover?"

Hana glared at him. "Don't be ridiculous! He's like a brother to me!"

"He wasn't looking at you like a brother."

Was that jealousy she heard in Antonio's voice? No—impossible. He never cared enough about any woman to be jealous. She lifted her chin. "Why do you care?"

"I don't."

She felt an ache in her throat. "If you only came to yell at me, then I'm going back…"

But as she turned, he stopped her with his husky voice. "Wait. Please."

"Wait for what?" She lifted her chin. "For you to find new ways to insult me and hurt me? I've had enough of that."

"No. Damn it." He clawed his hand through his dark, rumpled hair. "I'm doing this all wrong. I came…" Taking a deep breath, Antonio came closer. "I came to tell you I'm sorry."

Hana's jaw dropped. In two years of working for him, she'd never heard him apologize to anyone. For anything.

"*Sorry,*" she repeated numbly.

"Yes." He came closer, not touching her. "Please. You have to let me explain."

Antonio Delacruz, who never explained himself to anyone, wanted to explain to her? Her mouth was dry as she said, "Go ahead."

He stood in front of her, starkly handsome and broad-shouldered in his sleek black suit and long coat. Behind him, the park was a kaleidoscope of color, green and pink and white, beneath the sun's golden light and bright blue sky.

His black eyes seemed strangely vulnerable, in a way she'd never seen before. "This isn't easy."

"Good," she said, refusing to show him any mercy.

"I treated you badly," he acknowledged.

"Badly?"

He gave a crooked smile. "Really badly."

"It took all of my courage to tell you I was pregnant. I know how you are. I knew you wouldn't exactly be overjoyed at the news. But I never thought you'd accuse me of lying to you!" She shook her head fiercely. "Even with a condom, you know sex always comes with some risk of pregnancy, you know that, right? Plus, you know *me*! How could you do that?"

Antonio looked down at her. "I had a vasectomy, Hana. Eighteen years ago."

In the distance, she could see the tips of modern buildings gleaming over the park, against the vivid blue sky. "Wh-what?"

"It's true."

"You were just a teenager then!"

"Barely eighteen."

"But why—why would you do something so permanent to yourself? How could you?"

Setting his jaw, he shook his head. "Why I did it doesn't matter. Not anymore." He gave a sudden snort. "And as it turned out, it wasn't so permanent."

"What do you mean?"

"After you told me you were pregnant, I couldn't think about anything else. So I canceled the business meeting—"

"You did what?"

"And I went to a doctor, where I was told that, somehow, my body had healed itself. It's rare, the doctor said. The rate is less than one percent. But it happens. And it happened to me."

She was staring at him openmouthed. "You canceled the meeting?"

He gave a wry smile. "*That's* the thing that surprises you?"

"You've been working like a madman for months—"

"I had to. I thought I knew you. How could you be a lying gold digger, trying to lure me into bed and trick me into marriage?"

"I wasn't!" she said indignantly.

"But there was no other explanation, don't you see? I'd had a vasectomy. I couldn't be the father of your baby. You couldn't possibly be telling me the truth." He paused. "I went to a private clinic so I could prove, once and for all, that you were lying." He gave her a rueful smile. "But it turned out that I was the one who was wrong. And you were right."

A soft breeze stroked the blossoms lazily, and ruffled his dark hair against his forehead. She fought the sudden impulse to brush it back with her fingertips.

Tightening her hands at her sides, Hana looked past him, to the families with blankets spread out beneath the flowering trees, enjoying a late lunch in the festive tradition of *hanami*. She looked at the nearest family, a smiling young couple with a toddler, picnicking together on a blanket.

"I was wrong to accuse you of lying," Antonio said, bowing his head. "I'm sorry. I won't insult you by asking for a paternity test. I know the baby's mine."

She looked at him. "Just like that?"

"Just like that."

For a moment, their eyes locked, and she felt the electricity of his gaze go straight to her heart.

Then his jaw tightened, and he looked away. "But you and I both know I'd be no good at raising a baby."

The lump returned to her throat. "Yes. I know."

"You aren't going to argue?"

She gave him a wistful smile. "I know you, Antonio. Of course you don't want to raise a baby. I only told you about the pregnancy because it was the right thing to do. But I know you're not interested in becoming a husband or father."

"Oh." He blinked, then continued awkwardly, "I will of course pay child support. And give you a large settlement to provide for the baby—"

"I don't want your money." It was exactly what she'd expected, so why did she feel hurt? Of course he'd offer her money for her baby. What else could he give? His time? His love? She said thickly, "We'll be fine."

He frowned. "But of course you will have a settlement. You deserve it. You earned it."

"Earned it how?" Her pride suddenly flared. "On my back in your bed?"

He scowled at her. "I didn't mean it that way—"

"I know," she cut him off. She'd been rude. But her heart was aching as she thought how different it should have been, sharing the joy of her pregnancy news. How happy and sweet today would have been, if she'd just taken her grandmother's advice and waited for marriage! If she'd waited until she'd found her true partner and home!

Swallowing, she looked across the beautiful cherry tree blooms against the wide blue sky. "You've paid me a very good salary, and I've saved most of it for the past year. Working and traveling so much, I had no time to spend it."

She lifted her chin. "*That* is what I've earned. And until I get a new job, the baby and I will be fine."

"Hana, you're being unreasonable."

"It's my choice. I don't want your payoff money."

"It's not a payoff."

"Of course it is."

He ground his teeth. "What is it you want, Hana? Marriage? We both know that's not going to happen."

A low, bitter laugh came unbidden from her throat. "You think I want to marry you?" She shook her head. "It must be amazing to be you, Antonio, always confident that you're the center of the world."

"Come on, Hana. You've spent two years at my side. You know how I am."

Yes, she did. She remembered all the women who'd tried so desperately to marry him over the last two years. How sorry she'd felt for them. She'd always been attracted to her boss, but she'd heeded the warnings. She would never love him. Her own parents' intense, almost teenager-like relationship had soured her on the idea of romantic love anyway.

Besides, it was bad enough that, as his employee, she'd based the last two years of her life entirely around Antonio's needs. She'd traveled when he traveled, lived where he lived, worked when he worked. The opposite of the life she actually wanted.

Since her rootless childhood, Hana had yearned for a real home. But when her beloved grandmother had become sick, Hana had dropped out of college. Desperate to provide Sachiko with the comfort and care of the best medical facility, she'd gotten a job. Giving up her own dreams, she'd taken increasingly demanding, high-paying secretarial jobs requiring her to travel constantly around the world.

Her grandmother had died a year ago. Hana could have quit her job then. But she hadn't.

Because as challenging as it was to work for Antonio, she'd come to love it. Somehow, his house in Madrid had become like home.

It shouldn't have felt that way. With all their traveling, they only lived there part-time. And though she'd become friends with the house staff, the palace still wasn't exactly homey, but ridiculously big with a ballroom and vast echoing hallways.

And yet, two months ago, when Antonio announced out of the blue he was going to sell the Madrid house and move the company's headquarters to New York, she'd felt a pain in her heart she hadn't expected. "Time to move on," he'd told her casually as he looked around the home office where they'd spent untold hours together. He'd shrugged. "There's nothing I care about in Madrid anymore."

A few hours later, he'd been astonished to find her crying in the *palacio*'s hallway. Shocked, he'd demanded to know the reason. But how could Hana explain, when she didn't understand it herself?

She had no claim on his house in Madrid. Just as she had no claim on Antonio.

It was time for her to go, she'd realized. To quit her job and move on, so she could finally find a home that no one could ever take from her.

But even as she'd had the thought, she'd suddenly lifted up on her tiptoes and kissed him. With an intake of breath, he'd stared at her. Then he'd grabbed her and kissed her back with passionate need.

Leading to her pregnancy now.

She never should have let herself trade their professional relationship for a personal one. Their argument this morning notwithstanding, Antonio had always treated Hana with respect far greater than he gave his mistresses. If anything, he seemed to enjoy treating his girlfriends badly. Almost as if he *wanted* them to leave him as soon as possible.

She'd felt such great pity for his last mistress, a beautiful Instagram fitness model who'd clung to him in the face of all his rudeness, that Hana had actually arranged a Christmas gift for the girl, a rare vintage camera. She'd signed Antonio's name to the card. As his secretary, Hana figured it was her job to try to make it at least *appear* that Antonio had normal human feelings—her job to make him look good, or at least less bad.

But it had been useless. Antonio had been furious at her interference, and he'd broken up with his mistress anyway. On Christmas morning, too. Well, at least the girl still had the camera as a parting gift.

Hana looked at him now beneath the cherry trees.

"You're right," she said in a low voice. "I do know you. It's probably for the best you don't want to be part of our baby's life. You'd be a horrible father, and we both know it. And as a husband—" She rolled her eyes heavenward, as if there were no words.

For a moment, Antonio's face was shocked. Then he looked inexplicably offended. "*Horrible* seems rather a strong word—"

She held up her hand to stave off his protest. "I'm just agreeing with you. You're incapable of being a father. You have absolutely nothing to offer us except money. And since I don't need that, there's nothing more to discuss, is there?"

Antonio opened his mouth. Closed it. Finally, he said tightly, "I apologized. Why are you still attacking me?"

"Attacking? You should be glad!"

He ground his teeth. "Glad you're telling me I'd be a poor excuse for a father and an even worse husband?"

"Glad I'm not trying to change you!" She shook her head. "You can move on with your life, Antonio. Get your air routes into Asia. Expand the company worldwide, gather more billions into your bank account. I won't bother you." She lifted her chin. "You won't be my baby's father, you're no longer my boss. You're not my lover, nor even my friend. So I think we can agree there's no reason for us to ever see each other again." She stuck out her hand. "Goodbye, Antonio."

He looked down at it. She felt the sizzle from his gaze, and suddenly realized her mistake. She tried to pull her hand back, but it was too late.

Antonio took her hand in his larger one.

Just that simple contact, palm to palm, caused her to gasp. Electricity sizzled through her, from her scalp to her toes.

His expression changed, and his hand tightened on hers.

"I can't let you go," he said quietly.

"You can't?" she breathed.

"Maybe I won't be a good father. Maybe I can't be a husband. But I still don't want to let you go." Antonio pulled her closer, searching her gaze intently. "Stay with me, Hana. As my mistress."

"Mistress?" The word was slippery on her tongue, causing a flood of desire to pulse through her blood, tightening her nipples as tension coiled low and deep inside her. *Mistress.* "For how long?"

He gave her a sensual smile, lifting his other hand to her cheek. "As long as we want."

Barely able to breathe, Hana stared up at his handsome face, his dark eyes, his sculpted cheekbones, the five o'clock shadow on his hard jawline. His cruel mouth.

As long as we want.

He meant as long as *he* wanted, she realized. A month. A week. Even a night. She'd seen it play out, time and time again. Hadn't she just been pitying those foolish women who fell for him, just seconds before?

And yet she'd never expected to be asked. Not like this. It felt strangely difficult to refuse, with his dark eyes burning through her as the memory of their night together pounded through her blood.

"And the baby?" she said hoarsely.

Antonio shrugged. "We'll see. Maybe I could be some kind of father to it. Who knows?"

Maybe? A father to *it*?

A shudder went through her. *Maybe* had nothing to do with her idea of family. Family was forever. Family was all a person had to cling to in a chaotic, uncertain world.

What he was talking about was something else entirely. He was a petulant boy, not wanting to be parted from a toy.

Hana ripped herself away from the temptation of his touch. "You can't just amuse yourself for a while and then toss us aside when you're bored. I won't let you do it. Not to me and definitely not to the baby!"

He stared at her incredulously. "Don't you understand, Hana? I'm offering to let you live with me. That's more than I've ever offered any woman."

Antonio actually believed he was offering her something precious. She saw that in his handsome face. He expected her to squeal with delight, throw her arms around him and scream *"Yes!"*

He was inviting her to live with him, but he didn't seem to realize she'd already done that for two years, living at his beck and call.

The only difference was that now she'd also service him in bed. She'd live with him as his girlfriend, at his whim and on his schedule, grateful for any time and attention he chose to give her or their child, assuming their relationship even lasted until the baby was born. And when Antonio chose to leave, she'd be expected to let him go without complaint. She wouldn't even have the dignity or security she'd had as his secretary.

That was the deal he offered her. He'd possibly be a father to their child, or possibly not; he wasn't willing to commit, but still, either way, she was supposed to be grateful, and put her heart on the hook to twist whichever way his wind blew.

Her body reacted before her brain, snapping her spine straight. Anger washed through her like a flash flood, knocking out every other emotion as she looked up at him in cold fury.

"No," she said flatly.

No? *No?*

Antonio stared at her in shock, hardly able to believe he'd heard her right.

No?

He couldn't remember the last time he'd heard the word *no*, from anyone, for any reason. Hearing it from a lover was particularly shocking, especially after he'd fought for the last hour to resist his need to possess her, and stick to his original plan.

He'd never expected, if he surrendered to his overwhelming desire for her—even offering to give up his precious freedom and allow her to live with him, in his house—that she might refuse.

Antonio glared at her, feeling somehow betrayed, as if she'd lured him into this moment, just so she could reject and humiliate him.

"Why?" he demanded. How could she say no? She wanted him as much as he wanted her. *Didn't she?*

Hana raised her chin. "I went to see a doctor this morning, too." She looked down at her waistline beneath her white skirt suit. "I heard our baby's heartbeat."

The baby's heartbeat. What a strange idea. "And?"

With a slight smile, she put her hand on her belly. "Everything is coming along just fine," she said softly. "I'm due in mid-October."

Beneath the warm sun in the Tokyo park, his gaze followed hers. The barest curve beneath her white fitted jacket hinted at the child growing inside her. A baby. His baby. Setting his jaw, he pushed all emotion away. "Another reason for you to live with me."

She narrowed her lovely brown eyes. "I don't want my baby to be part of your world. Whatever made you become like this…"

"Like what?"

"So cold, so distant, so untrusting." Hana took a deep breath, then added, "So broken."

Broken? Anger shot through him. He said tightly, "You don't know me. You don't know anything about me."

"Don't I?" Hana gave him a wistful smile as the sun went behind a passing cloud. "I know you don't want a family and won't commit to anyone, ever. Why would I want to raise my child with a man like that? Even if I thought you'd actually stick around. Which I don't."

His lips parted. He wanted to defy her words, to tell her that he could commit anytime he wanted, he simply chose not to. But the words dried up in his mouth.

Her expression changed as she watched him. She shook her head, looking yearningly toward the happy young family picnicking nearby beneath the blooming cherry trees. "My parents were teachers and we moved to a new country each year. I was rarely in one place long enough to make friends. Growing up, family was all I had."

"I find that hard to imagine." Antonio remembered her grandmother's funeral last year, when so many people had come forward to comfort Hana. "You seem to make friends wherever you go." His lips suddenly tightened. "Like Ren Tanaka."

"He's my oldest friend," she said softly. "Almost like family."

"How is it that I never knew of his existence?"

She lifted her eyes. "Because you don't pay attention to anyone's life but your own."

"That's not true."

She gave a humorless smile. "I know you, Antonio."

"You don't know everything," he said tightly. No one knew about his childhood—he'd made sure of that. He himself had tried to forget how he'd been shown, over and over, that he hadn't been wanted as a child, not by anyone. Twice, foster families had brought him home from the orphanage. Twice, he'd been sent right back. The final time, when he was six years old, it had been because his foster mother had unexpectedly become pregnant. "Nothing personal, boy," his foster father had explained kindly. "But we're having our own baby now, so we don't need you anymore."

Broken.

Yes. Hana was right. She did know him. She'd seen the dark truth in his soul that he'd spent his life trying to hide. The secret no one else knew about Antonio Delacruz, playboy airline billionaire: there was some huge flaw in his soul. Something monstrous about him that had made his birth parents decide to abandon him when he was just hours old, leaving their nameless newborn in a basket on the steps of a Spanish church in the middle of the night.

"What happened to you?" Hana asked gently, drawing closer. "Why would you have a vasectomy when you were only eighteen? How could you already know you never wanted to be a father?"

Her questions felt like stabs through his heart. He couldn't let her see through his armor to the weakness beneath. He couldn't. Not anyone. But especially not her.

She was getting too close. Fortunately, he knew exactly how to push people away—by attacking their weaknesses, to distract them from seeing his.

Stepping back from her as the soft cherry petals whirled around them in the park, he said in a bored voice, "Why did I get a vasectomy? Because I'm a selfish bastard, obviously. Which as you said, you know better than anyone. Which begs the question." His eyes pierced hers. "Why did you kiss me that night?"

Hana's cheeks darkened to deep pink as she looked away. She mumbled something.

"What?"

Looking at her feet, she said, "When you told me you were going to sell the house in Madrid," her voice became stilted, "it made me sad."

Antonio didn't understand. "Why would you care if I sold the *palacio*? We're only there a week or two a month."

"Because I was happy there. I made friends there. It felt almost like…like home."

He didn't know what she was talking about. The *palacio* was a trophy to him, nothing more. He'd bought it as a big middle finger to everyone in Spain who'd thought him worthless as a boy. But he didn't need it anymore. He was ready to move on. Strange that she'd come to think of it as home.

He licked his lips. "That still doesn't explain why you kissed me."

Hana took a deep, agonized breath. "It was a mistake. I never should have kissed you. No matter how many years I'd wanted you."

Antonio couldn't move. She'd wanted him? For years?

"I should have quit my job right then," she said. "I've spent too long traveling from place to place, when all I've ever really wanted is a real home. A place in the world that's mine. A home no one can ever take from me."

He stared down at her.

"I never wanted a home," he said finally.

Her lips curved at the edges. "I know. You built an airline to make sure you're never stuck in one place too long. Not with one place. Not with one person."

Antonio's gaze fell to her lips. He felt a flash of heat. Everything she'd said about him was true.

So why had he been faithful to Hana—not just since their night together, but even before, since Christmas Eve?

For years, he'd tried to deny his attraction to her. He was her boss, and she was his valuable employee. But his desire for Hana had never ended. Even now, he was still racked with it, body and soul. More than ever. His nerve endings strummed with need. He felt her every movement, her every breath.

"I never should have slept with you," Hana choked out. "I should have waited for a man I could marry."

Antonio clamped down on a sudden emotion in his heart, emotion he didn't want to identify. He said harshly, "So you admit you want marriage."

"Of course I do." She looked again at the families picnicking in the April sunshine of the park, beneath the flowering cherry trees. "I want a man who will be my partner. A man who will help me build a home. Who will love our child and be there for us, every single day." Her eyes focused on Antonio. "That man won't be you."

He felt a strange twist through his solar plexus. As two men passed by on the path, Antonio saw their eyes linger on her.

Hana wouldn't be alone for long, he knew. She was too beautiful, too kind, too warm. He'd seen the way men looked at her. She could have any man she wanted, begging to bed her, to wed her, to raise her child. Starting with Ren Tanaka.

With her early pregnancy, there was a new lushness about her, not just her ripening body, but her lovely face, her dark eyes glimmering with new confidence and power. She wasn't deferential to Antonio as she'd once been. Why would she be? He was no longer her boss. No longer her lover. She'd already rejected him as her baby's father. With better reason than she even knew.

Antonio took a breath. Wasn't this what he'd wanted? So why did he feel as if he were the one being dumped?

Was it just because he'd never had a woman reject him before? Or did it go deeper than that?

"Goodbye, Antonio," Hana said quietly. This time, she didn't reach out to shake his hand. She just turned away, and he suddenly knew he might never see her again. She intended to disappear from his life, and take their baby with her. To take her sweetness and loyalty and warmth to some other, more deserving man.

The strange tension lifted from his belly to his throat, making it suddenly hard to breathe. "Wait."

Hana looked at him. "For what?"

She was close, so close. Just inches away. He could imagine her body against his. It would be so easy to take her in his arms and kiss her.

No. He couldn't. If he did, he would want more. He cursed silently to himself. He *already* wanted more. He'd never stopped wanting more. From the moment he'd possessed her. No. From the moment he'd first hired her. Hana was his weakness, the one and only desire he hadn't been able to push aside in obedience to the coldly ruthless dictates of his brain.

But he wouldn't kiss her.

Couldn't.

It was absolutely *forbidden.*

As Antonio looked down into her brown eyes, so deep with sadness, shining beneath all the lush colors around them, he suddenly felt like all the world was bursting into spring around them. Only he was still frozen. And if she left, the cold gray winter he lived in would last forever.

His gaze fell to her full pink lips. He saw the way her even white teeth worried against the tender lower lip.

"You can't go," he said, searching her gaze. "Not until I kiss you goodbye…"

Without letting himself stop, without letting himself think, he reached for her. In the middle of the beautiful park, as cherry blossoms blew in the soft spring breeze, he cupped her face with both his hands.

He had the brief image of her wide, startled eyes in her heartbreakingly lovely face. And then he lowered his mouth to hers, kissing her with all the emotion he could not let himself think, feel or say.

He felt the tremble of her lips beneath his own, before, like a miracle, she surrendered to him with a small shivery sigh.

But almost at once, his self-control started to fray.

He wrapped his larger body around hers, holding her tight against him as he deepened the kiss, plundering her mouth until the whole world felt like it was whirling around them, as if they were the eye of the storm.

He was pulled into a vortex of desire. Suddenly he felt lost, drowning in the intensity of his need. Nothing mattered—but this—

She roughly pulled away. She looked up, her face stricken. "Don't!"

"Hana—"

"Stay away from me!"

And she turned and walked away. Antonio watched her wan figure disappear, her shoulders slumped, crossing back through the park. A cool wind blew against his face, as white petals danced in the breeze, brushing against his black cashmere coat. Burning, he was frozen, watching her.

Could he really, truly let her go?

CHAPTER FOUR

HANA FELT A lump in her throat as she walked past the bowing doorman into the Tanaka hotel. She wasn't going to let herself cry. She wasn't! Antonio wasn't worth it!

She blinked fast as her eyes burned.

She'd known all along he wouldn't want to be part of their baby's life. She'd known it even before he'd made love to her, when he'd told her outright that their affair had to be brief, forgettable and consequence-free.

So why, after telling her he couldn't be part of their baby's life, had he suddenly asked her to be his mistress—and worse, kissed her?

Her lips still burned from his kiss. Why would he do such a thing? Just to prove the power he still held over her? He'd have that power for the rest of his life, with the child that would link them until the day Hana died.

But her baby needed a real home, a real family, a real father, not someone who would leave or neglect them at his whim. Antonio would never be the man her baby needed. He'd had a vasectomy, for heaven's sake. At *eighteen*. Could he make it any more clear that he never wanted to be a father?

Better to have a clean break.

As Hana entered the hotel, she saw Ren's handsome, worried face across the lobby. She suddenly wished he could have been the father of her baby, instead of Antonio.

Her best friend was a good man, smart, loyal and kind. Any child would be lucky to have him as a father.

But for Hana, he was a dear friend, nothing more. And she had to make him see that, too.

Ren took one look at her tearstained face, and his dark eyes turned grim. "What did Delacruz say? What did he do?" He set his jaw, glaring out the window. "I'm going to find him and—"

"Don't. He didn't do anything," she said wearily. "It's finished. I'll never see him again."

"You still love him." Ren's voice was flat as he looked at her. "Even after he's treated you so badly."

"No," she protested. Love? Ridiculous. Knowing what she knew, she'd have to be the stupidest woman on earth, or the worst sort of masochist, to fall in love with Antonio, and she was neither.

Something had broken him, something that left him unable to open his heart to anyone. She wasn't sure he *had* a heart.

And yet, sometimes… He did something that surprised her.

Like when her beloved grandmother had died last year from complications of dementia. Hana had been grieving her loss for years, even before her death, when Sachiko had stopped recognizing her, then stopped speaking at all. But losing the last member of her family had been a devastating blow.

And yet, initially Antonio hadn't wanted Hana to go to the funeral. He'd tried to convince her that it would be a waste of time for her to leave Madrid. "Your grandmother won't even appreciate it," he'd said firmly. "She's dead. And I need you here."

Then he'd looked at her tearstained face. And something had changed in his dark eyes.

"I'll come with you," he'd said quietly.

"It's not necessary," she'd said, her voice clogged with tears.

"I'm coming," he'd cut her off.

And he had. He'd had a million other things he should have been doing, billion-dollar deals waiting to be made, but he'd taken Hana on his private jet to rural California instead. He'd sat silently beside her at her grandmother's funeral, and afterward, when Sachiko's many friends had shyly come forward to hug Hana, whom they hadn't seen in years, Antonio had introduced himself not as her boss, but as her friend. He'd remained in California with her for two days, a comforting presence in the background, giving her the strength to go through her grandmother's things and begin arrangements to sell off the heavily mortgaged farm. Then, when it was over, he'd taken her home to Madrid.

Home. To Madrid.

A home she'd never see again now.

Hana's shoulders sagged. After everything she'd gone through today, she felt bone-tired, more tired than she'd ever been in her life.

"Are you all right?" Ren asked.

She rubbed her eyes. "Just tired."

"Don't worry, Hana," he said softly, as he looked down at her in the hotel lobby. "I'll take care of you."

The possessive look on his handsome face troubled her. She blurted out, "Ren, please, you can't think—"

He abruptly turned away. "Your satchel was dropped off earlier. I had it taken to our best suite. You can rest there."

"Thank you." She bit her lip. "I'll pay for the room—"

"Don't be ridiculous," he said. "You're my best friend. You think I would take your money? I want to help. I am proud to have a hotel to offer you."

Hana disliked the feeling that he was offering her not just a room for the night, but himself for a lifetime. But they were best friends. She wouldn't have even questioned his offer, if she didn't fear—*know*—his feelings went deeper.

"Ren," she said gently, speaking quietly so no one else would hear, "I'm so grateful. But," she hesitated, "you have always been like a brother to me…"

He looked away. "I must go to Osaka for a few days," he said in an expressionless voice. "A business trip with suppliers. If you need me, I could cancel my trip—"

"No, I'll be fine," Hana said, relieved to put off further discussion of an issue that would be awkward at best, and at worst, horrifyingly painful for them both. It might even cost her Ren's friendship entirely, and that was a prospect she just couldn't face today. Rubbing her eyes, she confessed, "I feel like I haven't slept in a year."

He gave her a kind smile. "Come with me."

Twenty minutes later, she'd kicked off her shoes and was comfortably ensconced in a luxurious penthouse suite. He indicated her overnight bag. "If there is anything you need, anything at all, my staff will be glad to assist you."

"Thank you, Ren."

"It is the least I can do," he said, and she hated the way he looked at her. "Until I return." With a formal bow of his head, he left.

Hana exhaled, shivering with exhaustion as the aching hollows of her feet rested against the tatami mat on the floor. Picking up her bag, she silently blessed Ramon Garcia, who must have noticed she'd left her satchel and arranged to have it dropped off at the hotel. It certainly wouldn't have occurred to Antonio. No way.

But she wasn't going to think about him. She was not!

Pushing aside the sliding paper doors, she went past the main room of the suite, into the bedroom. Though exquisitely decorated in traditional Japanese style, the room still had some Western elements—like a king-size bed.

Which again, in spite of her best efforts, made her think of Antonio.

Setting down her overnight bag, she looked out the bedroom's wide windows. In the distance, she could see the bright neon lights of a busy shopping district. So different from the tranquil park where he'd just kissed her amid all the beautiful pink-and-white flowering trees.

She could still hardly believe Antonio had asked her to be his mistress—and she'd told him no.

It was the right thing to do, Hana told herself wearily, leaning her hand against the window. For Antonio, there was only one thing that was always right: strength. One thing that was always wrong: weakness.

If he crushed his opponents, it was their own fault. He'd say they had been weak, letting themselves become takeover targets or badly managing their businesses. If he bruised the hearts of his mistresses, it was the women's fault for not believing him when he told them he would never love them.

No matter how incredible their night together had been, no matter how every time she remembered their passion her body burned from her fingertips to her toes, sex wasn't enough. Antonio would never be the man she needed him to be.

Yes, she'd done the right thing, refusing to be Antonio's mistress, when it would have brought only brief pleasure at the expense of endless grief. The right thing for her. The right thing for their child.

So why did Hana feel so miserable?

Her shoulders drooped as she went into the gleaming, ultramodern bathroom and turned on the shower. She washed her hair with the orange-blossom-scented shampoo and felt the blast of water massage her skin.

Best to make the best of things. Her mother had been forty-two when Hana was born, a surprise to the married couple, who'd already spent nearly two decades teaching and traveling the world. Restless hippies both, they'd believed problems could be solved just by changing the country one lived in.

Wherever they'd traveled, Hana had been a chameleon, fitting in everywhere—and feeling like she belonged nowhere. With Hana's mixed heritage, no one looked exactly like her, certainly not her pale, red-haired father or her olive-skinned, dark-haired mother.

Her parents had had a passionate relationship—full of arguments and moaning kisses—almost like teenagers. Sometimes they'd seemed to forget they even had a daughter. Sometimes Hana had felt like *she* was the grown-up in their family.

Every time she started to make friends and actually become part of a new community, her parents would inevitably have a big fight, or declare themselves bored, and then grandly announce it was time for another "adventure" in a new country.

"It's wonderful to be free," they'd say, toasting each other with cheap wine, scorning the "poor slobs" who were "trapped in one place till death."

To Hana, without friends or roots and often feeling even excluded from her parents' tight relationship, being trapped in one place sounded like heaven. Her beloved grandmother Sachiko, a widow who was her last living grandparent, had been her only true source of stability. Whenever her parents had needed space from the onerous demands of child-rearing— "Grown-ups need time just to be romantic, darling, just for ourselves, you understand"— they'd send Hana for a few weeks to her grandmother's rural almond farm in northern California.

Sachiko was the one who'd taught her Japanese. Each time she felt her grandmother's warm arms around her, and look up into her calm, wise eyes, Hana would vow, when she grew up, she'd settle down nearby and never leave again.

But Hana had barely started college in nearby Sacramento before her father suddenly died of a stroke in Tasmania, leaving her mother in shock. No one was sure whether it was an accident when Laurel's rental car had gone off a cliff in Thailand six months later. And the very next month, her grandmother had the first onset of dementia that would eventually claim her life.

Now Hana was alone.

No, she remembered. Not alone. She'd never be alone again. She put her hand over her belly. She was going to have a baby.

Hana was going to be a mother. She'd build them a home. She had enough money so she could wait to get a job, until her baby was a few months old. She could be choosy. So she'd lost her home in Madrid. She told herself there were other places in the world.

The world is your oyster, kid, her father had always said when he was proud of her. Hana took a deep breath.

Somewhere. Somehow. She'd make the two of them a home.

As she got out of the hot shower, she dried off, brushing her long dark hair, then pulled on an ivory silk nightgown and robe from her bag. Her stomach growled, and she remembered she hadn't eaten since she'd arrived in Tokyo.

But as she was reaching to call room service, the phone rang. Nervous it might be Ren, she snatched it up. "Hello?"

"You turned off your mobile." Antonio's voice was accusing.

She gripped the receiver. "How did you find me?"

"It wasn't hard to guess you'd be staying at Tanaka's hotel," he said sardonically.

"What do you want?"

"We need to talk." His husky voice made her toes curl in spite of herself. She hardened her heart.

"We already did. In the park."

"I have more to say—"

"Don't call me again." And she hung up.

Almost immediately, the penthouse's phone began to ring again. She picked up the receiver and slammed it back without saying a word. Then she called the front desk of the hotel and told them to hold all calls to her room.

Antonio either couldn't believe she'd turned down his *fantastic* offer to be his temporary mistress, or else he had urgent questions about business negotiations. But she didn't have to put up with his whims or worry about his ego anymore.

So she wouldn't.

Feeling too exhausted to think, Hana curled up on the enormous bed.

Her eyes flew open when she heard a hard knock on the door. *Antonio*, she thought groggily. But he couldn't know her room number. Surely none of the staff would give that information to a stranger. Stumbling to her feet, she went to the door and looked through the peephole.

She saw only a uniformed member of hotel staff.

Tightening the belt on her silk kimono robe, she opened the door the barest crack. "Yes?"

"Flowers, ma'am," the young man said, an explanation that was utterly unnecessary because five uniformed staff members stood behind him in the hallway, all holding huge full vases—red roses, pink tulips and other, more exotic flowers, enough to fill an entire shop.

"All of these—for me?" she stammered.

"Yes, miss."

"Who sent them?"

The man handed her a card. Tearing it open, Hana saw a brief sentence in Antonio's arrogant scrawl.

Talk to me.

Her heart leaped to her throat. Antonio could be ruthless and utterly single-minded when he wanted something. Had that one simple word—*No*—suddenly made him decide he wanted her? For his bed? For the boardroom? Where?

It didn't matter. He couldn't have her. He couldn't just fire her, reject her—then think he could have her back whenever and however he wanted!

"Stop," she cried, blocking them from entering her penthouse suite with the flowers. "I don't want them!"

The staff members looked at each other in bewilderment. "What shall we do with them, ma'am?" one ventured.

"I don't care—send them to the hospital—or you can have them! Do whatever you want with them, but they can't come in here!"

Closing the door in their faces, Hana exhaled, sagging against the door. But she could still smell the sweet scent of roses wafting through the air, messing with her mind. Her eyes narrowed. She started to reach for her cell phone, to call Antonio and tell him angrily what she thought of his ploy.

Then she stopped herself. That was just what he wanted. She wouldn't give him the satisfaction!

Hana paced the length of the hotel suite, trying not to think about him. She wouldn't remember all the days they'd spent together, or the night he'd taken her virginity, or the fact that she carried his child inside her. She wouldn't!

Two minutes later, the hotel suite's doorbell rang.

"Oh, for the love of…" Choking back a curse, she looked through the peephole again. Her hands trembled as she opened the door.

Another line of hotel employees stood in the hallway, weighed down with chocolates and elegant treats with the distinctive wrapping of the finest candy boutiques in Tokyo. And the uniformed staff member at the back held a silver tray spread just with different Kit Kat flavors, the *sakura* with its wrapper of delicate pink blossoms, sweet potato, wasabi, green tea and other, even more exotic flavors that she knew from experience were notoriously hard to find, exclusive only to certain cities in Japan.

She ground her teeth. This was a low blow—he was perfectly aware she had a sweet tooth. Antonio knew just how to tempt her.

No! She wouldn't give in to weakness!

"Take it all away," she told the hotel staff firmly, and shut the door again.

Hana's hands shook as she went to the low table that held a tray with a traditional tea service. She filled the kettle with water, waited, then poured hot steaming water into the delicate ceramic cup and placed herbal leaves to steep. She took deep breaths of the fragrant chamomile and tried to calm down. Peaceful, she told herself. The world is my oyster. He doesn't exist.

Then she heard another loud knock.

Setting the cup down hard on the table, she stalked to her door. Opening it, she glared at the unfortunate hotel staff, all standing there sheepishly holding large black velvet boxes.

"What now?" she snapped.

"I'm sorry, Miss Everly," the first one said unhappily, bowing, "but we were ordered to bring you this."

Glancing at the others, he gave a signal. And all five of the uniformed staff opened their flat, wide black velvet boxes at once.

Hana almost screamed.

Five necklaces sparkled at her from black velvet, each more ridiculously over-the-top than the last, necklaces that must have cost many millions of yen, that would have made Marie Antoinette blush. Brilliant diamonds, as big as robin's eggs, emeralds, sapphires, all gleamed and glistened and whispered wickedly sensual desires to her.

Against her will, she snapped back to the memory of Antonio's husky voice when her body had been naked against his in the bedroom of his *palacio*.

"I'd like to see you in jewels," he'd breathed, brushing back a long dark tendril of her hair, kissing down her collarbone. "Jewels and nothing else."

But she hadn't cared about jewels that night. Just having Antonio in her arms, after two years of helpless, hopeless desire, she'd felt like the world was exploding around her with passion and joy.

Did he really think she could be bought?

"Take them…away," she croaked out to the hotel staff.

The employees looked at each other with wide eyes. "You don't want these jewels, Miss Everly?" one ventured.

"No!" she nearly shouted. Closing the door, she sagged back against it. Why was Antonio doing this? To torture her? How dare he send her flowers, candy and jewels! Enough!

Stomping across the penthouse suite, she grabbed her cell phone from her purse. Turning it on, she dialed. She took a deep breath.

"Yes?" Antonio answered innocently on the second ring. His voice was calm, while her emotions felt like they were spiraling out of control. It enraged her further.

"Stop sending me gifts."

"Yes, I heard you sent them all back." He paused. "It surprised me that you resisted the candy."

Her cheeks burned, as she remembered all the times over the last two years when he'd teased her about her love of chocolate. All the times she'd eaten candy in the middle of the night, as he had a glass of scotch—each of them picking their own particular poison as they worked long, laborious hours on various deals. But it wasn't candy that was most forbidden. She could resist chocolate, if she needed to.

Antonio Delacruz was the most dangerous temptation. Definitely bad for her health.

Hana glared out the window toward the bright neon signs of the nearby commercial district. "How much clearer do I have to be? I don't want you in my life. Stop calling me."

"You called me," he pointed out.

"I'm hanging up."

"If you must."

"There's someone knocking at my door," she said. "If it's another ridiculous gift, I'm throwing it out the window."

"I'm hanging up now," he said smoothly.

"Good," she choked out, and flung open the door.

Hana felt her heart lift to her throat as she saw Antonio in the doorway, broad-shouldered, tall and devastatingly handsome in his suit and black coat. His cell phone was still to his ear, against his mussed black hair, and his hard jaw was scruffy as he looked right through her with his searing dark eyes.

"Will you talk to me, *querida*?" he said huskily.

CHAPTER FIVE

ANTONIO STARED DOWN at her. He couldn't remember the last time he'd pursued any woman like this. Never, not since he'd turned eighteen. But the stakes had never been so high.

Standing in her hotel room, Hana looked up at him, her brown eyes wary, one hand against the door, as if she yearned to slam it in his face. He couldn't take that chance. Bracing his hand against the door, he ruthlessly pushed into her hotel suite, closing it softly behind them.

They faced each other in the fading afternoon light of the entryway.

"What do you want?" she whispered, backing away, past the open paper doors into the main room. He followed her.

"Stop," she cried. "Kick off your shoes!"

"My shoes?"

"Japanese tradition!"

Tradition? With a snort, he started to refuse. Then the words stopped at his lips as he saw her face.

Hana *expected* him to refuse. She thought she knew him. She didn't just think he was selfish. She thought he was broken and unredeemable. She thought he was heartless. Soulless.

He suddenly wanted to prove her wrong. To wipe away the scorn he imagined he saw in her eyes.

Antonio kicked off his handmade Italian shoes. Her eyes widened in surprise as he walked toward her on the rough reed mat. He stopped when he was just inches away from her, standing between the low-slung sofa and the wall of windows facing the city and darkening April sky.

His gaze traced her silhouette against the wide windows. She'd never looked so beautiful to him, so vulnerable—a strange thing to think, he thought wryly, when she had all the power in this moment. She had his baby inside her. The baby he'd never imagined he wanted.

But he'd discovered, to his shock, that he could not let them go—either of them. For the first time in his life, he was unable to walk away.

"You took off your shoes," Hana breathed, tilting back her head to look into his face.

Antonio gave a slight smile. "You told me to."

"I didn't expect you to do it."

"So you admit it."

"What?"

"I can surprise you." Of its own accord, his hand stretched out to trace her long dark hair, tumbling down her creamy silk robe with its elegant floral pattern. The robe's tie had become slightly loose, revealing a matching silk nightgown. His gaze traced over her bare collarbone to the neckline, which hinted at the full shape of her pregnancy-swollen breasts beneath.

Abruptly backing away, she glared at him, tightening her silk robe around her waist. "What do you want, Antonio?"

That was a strange question.

What did he want?

He thought he'd known the answer to that since he was six, when he'd returned to the orphanage after a month spent with the foster parents who'd decided not to adopt him after all. He'd cried that first night, and the older boys had bullied him for it.

Giving up all hopes of being adopted, he'd frozen his heart as a means of survival. When other children cried in the night for someone to love them, he'd become the one to tell them to shut up, to be tough, to go to sleep, so they'd be stronger to face whatever fresh hell the next day could bring.

When he'd left the orphanage on his eighteenth birthday, he'd met a pretty waitress. Isabella had been older, experienced, and was amused when Antonio fervently declared his love for her after their first night in bed. She'd been equally amused by his broken heart when she told him a few months later she was leaving him for a squat businessman three times her age.

"Sorry, Antonio." She'd shrugged. "Pierre has a new BMW and a flat in Paris. You have nothing to offer."

"Nothing but my heart," he'd choked out.

"Money is what matters. Money is what lasts." She'd patted him on the shoulder like a dog. "You're young. You'll learn."

And he had. Isabella had helped him see that, whatever awful flaw had caused him to be constantly rejected since he was born, it could be hidden by a big enough fortune.

He'd gotten a job on a small airfield and soon started his first airline with a single rickety, leased plane. He'd built his company through sheer tenacity and will. He'd succeeded where better-funded, better-connected men had failed.

And five years later, when Isabella had come crawling back, this time he'd been the one to be amused. He'd tilted his head, coldly looking her over. "Sorry. You have nothing to offer."

Antonio didn't make excuses. He didn't give in to feelings. He controlled his own fate.

Then how to explain the inexplicable reaction now pounding through his body?

What did he want?

He wanted Hana as his mistress. But could he want more? Did he want to be a father?

A baby. Antonio tried to even imagine it. A child growing up, learning to walk and talk. Going to school. Learning sports, learning to read. A child. A son or daughter, looking up at him with smiling eyes—

"Why are you pursuing me?" Hana demanded, breaking his reverie. "I've already given you my answer. I won't be your mistress. What else can you possibly hope to gain?"

"Where is Tanaka?" he said suddenly. "Why isn't he here guarding you?"

"Ren had to leave for Osaka," she said unwillingly.

His dark eyes gleamed. "So you told him you didn't love him, and he couldn't take it."

Folding her arms over her chest, she said pointedly, "He didn't need to guard me. I didn't plan to see you again."

"We need to discuss our baby—"

"*My* baby," she said fiercely. "Just mine. It's what I want. It's what you want. So why won't you just go?"

Pacing a few long strides across the suite's luxurious main room, he stopped. He glanced out the windows, where twilight had begun to fall. He slowly turned to face her. "I can't."

He was startled to see sudden tears in her eyes. "You only want me because you think you can't have me. If I actually let you into our lives, if I tried to depend on you, you'd be gone in a second!"

"Hana—"

She turned her body away from him. "Just go. And this time, don't come back. I mean it."

Antonio's hands tightened at his sides.

How could she be so unfeeling? How could she not see how difficult this was for him? He was struggling with the question of his life: Who was he as a man? Could he be more?

Then he suddenly realized.

She didn't understand because he hadn't told her. There was only one way to change that. Just the thought made his stomach churn. But there was only one option that was worse. Leaving Hana and his unborn child behind.

Taking a deep breath, he said hoarsely, "You're right. I never wanted to be a father. That's why I had a vasectomy at eighteen."

Slowly, she turned to face him, her eyes wide.

"What did I know about fatherhood?" he continued, his jaw clenched. "I never even knew my parents. They abandoned me in a basket on the steps of a church in southern Spain the day I was born."

"What?" she breathed.

"The nuns found me. Gave me a name. Sent me to the nearest orphanage." The words came slow and halting from his lips. "When I was a few months old, I was brought home by a family who said they intended to adopt me. But they sent me back."

"Back? Why?"

He shrugged. "I never learned. Maybe I cried too much. It doesn't matter. I don't remember them." Every syllable tasted like rust in his mouth. "But I do remember the child-less couple who brought me home when I was six. Then they got pregnant, and decided they didn't need me. The night they sent me back to the orphanage, I made the mistake of crying about it. The older boys said they'd give me something to cry about." Pulling back the hairline at his left temple, he revealed a raised scar. "I quit crying, all right. I was in bandages for weeks." His lips curled sardonically. "After that, no one tried to adopt me again. I made sure of that."

"Oh, no." Hana's lovely face looked stricken as she whispered, "I'm sorry."

"Don't be."

"It's not your fault—none of it is your fault!"

"I know," he lied. He shrugged. "It helped me, really. Made me stronger. Gave me ambition."

"Did you ever find out why your parents left you on those church steps?"

"No."

"There had to be some reason—"

"It doesn't matter." His voice held an edge. "I just wanted you to understand why, even at eighteen, I knew I didn't want to be a father." He thought of telling her about Isabella, but that was a step too far. He took a deep breath. "But you're pregnant. Everything has changed."

She gave a weak smile. "Because the vasectomy failed. For all you know, you might have children all over the world you've never heard about."

He rolled his eyes. "Unlikely."

"How do you know?"

"Because no woman has come to my house with a baby in her arms, begging for her fair share of my fortune."

"You really do believe the worst of everyone."

Antonio looked at her.

"Except you," he said quietly.

Coming forward, he gently traced his hands along the shoulders of her silk robe. He felt her shiver beneath his touch—or was he the one who was shivering? He dropped his hands.

"I can't abandon you, or this baby," he said in a low voice. "I might not have planned for this, but now it's happened, I can't leave my child to wonder, night after night, what flaw he could have possibly had from birth, that made him unworthy of a parent's love, unworthy of family or home."

Hana gave a choked gasp. "My baby will never feel that way! I will be there. Always."

"Yes. But he'd always wonder about his father." Emotion

went through Antonio. He couldn't let this baby feel as he once had. Unworthy. Unwanted. Rejected.

"I will find someone…"

Her voice trailed off at his sharp gaze. "Tanaka?"

She shook her head. "But…but someone. A partner."

Antonio exhaled, knowing she was right. "Any man would want you," he said quietly. "But even with the best stepfather on earth, the baby will always wonder about me. Why I left. What will you tell him?"

"The truth." Her hands tightened at her sides, and her beautiful face looked down as she added, "There's no other answer."

The truth. That Antonio was a selfish, shallow playboy, more interested in his airline than his child. That he didn't have the capacity, or the desire, to commit. Not to his child. He looked at Hana. Not to her.

Unless…

Staring at her bowed head, he blinked, and the world seemed to spin on its axis. Suddenly, the solution was astonishingly clear.

The only way to get everything he wanted. To protect his child. To have Hana in his bed. Everything.

As they stood across from each other in her hotel suite, he said bluntly, "You know I don't love you."

"Of course you don't." She rolled her eyes. "Luckily, I don't love you either. Heaven help any woman who does."

He gave a wry smile, then his expression became serious. "But you've never betrayed me. Not once. You're the one person I trust most on earth. The one I most respect."

"Thanks." Hana snorted a low laugh. "That changes nothing."

She was trying to protect herself from hurt. He knew that cynical tone. He'd used it himself. "It changes everything."

"How?"

"I want you in my bed. I want you in my company and in my life. And…" He took a deep breath. "I want to be a real father to our baby."

Her lips parted as she said hoarsely, "What are you saying?"

His lips curved as he looked down at her. "I want you to marry me, Hana."

Hana stared at him.

The twilight from the hotel penthouse's windows left a strange reddish glow on his hard, handsome face, leaving a shadow behind him on the translucent *shōji* doors of the suite.

Had he gone crazy—or had she?

Marriage?

"Is this a joke?" she choked out.

"I'm deadly serious."

She stammered, "You don't want to marry anyone."

"I just asked you." Antonio lifted his dark eyebrows. "But perhaps I didn't do it properly?"

In front of her horrified eyes, he folded his powerful body, falling to one knee before her. Taking both her hands in his own, he looked up. "Hana Everly, will you do me the honor of becoming my bride?"

"Stop it," she hissed, tugging on his hands. "Stand up."

Slowly, he rose back to his feet. His dark gaze burned through her. "Will you?"

"You're being ridiculous."

"I need an answer."

"My answer is no!"

The humor fled from his face. He said tersely, "Might I ask why?"

"For starters—you just said you don't love me!"

"Love only brings pain."

Hana thought of her parents' passionate love, their constant drama, and had to admit he maybe had a point. Then she raised her chin. "How would you even know?"

"I tried it once," Antonio said quietly. "A waitress. When I was eighteen and broke and stupid."

Hana's jaw dropped.

"You—loved someone?" she gasped. *"You?"*

"I was a virgin," he said ironically. "I thought I loved her because she took me to her bed. She told me it was hilarious and dumped me a few months later." He tilted his head. "And you, Hana? What experience have you had with love that makes you think it's necessary, or even good, for a marriage?"

She thought again about how excluded she'd felt, as her parents had focused solely on each other, on fighting and kisses, dragging their daughter around the world almost like an afterthought.

Biting her lip, she looked away.

"So," Antonio said softly. "You do have some experience with love after all."

"Not me," she said unwillingly. "But my parents. They were so in love, they—they sometimes forgot about me."

He took her hand. She felt the comfort of his touch, the heat of his palm against hers, and her whole body shivered.

She heard herself ask, "What happened to her?"

"Who?" His fingers tightened around hers.

Her cheeks burned. "The waitress."

"Ah." His lips curved. "She left me for a rich, elderly Frenchman. But she came crawling back when she heard I'd made my fortune."

"And?"

He shrugged. "I was no longer interested."

"Of course not." She looked up at his handsome, implacable face. "But marriage is a commitment for a lifetime."

"You think I don't know that?"

"Your longest love affair lasted six weeks."

His dark eyes flashed with amusement, his shoulders suddenly relaxing beneath his sleekly tailored coat. "You were paying attention?"

She bit her lip, hating that she'd revealed so much. She said defiantly, "It was my job to pay attention. To clean up your messes when you ghosted a girl and she came sobbing to me, wondering why you'd suddenly stopped calling when she'd thought she was on the fast track to earning your heart!"

"So that's why you brought Madison the camera for Christmas? You wanted her to think I was a good boyfriend?"

"For all the good it did." She scowled. "I can't believe you'd break up with someone on *Christmas morning.* Not even you."

"It seemed the only decent thing to do."

She choked a laugh. "Decent?"

"Yes. Decent." His eyes met hers. "Because when you showed up with her gift that night, I realized you were the only woman I wanted. How could I be with Madison after that?"

Hana's throat went dry.

"I've been faithful to you ever since then." He shook his head ruefully. "Against my will. I had no choice. Because I wanted no other woman. Just you."

Her heart was pounding. "Why didn't you say anything?"

"I couldn't let myself seduce you."

"Why?"

"You were too important. I was afraid if I took you to my bed, I'd end up breaking your heart, and then my company would lose the best damn secretary in the world."

"Then you fired me anyway."

Antonio gave a rueful laugh. "Not my finest moment. Can I hire you back?"

"I haven't decided," she said faintly. What was happening? The hotel suite was spinning around her. Antonio, proposing marriage? Was this all a dream?

"Marry me, Hana," he said in a low voice. "I'll be faithful to you until the day I die."

"How can you be sure?"

"You're the only woman I desire." He cupped her cheek. "The one I trust."

She shivered at his nearness, trying not to notice the weight and warmth of his hand against her skin, sending a spiral of sparks down her body. She was suddenly aware that she wore only a creamy silk negligee and robe against her skin. She wasn't even wearing panties beneath.

His hand moved slowly down the edge of her bare neck. He repeated, "Marry me."

She trembled as he pulled her into his arms. Standing in the middle of the penthouse suite, her feet bare on the tatami mat, Hana tilted her head to look up at his handsome face.

"You're going to have my baby." He gently placed his large hand against her belly, sliding over the sensual silk of her robe. "You belong to me," he said huskily. Lowering his head toward hers, he whispered, "As I belong to you…"

Her knees went weak as his lips possessed hers. He was so much larger than she was, so broad-shouldered and strong. She surrendered to his embrace, lost in sensation as their kiss intensified.

His hands cupped the back of her head, lightly brushing down her long dark hair as he caressed slowly down her back, causing the silk to slide over her naked skin.

Pressed against his fully clothed body, she felt his heat and strength, which he tempered and held back, holding her as if she were a precious treasure. Her nipples tightened as they brushed against his suit and tie, her swollen breasts sensitive and heavy. Tension coiled low and deep inside her.

How long had her body cried out to be in Antonio's arms, held with such passionate tenderness? How long had her soul thirsted to hear words like this from anyone?

No wonder the penthouse seemed to spin around her. She was dreaming. She had to be dreaming!

And she wasn't sure she ever wanted to wake up…

Her hands wrapped around his shoulders as she kissed him back with all the longing in her heart. As he deepened the embrace, she felt a sudden urgency, a need to have him closer, to block out the small voice in the back of her mind that was shouting that she needed to stop this, stop it before it was too late. Reaching under his dark cashmere coat, she lifted it off his shoulders and pulled it down his back.

She felt his approval, his answering need. Before the coat had even dropped to the floor, he was yanking off his tie and jacket, unbuttoning his cuffs. Never breaking the kiss, she reached to undo his shirt, desperate to feel the bare skin of his hard-muscled chest beneath her fingertips. The last button caught. Urgently, she yanked hard on the shirt, feeling it finally rip and give way as that too dropped to the floor.

With a low growl, he lifted her up in his arms, against his bare chest, and carried her into the bedroom. Looking up at him breathlessly, she ran her hand along his powerful muscles, lightly dusted with dark hair. His tanned skin felt like satin beneath her hands as she traced over the hard curves of his pecs, brushing his taut nipples with her fingertips, and down farther, to the flat, hard plane of his belly.

Releasing her, he let her slide down his body, the silk caressing her skin, and set her to her feet.

They faced each other in front of the enormous bed.

Reaching out, he undid the belt of her robe, pulling it off her shoulders. As it fell softly to the floor, he wrapped his arms around her, kissing her neck. With a soft gasp, Hana closed her eyes, letting her long dark hair tumble down her back, brushing against the bare skin of her shoulders. Her nipples felt exquisitely sensitive against her nightgown, which left her arms and collarbone bare.

"You belong to me, Hana," he whispered against her skin. "Say it."

"I…" She caught her breath, her heart pounding. It was true. She belonged to him. She had from the day they'd met, when he'd given her that carelessly charming smile and said, *So I hear you're the best secretary in the world and I'm a fool if I don't hire you immediately.* But if she told him she belonged to him, if she said the words aloud, she was afraid she would be lost—lost forever. What next?

Would she agree to marry him?

Raise their child together?

Fall in love with him?

No. That would be a disaster. As crazy as her own parents' marriage had been, at least they'd both loved each other. Hana couldn't imagine the lonely desperation of being trapped in a marriage with a man she loved, who didn't love her back.

And how long would she be able to keep her heart cold, if she married Antonio, and every day, she watched him be a loving father to their child, and every night, he made love to Hana with fiery passion in their bed? How long?

"Say it," he commanded.

Wordlessly, she shook her head.

Antonio gave a sensual smile. Lowering his head to hers, he whispered, "You will…"

His kiss was gentle, deepening until it was so passionate, it was almost overwhelming. She gasped as explosive pleasure ricocheted from her scalp to the hollows of her feet.

Reaching up, she held him tightly. But she couldn't give in to the temptation of being his wife. Perhaps once he possessed her again, he'd lose interest. Soon, perhaps tomorrow, he would remember that he was a workaholic playboy who had no interest in marriage or children. He'd leave her and the baby in peace.

But until then…

She couldn't stop. She couldn't let go. No one else had ever made her feel like this, so alive.

"Querida," he whispered against her lips. And she realized he was trembling. Was it possible that he felt the same overwhelming desire beyond reason that she did? No, surely not with all his experience. And yet…

"Kiss me," she breathed. She didn't want to talk. She didn't want to think.

He held her tight, plundering her mouth with his own, the tip of his tongue teasing and luring her until she no longer knew where he ended and she began. She felt him pull the straps of her nightgown from her shoulders, and it slipped down her body in a soft blur of silk, leaving her naked in front of him in the darkened bedroom.

He slowly looked her over, from her pregnancy-swollen breasts to the soft curve of her belly and hips. His hot gaze lifted, as he unbuttoned his black trousers and pulled off the rest of his clothes, until he stood proudly naked in front of her, his shaft huge and hard.

Falling back on the enormous bed, he pulled her against him, kissing her. Rolling her beneath him, he kissed slowly down her body, cupping her breasts, suckling her until she gasped with pleasure, her back curving up from the bed. She felt the roughness of his tongue swirling against the tight, aching flesh of her nipple, and panted for breath, nearly exploding.

"No, my sweet," he murmured. "Not yet."

He moved down her body, gentle over her belly, before he gripped her hips. He lowered his head and she squeezed her eyes shut, feeling dizzy.

He teased her, kissing along the edge of her hip as his

hands spread her thighs wide. She felt the warmth of his breath, causing prickles of need to rush up and down her body. Lowering his head, he took a long deep taste.

She gasped, shaking. The pleasure was almost too great, and she tried to twist her hips away. But he was relentless. The tip of his tongue moved delicately against her, twisting and swirling around her. He held her down, tempting her to accept the pleasure, working her with his tongue as he pressed a thick finger inside her, then another, pushing deeper, wider, until she exploded.

As she cried out, he moved, lifting his body to position his hips between her legs. Even as she was still shaking with explosions of pleasure, he took a deep breath, then pushed himself inside her, thrusting his full length so deep, deep, deep inside her, until the blazing fire consumed her, and she cried out his name.

Antonio held his breath. He was so deep inside her. He wanted to make this last. He was good at this; he always had been. He'd always had stamina. He could make sex last as long as he wanted. All he had to do was remove his mind from his body. All he had to do was not care.

He would make Hana agree to marry him. He would possess her forever. He just had to stay in control. He had to make her lose her mind. Make her surrender.

But as he felt Hana tighten around him, something felt different. *He* felt different. Shocked, he tried to pull his mind away, his heart, and not care.

But for the first time in his life, it didn't work.

He felt everything, every exquisite sensation. The brush of her soft body beneath his. The satin of her skin. The vision of her long dark hair spread across the pillow, the way her full plump breasts swayed against his arms straining to hold himself up from her.

And most of all, the pure ecstasy of being inside her,

rammed into her hot tight sheath. No—he couldn't—he scrambled to hold himself back. *I feel nothing, I feel nothing—*

Then he heard her scream his name as she exploded a second time, felt the rake of her fingernails against his back as she tightened around the full length of his shaft. Against his will, his body rushed forward like a careening train, leaving him helpless against the pleasure as with a shocked cry, he exploded, pouring himself inside her.

One thrust. That was all his famous stamina had been good for with Hana. *One.*

Still panting for breath, overwhelmed and stunned, he collapsed beside her on the bed, pulling her into his arms.

As reason slowly returned, he tried to understand what had just happened. He'd never had sex without a condom before. He'd never known how intense it would be. That had to be why he'd exploded like some teenaged virgin. Wasn't it?

Antonio looked down at Hana, nestled naked and warm against his chest. Her eyes were closed, her lovely face rosy, her expression hallowed by joy. She sighed with happiness, pressing against him. Kissing her sweaty temple tenderly, he wrapped his arms around her.

He knew he'd satisfied her. But he'd wanted to do so much more. He'd wanted to impress her, to dazzle her, to bring her to fulfillment not just twice, but three or four times.

Instead, he'd been the one who'd been dazzled and overwhelmed, by a girl barely more than a virgin. He took a deep breath. He didn't understand what had happened.

But he could never let it happen again.

Antonio had to remain in control. Always. Not just of others. Of himself most of all.

Strength came from not caring about other people. If you felt nothing, you could withstand injury. If you were impervious to pain, if you didn't give a damn about anyone, you could make it through anything. No one could hurt you.

He looked down at her, cuddled against his shoulder, naked and soft and warm.

One thrust.

She'd made him explode with one thrust.

The changing neon lights from the city below left patterns across her soft skin. He cupped a hand over her naked breast, and was awed when he felt himself start to stir again, when it had been only minutes since he'd had her.

Eyes still closed, she gave a soft, satisfied sigh, cuddling against him. He wondered if he'd ever get enough of her—if he'd ever be truly satisfied, or he'd always feel like a starving man when she was near.

How could he already want her again?

An incredulous smile lifted to his lips. Losing control over his body had been—interesting, at least. How had she made sex so thrilling and new? In the past, it had felt like satisfying an appetite, nothing more. But Hana made his body react in ways he'd never experienced. Even now, when he should have been completely satiated, lying naked beside her, he was once again hard as a rock.

Why? How? Because he'd wanted her for so long? The delayed gratification of finally possessing her after months of repressed desire—and the years before that?

He didn't know the reason, but she made everything feel new.

And he was going to marry her. No other man would be able to touch her—ever. She was his alone.

She would agree to marry him. Soon. Tomorrow, if he could convince her. And he would. When had he ever had trouble sweeping a woman off her feet?

When had he ever had to try?

Now. And he would. He would seduce her with everything he had.

Antonio started to turn away, to reach for his phone, intending to make plans—

Hana's eyes fluttered open as she yawned. "Don't go," she whispered, reaching for him. "Stay with me all night."

No man alive could have resisted her sweetly pleading voice, her softly enticing body, her breasts and hips half-covered by a cotton sheet. He pulled her back against his chest.

"I'm never leaving you again," he said huskily, and he meant every word.

CHAPTER SIX

HANA WOKE WITH a start to discover the gentle pink light of morning suffusing the hotel suite's bedroom. A smile was on her lips, then she remembered with a gasp everything that had happened last night, and looked next to her on the bed.

It was empty.

Antonio was gone.

A crushing disappointment filled her, even as she told herself it was exactly what she'd known would happen. Just as soon as he'd gotten what he wanted, he'd left.

If anything, she should be surprised he'd stayed so long. He'd made love to her three times last night. Her cheeks burned, remembering. Four times, if you counted the interlude in the shower. Her whole body ached with the sweet exhaustion of pleasure. She'd never imagined anyone could make her feel that good, over and over and over. No wonder all those women went so crazy over him. And no wonder he would not commit to any of them for long. He was probably already on the other side of Tokyo, focusing back on the negotiations for the codeshare with Iyokan Airways. His company was his only true love, his family and religion, and now that he'd possessed Hana so thoroughly, Antonio had moved on with—

"Buenos días, querida."

Her lips parted in a gasp as she saw him entering the

bedroom with a tray. He was wearing only a white terry cloth robe, which set off his tanned skin and gorgeous body to perfection. As he came closer to the bed, she saw he'd showered and freshly shaved.

"G-good morning," she stammered, unsure how to react. Even though he'd promised her he'd stay the entire night, she'd never imagined he'd actually do it. He never stayed the night with any of his mistresses. He either came home, or kicked them out, with the excuse of an early morning meeting that was, to be fair, always true.

"I thought you'd be hungry." Antonio set down the silver tray beside her on the bed. She saw a full breakfast of eggs and fruit and toast and other delicious things, beside a pretty red rose in a bud vase. Then she took a deep breath, and frowned.

"Um…thank you?"

"You're welcome." He gave her a sensual smile. "Coffee?"

Her stomach, which had been strangely finicky for the last few weeks for a cause she now knew was morning sickness, immediately rebelled, and she shook her head. "Actually," she said, careful not to sniff again, "Could you take that coffee into the other room? It…"

He looked at her. "The smell makes you sick?" He immediately grabbed the carafe and left the suite. He returned empty-handed a moment later. "Orange juice?"

"Thank you."

He poured it, then handed her the glass. Now that the coffee smell was gone, she took a deep breath, inhaling his delectable scent of clean male and woodland spice and something indefinably him. Now *that* smelled good to her. Too good, even.

He sat down on the edge of the bed, looking down at her tenderly. "How did you sleep?"

"Not long enough," she said, blushing a little.

Antonio gave her a wicked grin. "Perhaps we'll need to take a nap later, eh?"

Based on the way he was looking at her, she doubted it would involve much actual sleep.

How could she already want him again? How was it possible? Was she really such a wanton?

Yes, she realized, looking up with a shiver into his dark Spanish eyes. She was utterly a wanton where Antonio Delacruz was concerned.

Oh, this wasn't good at all. She'd believed with all her heart that one more night would make him lose interest, and stop him from trying to tempt her with dreams that couldn't possibly come true—dreams of marrying him, of raising their child together. She couldn't let herself hope, when after two years of watching him, she knew it was a hopeless fantasy. Men like Antonio never changed!

But as she felt his hot gaze on her, she felt the answering tremble of desire across her body. She quickly set down her orange juice. "Aren't you heading back into the office this morning? To finish the Iyokan deal?"

He shook his head. "I thought I might show you around Tokyo."

Wide-eyed, Hana looked at him, then her lips lifted at the edges. "I've been here a few times. I speak Japanese fairly well. And you're going to show *me* around?"

He looked disgruntled. He was accustomed to being the one with all the answers, the one in control.

But after last night… Hana thought of the first time they'd made love, when he'd exploded almost the very moment he'd pushed inside her, when she was still lost in the swirl of her own pleasure. He was a famous lover. That couldn't have been his plan.

Something had made him lose control.

Though perhaps this was a normal changeup in his repertoire. How would she know? She'd been screaming his name—she blushed at the memory—so he'd known there was no reason to wait. The etiquette of sex was still a mystery to her. But he'd certainly made it last longer the next three times. *Lots* longer. They'd been in bed the first time. After that, it had been against the wall. In the shower. Against the windows overlooking the neon lights. Her eyes became unfocused as a flash of heat went through her, lost in the memories.

"We can't stay here," Antonio said huskily. She blinked, her cheeks warming as she paused chewing her toast. Was she that transparent? Could he see that she'd been picturing just that?

"Of course not," she said hurriedly. "You think I want to stay in bed all day?"

He looked at her knowingly, and her blush deepened.

Then, shaking his head, he scowled. "The waiter wouldn't let me pay for room service. Apparently your dear friend Tanaka," his voice held an edge, "gave his staff orders that this penthouse suite is not to be charged for anything."

She couldn't imagine a proud man like Antonio allowing another man to pay his way. Particularly not someone he saw as a rival. Biting her lip, she said awkwardly, "Ren is a dear friend…"

"We will move to my hotel room tonight," he cut her off.

"It's not up to you." She lifted her chin. "I can sleep where I please."

Antonio gave her an easy smile. "Of course." He moved closer to the bed in his white terry cloth robe, and she had a flash of tanned, powerful legs and his hard-muscled chest. "Do you want more breakfast?"

Looking down at the tray, Hana realized she'd somehow gobbled it all down. "No…"

His sensual lips curved. "Perhaps I'm being hasty to

want to tour the sights of Tokyo. We could stay in, and order more…"

Pushing the tray aside, she jumped out of bed, snatching up her silk robe, which had been left in a puddle on the floor last night when they'd…but she wasn't going to think about that. She wrapped the robe around herself and tied it firmly. "How did the negotiations end yesterday?"

"A total disaster," he said cheerfully.

"Don't you want to try to save the deal? We've been working on it for months!"

Antonio shook his head.

"You're just letting it go?" she asked in astonishment.

He looked down at her, as they stood together next to the enormous bed with its tangled sheets warmed by golden light. He murmured, "I have a different priority today."

She didn't have to ask what it was. He'd made his determination plain. But it seemed incredible to her that Antonio Delacruz was putting his desire to marry her as a greater priority than the business deal that would give him routes into Asia. She snorted. "Are you trying to impress me by giving up the deal just to spend time with me?"

"Would that work?"

"No," she lied, "and I think it's ridiculous when you know how important this deal is to CrossWorld Airways. Do you want to expand into Asia or not?"

Antonio came so close to her, their bodies almost touched. He looked down at her, his darkly handsome face serious. "I want to marry you."

Her mouth went dry, and with an effort, she turned away. "This isn't a game!"

"You're the only one who seems to think it is."

"I'm not going to marry you, Antonio. Never ever!"

For a moment, his dark eyes looked vulnerable. Then a veil came down over his gaze. "We'll see."

She must have imagined that look in his eyes, she decided. Antonio Delacruz had no feelings. He was heartless. He prided himself on it.

But he was starting to get to her. Could Antonio really care about this baby? Could he actually commit to raising a child? Hana shivered. Could he commit to *her*?

She was still stunned by what he'd told her of his childhood. He'd always been notoriously closed-lipped about his past. What people knew about him was mostly the business legend, how he'd taken one small leased airplane in the south of Spain and turned it into an empire through hard work and grit. He'd taken big chances, and somehow made those risks pay off.

But no one knew the story of the newborn baby left on the church steps. The young boy who'd been taken home by two different families, then heartlessly rejected. The teenager who'd offered his heart to his first lover, only to be spurned.

No wonder he'd never wanted children. No wonder his company was his only family and money his way of keeping score. Who could blame him for having no heart after that?

"Why is marriage suddenly so important to you?" she asked. "You've never wanted it before."

"I told you. My child must always know they were wanted. He—or she—will have a name. A home."

A home. Emotion hit her. How could she refuse? Hana took a deep breath.

"Fine," she said quietly. "You can be in our baby's life. You're the father. The baby can have your name."

Antonio's shoulders seemed to relax slightly. He looked at her. "And you will marry me."

But on that precipice, she shivered with fear. Allowing him to help raise their baby was one thing. But to willingly promise to spend the rest of her life with a playboy who'd never love her? Her heart wasn't as cold as his.

But he was offering her everything she'd once dreamed about. A real home for their baby. Marriage. A settled family. Stability. Security.

"Where would we live?" she heard herself ask in a small voice.

"Madrid," he said huskily. "In the house you already love."

Madrid. She looked away, her heart in her throat. She thought of the *palacio*, all the people she'd come to care about, the company's world headquarters, the warm Spanish sun and palm trees rustling softly in the wind. Madrid. "I… I don't know."

Silence fell.

"Get dressed," he said suddenly.

Surprised, she looked at him. "For what?"

Antonio gave her a crooked smile. "Didn't you offer to show me the sights of Tokyo?"

"Yes, but…what about the Iyokan deal?"

"It can wait." He went back to the foyer, returning with an expensive designer overnight bag. He flashed her a grin. "Garcia delivered this an hour ago when I called for room service."

She watched as he opened the bag. "What are you doing?"

Glancing through the window at the bright sun and blue sky, he pulled out a black jacket, white button-down shirt and black trousers. "You're going to show me what you love about this city." His lips curved as he looked up at her, then glanced suggestively at the bed. "Unless you'd rather linger…"

"No," she said quickly. Any more time in bed would surely end with his engagement ring on her finger. She had to resist. *Had* to. Until he came to his senses and realized marriage was the last thing he wanted. In the meantime she couldn't let her heart talk her into surrendering her body, her soul and her life!

Safer to be out on the streets, where she wouldn't be tempted into wicked pleasures that might lure her into becoming his bride.

Or so Hana thought.

But for the next few hours, as she took Antonio to see the most famous tourist sights of Tokyo, even convincing him to leave his driver and bodyguard behind so they could experience the sidewalks and the notoriously crowded subways, she wasn't so sure.

Because she'd never seen Antonio like this, so attentive, so good-natured, so darkly charming as he told her amusing stories about how he'd broken into the aviation business, long before they'd met, and the foibles of wealthy acquaintances, stories she'd never heard as his secretary. She was dazzled by his graveled, sexy voice, with its slight Spanish accent, and the burn of his dark eyes every time he looked at her. She kept thinking that any moment, he'd remember the critical importance of the business deal, and announce his departure. But he didn't.

They visited shrines, parks, museums, peered at buildings constructed for the Olympics, then the noodle museum and lunch. He was always beside her, his hand protectively at the ready. Later, as they took a boat meandering down a waterway that had once been a moat around Edo Castle, she started to shiver in her pale pink sundress and sandals, and he'd pulled off his jacket and wrapped it around her shoulders. But she wasn't shivering from the cold.

Looking up at him as their small boat went slowly down Chidorigafuchi Moat beneath the blooming cherry trees, Hana's heart was filled with yearning. How she wished this could be real—that he could be her husband, and she could be his wife, that they could be partners, forever and ever. But she knew the risks. What if he changed his mind? Or worse—what if she gave him her heart and he rejected it?

"What are you thinking?" Antonio said softly. Another

thing he'd never said to her before, and that she doubted he'd ever said to any woman.

"Nothing," she said, looking away. She heard his phone ring from his jacket pocket. Again. It had been ringing incessantly since they'd left the restaurant. "Oh." Reaching into his jacket still hanging over her shoulders, she handed him the phone, careful not to look at it so she didn't seem like she was invading his privacy. "Here."

Taking it, Antonio frowned.

Hana shrank a little, watching him. Who was calling him? Few people had his direct number. Was it another woman? He'd had many mistresses in the past. And time after time, she'd seen him treat those women so casually, discarding them like drive-through wrappers after lunch. Easily consumed, easily forgotten, easily replaced.

Glancing at the phone, Antonio turned it off without comment. He gave it back to her. "Sorry."

"It's fine." Putting it back in the jacket pocket, she told herself she wasn't going to ask. She had no intention of marrying him, so why would she care who called him?

She was grateful, in fact. It reminded her why she had to stay strong and resist his marriage proposal.

Because she was tempted. After they reached the end of the boat ride, as he held out his hand to help Hana out, she couldn't help but imagine what it would be like if every day could be like this. Having a home together. Working together. Raising a child together. Being happy.

But this feeling couldn't last. Even if Antonio could be faithful to her as he vowed, he was a workaholic who loved only his company. He'd never make room in his life to be a full-time husband and father. That wouldn't change. Ever.

Although, she suddenly realized, he'd just given up a critical business deal, just to spend the day with her and see the sights of Tokyo…

"What about shopping?" Antonio asked, his dark eyes

crinkling in a smile. "I heard Tokyo has some of the best
luxury shops in the world."

She paused. "Yes, it does. Why? Do you need something?"

"Yes," he said firmly. "I do."

Hours later, they came out of yet another lavish Ginza
boutique, a toy store so enormous it was five stories high.
Going out onto the main shopping avenue of Chuo-Dori,
Hana was still shaking her head.

"The baby won't be born until October," she chided.
"And this is too much! Don't you think you should wait?"

"Wait for what?"

"You haven't even seen a scan yet. I'm only ten weeks
pregnant."

He stopped. "Did the doctor you saw hint there might
be a problem?"

"No, she said everything looked perfect. But it just
seems—"

"What?"

"Like tempting fate!"

Looking down at her, he said gruffly, "I make my own
fate."

That was certainly true. Hana shook her head with
a laugh. "Toys, baby clothes. The most expensive baby
stroller I've ever seen. I've seen cars that cost less! It's just
a good thing the shops deliver, or you'd have needed to hire
a van and staff to carry it all."

"I wanted to buy more." Standing beside her on the busy
sidewalk, he looked down at her seriously. "I wanted to buy
things for you. Why won't you let me?"

Hana looked away, feeling her cheeks burn. "I'm not
your responsibility."

"I'd like you to be." The intensity of his dark gaze
burned through her. She couldn't bear it. Tugging on his
hand, she started walking. They passed other lavish lux-

ury department stores and boutiques. Glancing down the street at the enormous, exclusive Bulgari flagship on the corner, he stopped her. "I want to buy you a ring, any ring you like, the biggest damn diamond in the entire store."

"I don't need a big diamond," she objected. All around them, Tokyo's traffic whirled past, making her dizzy.

"I'd give anything," Antonio said gruffly, "to get down on one knee and propose marriage in any way that would make you say yes. With a twenty-carat diamond ring, a sapphire, an emerald—even a damn ring from a gumball machine." He looked at her. "What would it take, Hana? Tell me. Whatever it is, I can do it. Just tell me."

Her heart was in her throat. Her eyelashes fluttered, brushing her cheek as she looked down at her own hands. She couldn't look him in the eye. He couldn't know how close she was to falling. If he had any idea of how tempted she was to surrender—

"Mr. Delacruz!" a voice called loudly. *"Señor!"*

Turning, she saw Ramon Garcia's hulking form waving at them through the crowded sidewalks. "There you are," the man panted. "We've been looking for you. All over. The lawyers are frantic."

"What do you want?" Antonio demanded, clearly annoyed.

"It's—the Iyokan deal." The muscular bodyguard leaned over, gasping to catch his breath. She wondered how long he'd been running. "Another company made—an offer. Iyokan says if they don't get a—sweetened deal—by the end of the day, they're going to walk. Please." He waved desperately toward the street. "The car is around the corner. Come now."

"I turned off my phone for a reason," Antonio said coldly. "Tell the lawyers I'm busy." And he turned back to Hana. "What's next?"

She stared at him, thinking of the hundreds of hours

she'd spent over the last few months, helping him assess and prepare the legal and financial documentation for the negotiations. This deal was CrossWorld Airways's entrée into the Asian market, the key to make his company a truly global power.

"Are you crazy?" she demanded. "Go! Go now!"

"I don't care. Let it fail." Antonio looked at her steadily. "I'm not going anywhere. I'm here. For you."

Her jaw dropped.

He was truly willing to fail, and let a competitor win in his place? Just to impress her? Just to *woo* her?

No. No way.

"Forget that." Hana's eyes narrowed. "We're going. Right now."

"We?" Antonio blinked. "But I thought—"

"You thought I'd let the deal we've both killed ourselves over for months just disappear up in smoke? No way!" She turned to the bodyguard. "We're coming now."

She heard Antonio's ragged intake of breath.

"Querida..." he breathed, and, pulling her into his arms, he looked down at her with such pure joy that it melted her right through. She beamed back at him, and then her smile slid from her face.

Oh, she was in so much trouble.

CHAPTER SEVEN

Two HOURS LATER, as Antonio walked out of the board-room with the Iyokan Airways deal signed and delivered, he looked down at the amazing, intoxicating woman beside him.

"We did it," he said, still slightly dazed.

Hana turned to him, smiling. "*You* did it."

Antonio shook his head. She was the one who'd known every detail necessary to hammer out the negotiations and get everything signed. Her beauty hadn't hurt either, or her fluency in Japanese. The CEO of Iyokan Airways had obviously been charmed. Even now, as they walked out of the office toward the elevator, trailing lawyers in their wake, Antonio still wondered if the other airline had made the deal in order to partner with CrossWorld Airways—or to partner with Hana Everly.

Either way, with one stroke, Antonio's airline now had the international reach he'd always dreamed of.

"The deal was signed because of you," Antonio said quietly.

"I couldn't let you lose it. Not when it means so much to you."

He thought of how hard she'd worked, at his side, night and day. "And you."

"I love our company, too," she said simply.

Our company.

He'd never thought of it that way before.

"We're all going to celebrate," Emika Ito, the pretty young director of the Japanese lead team, called out to them. "Come join us!"

"Thanks, but we have plans," Antonio replied automatically, not looking away from Hana's beautiful face.

"We'll be at the hotel bar in Ginza if you change your mind!"

"What plans?" Hana asked him.

Plans? Antonio's only plan was that he wanted to feel like this forever, triumphant after their business deal, with this sensual, brilliant woman in his arms. No one else could have done it—none but Hana.

"You're right. The company isn't just mine," he heard himself say suddenly. "It's ours."

"I know," she said cheerfully. "You couldn't possibly succeed without me." Then she saw his expression. Her forehead furrowed. "What are you trying to tell me?"

Yes, what? His heart was suddenly pounding. He could hardly believe he was saying it. But he slowly said, "You know this company is my life. My family. But you and the baby are part of that now. You should be with me."

"You—" Licking her lips, she said, "You want to hire me back as your secretary?"

"Not my secretary." He took a deep breath, then plunged in. "My full partner."

Her lips parted. "Wh-what?"

Antonio took her hands in his own. "Maybe I can't offer you love like in the fairy tales. But we could have an incredible marriage. We'll work together, create a worldwide empire—a legacy that someday our child will inherit."

Her warm brown eyes met his. They looked equal parts terrified and dazzled. "We'll spend our days together, as a team? Working together like before?"

"Better than before. This time, we'll be partners. Our

family. Our company." Running his hands through her long dark hair, he whispered, "I can imagine nothing better than spending our days together running our empire, and our nights setting the world on fire."

He heard her gasp. Her cheeks were pale as she looked up at him in shock. "You'd give me half your company—just like that?"

Antonio could hardly believe it himself. His heart was pounding. He felt almost sick if he let himself think about it that way. His company meant everything to him. Even now, part of his heart was screaming that he couldn't risk this, couldn't, not even with someone he trusted as much as Hana. His company was everything he had.

But what risk? He needed her in his company. He needed her at his side, slaying dragons. Almost as much as he needed her in his bed.

He wanted to marry her. If she refused this, he did not know what more he could offer her.

Standing by the elevator on the top floor of the Tokyo office, he looked at her. "What do you say, Hana?" he asked in a low voice. "Will you have me?"

"If you would offer me half of your company, then some part of you must—"

She stopped.

He prompted, "Must?"

"Must…really want to marry me."

He had the strange feeling that she'd been about to say something else. "How much clearer can I be?"

Hana looked up at him, her eyes shining. "I thought I knew you," she whispered. "But maybe I don't. Because the man I knew could never do what you've just done."

Antonio felt a drop of cold sweat go down his back. Half his company. How could he have offered her that? How?

But he had to win. He could not lose Hana. She was the

heart of CrossWorld Airways. She was the mother of his unborn child.

"Does that mean yes?" he asked quietly.

Her eyes were suddenly full of tears. "What if you regret it?"

"I won't," he said harshly, praying he wouldn't.

The elevator dinged as the door slid open. Behind them, more lawyers were coming out of the boardroom with their assistants and briefcases. Grabbing Hana's hand, Antonio pulled her inside the elevator, away from prying eyes.

Taking her into his arms, he whispered, "Say you'll be mine."

He could feel her trembling, tottering on the brink of surrender.

"Just...just let me think," she breathed.

Antonio's mind whirled. They were both exhilarated after signing the deal. Perhaps tomorrow she'd have a clearer head. Perhaps tomorrow, Ren Tanaka would be back from Osaka and convince her she could do better than Antonio. He looked down at her.

Which she could.

Cupping her face in both his hands, he vowed, "I'll make you happy, Hana. We'll have a marriage. A home. I'll be a good husband and father. Everything you ever wanted. I swear it. Marry me. Marry me now. Today."

For a moment, he thought she was still going to say no, and his heart thundered in his chest. He'd never let himself be so vulnerable, not since he was eighteen. In fact, he'd created his whole life to make sure he never felt vulnerable like this.

Hana took a deep breath.

"Yes," she said quietly.

"You will?" Antonio felt a rush he'd never felt before. Every business deal he'd ever made, even the first one that had allowed him to lease a plane for little more than a promise of a percentage of future profits, paled compared to this. He needed Hana in his bed. Tonight. Knowing he would possess her, now and for always.

He needed her as his wife.

And so it was that an hour later, they were signing the document in a plain civil registration in a government office in the city. Hana seemed slightly bewildered, as if she wasn't sure how it had happened so fast. But with Tokyo's straightforward marriage laws, there was no need to wait. Neither of them had ever been married before. They'd just needed passports, his driver and Ramon Garcia as witnesses, and a simple document from their embassies. They wore the same clothes as when they'd left Tanaka's hotel that morning, Antonio in a white shirt and black trousers, Hana in her pale pink sundress, clutching the tiny bouquet of cherry blossoms he'd impulsively bought from the flower shop across the street.

And just like that, it was done. They were married.

After a lifetime of being absolutely sure he would never, *could* never, marry anyone, he could hardly believe how easy it had been to marry Hana.

They left the small government office and came out into the fading afternoon light, Antonio holding the marriage document with one hand and Hana's arm with the other. As they came out of the building, a beam of light fell on her, and he stopped.

Golden light caressed her long dark hair like a halo, frosting her soft cheeks, her pale pink sundress and sandals. She looked fresh-faced, sweet and innocent as a country girl—except for the big diamond ring on her finger, which he'd insisted on buying at Cartier en route to their civil ceremony. It wasn't the biggest diamond in the store, but it had been the most expensive, because it was perfect.

Like Hana, Antonio thought, dazzled. Perfect in every way.

And now she was his—forever. He shivered. He couldn't wait to get her into bed. He'd made love to her four times last night, but he still wanted her to the point of madness. It was insane, the grip she had over him. Normally that sense of lost control might have scared him. But that was nothing.

Not compared to the fact that he'd just married her without a prenuptial agreement.

He could hardly have asked for one, after his big speech about wanting to share his company with her. And the last thing he'd wanted was to wait for his lawyers, when he'd been desperate to marry her today before the municipal office closed. They'd barely squeaked in before closing time as it was. He hadn't wanted to give her a night to think it over or change her mind—especially since he'd heard her call Ren Tanaka as they left the skyscraper in Marunouchi, leaving him a message about her hasty wedding.

But now, thinking of what he'd just done, Antonio felt ice slide down his spine.

He'd promised her half his company. He'd married her without a prenup.

Without his airline, Antonio was nothing. He was still that dirty, worthless little orphan no one wanted, no use to anyone, not even his own family—

With a deep breath, Antonio pushed the old fear aside. He could trust Hana, damn it. She would never leave him. She'd never try to wrest control of CrossWorld Airways from him. She would respect his decisions. At least she always had before.

Before he'd given her everything...

"Congratulations, you two!" Ramon Garcia exclaimed, interrupting Antonio's unsettling reverie. "How are you going to celebrate? Join the team at the bar? Wait until they hear!"

Antonio's gaze traced from the delicate corner of Hana's neck to the full curves of her breasts. "I have something else in mind."

All he wanted to do was get back to his own lavish hotel suite—far from Tanaka's hotel—and make love to his wife.

His wife!

"Oh, please." Hana turned to him with her big brown eyes. "Can't we meet with the others?" She added wistfully, "I'd love to celebrate with everyone…"

There was no way he could deny her anything right now.

"If you wish it, *querida*," he agreed, and Garcia and Haruto Nakamura, the Japanese driver, cheered. His wife, with an adorable smile, lifted on her tiptoes to place her hands around his shoulders, one hand still holding her small bouquet.

"You've made me so happy," she whispered, and Antonio's fear melted away as his heart swelled with pride. All he wanted to do was keep the joyful light in her eyes, and know he'd caused it to be there, now and forever.

As Nakamura went to get the car, Antonio gripped Hana's hand. In the back seat, even when they reached his luxury hotel—the biggest, most glamorous international hotel in Ginza—he never let go. As they walked into the hotel bar, which was sleekly black-and-white with high ceilings and modern art, the two of them were met with thunderous applause.

"Congratulations!" Emika Ito cried, holding up a champagne toast toward them. Stopping in the doorway, Antonio looked around in astonishment. Had everyone already heard about their wedding? But how?

The young woman continued, "The deal was lost, then it was struck. To the couple of the hour!"

Everyone applauded wildly, the entire Japan lead team,

and the New York lawyers who'd been staying here the last few weeks to prep for the Iyokan deal. Emika had not been referring to their wedding, but the deal he'd actually forgotten about in all the excitement of marrying Hana.

He really was losing his mind...

Nestling close, Hana looked up at him with a blushing, intimate smile that he felt all over his body. Looking back at his employees, Antonio held up his hand for silence.

"Thank you to everyone who made this deal possible today. You will take CrossWorld Airways into not just Asia, but the future!" He paused to allow for applause, taking champagne from the tray of a passing waiter. Hana held her flute, but did not drink it. "But I have other news, even more important to me personally."

"What could be more important than business?" one of his lawyers hollered. Antonio smiled, then looked down at Hana in his arms.

"This wonderful woman, whom most of you know as my executive assistant, just became more. She's become, this very hour, my wife."

There was a gasp.

Hana looked up at him, biting her lip nervously. Antonio hesitated, wondering if he should hide the baby news for a few weeks more. But why? Half the people in the room had probably already guessed it, just based on the quickness of the marriage. Best to get all the juicy scandal out at once, and be done with it. "There's more." He paused. "We're expecting a baby."

The gasp became a roar, followed by more applause, as people surged forward to congratulate them, their faces all various degrees of shock and delight.

Hana was immediately circled by a group of women exclaiming over her and asking questions about the sudden wedding, and about her pregnancy. Antonio had a brief glimpse of her shy, happy smile as she was led away, before his view was blocked by one of his sharpest New York lawyers, coming forward with a well-cut suit and a big grin.

"I can't believe it, Mr. Delacruz! Here I thought you were immune!" The man shook his head, rolling his eyes heavenward as he held up his martini glass. "A toast to love! It gets the best of all of us, sooner or later!"

"We should toast marriage," a female lawyer chirped behind him. "Half our firm's billable hours come from divorce!" At the head lawyer's harsh glare, she blanched and mumbled, "Er, not that that will ever happen to you, Mr. Delacruz."

"Of course not." The head lawyer, a corporate shark whose going rate was three thousand dollars an hour, turned back to him with a blinding smile. "We've never handled Mr. Delacruz's personal matters. So tell me," he leaned forward confidentially, "Who did your prenup? I never heard a whisper. Tokyo's top firm, I assume." He gave a jovial laugh. "Obviously. It's not like you'd want to just *give away* half your company."

It hurt to hear those painful words out loud. Antonio flinched, feeling like he'd just been punched in the face, knocked out of his sensual dream into a harsh, cold reality.

Heart pounding, he slowly turned toward Hana. Across the room, she was smiling happily as she showed the other women the sparkling diamond on her finger. Then, suddenly, she looked up at the door, and her face lit up. With a gasp, she ran toward the door, her dark hair and pale pink sundress flying behind her.

Ren Tanaka stood in the doorway, his handsome face blank as he dropped his suitcase to the floor with a bang.

Watching as his wife threw her arms around the other man, Antonio felt suddenly sick inside.

He'd just given away his life, everything he cared about, everything that gave him value, to a woman who could now ruin him with a mere flick of her finger.

If Hana ever wanted to destroy Antonio, she could now. She could burn him to the ground. Leave him desolate and worthless and alone.

What had he just done?

"You're here!" Hana cried, throwing her arms around her best friend. "I didn't think you'd make it!"

"I didn't," Ren said grimly, pulling away from her impulsive embrace. "I dropped everything and took the bullet train from Osaka. But I'm still too late."

She'd texted Ren her current location, after having left a long, rushed message on his phone hours before. She'd hoped and feared in equal parts that Ren would somehow make it to their wedding—hoped, because he was her only family, and feared, because she was afraid he'd try to talk her out of it or make a scene.

The truth was, Hana still couldn't quite believe she'd done it. She'd married Antonio.

But he'd offered her everything she'd ever wanted.

A home. A real father for their baby. Marriage. Passion.

And half the company. That was most shocking of all. Antonio—offering to share his airline?

For all this time, she'd told herself that a selfish playboy workaholic like Antonio Delacruz would never change.

But the truth was he already *had*. In the space of two days, he'd gone from rejecting her, to offering child support money, to asking her to be his mistress, to proposing marriage and asking to share full-time parenting.

Hana thought of what she'd learned about his heartbreaking childhood. And yet he was still willing to take the risk.

The more she learned about Antonio, the more she—cared.

And he was starting to care for her as well. He had to be. Because there was no other reason he would have offered to share his company.

If he was willing to share his most precious possession with her, didn't that also have to mean he'd be willing to truly share his life?

"How could you do it, Hana?" Ren demanded. "How could you marry him?"

Blinking, she looked at her friend in the elegant, crowded bar. His handsome face looked so strange. She said slowly, "Antonio is the father of my baby."

"And when I left Tokyo, you said you'd never see him again."

"He changed my mind."

"How?"

"He's not the man I thought he was, Ren. He wants to settle down, and be a father to our baby. Look, I know our wedding was a little sudden…"

"*Sudden*." Ren's face looked grimmer still. "Is that what you call it?" He looked around the modern bar, filled with Antonio's employees and lawyers in their office clothes, getting drunk on martinis and sake. "This is your wedding reception?" He glanced at her pale pink sundress, which was starting to look a little limp after a full day of wear. "That's your wedding dress?"

She stiffened. "Do you really think I care about the wedding details?"

Ren stared at her, and she blanched as she remembered all the times as a girl that she'd described ridiculous dreams about her faraway, someday wedding.

Her throat suddenly hurt. A moment before, she'd convinced herself that their impulsive ceremony had been perfect. Efficient. No plans, no worries, just done and over with.

But now, it suddenly occurred to her that she'd never have another wedding. Or the chance to experience romantic, fairy-tale love.

Good, she told herself. So their child would never know how it felt to be excluded, as Hana had.

But the reassurance felt hollow.

"You don't even have a wedding cake," Ren said contemptuously, looking around. "Where are your seven tiers with white buttercream frosting flowers?"

"I don't care about cake." She lifted her hand defiantly. "Besides. He got me this."

Grabbing her hand, Ren closely examined the enormous platinum-set diamond ring. Then he snorted, releasing her hand. "That had to be his idea. Not yours."

Pulling back her arm, she said stiffly, "It doesn't matter. The wedding doesn't matter. Just the marriage. We're having a baby. We're a family now. Partners."

Silence fell between them, even as all around them people laughed over the bar's loud, raucous music. One of the New York lawyers was yelling, "A toast! To annual growth next year of eight percent!"

"Nine!" someone else roared, sloshing his drink.

Ren looked at her in the shadowy entrance of the bar.

"Partners," he said sardonically. "Very romantic."

Her cheeks heated. She couldn't meet his gaze. "You know I never asked for love."

"Yes," he said. "I know."

With an intake of breath, she looked up, and saw the blatant pain in Ren's dark eyes. Putting a hand to her mouth, she whispered, "I'm sorry. I'm so sorry. It's so hideously unfair. I never meant to—"

"I know." He tried to smile. "I was stupid to let myself love you when I knew you wouldn't love me back. But I convinced myself—" He turned away. "It was stupid."

Hana felt grief that she'd hurt her best friend. And on the edges of that grief, she felt fear.

I was stupid to let myself love you when I knew you wouldn't love me back.

No, she told herself. She wouldn't let herself fall in love with Antonio. No matter how charming or wonderful her husband might be. Because no matter how much he'd changed, she knew he'd never love her back. That miracle would be a step too far.

But as she looked across the crowded room, she saw her husband sitting at the bar. He lifted his head and his dark eyes burned through her soul.

Taking a deep breath, Hana quickly turned away. "Please, Ren. Just be happy."

"Don't worry about me." His eyes narrowed. "But if your husband ever does the slightest thing to cause you pain—if he hurts you or disappoints you in any way—"

"He won't," Hana assured him. "Will you be all right?"

"I'll be fine."

"I never meant to—"

"Stop." A low strangled curse came from his throat. "I'll get over it, Hana."

"Get over it?"

He looked at her. "Loving you."

She'd never thought she could feel so sad, standing beside her best friend on what was supposed to be the happiest day of her life. Her view was suddenly blocked by Emika Ito.

"Congratulations again," she told Hana warmly. "Married, and expecting a baby!" She shook her head, grinning. "No one thought Mr. Delacruz would settle down. I've always heard you were an amazing person, Hana. Now I think you're a rock star!"

"Oh," said Hana, who didn't feel remotely rock star-ish at the moment.

Emika turned to Ren. "Mr. Delacruz wants to talk to you."

His eyes darkened. "He does?"

"Alone."

Antonio and Ren—talking alone? Anxiety ripped through Hana. "I'll come with you."

"No," he said.

"You don't have to do it—"

"You're wrong," Ren said grimly. He looked toward the bar. "I can hardly wait."

Glancing toward the doorway from where he was sitting, Antonio saw Ren Tanaka coming forward with a glower and turned back to the bartender. "Double scotch."

As the drink was placed in front of him, Antonio took a sip, letting the harsh liquid burn him from the inside. Scotch for a wedding reception. It should have been champagne, with toasts to the bridal couple, instead of to the future profitability of CrossWorld Airways. But then, as Antonio had told Hana, they weren't a normal couple.

No. Any normal man in his position would have insisted on a prenup, instead of stupidly offering up half his fortune.

He could trust Hana, he told himself. He could trust her. He did trust her.

Antonio pressed the glass against his forehead, to cool his hot skin.

"I hope you're proud of yourself." Tanaka's voice was cold as he slid into the empty bar stool beside him.

Turning, Antonio bared his teeth in a smile. "If you mean proud of marrying Hana, then yes, I'm very proud. She's carrying my child and I've done right by her."

"*Right*," Tanaka sneered. He glanced back at Hana, who was still by the doorway talking to Emika Ito, throwing them worried glances. "The right thing would have been to set her free to marry someone who's worthy of her."

"That's you, I suppose."

"More than you'll ever be." Tanaka looked around. "This is how you marry Hana? No cake, no wedding dress, just some office party in a bar?"

The last thing Antonio needed was to be criticized just when he was already kicking himself about the prenup. His lip twisted in a snarl. "She doesn't love you, Tanaka. Get over it."

"She might have found a way to love me, someday, if you'd just left her alone. But you couldn't, could you? You selfishly took her for yourself."

"She kissed me first," Antonio took malicious pleasure in informing him. "I didn't seduce her. *She* kissed *me*."

The younger man's eyes flashed, then his jaw set. "You're a selfish bastard, Delacruz. You jump from one place and person to the next, because you're afraid if you stick around anywhere too long, people will realize you're nothing. An empty husk."

From long practice, Antonio kept his expression amused, so the other man wouldn't know he'd hit his target. His voice was cool as he pointed out, "And yet Hana still chose me over you."

"A choice you'll make her regret, won't you? Starting with this pathetic wedding."

"I've planned her an amazing honeymoon," said Antonio, who'd just that moment thought of it.

Tanaka muttered something in Japanese.

Antonio bared his teeth. "Consider your friendship with her over. Stay away from my wife."

"You'll never be good enough for her," the younger man replied coldly. "You know it. I know it." As the two men looked at Hana across the room, she turned and met Antonio's gaze. Almost at once, her stunning face lit up, and he unwillingly felt his heart rise. Then he heard Tanaka add under his breath, "And someday soon, Hana will know it, too."

CHAPTER EIGHT

HEAVEN. SHE WAS in heaven.

The hot Caribbean sun was shining on a sea that was so impossibly blue it burned Hana's eyes to look at it from the pink sand beach.

Looking out from the lounge chair beneath the open-air cabana, where she was stretched out in a turquoise string bikini, she lifted her sunglasses and watched her husband rise from the sea.

Rivulets of water ran from his dark hair down his thick neck and over the muscles and hollows of his torso, to the edge of his swim trunks. All that water, and as she looked at him, her mouth went dry.

Coming over to the cabana, which was just wooden pillars, a slatted roof and white curtains perched over the sand, Antonio smiled down at her, his eyes crinkling. "You should have joined me in the water."

"I was reading…" Then she saw that her book had fallen from her lap, and lay upside down in the sand, and blushed. His smile widened, and he sat beside her on the lounge chair.

"I have other ways to entertain you," he said softly, running his large hand from her neck down the valley between her breasts, to her belly, naked and warmed by the sun. Her breathing quickened.

Her husband. Antonio was her husband now. She still

couldn't quite believe it. When they'd left their reception in Tokyo, he'd surprised her by taking her on a honeymoon to his private island in the Caribbean, where she knew for a fact he'd never taken anyone. It had always been his private demesne, where he went to get away from the world.

But he'd brought her here.

"You're so good to me," she said.

"So you don't mind not having the wedding of your dreams?"

Not for the first time, Hana wondered what Ren had said to him in Tokyo. The last thing she wanted was for Antonio to feel bad. "I didn't need a romantic wedding."

Antonio gave her a skeptical look.

"Well, the honeymoon has more than made up for it," she said, sighing with pleasure as she leaned back on the lounge chair, and that, at least, was utterly true.

After three days on his private island, she felt deliciously good all over. It was the longest vacation either of them had ever had. With their phones turned off and the company's decisions temporarily delegated to the COO, there had been nothing for them to do but enjoy each other.

Instead of thinking about work, they'd spent their days making love. Staying in a luxurious, sprawling villa, cared for by a live-in staff of ten, they'd laughed, splashing on the beach, kissing in the shallow blue water, drinking virgin piña coladas and eating seafood brought fresh from the sea.

"You look tense," her husband informed her now with a wicked smile. "Let me give you a massage."

Hana shivered as he slowly ran his hands down the length of her bare legs. As she felt his fingers caress and stroke the hollows of her feet, her gaze traced dreamily over the satin smoothness of her husband's powerful body. His muscular thighs, his flat belly. His thick forearms, laced with dark hair. The hard line of his cheekbones and jaw, shadowed with bristle. His cruelly sensual lips.

Dappled sunlight flashed through the slatted roof of the cabana. A warm fragrant breeze, scented of sea salt and lush tropical flowers, caressed her skin, blowing against the gauzy white curtains that protected them from the eyes of the villa's well-trained, discreet staff.

This cabana had become one of her favorite places on the private island, on the edge of the pink sand beach, with a breathtaking view of the Caribbean, separated from the bright blue horizon only by the sweep of green palm trees across the cove. And she'd never loved it more than now, on their last precious day before they returned to Madrid.

Antonio's hands stopped, and his dark eyes seared hers.

"I want you, *querida*," he growled.

She caught her breath. In spite of the hours he'd spent making love to her day and night since they'd arrived at this island, she wanted him as badly as if they'd never even kissed, as if she weren't already carrying his baby inside her.

How was it possible that each time they made love, instead of satiating their desire, it only caused their fire to burn hotter?

Sitting up in the lounge chair, she reached out to stroke his rough cheek. His dark hair, still wet and plastered back, revealed the scar on his left temple where the awful boys at a Spanish orphanage had once beaten a six-year-old boy for crying. Gently, deliberately, she ran her fingertips over the raised scar.

With an intake of breath, he caught her wrist.

"Kintsugi," she whispered.

His eyes widened. "What?"

Pulling her wrist from his grasp, she explained, "It's a Japanese art, when broken pottery is rejoined by molten gold. But it's more than that. It means something broken and repaired is more precious and beautiful than something unused and whole." Her eyes met his. "It shows history. It shows life."

He gave a low, rueful laugh. "Oh, Hana," he said softly. "You make the world new. I wish you could always look at me the way you are now."

"I will." She ran her hand slowly down his bare, warm chest, still traced with droplets of water from his dripping wet hair, feeling the softness of his skin over his hard muscles.

Tensing, Antonio looked toward the sea. "Tanaka—"

Her hand froze. "What did Ren say to you?"

"It doesn't matter." He looked back at her. "I don't want you to see him again."

"How can you say that? He's my friend."

"And you're my wife."

She drew away, the good feelings lost. "You're being ridiculous."

But as she started to rise to her feet, he pulled her back. "Fine. We won't waste our honeymoon talking about Tanaka." Running his hand down her naked belly, he slowly lowered his lips to hers. "I have something more fun in mind, anyway…"

Any further discussion was impossible as he kissed her. But his lips were barely on hers before there was a wrench below them, as the lounge chair cracked under their mutual weight. At lightning speed, Antonio was on his feet, catching her in his arms.

Held protectively against his bare chest, she looked at him in amazement. "How did you do that?"

"I'll never let you fall." He gently lowered her to her feet in front of him, their skin touching, his arms still around her waist.

Behind his handsome face, edged with wild dark hair, she saw the bright blue Caribbean. She felt the warm breezes off the sea.

And she felt it again, her heart swelling inside her as she'd never felt before, rising until she felt like she was nothing but heart, through muscle and bone, to the very edge of her skin. It terrified her.

She was falling in love with her husband.

Every time he made love to her, every time they talked and laughed together, every time he looked at her the way he was looking at her now, she fell a little deeper.

She heard herself say in a small voice, "You won't?"

"Never," he whispered. Gently, he lifted her chin, smoothing back long dark tendrils of her hair. "I'm your partner. In bed." He kissed her cheeks. "In business." He kissed down between her full breasts, letting the tip of his tongue taste with a flick a tiny bead of sweat. "In life."

Her knees went weak as she staggered back a single step, bracing herself against a thick wooden post on the edge of the large cabana.

"I trust you," he said. Something in his dark eyes made her wonder if he was speaking to her, or to himself. There was something he wasn't telling her. Some hidden fear.

But as her lips parted to ask, he fell to his knees on the sand in front of her. Leaning forward, he tenderly kissed the bare skin of her pregnant belly before he looked up past the full breasts straining the bikini top, to her luminous eyes.

"Forever," he murmured.

Hana looked down at him. She heard the soft roar of the sea against the shore, the birds soaring through the palm trees above. She felt hot, trembling all over.

Silently, he reached around her back and loosened the tie of her bikini top, letting it fall to the sand. He cupped her breasts with his large hands. Leaning forward, he gently suckled a pink nipple, swirling it with his tongue, making her gasp before he moved to the other.

Still kneeling on the sand, he stroked down her waist

to her hips, then undid the ties of her string bikini bottom, and that, too, fell to the sand.

He leaned forward, lifting one of her knees over his shoulder. He breathed in the scent of her, then kissed her there, between her naked thighs.

Holding her breath, she looked down at him kneeling between her tanned legs. Behind him, the gauzy white curtains shielding the cabana blew softly in the breeze, as flashes of golden light stroked patterns on his skin.

He lowered his head between her legs and tasted her, making her shudder with desire. Gripping her hips with his hands, with one of her legs still tossed over his shoulder, he licked and suckled her most secret places, until she began to shake, gripping her hands on the wooden pillar behind her as she cried out.

He rose to his feet, and yanked off his swim trunks almost violently, the hard shaft jutting from his body. Grasping her backside, he lifted her off the ground, pulling her legs to wrap around his hips. Leaning her against the pillar, he pushed slowly inside her, filling her inch by inch. She gasped, straining against him as he stretched her to the limit. He thrust again, and again, increasing the rhythm until he rode her, hard and deep. Panting for breath, she felt the world spinning around her, in Caribbean blue and pink sand and green palm trees, and at the center of it all, the man she…

The man she…

Tension twisted inside her, higher and higher, until her body shattered into a million pieces.

Across the beach, the seagulls echoed her cry, and with one last thrust, he roared as he exploded inside her.

Slowly, she came back to earth. She lowered her feet once more to the sand. Her husband held her, the two of them naked together in the cabana on the private pink sand beach. And he tenderly kissed her.

But as she pressed her cheek against his chest, her heart was pounding at what she could no longer deny.

She was in love with her husband.

It's all right, Hana told herself desperately. It'll be all right.

"You're crying, *querida*," Antonio said, touching her cheek. He gave a sudden wicked smile. "Am I just that good?"

"Yes," she managed. "You're just that good."

And she tried not to think about how he'd told her from the beginning he wasn't capable of loving anyone. She tried not to remember the pain in Ren's words. *I was stupid to let myself love you when I knew you wouldn't love me back.*

And Hana felt a cold hollow in her belly.

Happiness suffused Antonio's body as he held his wife in the beachside cabana, the two of them still standing naked in each other's arms. She was everything to him, he thought drowsily, playing with the ends of her long dark hair. Everything.

Then his eyes opened as he stared past her, out at the sea.

Yes, she was everything. She owned him now. Half of him. Half this island. Half this villa. Half his company. Half his soul. She could cut him right in half, anytime she chose. Cut him in half and just walk away—

You'll never be good enough for her. You know it. I know it. And soon, Hana will know it, too.

How long would it be before she realized Antonio was utterly unworthy of her? How long before she saw the deep, mysterious flaw that had caused everyone, starting with his own parents, to steer clear of him?

Kintsugi, indeed. Nothing broken was ever better than something unused and whole, he thought bitterly. No philosophy would ever make him believe otherwise. Not against the experience of his life.

Antonio tried to fight the panic rising inside him. He repeated to himself, over and over, that he could trust Hana. Hadn't she proved that, time and time again?

He trusted her. He trusted her. He repeated the words like a spell of protection. Hana alone had never lied to him, never betrayed him. He could trust her, he told himself. He could trust her. He had no choice.

But what if he couldn't? What if she left—and took everything, leaving him utterly destroyed? How could he just stand by and wait for it to happen?

CHAPTER NINE

HANA WASN'T SURE how it started, or why.

The week they were married was the happiest of her life. But every day after that, there was a little less happiness, like air let out of a leaky tire.

For the last six months, they'd lived as husband and wife in Madrid, working each day in the CrossWorld Airways headquarters, a glass and steel skyscraper in the financial center of the city, then sleeping together each night in the gorgeous bedroom of their nineteenth-century *palacio*, with its wrought-iron veranda covered with bright pink bougainvillea.

Their lives should have been perfect. And they were—on the outside.

But on the inside…

She still didn't understand what had happened. All summer, from the moment she'd married him in Tokyo last April, she should have felt like the luckiest woman on earth. So, except for the happy day in June when they'd found out they were having a daughter, why did it feel like each day, she had less than the day before?

Like now. Coming to tell her husband it was time to leave for the party, Hana froze in the hallway as she heard the COO's voice carry through the partially open door of Antonio's office.

"I understand Señora Delacruz isn't getting paid. She doesn't even have a title. Why?"

"I haven't decided yet what my wife's place should be." Antonio's voice was cold.

"You could add her to the board. Even as chairman." The man gave a low laugh. "You must know CrossWorld couldn't do without her."

"I know." Her husband's voice became colder still. "She is very popular with the staff."

"Popular with everyone... But it's awkward, since no one is quite sure what her official position is. It makes it confusing. Does she have a position here, or not?"

Hana strained to listen. She'd asked Antonio so many times over the summer when he would be making her new position in the company official, and giving her some title beyond just being his wife. But every time she asked, his expression closed up. "Later," he always said. And that was exactly what he said now.

"Later. We have more important things to discuss." Antonio paused. "Like how we can gain control of Lund Avionics..."

With an intake of breath, Hana abruptly pushed inside his door. "No. You can't take the poor man's company! It would be unthinkably cruel."

Her husband glowered at her. Looking around his sleek office with its beautiful view of Madrid, she saw not just the COO, but also his secretary and the head of acquisitions, all of whom were gaping at Hana now.

Antonio didn't like employees arguing with him, so they rarely did. Maybe that was why the COO, and everyone else at the Madrid headquarters, appreciated Hana. As his secretary, she'd been the only one to push back against Antonio, even gently. Now, as his wife and partner, she did it full bore.

She didn't hold back. She couldn't be afraid to argue for

what she thought was right for the company. It was their family's airline, after all, that would someday be run by their daughter.

So now, in response to Antonio's furious glare, Hana coolly lifted her chin.

Let others be yes-men and toadies. She was his wife. This company was half hers, even if she didn't yet officially have the title or shares to prove it.

Once, her job had been to make him look good. Now, it was to be fearless enough to point out when he was wrong.

As he was now.

"Lund Avionics is one of our core suppliers," she said firmly.

His black eyes glittered. "Exactly why we should acquire it. They're vulnerable to a hostile takeover right now."

"Vertical integration doesn't make sense in this case." She glared at him. "Plus, I don't like kicking someone when they're down."

Antonio folded his arms, pulling up his tall, powerful frame in his sophisticated suit. "It's already decided."

"I know it is." Folding her arms over her hugely pregnant belly, she matched him toe to toe. "We're not doing it."

The others in the room looked back and forth between them, wide-eyed, as if they were at a tennis match.

Antonio narrowed his eyes as if he hated her. And for the first time since they'd returned to Madrid, Hana felt shaken.

He abruptly turned away, speaking to the COO and VP of acquisitions on other topics before dismissing them a few minutes later. The COO paused, looking at Hana as he left.

"Nice work lining up the New York union negotiations, Señora Delacruz."

"I just wish I could be part of the negotiating team," she said ruefully. Antonio had convinced her it would be unwise, this close to her due date, to travel to New York for a week of stressful, contentious negotiations with the employees union.

"I do, too. You have a magic touch with employees. With customers and suppliers, too. And your new charity initiative—genius! Which reminds me." The man looked at his watch. "My wife will have my hide if I don't head home to get ready."

"We need to do the same." But as Hana glanced at her husband, her shy smile fell away. Antonio looked so strange, almost green. As if he'd just been kicked in the teeth. She didn't understand. "Antonio?"

"Yes," he said tersely, not looking at her. "We should go."

But as the chauffeur drove the two of them home through the streets of Madrid, her husband barely looked at her.

Hana was at a loss. Surely he couldn't be upset at her for making her mark at their company? Or for having a different opinion, when they were both simply trying to do right by everyone?

Whatever the reason was, from the moment they'd returned to Madrid, to the place she'd thought would be her forever home, Antonio had seemed more cold and distant each day.

Could he have somehow learned her secret? Glancing at him again in the back of the Bentley, Hana took a deep breath. Was it possible he was actually trying to drive her away, as he'd done with all his mistresses before?

But she wasn't a mistress. She was his wife.

So why? When had Antonio started to pull away from her? Had it been on their honeymoon? She tried to remember. The Caribbean sun had been spun gold on the pink sand beach. For four days, she and Antonio had splashed in the sea and made love. A blush suffused Hana's cheeks as she remembered that time in the cabana, when he'd lifted her legs around his hips as he'd plunged into her, riding her hard.

That would be impossible now. Her belly had grown in

the last six months. With only a few weeks until her due date now, she was huge. The Spanish summer had nearly melted her with heat. Thank heavens that finally, in late September, the autumn air had grown cooler.

But the nights were hotter than ever, at least in their bedroom. Sex wasn't their problem. Antonio seemed to think it was his duty to bring her to explosive, gasping fulfillment at least twice a night. Last night, he'd done it three times.

It had become harder and harder for Hana to hide her feelings. Since their honeymoon, she'd buried her love for him deep in her heart. She tried to forget. She couldn't risk him knowing. Because if he couldn't return her love, he'd scorn her, or worse—pity her.

What would she do then? Could she still bear to be his wife, to live by his side, to sleep in his bed, if she knew for certain he'd never feel anything for her beyond friendship?

No. She wouldn't break up their family and home, just because her husband didn't love her back. Home and stability were far more important than love.

Weren't they?

The crowded city streets of Madrid in the early evening rush hour were flooded with the last rays of autumn sunshine as they went home. They were running late for their own party. But Hana could barely think about the charity ball that had been her project for the last two months. She kept giving Antonio side glances in the back of the Bentley, as, in the front seat, Ramon Garcia kept up a stream of affable chatter in Spanish with the chauffeur.

Antonio pressed the button to slide up the privacy screen.

"I didn't appreciate you contradicting me in front of the staff."

Antonio's voice was terse in the seat beside her. Her hands tightened in her lap.

"You mean about the avionics deal? I just don't think it's right to take advantage of the poor guy's divorce, that's all."

"If we don't take advantage of it, someone else will." His expression was hard. "And his liquidity problems are his own fault, for not making his wife sign a prenup."

"Don't be too hard on him. After all," Hana tilted her head with a flirtatious smile, trying to lighten the mood, "you didn't make *me* sign one…"

His dark eyes were grim. "That's something I've been meaning to discuss with you."

The smile slid from Hana's face. "You want me to sign a prenup?"

"A postnuptial agreement, yes." Antonio looked calmly handsome in his perfectly tailored dark suit. "And perhaps you should stop coming to the office."

Hana's jaw dropped. "You're kicking me out?"

"Nothing so dramatic," Antonio said gruffly. "It's just that you're about to become a mother…"

"You're about to become a father, but I don't hear anything about *you* leaving your job."

"Our baby will be so tiny," he persisted. "Helpless. Surely you would not wish to abandon a newborn to the care of nannies."

His words felt like an attack. Like he was trying to give her an argument that she could not fight, rather than tell her his real reasons. "I'm planning to stay home for a while, yes. But CrossWorld Airways is part of our family. Even the name comes from our surname. In a few months, I'll return to work and bring the baby with me."

"It's an office, not a nursery," he said coldly.

"Why are you acting like this?" Hana glared at him. "Just because I didn't want us to buy that poor man's company at fire sale prices?"

"Since you mention it, I think it does confuse some of my employees when you give orders, since you don't have an official position at the company."

"I'm your equal partner," she said.

He said nothing.

Searching his closed face, she pressed, "I am, aren't I?"

"The post-nup is fairly standard." Antonio suddenly wouldn't meet her eyes. "It just says, in case of a split, we'll each keep the assets we came into the marriage with. You also get a generous settlement, of course."

The passing streets of Madrid seemed to whirl in front of her eyes. "You...you don't want to share the company with me."

"Don't say it like that."

"Like what?"

"Accusingly," he accused.

Hana stared at him.

After all his fine words about wanting their airline to be a family company, he was going to go back on his word and keep it for himself alone?

The foundation of everything she'd believed about their marriage shifted beneath her.

"You lied to me?"

"I've reassessed the situation."

"You said the company was ours," she said. "That we'd share it, and build it together for our child."

Antonio looked at her emotionlessly in the back seat of the car. "You're not the one who created an empire from nothing. It's mine. I built it. All you did was help me a little."

Turning, Hana stared blindly in front of her, at the blank privacy screen. She felt the soft calfskin leather of the Bentley's leather seat beneath her fingers.

"Then..." Hana looked down at her swelling belly. She said in a low voice, "By that argument, our daughter is only mine."

Antonio glared at her. "That's not fair, and you know it."

"Fair?" Hana thought of all her effort and love she'd put into CrossWorld Airways over the last two and a half years, working every bit as long and hard as Antonio had. And for the last six months, she'd done it without salary or title. She'd done it for love. Because she'd thought they were building something. As a couple. As a *family*.

No wonder she'd felt a growing emotional distance between them. She was the only one who'd even thought they were a team. The lump in her throat turned to a razor blade.

"Did you ever intend to share it with me?" she choked out. "Or was it just a ploy to make me marry you?"

Looking at her evenly, Antonio countered, "Is that the only reason you married me? Because you wanted to get your hands on half my company?" He shook his head furiously. "I never dreamed you'd challenge me at every step, luring the staff to your side, trying to take it from me like this!"

"I'm not!"

"Then what are you doing?"

Staring at him as the car stopped, she whispered, "Trying to make it better."

She dimly saw the *palacio* ahead on their elegant, tree-lined street. As the Bentley paused, waiting to turn into the gated driveway that led into the *palacio*'s courtyard, Antonio suddenly narrowed his eyes, trying to see through the window. He pressed another button and spoke through the car's intercom. "What is it, Carlos?"

"I'm not sure, *señor*," the driver responded. "Someone is blocking the gate."

Hana didn't understand how her husband could be talking about the stupid gate, when he'd just ripped out her heart. "What made you like this?"

"Like what?" Antonio bit out, turning back to her.

"Suspicious. Cruel!"

"Experience," he said coldly, and got out of the car.

Hana blinked, feeling sick and shivering in her maternity suit. For months, she'd been excited about tonight's fund-raiser ball, the kickoff of the new charity initiative she'd created for the company. She'd spent weeks choosing an exquisite gown from one of the top designers in Madrid. She'd never worn a dress so fancy in her life. It was fit for a princess, far more glamorous and fairy-tale-like than the simple pink sundress that had been her wedding dress. She'd been so excited for Antonio to see her in it. In spite of being so pregnant, she'd dreamed of a romantic night, of him taking her in his arms on the dance floor. *I love you,* querida. *I never realized it till this very moment. My heart is yours, now and forever.* And it was then, only then, that she could confess her love.

Stupid dream!

Instead, they'd have to pretend to be a happy couple in front of all their high-powered guests, so the share price of CrossWorld Airways didn't drop at rumors of a potential marital split. The stock market was ruthless. The party was due to start in an hour, and she still had to take a shower and get ready.

"Something's happening at the gate," their bodyguard said, getting out of the car. "Stay here, Señora Delacruz."

At the guarded gate at the end of the tall, wrought-iron fence, Hana saw her husband approaching a strange man with his back toward them, arguing with their security guard.

Getting out of the car over the driver's protests, she followed Antonio and their bodyguard past the privacy hedges toward their *palacio*'s gatehouse.

Could it be Ren? she thought with sudden longing. She hadn't spoken to her friend since the wedding. She'd tried, but he hadn't returned any of her messages. Could Ren have come to Madrid after all this time to say he was ready to be friends again?

Then the man's hat fell off, and she saw he was a white-haired stranger, nothing like Ren at all.

"If you don't leave, I'll call the police…" the security guard was saying in Spanish, glaring at the stranger.

"But if you'll just give him this letter…" Then the elderly man saw Antonio, and his face lit up with relief. "Señor Delacruz. It is you, is it not? I've seen you in the newspaper."

Antonio glowered at him. "Who are you?"

"Please—this is for you." The old man held out a white envelope. Antonio didn't take it.

"Back away." Ramon Garcia held up a brawny arm to ward off the elderly stranger.

Why such a fuss? In another moment, they'd be calling for police with sirens blazing. And all for an old man who just wanted to give Antonio something.

"What do you want, *señor*?" Hana asked him kindly.

The man straightened. His eyes were rheumy and red, and in spite of his carefully pressed, if outdated, coat and trousers, he smelled of wine. But he still had a strange dignity as he held out a small white envelope. "Please, *señora*."

"Don't take it," Garcia warned, but she ignored him. She took the envelope.

"Bless you," the elderly man whispered. "She doesn't have long. I couldn't let her life end like this."

"What are you talking about?" Hana said, alarmed. "Who are you?"

"I'm Dr. Mendoza from Etxetarri, to the north." He slowly looked at Antonio. "I delivered you when you were born."

Antonio's jaw dropped. It would have been hilarious to see him so surprised, if Hana hadn't felt the same shock.

The doctor's rheumy eyes fell as his shoulders sagged. He whispered, "Then I took you south to Andalusia, and left you in a basket."

Hana caught her breath. No one knew that story—no one. Glancing at her husband, she waited for him to say

something, anything. When he did not move, she said anxiously to the man, "Please, come inside." What did the
charity ball matter, compared to this? "We have so many
questions…"

Shaking his head, he looked back at Antonio. "Your
mother is dying. You must go to her—"

"Get off my property," Antonio said grimly. "Now."

"Antonio!" Hana cried, scandalized.

"Read the letter," the man pleaded. "Before it's too late."
Turning, he shuffled away, his gait uneven.

"My apologies, *señor*," the gate guard said to Antonio,
hanging his head.

"You should have called the police immediately," Garcia reprimanded him, then turned to Hana. "*Señora*, give
me the envelope."

"Why?" she said, still watching the elderly man disappear down the street.

"I'll dispose of it. Have it tested for anthrax, poisons,
blackmail attempts, then thrown away."

"How can you be so suspicious and rude?" Her eyes
snapped to her husband. "And you!"

Antonio didn't even look at her. Without a word, he
turned on his heel and walked through the gate toward
the *palacio*.

Still gripping the letter, she hurried after him.

Inside the courtyard, a steady stream of caterers and
florists carried canapés and flower arrangements into the
elegant, nineteenth-century palace, constructed of lime-
stone in the classical style. It was difficult to keep up with
his stride, so she increased her pace as much as a heavily
pregnant woman could. It was almost as if Antonio didn't
want her to catch up.

Inside the *palacio*'s grand foyer, with its soaring ceiling and dazzling chandelier, she saw Manuelita, the housekeeper, directing traffic. "You're back!" the older woman

said, beaming at her. Hana and Manuelita had been friends for years, since she'd only been a secretary. The woman was almost like a mother to her, or at the very least an aunt. "There are some questions about the music—"

"I'm sorry, it will have to wait," Hana called, hurrying after Antonio, who was already disappearing down the long hall, past the antique suit of armor, toward the stained glass window. When she finally caught up with him in the study, she was panting for breath.

"Antonio!" she said accusingly.

Plantation shutters blocked the sunlight, leaving her husband's face in shadow as he looked up calmly from his dark wood desk. "Yes?"

"This letter!" Holding it out anxiously, she went to the desk. The room was masculine and dark, with bookshelves and leather furniture. A fire crackled in the fireplace. "Don't you want to rip it open?"

He leaned back in his chair. "Not particularly."

"Are you kidding?" She looked down at the envelope. Antonio's name was written on it in spidery, uncertain handwriting. "But you've wanted to know about your past all your life!"

"Maybe once I did. Now I really don't care." Tenting his fingers on the desk, he curled his lip. "And the man hardly seemed credible. I smelled alcohol on him from ten feet away."

"Just open it!" She dropped the envelope on the desk in front of him. When he didn't move, she tilted her head challengingly. "Unless you're afraid."

His forehead furrowed as he stared down at the envelope. He picked it up.

Then, without reading, he abruptly crumpled it into a ball. "It is nothing."

"You didn't even open it!"

"I am wealthy. I am known." He rose to his feet. "There

are always crackpots who want to cause trouble, who scheme to get money."

"But he didn't ask for money. You heard him. He said he left you in a basket as a baby. Who even knows about that?"

His expression was hard as granite. "I've heard enough." He went grimly toward the fireplace.

"Wait," Hana said, alarmed, "you're not going to—?"

She gasped as Antonio tossed the crumpled ball into the fire.

"How could you?" she whispered, staring at the envelope, as the spidery handwriting burned. "You don't even want to know the reason your parents abandoned you?"

"I don't give a damn."

"I would give anything to have my parents or grandmother back. To have family." Her voice became shrill. "Your parents might be alive and you don't want to know? You won't even give them a chance to explain?"

"No." His voice was cold.

"Why?"

"If my parents showed up begging on their knees, I still wouldn't speak to them. They made their choice. The doctor, if that's really what he was, made his choice, as well." He lifted his chin. "Let them all live with it."

"But—"

"Never speak to me of this again." Going back to his desk, Antonio opened a briefcase and held out a stack of papers.

"What's this?"

"The postnuptial agreement," he said coolly. "Read and sign it before I leave for New York tomorrow. Tonight, if possible." Antonio gave a cold smile, his black eyes icy as a January night. "I'm going to get ready for the party."

And he left.

Holding the post-nup in her numb hands, Hana stared

at the open doorway, in shock over what she'd learned in the last hour.

Her husband had betrayed her. She thought he'd changed, but he'd never had any intention of sharing either his company or his life with her. And she knew, if she wasn't at the office, they'd lead separate lives. He routinely worked sixteen-hour days. How could he possibly be a real father? A real husband?

He hadn't changed. He still wouldn't let anyone have the slightest control over his life, or his heart.

Perhaps his heart had been broken by his parents' desertion, the day he was born. But Antonio wasn't even interested in trying to heal or learning to trust again. He preferred to continue living as he was—with a cold heart, and an iron grip on his company and fortune. Their only real connection was when he made love to her so passionately at night. But how long could Hana continue to share her body with him, after he'd betrayed his promise to her that they would be equal partners and share their lives?

If she stayed with him, she would be his possession. His servant, almost. Servicing him in bed, running his home, raising his child.

If she stayed?

She looked around the house she'd dreamed could be her home, then down at the postnuptial agreement in her hands. *In case of a split,* he'd said.

There was only one play she had left. One last chance to see if she could convince him to change, to heal his heart. What did she have to lose now by taking the risk? Hana crushed the papers to her chest.

Nothing. Nothing at all.

CHAPTER TEN

ANTONIO PACED IMPATIENTLY at the bottom of the *palacio*'s sweeping staircase.

An hour. An hour since he'd left her in his study and told her to get ready. It wasn't like Hana to be late. But apparently that had changed. Just as it once hadn't been like her to attack or purposefully provoke him. But that, too, had become a habit with her lately.

At first, working with her had been good, just like when she was his secretary. All summer, they'd shared the thrill of closing the deals that gave CrossWorld Airways the routes they needed for exponential growth. First had been Tokyo, then Rio, then Nairobi. Tomorrow, he'd leave for New York to deal with the union. Once he built out North America, it would be the final piece of the puzzle.

But over the summer, Hana had changed. She'd started to flaunt her growing influence. Which was a problem. Because while Antonio's employees respected and feared him for his vision, hard work and ruthlessness, they *loved* Hana.

He didn't understand why she'd changed, when she'd never once tried to work against him before. Gaining the loyalty of his company's leadership team! Contradicting Antonio's orders!

Hearing her defy his decisions in front of his staff that morning, after the COO had actually demanded for Hana to be on the board—as chairman, second only to Antonio's status as CEO!—had been the final straw. He'd known he had to get her out of the company for good. It was bad enough that she already had so much power over him as his wife and the mother of his child. He couldn't let her seize the leadership of his company from him, along with everything else.

He'd been insane to ever offer to share his airline with her. He'd been out of his mind at the time, desperate to convince her to marry him. But he'd never imagined Hana could act like this, trying to seize control, to push Antonio out of the company he'd built with his bare hands. Without the company, who was he?

No one.

Well, he'd come to his senses. Hana would sign the post-nup. He didn't truly believe she wanted to lead the company. He didn't know why she'd become so focused on business. What she really wanted was a home and family. How many times had she said it? And that was what he'd given her. He'd kept the headquarters in Madrid because she wanted to live here, where she'd made friends. He would be glad for her to run her new charity initiative, as long as she stopped trying to run his company.

So why was she late for her own fund-raiser? Antonio straightened in his well-cut tuxedo, gritting his teeth as he looked up the staircase. Did she expect him to greet their guests alone?

Stopping his pacing, he scowled, narrowing his eyes. His hands tightened at his sides. Perhaps she'd gotten distracted listening to a staff member's problems. Her caring heart left her an easy mark. Like the way she hadn't wanted to do a hostile takeover of Lund Avionics, because it was "unthinkably cruel." Or how she'd fallen for the story of the elderly so-called doctor who'd dropped off that ridiculous letter claiming to be the truth about Antonio's parents. He scowled. He'd barely picked up the envelope before his hands had started shaking so hard he'd known there was only one thing to do—destroy it.

Just open it. Unless you're afraid.

He couldn't believe Hana would ambush him that way. Why would she ever think he'd want to open some crackpot's letter?

There'd been no reason for him to read it. Either the old man had been lying, in which case reading it was a waste of his time, or else he was telling the truth—in which case, Antonio *really* didn't want to read it. If the parents who'd cold-bloodedly abandoned him as a newborn suddenly wanted to worm their way back into his life now they'd discovered he was rich, Antonio wanted no part of it.

Let them suffer with the knowledge that the baby they'd thrown away could have made their fortune. He'd turned out to have some worth, after all. And they'd blown it.

He had a new family now. A beautiful wife here at home, raising their child, supporting him while he built his empire alone.

His heartbeat slowed to normal pace. He looked at his platinum watch. Guests had already started to arrive in the ballroom, without either host or hostess to greet them. Where was Hana? This was her party, damn it!

"Antonio."

Hearing his wife's soft voice calling from above, he looked up, and his jaw dropped.

There at the top of the sweeping staircase, he saw a princess.

Hana's long dark hair had been twisted into a ballerina bun at the top of her head, surrounded by a delicate diamond tiara. She was wearing a blue gown, cut Regency-style, with a very low bodice that showcased a diamond and sapphire necklace, as well as her overflowing breasts. Layers of baby blue fabric skimmed lightly over her full, pregnant belly, and she wore white gloves that went up past her elbows.

Her brown eyes were guarded as she came down the staircase, her gloved hand skimming over the handrail, floating so lightly that he looked at her feet to see if she were being carried by doves, or at least glass slippers. No, just stiletto sandals in matching baby blue.

"You look stunning," he said when she reached the bottom of the stairs.

She smiled, but it seemed strangely sad. Why? Because he'd informed her he wouldn't give her half the company? No, that couldn't be it. Hana was no gold digger. All along, she'd wanted to focus on their family and home. He was simply helping her do that.

But in this moment, she looked so glamorous he almost couldn't recognize her. Hana's lips were full and red, her brown eyes rich and expressive beneath the extravagant sweep of dark lashes.

She paused. "I read the post-nup."

"And signed it?"

"And…we'll talk about it later."

"You will sign," Antonio said, holding out his arm. He knew it was the only way they could both be happy.

Lowering her gaze, she gently placed her gloved hand around the arm of his black tuxedo jacket. "Shall we greet our guests?"

As they entered the *palacio*'s ballroom, Antonio saw it had been transformed. The gilded mirrors were now covered with red roses, like a romantic fantasy.

Strange. He'd owned this *palacio* for a decade. He'd bought it as a symbol of how far he'd come, a way to prove to everyone, especially himself, that he was no longer a scruffy orphan, a pathetic squalling foundling who'd had to be given a name by the shocked nuns at a church.

This palace had been commissioned in the early nineteenth century by a young nobleman who'd come to a bad end in a duel, dying for love, "which," Antonio always finished smugly when he'd told the story, "shows he was too stupid to deserve such a magnificent home." It had taken several years of remodeling to bring the palace into the current century, with modern comforts and technology.

But Antonio had left this ballroom almost intact, from the gilded mirrors to the vibrant frescoes of Cupid and amorous couples on the ceiling. The ballroom had seemed a useless anachronism, so ridiculously romantic he'd never bothered with it. And it had never been more romantic than now, covered with flowers and filled with guests in tuxedos and ball gowns.

But somehow, he didn't hate it.

Antonio looked at his regally beautiful wife on his arm, listening as she greeted each guest courteously and intelligently, thanking them for attending CrossWorld Airways's charity fund-raiser in several different languages. He felt a swell of pride.

The evening passed in a swirl of conversation and laughter, with three hundred people in the ballroom all charmed by his wife, unable to resist her sweet pleas that they should donate to the CrossWorld Kids charity, which in addition to raising funds for medicine and supplies would offer free transport to medical teams. As she told heartfelt stories of the good that could be done, he was mesmerized by her beautiful face and the tremble of her voice. He congratulated himself on marrying her.

Antonio felt strangely reluctant to leave her side during the ball. He was irritated when he was interrupted by Horace Lund, the recently divorced owner of the American avionics firm that had lately become a takeover target, the same company Hana had pleaded with him to leave alone. But how could he, when Lund Avionics was so ripe for the taking?

As the pudgy, sweaty, anxious man pulled him into a quiet corner of the ballroom, Antonio gritted his teeth. "What do you want?"

He braced himself, wondering if the man would burst into sobs and beg for money. Maybe he should call security before Lund ruined the whole charity ball.

Horace Lund took a deep breath, then said unhappily, "I want you to buy my company."

Antonio's jaw dropped, then he caught himself. "Because you know I will take it, whether you wish it or not."

"My company is a picked-over bone being fought over by dogs. And there's no way I can consolidate our debts, not in the middle of this divorce." The middle-aged man wiped his eyes. "I'd rather sell my company to you whole than risk another corporation getting it. At least I know you won't break my company up for parts and fire all our employees." He took a deep breath. "As long as my employees still have jobs…"

The older man cut a pitiable figure. Antonio discovered he felt sorry for him. But why should he? The man had done it to himself. Lund had been an idiot for not asking his wife for a prenup before she divorced him. Just being around the sad, hunched man made Antonio feel edgy. It made him more determined than ever to make Hana sign the papers tonight, no matter how proud of her he was in this moment.

He looked back at Hana, glowing onstage as she spoke so earnestly about CrossWorld's new charity. He remembered her voice. *Plus, I don't like kicking someone when they're down.*

"No," he heard himself say suddenly. "I won't buy it."

"You're going to let the other airline take it?" The other man's eyes filled with fear. "They're heartless. They'll fire everyone—"

"I'm offering you a loan, Lund," he said abruptly. "On reasonable terms."

Lund almost staggered with shock. "You—want to *help* me?"

"You're the best electronics supplier in the business," Antonio said. "It would be inconvenient for me if you went bust."

"How can I ever repay you," the man whispered, choking up, reaching out to shake his hand.

Antonio pulled away, pushing a card into his hand. "Don't thank me. Just contact my lawyers."

Lund shook his head in wonder. "Why, Delacruz? You've always been a shark. Why would you save me?"

"It's a business decision, nothing more," Antonio blurted out, and fled. Stepping out into the privacy of the hallway outside his ballroom, he called his lawyers. Afterward, as he returned to the crowded ballroom, with all its music and flowers, he still couldn't understand why he'd done it. He'd had an excellent chance of buying the shares cheap and taking control of the company at a stellar profit. What was wrong with him?

Hana. She was what was wrong. It wasn't enough that she'd gained the loyalty of his employees and tried to take over his company. She was starting to make Antonio doubt his own priorities.

You've always been a shark.

His hands tightened. It wouldn't be enough to get Hana out of his company, he suddenly realized. He needed her out of his soul. Out of his heart.

Antonio felt the shiver of ice down his spine, the one he always felt when he felt the air around him changing. Gritting his teeth, he pushed the feeling aside. He just liked the American company's cockpit instrument displays, that was all. As Lund had said, the bigger airline would have consumed it whole. Their CEO was a corporate bloodsucker.

It had been a stone-cold business decision, nothing more. His priorities were strength and profit, like always.

He hadn't changed. He was his own man. He made his own fate.

Hana would sign the post-nup tonight, and tomorrow he'd fly off to New York. For the foreseeable future, he would be so busy building his empire that their only connection would be in bed, or to discuss matters regarding their child's welfare. He'd give his wife free rein at home and she'd have no complaints.

Grabbing a glass of scotch, he drank it down in a single gulp and deposited the empty glass on a passing tray. He saw his wife speaking to some French aerospace executives he recognized. As he approached, he heard the executives eagerly telling Hana about their latest technology. She responded with sharp, incisive questions that made the other men laugh, with admiring glances. Coming from behind, Antonio kissed her softly on the temple.

Hana turned to look at him. "Where have you been?"

"Investing in avionics," he said lightly.

"We'd heard about your wife," one of the executives told him jovially, smiling at Hana. "But the rumors didn't do her justice. It's a pleasure, madame."

She grinned. "Just remember that when we discuss that discount for our next order."

"You drive a hard bargain."

She was obviously still representing herself as a leader in his company. Repressing his irritation, Antonio gave the executives a bland smile. "Will you excuse me, gentlemen? My wife and I are supposed to lead the first dance."

As he led Hana onto the dance floor of the *palacio*'s ballroom, a hush fell across the crowd. At his sign, music began to play from the orchestra. Pulling her into his arms, Antonio held her against his tuxedo-clad body, the two of them alone beneath a spotlight on the ballroom dance floor.

Her arms in long white gloves wrapped around the shoulders of his black jacket, as the skirts of her blue ball gown fluttered against his legs. Her baby bump pressed against his muscled belly as his hands went to the small of her back. He felt her sway. Her brown eyes glowed with warmth, and her diamond tiara and jeweled necklace sparkled with fire beneath the chandeliers high above.

Hana was so beautiful. His hands tightened on her back. In this moment, in spite of all his promises to himself to be his own man and make his own fate, all he could feel was her.

Right here, in his arms, Hana was everything he'd ever wanted.

I love you. Just three little words. Why were they so hard for her to say?

As Hana swayed in her husband's arms, beneath the ballroom spotlight, as she looked up into his dark, unfathomable gaze as the orchestra's music swelled around them, telling him she loved him wasn't just hard—it was impossible.

All too soon, other guests joined them on the dance floor, bumping up against them, watching them, smiling at them—and the moment was lost.

She had to tell him. It was her only way to change the course of their lives. She had to be brave enough to finally speak words she could never take back.

Either Antonio would realize he loved her as well, and they could be happy…or else he'd tell her he couldn't. And they wouldn't.

The stakes were so high, it terrified her.

She couldn't say the words.

Hours later, when the ball finally ended and the last guest departed in the wee hours of the morning, Antonio turned to her with a smile. "Are you pleased?"

"Pleased?" she repeated, searching his gaze.

"You did a good job, Hana." He tilted his head. "You

raised a lot of money tonight for charity, and gained good-will and good press for CrossWorld." He paused. "Perhaps you could continue running the kids' charity. From home."

"I suppose." It had been a long day. They'd already told the house staff to go to bed. Tomorrow would be soon enough to tidy up.

Hana felt weary as she looked at Antonio in the darkened ballroom. The sweet smell of wilting flowers wafted around them as candles flickered to an end. She asked in a low voice, "Why don't you want me in the company anymore?"

Antonio hesitated. "You know why."

"Why?"

"Because I want you to have the freedom to be home. Taking care of our baby."

"But there's more to it than that, I know there is—"

"Did you sign the post-nup?"

"Yes." Her heart was pounding. *I signed it because I love you.* Why couldn't she say it?

"Where is it?"

"I left it in the bedroom."

"So you agree to the terms?"

"Yes." She'd barely skimmed the contract, as she'd been in a hurry to get ready for the party. But she'd have physical custody of their child, which was all she cared about. The money didn't matter.

"Good." He gave a brief nod. "I hope you feel the financial settlement was generous."

"Yes. Thank you," she said numbly, because he seemed to be waiting for a response. Did she expect her to be grateful to him for carefully planning their divorce, when all she wanted was for him to love her?

She had to tell him.

Her body temperature suddenly went up twenty degrees. Feeling hot and afraid, she pulled off her long white gloves.

Abruptly changing the subject, she said brightly, "I heard a rumor this evening."

"Rumor?" Antonio watched her peel the long gloves down her arms, one by one. A hunger came into his eyes.

"I can hardly believe it," she continued.

"Believe what?" His gaze fell onto her lips, his hard-edged face half in shadow. He looked devastatingly handsome in his perfectly cut tuxedo.

She smiled. "I heard a rumor that you not only let Horace Lund off the hook, you gave him a loan so his company would survive."

His dark eyes flashed up to hers, looking almost vulnerable, as if she'd caught him doing something wrong.

"So?" His tone was dismissive.

She didn't understand. "I'm glad."

His jaw hardened in the guttering candlelight. "You need to stop trying to interfere with my company."

His company. For such a brief amount of time, it had been *their* company. The lump returned to her throat and she looked away. "You mean when I was discussing the new aircraft with Pierre."

"It's not your place."

Heart aching, Hana lifted her gaze to his and said, "I don't know where my place is anymore."

Taking her hands in his own, he lowered his head and kissed the back of each one.

"In my home," he whispered. "In my bed."

Their eyes met. Still holding her hand, he led her out of the shadowy ballroom and down the hall. He pulled her up the sweeping staircase, beneath the chandelier soaring high overhead, and the gaze of the angelic cherubs regarding them from the painted ceiling.

The *palacio* was strangely quiet, in the darkest hours of night, with all the servants long gone to bed. Their footsteps echoed against the tile as he led her down the hallway to their bedroom.

Closing the door behind him, he set her back gently on the bed, then fell to his knees on the priceless Turkish rug in front of her. Without a word, he untied each of her stiletto sandals, one by one, sending them skittering to the floor.

Rising to his feet, he slowly undid his cuff links and pulled off his black tuxedo jacket. His hard, handsome face was edged with moonlight from the window as he unbuttoned his shirt.

Her heart started to pound, in rhythm to the words she could not say. *I love you.*

His hard-muscled chest was lightly dusted with dark hair, his skin hot and smooth beneath the rough bristles as he lifted her back to her feet as if she weighed nothing. Unzipping the back of her blue Regency-style ball gown, he let it drop to the floor, leaving her standing in front of him in nothing but white lace panties, cut low to fit beneath her swelling belly, and a white lace demi-bra that barely contained her overflowing breasts.

Reaching around her, he undid the clasp, and her bra dropped to the floor as her breasts sprang free. With a flick of his fingers, he ripped the edges of the panties, and that white scrap of lace, too, fell to the floor.

"You don't have to destroy them—" she protested, then her mouth went dry when she saw the heat in his dark gaze.

Antonio cupped her face with his hands. "This is just as I always pictured you," he whispered. "Naked, filled with my child." His fingertips lightly stroked the diamond and sapphire necklace above her bare collarbone. "Covered only with jewels."

She could not make herself say the words. *I love you.* But perhaps she could show him...

Hana pushed him back gently against the bed. Surprised, he looked up at her with smoldering eyes.

Leaning over, she kissed him. His sensual lips were warm and intoxicating. She wondered if he, too, was trying to tell her he loved her, because that was how he kissed her. Oh, if only it could be true...

Looking down at him, she pulled off the sparkling diamond tiara and set it on the nightstand. As if it were a striptease, she slowly pulled off all the hairpins from her ballerina bun, one at a time, tossing them to the floor.

Lying on the bed beneath her, he watched her, his eyes wide, his lips parted.

Looking down at him through her sweep of black eyelashes, she deliberately pulled the last hairpin from the bun. Shaking her head, she let her long dark hair tumble down her naked shoulders in the silvery moonlight.

Lowering her head, she kissed him, as the dark curtain of hair fell around her, brushing against his chest. Reaching up, he gripped her shoulders and kissed her, long and hard, his tongue plundering hers.

"Careful." Pulling back, she gave a low laugh, running the tip of one fingernail down his hard-muscled chest. "Remember I'm pregnant." She let the nail dig a little deeper. "You have to be very, very gentle with me..."

"I'm always gentle," he growled, his deep voice booming against the high ceiling of the nineteenth-century Spanish bedroom. Taking a deep breath, he repeated in a calmer voice, "I can be gentle." But even as his grip on her shoulders loosened, she saw the barely restrained wildness in his eyes.

As she kissed him, as she pulled off his tuxedo trousers and silk boxers beneath, she controlled the pace. If he tried to hold her, she stopped. If he tried to kiss her too passionately, she pulled away. She was tender. Gentle.

Finally, when she'd tortured him enough, she climbed

over his naked hips and spread her bare legs wide over his thighs. She lowered herself on him, inch by inch, until beads of sweat appeared on his forehead from the effort of restraining his desire. She began to ride him. Slowly. Deliberately. Until he was gasping and gripping the comforter beneath him and nearly weeping as he held himself back. Tension coiled inside her, delicious and sweet, until she soared with a loud cry. A split second later, with a shout, he exploded inside her.

She'd been trying to show him that she loved him with her touch, since she was too terrified to tell him with words. But as they held each other afterward in bed, naked, sweaty and spent, as he kissed her tenderly on the forehead and said huskily, "You're incredible, *querida*, there's no other woman like you on earth," suddenly, Hana was no longer afraid.

"I need to tell you something," she whispered in the darkness. Wrapping his arms more securely around her, he pulled her back against his naked chest.

"What is it, *querida*?" he said drowsily, nuzzling her neck. His muscular body felt so warm against her own, making her feel safe. She took a deep breath.

"I love you, Antonio."

CHAPTER ELEVEN

ANTONIO'S EYES FLEW open in the dark bedroom.

I love you.

He'd been exhausted and content, holding his naked wife in his arms in the moonlight. But when he heard her whisper those three words with a mix of shyness and pride, he felt a rush of emotion.

I love you. Those soft, warm words poured like honey into all of his broken places.

I love you. Strange. Women had said those words to him before, but he'd always been cynical about it, assuming they were an obvious ploy meant to lure him into marriage.

This was different.

Hearing Hana say she loved him was like the first time he'd made love to her, when her innocence had almost made him feel as if he, too, were a virgin. Now, as he looked down at her in his arms, naked in their bed, he felt his heart swell all the way to his throat as he realized that he—

His shoulders stiffened as a cold sweat broke out along his spine.

No. Coldness rushed into his soul like wolves howling in a winter forest, biting the edges of his heart, making it shrink, making it bleed.

Antonio couldn't love her. He couldn't love anyone. If he ever really opened up, if he ever showed her all his flaws and darkness, her so-called love would evaporate like mist in the brutal Spanish sun.

Even his own parents hadn't wanted him. Neither had any of the foster parents who'd tried, or that waitress he'd naively tried to love at eighteen. They'd all seen some monstrous flaw in him. Why should he think that Hana, so intelligent and wise, wouldn't as well?

You'll never be good enough for her. You know it. I know it. And soon, Hana will know it, too.

Squeezing his eyes shut, he tried to push away Tanaka's words and return to that drowsy, contented feeling of a moment before. But it was impossible.

Hana was looking at him with her brown eyes full of tortured hope. She'd just told him she loved him. She was waiting for his answer.

But even if she believed she loved him now, it wouldn't last. Soon she would open her beautiful brown eyes and see that he was unworthy of her. She'd turn away. She'd scorn him.

She'd leave.

At the thought, ice spread across Antonio's body, from the tips of his fingers and toes toward his center, flash-freezing every cell and nerve, racing up his spine. Ice reached his heart, cracking into shards.

Hana sat up in bed, her lovely face worried. "Antonio?"

"I—" Was he having a heart attack? Was he dying? His breathing was hoarse. His heart felt like it had stopped beating. He had to control the situation. He couldn't let her realize the truth—

"What's wrong?" she said anxiously, putting her hand on his bare shoulder.

Jerking away, he nearly fell out of the bed. "Where is the post-nup?"

With bewildered eyes, she pointed to the end table by the fireplace. Stumbling over, he found the pages, saw her signature at the bottom. *Hana Delacruz.* The postnuptial agreement had been more generous than his lawyers had liked, but they'd mostly been relieved that one now existed. "You have to get her to sign this immediately, *señor.* Your whole life is at risk."

But Antonio didn't feel better now that he held the financial document in his hands. Because it wasn't just his business empire that was at stake.

He couldn't look at her, at those brown eyes that had started to lose hope. Grabbing clothes from the enormous walk-in closet, he pulled on jeans and a long-sleeved T-shirt. He grabbed a Louis Vuitton duffel bag.

"Where are you going?" Hana exclaimed.

He kept his voice expressionless. "New York."

"So early? Surely you don't have to leave in the middle of the night!"

"My competitors don't rest. Neither can I."

She seemed to shrink a little on the bed, pulling the blanket up higher, over her belly, all the way to her neck.

"How can you leave me like this?" she whispered. "I just told you I love you!"

Antonio didn't look at her as he roughly put clothes in the duffel bag. "I never asked for your love."

"I know." She took a deep breath. "When we married, I didn't want your love, either. I was afraid if we fell in love, our child might feel excluded, as I once did, from parents focused only on each other. But now I know it doesn't have to be that way. I can love you both. So much."

He paused. "You can love me if you want. But I'm not like you. I don't have…"

"Feelings?" she choked out.

"The ability to love you in such a sentimental fashion. I'll never be like Tanaka, mooning over you all the time. I care for you and our child. Caring is an action, not an emotion. I will always provide for you and the children.

But CrossWorld Airways is what I love. It's the only thing I can control. The only thing that lasts."

"Family doesn't last? Love?"

He gave a low, bitter laugh. "No. Love doesn't last."

Hana's expression suddenly changed. "Why don't you admit the truth?"

"And what's that, Hana?"

"You're afraid to love me. Just as you're afraid to find out the truth about your parents. But the worst thing is, you *like* being afraid. Because it's safe." She lifted her chin. "You're a coward, Antonio."

His body recoiled.

Then cold anger snapped his spine straight, made his shoulders broaden to their full width. He looked at her, his soul like ice. "Enough." He snapped the bag shut. "If you ever speak of love again, this marriage is over."

And without looking at her again, he left.

Hana woke to hear the shutters opening. Rich Spanish sunlight poured in from the wrought-iron veranda overlooking their grand tree-lined avenue in Madrid.

"*Buenos días*, Señora Delacruz," Manuelita chirped happily.

But it wasn't a good morning. With a sudden sick feeling, Hana remembered everything that had happened during the darkness, hours before.

Her husband didn't want her love.

So much so that when she'd told him she loved him, he'd literally packed his bag and left the country.

Hana's whole body hurt from a night of tossing and turning. Glancing at the gilded clock over the marble fireplace mantel, she saw it was nearly eleven. She must have fallen asleep shortly before dawn. Now, sunlight flooded their bedroom.

But it might as well have been pouring rain.

She sat up stiffly in the big four-poster bed, yanking the comforter up over her nightgown. Her joints ached, and her lower back. Her hugely pregnant belly felt heavy. So did her heart.

Picking up a breakfast tray from a nearby table, Manuelita brought it to the bed. "Señor Delacruz told me yesterday that whenever he travels, we must take extra good care of you." She smiled. "He asked me to wake you up each morning with a tray, and your favorite flower."

Hana looked down at the tray in her lap. The breakfast had all her favorites—fruit, yogurt, crusty toast and jam, scrambled eggs, with orange juice and herbal tea. And in a tiny, perfect crystal vase, a tiny, perfect pink rose.

"Thank you, Manuelita," she whispered. Smiling, the older woman left with a satisfied nod, as if proud of representing her employer, who had obviously become a romantic, leaving his pregnant wife to sleep in and arranging breakfast in bed, even remembering her favorite flower. So romantic, so loving, so thoughtful.

But it didn't feel that way to Hana. Antonio had no problem paying people off with money or gifts. He'd asked his housekeeper to take care of Hana. But giving her anything real of himself—his time, his trust, his *love*—forget it.

Hana gulped water, dehydrated after her night of tears. She tried to eat a few bites of food, but it all tasted like ash in her mouth.

Staring at the little flower, she resisted the urge to crumple it in her hand. Rather than trying to comfort her over the painful fact that he couldn't love her, or apologizing over the way he'd kicked her out of the company she'd come to love, Antonio had simply left. So she couldn't argue with him. She didn't even have a chance.

It was a coldhearted way to win. Ruthless. Exactly the way Antonio always dealt with his mistresses, opponents and rivals.

She'd just never thought he'd treat her like that.

Pushing the breakfast tray aside, she walked across the cool tile floor with bare feet. She pulled on a red silk robe with an embroidered dragon on the back. Opening a side door, she peeked into the baby's empty nursery. She'd spent hours tenderly picking out the furniture, the crib, the glider, the books, the toys. A huge stuffed polar bear rested against the corner of the pale pink walls. She loved this room, where very soon they'd bring their baby home. Her husband had barely looked at it.

Just as he'd barely looked at Hana when he left.

Turning back to the master bedroom, she opened the French doors. With a deep breath of the fresh, cool air, she went out onto the balcony, overlooking the historic neighborhood of Madrid where they lived.

Vivid pink bougainvillea hung on the edges of the wrought-iron balcony. Blinking fast, she looked out at the classical cream-colored buildings and palm trees beneath the golden sun and blue sky. A cold wind blew against her skin. Autumn had truly come at last. And along with it, the cold truth she hadn't wanted to face.

Her husband was broken, and her love could not save him. Because he did not even want to be saved.

Hana's hands tightened on the wrought-iron balcony. She had to find a way out of this. *Had* to. Why had he forced her to leave the company? They could easily set up a nursery in the office after the baby was born. Since she knew Antonio had no intention of spending less time at work, their only hope to be close as a family was for their family to be at work, as well. Surely he had to see this.

But he didn't want to see it. He was deliberately pushing her and the baby away.

Her cell phone rang from her bag inside. Turning back to the bedroom, she grabbed it, praying it was Antonio calling to make amends. But it wasn't her husband's name displayed on her phone, but someone even more surprising.

"Hello?" she said, a little nervously.

"Hana." Ren Tanaka's deep voice was tentative. "I almost didn't expect you to answer."

"Ren," she whispered, feeling low. "How did you know?"

"Know what? Is something wrong?"

She bit her lip. They hadn't spoken since her wedding day in Tokyo. She didn't know where to begin. "I…it's hard to explain."

"I'm sorry. I shouldn't have ignored you for the last six months," Ren said quietly. "I just…didn't know how to deal with everything."

"I know."

"I'm in Paris. I wondered if I could come see you." He paused. "I have some news."

Hana knew her husband wouldn't like her seeing Ren. He'd made his thoughts clear on her having a best friend who was a man: it wasn't allowed.

But it was so unfair. Antonio had abandoned her, cutting her off even from work. Did he expect her to remain a lonely prisoner in this house?

Forget that.

"Please come as soon as you can," she said, her voice cracking. "I need a friend today."

After they hung up, she paced all afternoon, staring at her phone, wishing Antonio would call her, trying to resist the urge to call him. He'd surely arrived in New York by now. She wondered how the negotiations were going with the labor union. Hana had always been the buffer.

Finally, she could resist no longer. Snatching up the phone, she dialed his number.

Antonio didn't answer. It rang and rang, then went to voice mail. She tried again. The same. She felt sick, questioning the future of their marriage. She was desperate to find something, anything, that would give her hope.

In the meantime, Antonio couldn't even be bothered to answer the phone.

She didn't leave a message. What was there to say?

When Ren showed up at the door of the *palacio* later that night, they hugged awkwardly over her enormous belly. Ren looked different, Hana thought. He'd grown a beard, and his clothes were more youthful.

Manuelita brought tea into the salon, then left, looking back between them suspiciously.

"Does she think I've come here to seduce you?" Ren said, his lips quirking.

Hana tried to smile, blinking so fast he wouldn't see the tears in her eyes. "Yes, a heavily pregnant woman is always a seduction magnet."

They sat on opposite couches in the salon for an hour drinking tea, making small talk about inconsequential things, people they knew, the expansion of the Tanakas' hotel business in Tokyo. Finally, with the pastries all gone and the tea grown cold, Ren looked at her across the coffee table.

"You look well, Hana," he said softly. "Are you happy?"

She set down her china teacup and changed the subject. "What's your big news?"

Leaning forward, Ren pulled a small black velvet box out of his pocket. Opening the lid, he held it out to her. A huge, sparkling diamond engagement ring.

Hana's mouth fell open with horror. "Oh, no—Ren, you know I'm already...and besides—"

"Hana, relax!" With a laugh, Ren snapped the lid closed. "It's not for you!"

"Whew!"

Staring at each other, they both burst into laughter, the awkwardness suddenly gone.

"You should see your face," he said, grinning.

"I'm sorry," she said. "But you scared me! For six months, you haven't answered my messages. I had no idea what you were feeling!"

"I know." His face grew serious. "The night you left Tokyo, you broke my heart."

Hana felt awful. "I never meant to."

"I know." He squared his shoulders. "I came to thank you. For telling me what I needed to hear."

"Even though I broke your heart?"

Ren shook his head. "It hurt, but not as much as my years of silent longing and hoping before. It's why I hated Delacruz from the moment you started working for him. I could hear the way you spoke about him." He paused. "But when you told me you'd never love me, as hard as it was to hear, it freed me. I was finally able to move on. And now... I'm happier than I've ever been."

"You've found someone else," she guessed.

He nodded shyly. "That's the other news I wanted to share. Emika Ito—you remember her?"

"The head of the Tokyo lead team?"

Ren nodded. "The night of your wedding, she came over and started talking to me. She's a good person, a kind person."

"And pretty," Hana added slyly.

"Yeah. That, too." He grinned. "We ended up doing shots at the bar and then..."

"Then?"

Happiness glowed from him. "The next day, she wanted to check on me, just to see I was all right. And gradually, our friendship turned into more." Ren shook his head. "It's strange. When you left Tokyo, I thought my heart would be broken forever." He looked down at the ring. "I never imagined how wonderful it could be to have someone love me like Emika does. And the way I love her! It makes me realize… My love for you was never real." He gave her a crooked grin. "I hope you're not offended."

"I'm thrilled!"

"Yesterday, I was finishing a conference in Paris, and I decided I couldn't wait any longer. I went to a jeweler and bought this ring. I'm going to ask her to marry me as soon as I'm back in Tokyo. I'll throw a big party, do everything I can to show her how much I love her. And I thought…" He lifted his gaze. "Who else could I share this big news with, if not my best friend?"

Tears lifted to Hana's eyes. Ren was in love. He was getting married. And in spite of all their past troubles, he'd come to share the news with her. "I'm so glad."

"Thank you." He tucked the black velvet box back in his pocket. Then his voice changed. "But what about you? Are you happy, Hana?"

"Of course," she said automatically, then flinched at the wobble in her voice.

Ren's jaw tightened. "Tell me what's wrong."

She gave him a sad smile. "You might be my best friend, but I can't tell you about my marriage."

"I understand."

"You do?"

He shrugged. "I've always thought Delacruz was a jerk. You know that. But if Emika and I were having a fight, I wouldn't want her to run tell some other man about it. I'd want her to talk to me, so we could work through it."

"Some things can't be worked through," Hana whispered.

His eyes narrowed. "He's hurt you—cheated on you?"

She was aghast. "No!"

"Then?"

"He…he just doesn't want to share his life with me, not really. He doesn't want to share his heart."

"Maybe he's afraid." His eyes met hers. "I get it. But love

can fix the broken pieces. I've learned that better than anyone. Maybe your heart won't be the same as it was, but—" the corners of his lips lifted "—it can be repaired, and more precious and beautiful for all that."

Her throat ached with pain. *"Kintsugi."*

Ren looked thoughtful. "Yes, I suppose you could look at it like that. A broken heart repaired by love."

Unable to speak, Hana looked out the large window of the *palacio*'s grand salon, overlooking the courtyard filled with orange trees. "But if Antonio doesn't love me..."

"There are all kinds of love." He snorted. "Maybe he has the kind of love that made him want to smash my face in back in Tokyo." He gave a sly grin. "Not that he would have succeeded, mind you..."

"He's possessive, yes. He keeps what is his." She strove to keep the bitterness out of her voice. "But that's not love."

Ren leaned over the coffee table. "Give him a chance, Hana. Tell him how you feel."

"I tried, and he...he just left."

"So try again."

Swallowing, she lifted her gaze. "But what if he really, truly can't love me?"

"Then at least you'll know." His eyes met hers. "Don't be like me, suffering for years in silence. Find out the truth. It's better to know, even if it hurts. It's the only thing that can set you free from a prison of hope."

A prison of hope. Hana shivered, looking down at her cooling tea. What a frightening thought. Even cold, awful freedom had to be better than that.

Ren looked regretfully at his watch. "I'm so sorry. I have to catch my flight to Tokyo." He rose to his feet. "You'll come to our wedding, won't you?" He gave a nervous laugh. "Assuming Emika says yes."

"Of course she'll say yes." Rising to her feet in turn, Hana walked him to the door. "And of course I'll come."

Pausing at the doorway, Ren said, "Give him another chance. Men can be fools." He added cheerfully, "And Delacruz is the biggest fool I've ever met."

"You two," she said, rolling her eyes.

He grinned. "We both love you. In different ways."

She returned his smile, then it faded. "He says he doesn't."

Ren sobered. "Maybe he doesn't. Or maybe he wants to, but he can't. Because of something he's gone through. Something he's lost," he said quietly. "Something he needs to get over, like I needed to get over you."

Hana thought of Antonio's childhood, the repeated abandonment when he was a boy. She said slowly, "What if he doesn't want to get over it?"

His eyes looked troubled. Then he shook his head. "Love can conquer anything. You'll see." He grinned. "Even that arrogant Spanish bastard."

After he was gone, Hana felt alone in the big, empty room. She paced, her angry footsteps echoing against the walls.

Love could conquer anything, could it?

But it hadn't! It couldn't!

Could it?

She stopped, clenching her hands at her sides as she looked out the big windows at the courtyard. She took a deep breath. After everything he'd gone through, it was no wonder Antonio wouldn't want to risk loving anyone, ever again.

If Hana could only find a way to heal him!

If he'd just been willing to learn why his parents abandoned him on those church steps the day he was born, she thought. Maybe the truth would hurt him—but like Ren had said, wouldn't knowing be better than always wondering? A wound couldn't heal until you removed the thing that was making it fester.

But Antonio had burned the letter. Closing her eyes, she tried to remember the doctor's name. Moreno? *Mendoza*. From some funny Basque-sounding village. Eche—something.

"Did your friend leave?" Manuelita called as Hana hurried back down the hallway.

"Yes." Going into the study, she grabbed her laptop and sat down at her husband's desk. Opening it, she started searching online. Hours later, after her shoulders ached with being hunched over the screen, she found it.

Dr. Mendoza. Of Etxetarri.

For a moment, she hesitated, knowing Antonio might never forgive her for intruding. But if her husband had no desire to heal his pain, no desire to love or be loved—no desire to even be in the same room with her!—how could they remain married? He'd told her if she ever mentioned love again, their marriage was over!

With a deep breath, Hana picked up her phone. Her hands shook as she dialed the doctor's listed number, and listened to it ring.

And when it was finally answered, Hana learned—everything.

CHAPTER TWELVE

WHEN ANTONIO GOT the first phone message from his wife, he ignored it.

And the second, third and fourth.

For the last three days, he'd been struggling in the boardroom of CrossWorld's New York office, dealing with his team of lawyers. Lauren, his new executive assistant in the New York office, hadn't done the prep work as thoroughly as Hana would have. Nor did she have the same charm.

But no one was as good as Hana. On top of all his wife's skills with language, logistics and the airline business in general, she'd also worked side by side with Antonio for years, and knew how to manage him almost as well as she could manage the labor union.

The negotiations hadn't gone at all well without her. Antonio had been off his game. He didn't know why. Maybe because he hadn't slept well alone in the luxury New York hotel suite. The bed felt empty.

So when he saw, on the third day as he'd come out of yet another fruitless, combative meeting, that Hana had left him yet another message, he'd just gritted his teeth and ignored it. He didn't need her at his company. He could do very well without her.

Especially if she was calling to gloat over his failure.

He glanced at his watch. He was late for a 9:00 p.m. dinner with Horace Lund. He'd think of Hana later.

I love you. He heard her voice. Remembered the pain in her eyes when he hadn't responded as she'd hoped he might.

No. Antonio couldn't bend. If he did, he was afraid he'd break.

Over appetizers in the elegant midtown restaurant, after Horace Lund toasted his gratitude for Antonio's loan, the older man spoke cheerfully about his business's potential. But by the man's third bourbon, he became morose. As he ate his fettuccine, he spoke about his recent divorce. By dessert, he was nearly crying over his cannoli.

"My wife always complained I didn't spend enough time with her," the older man choked out. "So last week, she said I should be happy she was divorcing me, because now I can work every single minute without guilt, just as I wanted…" And on and on.

Antonio, who'd indulged in only one glass of scotch, tried not to roll his eyes as he sipped bitter black coffee for dessert. He despised the man's tearful regret. If Lund didn't want this to happen, he never should have let himself love his wife. Why else was Antonio avoiding Hana? Even in spite of the unfortunate impact on his company.

The negotiations had gone badly again today, and the head of the employees' union had asked point-blank for Hana. "She, at least, knows what the employees are up against." Antonio had responded coldly, "You're up against *me*." And before he knew what was happening, the other man was stomping out of the meeting. Antonio ground his teeth.

"Now she's fallen for some yoga instructor," Lund moaned, as he stuffed cannoli into his mouth. "He doesn't have a penny but she doesn't care…"

Antonio regretted yet again that he'd ever agreed to meet the man for dinner. He coughed, then said tersely, "Pull yourself together. She's gone. It's time to move on. You have a company to reorganize."

"Yes." Lund brightened, then his lip began to wobble again. "Patricia helped me start it. It's not the same without her…"

Antonio was contemplating the possibility of flinging himself out the Italian restaurant's large glass window to get away from the man's whining when he heard his phone ping. Relieved for the distraction, he glanced at it. A message from Hana flashed across the screen.

I spoke with your mother. I know everything. You should come home.

Antonio jumped to his feet. His whole body was suddenly shaking. "I have to go," he said hoarsely, and tossed money on the table before he fled beneath the man's astonished eyes.

Getting into his Rolls-Royce waiting outside, Antonio was on the phone before his driver even pulled from the curb, contacting his new secretary. "Cancel tomorrow's meetings with the union."

"What?" Lauren's young voice was shocked. "Are you— are you sure, sir?"

He knew the question she'd nearly blurted out was, *Are you crazy?* A man messed with the union at his peril. But everything that had seemed so important suddenly meant nothing, compared to the acid hissing through his soul, searing everything in its path. "Have the jet waiting for me at Teterboro."

By the time his plane touched down in gray, rainy Madrid, it was early afternoon. Far from sleeping on the flight, he'd paced the aisle of his Gulfstream jet, his body so tight, his muscles hurt. As his driver took him to the *palacio*, through the city's crowded, lively streets in the autumn drizzle, Antonio looked out the window with a churning feeling in his belly.

What had Hana learned? The horrible thing that had made him a monster from the day he was born?

I spoke with your mother. I know everything.

The driver passed the *palacio*'s gatehouse and pulled into the courtyard. Antonio was already opening his door before the car stopped. Jumping out, he rushed inside, his heart pounding.

Empty. The *palacio* was empty.

Ice gripped his heart as he walked past dark rooms filled with antiques, past the salon on the main floor, with its big windows. Turning on a light, he went slowly up the sweeping staircase, feeling like he'd aged fifty years. He already knew what he would find: an empty bedroom, with all her clothes gone from their closet. All his attempts to hide his unworthiness from her had failed…

A light clicked on. He saw Hana sitting in the bedroom's armchair by the empty fireplace. There were dark circles beneath her eyes, as if she hadn't slept well in days, either.

Seeing her, Antonio felt a rush of joy. Then he was overwhelmed by fury. By betrayal.

"How could you?" Dropping his briefcase to the bedroom's tile floor, he ground out, "I made it clear I have no desire to learn about my past. Ever."

Hana lifted her chin, her eyes defiant. "I had to."

"Why? Do you hate me so much?"

She stopped, blinked. "No. I love you. That's why I did this. I'm trying to help you." Her expression became tender as she said softly, "You need to know the truth."

"But I burned that man's letter—"

"I remembered his name. I looked him up on the internet and called him." She paused. "Yesterday, I took the train up to Etxetarri."

"Where?"

"A little fishing village to the north." She took a deep breath. "I met your mother. In person."

"You. What?" Sudden vertigo made him light-headed.

"Please, just listen. You have to know. It could change everything. As Ren told me when he came here, the truth can set you free—"

Ren Tanaka? That made Antonio stop cold. All his fear and pain and uncertainty coagulated around this one point. "He was here?"

"You're missing the point—"

"You invited Tanaka to this house?" His eyes narrowed. "Behind my back? While I wasn't here?"

"*Behind your back?* Are you serious?" A hard laugh burst from her lips. "The only reason you weren't here is because *you left me.* In the middle of the night. After I told you I loved you."

Antonio thought of Lund's wife and the yoga instructor. "I told you I didn't want you to be friends with Tanaka anymore."

"Yes, you've told me a lot of things." She lifted her steady gaze to his. "Like when you said the company would belong to us equally. When you said we'd share our lives. But from the moment we arrived in Madrid, you've been pushing me away. And when I told you I loved you, you left."

She saw right through him. His weaknesses. He said coldly, "You keep bringing that up. But one has nothing to do with the other. And don't change the subject from Tanaka—"

"Ren came to show me the engagement ring he bought in Paris." For a split second, ice gripped Antonio's throat, before she continued, "He's going to propose to his girlfriend. Emika."

He stared at Hana blankly. "Emika?"

"Emika Ito," she prompted. "The head of your Tokyo office. Remember?"

"Of course I remember," he snapped. He took a deep breath, forcing his shoulders to relax. So Tanaka wasn't a rival after all. He felt dizzy with relief. "He came all the way to Madrid to tell you that?"

"Ren came to thank me. He told me it hurt him in April when I told him I'd never love him, but it also set him free," she said quietly. "When he was forced to give up old dreams, he was able to have new ones."

Her voice was strange. He set his jaw. "What are you trying to say?"

Hana's eyes met his. "You're afraid to let me love you. Because you're afraid to love me."

Antonio felt a wrench in his belly, a wild pounding of his heart even worse than when he'd heard about Tanaka's visit. *She knew.* This rocked the walls around his heart, the radioactive place he'd spent a lifetime being careful not to go. "Don't be ridiculous."

"But you don't have to be afraid. Not anymore." Rising to her feet, Hana came closer. Her eyes gleamed, her curvy pregnant body swaying as she approached. "I know the reason you were left on those church steps the day you were born."

"Stop," he said helplessly.

"Your mother's name is Josune Loiola. Here is her address. Her phone number." Hana held out a piece of paper. "Please go talk to her."

"No!" Ignoring the paper, he shook his head violently. "I don't want to know!"

"You have to hurry. There's not much time left. Your mother's sick. Dying..."

"I don't care."

"Only because you don't know what happened!"

"I know enough."

"You have to forgive her. So you can forgive yourself."

"Me?" Antonio looked at her incredulously. "I've done nothing wrong."

"Exactly. But you still can't move past it. And you must." Putting her hand on her pregnant belly, she murmured, "We need you."

"And this is how you try to help me?" Antonio said wildly. "By going behind my back, betraying me?"

"It's not a betrayal." When he still didn't move, she set the paper gently down on the side table. Coming forward, she put her hand on his arm. He imagined he saw pity in her eyes. "If you won't go see her, just listen. I'll tell you…"

Antonio yanked his arm away. "Stop it. Now. Or…"

"Or what?" As Hana stood apart from him, her lovely face suddenly looked sad. "Or you'll leave me again?"

"Yes."

He saw the exact moment hope died in her eyes.

Hana took a deep breath. "Don't bother."

Turning toward the door, she picked up a small overnight bag, the one she'd brought from Tokyo six months before. He frowned. "Where are you going?"

"To Tokyo," Hana said. "Ren's proposing to Emika at a big party tomorrow. If I leave right now, I can be there." She looked back at him. "With friends who actually want me to be part of their lives." She looked around the master bedroom where they'd spent so many passionate nights. "I thought this could be my home. But home isn't a place. It's people who love you."

Antonio stared at her. Outside the wrought-iron balcony, the lowering gray clouds rattled the lead windows with rain.

The bedroom seemed to whirl in front of his eyes as he looked at his wife holding the bag. Fear twisted through him. Anguish. Anger. He clung to the last emotion, the only one he knew how to deal with.

"You can't leave," he ground out. "You're my wife. Carrying my child."

"And yet you made it clear if I ever spoke about love again, our marriage was over."

Antonio narrowed his eyes. "Is this because I changed my mind about giving you half my company?"

"It hurt when you went back on your promise." She gave him a wistful smile. "Sharing the company was like sharing you."

Antonio's heart hammered against his ribs.

"But I was dreaming." Hana turned away. "I'm going to have my baby in Tokyo. I already booked myself on the evening flight. That, at least, is part of the post-nup I remember." She gave a smile. "Unlimited flights on Cross-World Airways for the rest of my life."

"You knew this was how tonight would end," he said slowly.

"I've tried everything I can to help heal you. But if you don't want to be healed, there's nothing I can do. Loving you isn't enough. I can't love you if you won't love yourself."

He stared at her, feeling numb.

She took a deep breath, trying to smile. "Our baby will have your name when she's born. You can see her anytime you want, no matter what the post-nup says."

"Hana," he choked out.

Her beautiful eyes were luminous in the shadows of their bedroom, as if her heart was breaking. "Goodbye, Antonio."

She left without looking back.

There was a flash of lightning outside the bedroom's windows. Antonio felt numb. As thunder rumbled across the sky a moment later, he felt a gut-wrenching pain.

How could Hana leave him? She had no right. He would not allow it. *She was his.*

And yet…he felt a strange trickle down his spine. His body was reacting strangely. Beneath the anger, he felt pain, yes. But also, buried in the cracks, another feeling he couldn't understand. One that made no sense. Relief.

Finally.

He'd always known this would happen. Even in their happiest moments. Even when he'd been making love to her on a pink sand Caribbean beach on their honeymoon, part of him had always known he'd lose her. No, even before that. On their wedding day in Tokyo, when Ren Tanaka had told him he wasn't worthy of his bride. *And someday soon, Hana will know it, too.*

That day had finally come.

His eyes fell on the end table. All he could see, all he could feel, was the small paper that Hana had left there. His mother's address. Her phone number. The answers to everything he'd feared most.

Turning, he fled the room.

Antonio went downstairs to his study to try to work, but he couldn't concentrate on his laptop. Words and figures swam incomprehensibly in front of his eyes. He thought of how he'd judged Horace Lund so harshly at the restaurant in New York, and wondered if he himself would soon be muttering wild-eyed over cannoli about the woman he'd lost.

He hadn't lost Hana to a yoga instructor. Not even to Tanaka, who though he still hated him, Antonio grudgingly had to admit he had a certain unwilling respect for.

No. Antonio had lost her on his own. Because of his fear to learn the truth about his own darkest flaws.

Pushing his laptop aside in disgust, he left the study and went down the hall, nearly walking into an antique suit of armor. That was what Hana deserved, he thought. A knight in shining armor. A man who wasn't so deeply cracked at the core.

Going back to his bedroom, he yanked off the business

suit he'd worn flying across the Atlantic, back when he'd thought he could still save their marriage. He put on exercise shorts, gym shoes and a thin T-shirt that stretched across his hard-muscled chest, then went back downstairs, past the kitchen, where he could hear Manuelita talking to her assistant and pounding the dough for bread. Going down the hall to his home gym, he turned on the light.

The gym was empty, gleaming, pristine. He pushed a button that lifted the automated blinds, filling the room with weak gray light.

I know the reason you were left on those church steps the day you were born.

Guzzling down some water from the cooler, he climbed on the treadmill. He set the speed faster and faster, trying to outrun his thoughts.

There's not much time left. Your mother's sick. Dying...

Going to the punching bag, he hit it without gloves. Once. Twice. He pounded it until his knuckles were raw.

I've tried everything I can to help heal you. But if you don't want to be healed, there's nothing I can do.

Antonio fell against the punching bag, wrapping his arms around it as his knees swayed beneath him.

Loving you isn't enough. I can't love you if you won't love yourself.

"Stop," he whispered aloud.

He didn't need her love. He had his business empire. His airline that allowed him to escape anywhere, anytime. He was a citizen of the world, beholden to no one and attached to nothing. He could replace Hana instantly. He...

Closing his eyes, Antonio leaned his hot cheek against the cool leather punching bag. He suddenly didn't care about his empire.

Money—what did that matter without being able to spend it on her?

Power—what kind of power could he ever have, if he didn't even have the power to be with her?

Sex—what appeal could meaningless hookups ever have, after the ecstasy of holding Hana in his arms?

His wife had tried to heal him. Ridiculous. Even she, with all her warmth and care, didn't have that power. He still couldn't believe Hana had tracked down the doctor and gone to speak with his mother.

There's not much time left. Your mother's sick. Dying...

A shudder went through him and he opened his eyes bleakly.

For the first time since he was a boy, he tried to picture his mother. Tried to imagine why she'd abandoned him. Was Antonio so awful as a newborn? Had he been colicky, crying for hours? Had she hated the man who'd impregnated her?

Had he been conceived, not in love, but out of some horrific act like rape?

It was his greatest fear.

Antonio thought of his childhood, of not even knowing who he was or why he'd been abandoned, of being sent back to the orphanage whenever he'd dared hope he'd found someone to love him, of getting beaten by the older kids for crying. He'd simply learned to stop feeling anything at all, just to avoid pain. He thought of the time he'd imagined himself in love with Isabella, giving his heart away so eagerly, only to have it thrown back in his face. *Money is what matters. Money is what lasts. You're young. You'll learn.*

But Hana hadn't cared about money. She'd only cared about him. Helping him. Healing him.

Loving him.

Antonio shuffled wearily out of the home gym. He stopped outside the doorway of the grand salon, a gracious, high-ceilinged room, in this palace once owned by a nobleman. The decor was elegant, with all the prestige money could buy. He'd done this to prove to everyone that he was no longer the pathetic orphan he'd been. But there was one person he'd never been able to convince: himself.

I can't love you if you won't love yourself.

Suddenly, Antonio knew he had to make a choice. One choice now that would separate his life forever onto two different paths.

Which would it be?

Gripping his hands at his sides, he looked out the wide windows toward the orange trees in the rainy courtyard. Would he keep the life he'd had? Where he felt nothing, and controlled everything—most of all, his own feelings— out of fear?

Or would he take a risk?

Suddenly, he was tired of being afraid.

He'd lost Hana. What could be worse than that? What more did he have to fear?

Antonio stood totally still. Then his chin lifted, his jaw set.

He would no longer be enslaved by his worst fears about his past. About himself.

His spine snapped straight, and he turned on his heel. Going up the staircase, he went into his bedroom. He picked up the piece of paper Hana had left. He saw his mother's name, Josune Loiola. An address. A phone number.

Grabbing his phone, he started to dial, then stopped. No. He couldn't do this on the phone. He had to see the woman in person, to see her face, to demand why she'd left him as a baby, helpless and alone, in a basket on those church steps.

He dialed Garcia instead. "Gas up the jet."

"Back to New York, *señor*?"

"No," he told his bodyguard. "North. Tell the pilot to find the closest airport to a village called Etxetarri."

It was early evening when Antonio got into the car that

awaited him on the tarmac of the tiny private airport on the northern coast. Getting into the car, he left Garcia and his pilot behind.

He had to do this alone.

Antonio's hands tightened on the wheel as he drove along the coastal road, following the directions of his GPS. The rain was thick here, and as the sun starting to lower toward the western horizon, a mist rolled in from the glassy gray sea.

Antonio felt butterflies in his stomach as he drove into the tiny fishing village with houses clinging to cliffs. Finally, he reached his destination, a squat stone building overlooking a bay filled with battered boats. And he blinked.

It was a hospice.

Its colorful shutters were bright against the gray stone and a profusion of flowers hung beneath the windows. Nervously, he parked his anonymous sedan behind the hospice and went inside. His clothes were anonymous as well, just a black T-shirt and dark pants. He didn't want this woman—this *stranger*—to imagine that he was trying to impress her. But his knees were shaking as he went inside.

"Who are you here to see?" the receptionist said, not looking up from her magazine.

"Señora Loiola."

"Her third visitor in two days," the girl murmured in surprise. "So many visits!" She looked up. "Are you expected, *señor*...?"

"Delacruz." Antonio saw the exact moment the receptionist recognized him. All those years he'd spent as the playboy billionaire of Madrid had apparently reached even this far north. "And no. She's not expecting me. We've never met."

"You're a friend?"

"Apparently—" he gave a hard smile "—I'm her son."

The young woman's jaw dropped. She rose hastily to her feet. "I'll show you to her room, Señor Delacruz."

Going down a short hallway, which was lit too brightly and smelled of antiseptic, she knocked on a door and peeked in. "Are you available for visitors, *señora*?" He couldn't hear the softly murmured reply. "There's a gentleman here who says he's your son."

The receptionist turned to him with a big, artificial smile. "Please. Go in."

Antonio hesitated, then squaring his shoulders, he turned to the door. From the corner of his eye he saw the receptionist surreptitiously taking his photo with her phone.

Inside, the room was dark, and filled with shadows. It took a moment for his vision to adjust.

Then he saw a small pitiful figure in the bed.

The woman was younger than he'd expected, perhaps in her midfifties, dark-haired and slender, with big dark eyes that seemed too large in her sunken, gaunt face. Especially now, when those eyes were glowing with almost painful hope.

"Is it really you?" she whispered. She took a shuddering breath. "My sweet boy?"

Antonio looked down at those dark eyes, so much like his own. And all of the air in his chest went out with a *whoosh*.

He'd come here to confront her, to accuse her of abandoning him as a baby, to berate her for what she'd done.

But he'd never once considered what might have happened to her.

He came forward into the shadowy room. On the table beside her, he saw a vase of fresh, vibrant flowers. Hana, he thought. It would be so like her to bring flowers to someone who was dying. Even a stranger.

"I'm Antonio," he said slowly. His voice cracked a little. "Delacruz is the last name the nuns gave me, when I was left on the steps of a church in Andalusia." He couldn't keep the recrimination from his voice.

The woman blinked fast. "I'm Josune," she whispered. "And I only learned yesterday that my baby lived. The baby I had thirty-six years ago." Tears were welling in her dark eyes. Her voice was almost too quiet to hear. She took a shuddering breath. "I was sixteen when you were born, and they told me you were dead. They told me—"

Her voice cut off.

He looked down at her.

His voice was strangely uncertain. "You…you didn't abandon me?"

"*Abandon* you!" Her black eyes blazed in her fragile face. "I never abandoned you, never!" She clasped her hands over the blanket in her lap. "Dr. Mendoza, my father, they both told me you died at birth. They wouldn't let me see your body. They said it would give me nightmares." She looked away sharply. Tears streaked down her face as she whispered, "If I'd known you were alive, if I'd ever even guessed…"

Antonio felt a razor blade in his throat. His voice was low and harsh. "Why would they tell you I was dead?"

She faltered, licking her cracked lips. "Your father was a backpacker from America. He'd come here to walk the Camino." She bit her lip. "I was very sheltered, and…"

Antonio could not breathe, looking down at her. His voice was a croak as he spoke his darkest fear. "He forced himself on you."

"Forced?" She snorted. "He romanced me. I wanted it to be love, but within the week, he was gone. He'd told me his name was John Smith. John Smith! Even my father could not find him, though he tried."

Antonio found himself sitting on the edge of her bed. "What happened?"

"My parents were ashamed their only daughter was

pregnant and unwed. For a woman to have a child alone is ordinary now. Back then, it was not." She sighed. "Especially in a small village."

He glanced out the window, at the tiny stone village clinging to the cliffs above the sea. "But you still stayed here all your life."

"I'd shamed my family. Lost my baby. What else was I to do? My mother was sick. She needed me. She died a few years later, my father last year."

"But you could have married—had other children—"

Josune shook her head, her eyes full of tears. "I loved a man once, and he abandoned me. I had a child I loved. I lost him, as well." She looked away, toward the wild sea. "I couldn't ever face that pain again. Especially when I knew it was my fault."

"Your fault?"

Tears streamed down her sunken cheeks as she choked out, "When you died, the day you were born, what else could it be but my fault? I did something wrong. I wasn't good enough to be your mother." Looking away, she whispered, "I wasn't worthy of that kind of joy."

I wasn't worthy of that kind of joy.

Emotion gripped Antonio's heart. He thought of how he'd pushed Hana away. How he'd felt unworthy of her. How he'd tried not to love her, because he'd known he would only lose her.

"But yesterday your wife came to me," Josune said, her hand trembling as she reached toward the fresh flowers. "I could hardly believe it when she told me you were alive. I called Dr. Mendoza in a panic. He came to see me and confessed everything. My baby boy had been born healthy, but my father convinced him it would be better if they said you were dead. He took you to Andalusia, where no one in my village would hear of the baby who'd been found there." Her dark eyes lifted to his. "Yesterday I didn't know what to think, feel. It was as if all my dreams had come true—and my nightmares."

He could see the desperate question in her gaunt face. He said slowly, "Dr. Mendoza came to see me in Madrid recently. Why didn't he tell you about me then?"

"He said he didn't want to hurt me." Her lips turned up bitterly. "He was afraid, if you refused to see me, that it would only stir up new pain as I was already dying." She looked down at her slender hands, held together tightly on the blanket. "Even your wife wouldn't tell me her last name. She said the choice had to be yours." Lifting her gaze to his, she breathed, "I didn't think you would come, even as I prayed for it every moment. When I learned you were alive, I knew you must hate me..."

It was true, Antonio realized. He'd hated her every day. And hated himself for whatever had made them give him away.

"Just tell me you were happy," she begged. "Tell me you were adopted by a family who loved you, as I would have loved you every day. I would have called you Julen." Her gaze wandered to the window, overlooking the misty coast. "Waking up, I'd think, today my son would have been three. Today he would have been six. Today he would be eighteen, and a man." She looked back at him, and her dark eyes shone with tears like rain. "When I learned yesterday you were alive, it was almost too amazing to believe. But now, all I can think is that I should have known. I should have sensed you were alive, and come for you." Her voice broke as she said, "Please just tell me you were happy."

Antonio closed his eyes.

When he was young, he'd imagined what he would tell the parents who'd abandoned him, if he ever had the chance. How he'd destroy them with guilt. And he saw, in this moment, how easy it would be to destroy Josune. All the pain and anguish of his childhood was pounding in his memory as he opened his eyes and took a deep breath, knowing he could take his revenge just by telling her the truth.

"I was happy," he lied in a low voice. "I was loved."

She exhaled in a rush of tears, covering her face with her hands as she choked out a sob. "Thank you." She wiped her eyes. "But your wife is not with you today? You are expecting a baby. You said you live in Madrid?"

Antonio stared at her. She had no idea who he was, he realized. She wasn't asking about his fortune, or his airline. She wasn't looking at his net worth to determine his value. She was asking about what really mattered. His family.

And in a flash, things clicked into place.

Antonio had always thought he was different. That he, alone on earth, was unworthy of being loved. It had driven him to build a worldwide company, a billion-dollar fortune, to prove everyone wrong. To escape his worst belief about himself.

But the truth was, far from being a monster, he was exactly like everyone else. Flawed. Making the best decisions he could, and sometimes failing. Sometimes being wrong. So wrong.

But all along, he'd been loved, though he hadn't known it, every single day by his mother, who'd mourned him. And he'd been loved by Hana, even as he'd tried so hard to push her away.

"Can you ever forgive me, *mi hijo*?" Josune whispered.

Reaching out, he took his mother's trembling hands in his own. "There's nothing to forgive, *mama*."

With a cry, she reached her arms around her much taller, broad-shouldered son. He leaned forward to hug her, and for a moment, they held each other. Then finally, he pulled back.

"I love you, Antonio," his mother said, wiping the tears still glimmering in her eyes. "And your wife. For bringing you back to me."

He lifted his head. "My wife…"

Josune gripped his hand. "Never forget to tell her you love her. We always must tell each other. Because you never know how many chances we have."

Antonio looked at his mother as a crack of brilliant, warm gold light finally broke through the gray clouds.

Memory stirred. Gold through the cracks. He heard his wife's voice, telling him about broken Japanese pottery rejoined by solid gold. *Something broken and repaired is more precious and beautiful than something unused and whole. It shows history. It shows life.*

"You're right." Rising to his feet, Antonio said, "I'll be back as soon as I can."

"Go, my son."

Turning, he started running down the hall of the hospice, out into the misty village above the sea. To find his wife.

To find his heart.

CHAPTER THIRTEEN

"YES, OF COURSE I will marry you!"

Hana smiled as she watched her best friend rise eagerly to his feet and embrace the woman he loved. He'd proposed on one knee, holding out the diamond ring he'd shown Hana in Madrid, at a party he'd organized in a fantastic bar near Shibuya Square, surrounded by their family and friends.

Of course Emika had said yes, Hana thought, watching as the Japanese girl hugged Ren, her pretty face crying with happiness. Ren was beaming, looking like the proudest man in the world.

Hana watched them with a lump in her throat.

It was strange to be back in Tokyo, at another party in another hotel, celebrating another union of two people. But this was very different from the last.

Her own sort-of wedding reception had been more of a business celebration, actually, and held at a sleek, sophisticated luxury hotel. Then, it had been April, with the cherry trees brilliantly in bloom.

Ren and Emika's party was different. This bar was modern and colorful and hip, with brightly colored manga on the walls. It was on the second floor, with huge windows overlooking Shibuya Crossing, with all its big neon signs lighting up the night. It was the busiest pedestrian intersection in the world, where two thousand people or more could cross the street each time the light changed.

And yet, even surrounded by people, Hana felt alone.

She'd thought her love could save Antonio. She'd hoped, when she left him, he might come after her.

He hadn't.

Since their wedding, spring had turned to autumn. All the bright, innocent hope she'd felt the last time she'd been in Tokyo had been lost. Just like the cherry trees—her happiness had bloomed briefly, then faded, then fallen.

It was October now, the haunted, wistful month of longings and regret. Her baby was due in less than two weeks, and her whole body ached. She put her hands on her belly, which had been tensing up strangely all evening. Braxton Hicks contractions, she thought. And her lower back had been aching for hours, but what did she expect, after such a long flight? But just in case, she'd go to the doctor first thing in the morning.

"Are you feeling all right, Hana?"

Looking up, she saw Ren's worried face.

"Of course." Trying to smile, she nodded toward Emika, who was showing her diamond engagement ring to her clamoring, excited friends. "I'm so happy I got to see your proposal."

"I'm just happy she said yes," he replied wryly.

Hana smiled. "She loves you. Anyone can see that."

He came closer. He had a strange expression on his face. "Delacruz loves you. I know he does. Give him another chance…"

"More chances?" She felt pain in her heart just at hearing her husband's name. "I never thought you'd be the one to sing his praises."

"Me either." He bit his lip hard, then said only, "Just wait another hour. Have another melon soda. I promise you'll feel better in an hour."

Another hour of watching other people's happiness and feeling the pain of her own broken heart? She didn't think she could manage it. She evaded, "I'm going to go congratulate Emika."

As the next half hour passed, Hana listened to the engagement toasts, looking at the dreamy, dazzled faces of the happy couple, kissing each other and toasting a blissful future. Finally, she could bear it no longer. Taking her coat from the coatrack near the door, without saying farewell to anyone, Hana quietly left.

Outside, the Tokyo air was cold, with the bite of frost already looming in the air. The sidewalks were crowded, as it was Saturday night. The neon lights of Shibuya Crossing were bright, casting moving colors against the streets below, with all the noodle shops and tiny boutiques. Pulling her coat closer over her belly, she ducked her head and walked with the crowd toward her hotel, on the other side of the crossing.

Did she hear someone calling her name?

She shrugged it off. Hana was a common enough name in Japan. All her friends were still upstairs at the party.

Shivering, Hana waited on the sidewalk for the light to turn. When it did, all the cars stopped in the streets surrounding Shibuya Crossing, to wait for pedestrians. She moved with the crowds of people walking in every direction, even diagonally, across the large square.

Again, she thought she heard a voice shouting her name. Grief must be making her crazy, because it sounded like Antonio. But her husband was back in Spain. Or perhaps he was already back in New York, negotiating with the employees' union. Because that was all he cared about: his empire. Not his wife. Not his child…

"Hana!"

This time, she couldn't stop herself from looking back.

And then she *knew* she was dreaming. Because there, in the middle of the street, she saw Antonio pushing toward her, his handsome face full of longing.

She stumbled in shock. It was only when he was suddenly there to catch her, and she felt the warmth and power of his arms, that she knew he was real.

"You're...you're here," she breathed.

"You left the party early..."

As he held her, she felt the current and flow of crowds passing all around them, but it was as if they were the only two people on earth as he lifted her gently back to her feet. Her forehead furrowed. "What are you doing here?"

His dark eyes burned through her. "I came for you."

"Why?"

"To tell you I was wrong. About everything." Antonio glanced around them as crowds continued to push past. "I saw my mother."

"What?"

Antonio gave a single nod. "I finally know the truth. About her. About myself. I've flown across the world to tell you what I've felt for a long time but was too scared to admit."

Her lips parted.

"You were right," he said simply. "I was a coward. You're the most incredible woman I've ever known. I was afraid I didn't deserve your love. And maybe I don't. But I can spend the rest of my life trying. Because you're my empire, Hana." Running his hands through her hair, he whispered, "You're my soul."

Glancing around them, she saw crowds thinning out. The crosswalk light was flashing green, indicating it was about to turn red, when the car traffic would return. "We should get off the street..."

"Tell me it's not too late," Antonio urged. "Tell me I still have a chance."

Looking up at him, she gave a low laugh. "Even Ren told me I had to give you another chance."

"I know. When I phoned him from the plane..."

Her jaw dropped. "You phoned Ren?"

"He wasn't glad to hear from me," Antonio said, rubbing his chin ruefully. "It took a lot of begging to convince him I deserved to see you again. He was supposed to keep you at the party till I arrived."

No wonder Ren had told her to drink another melon soda, and promised she'd feel better in an hour. An incredulous laugh bubbled from her as she shook her head. "You—begging Ren? That must have hurt."

Antonio snorted. "You have no idea." His grin faded. "But not nearly as badly as it hurt to think of losing you." His dark eyes seared hers. "I love you, Hana."

Her heart was pounding. They were still standing in the middle of the crossing. They had to move. She knew they had to move. But she couldn't. If this was a dream, she didn't want to wake.

They heard loud honks from the approaching cars.

"Hey, that's my pregnant wife you're honking at!" Antonio yelled at the cars, who really did have the right of way. Taking her hand, he gently pulled her to the sidewalk on the other side.

His hand tightened on hers as he faced her on the crowded sidewalk. His gaze searched hers beneath the moving lights of the electronic billboards. "I love you," he repeated. He leaned his forehead against hers as he murmured, "Am I too late?"

Shaking her head, Hana drew back, smiling. "It's never too late." Lifting her hand, she placed it on his scratchy cheek. "Because I'll never stop loving you."

She heard his intake of breath. Pulling her into his arms, Antonio lowered his head to hers. His kiss was passionate, gentle and hot at once, promising forever.

Then Hana felt it again. The strange, sharp pain around her abdomen. Just like she'd read about. This wasn't Braxton-Hicks. She wrenched away.

"Antonio—" she panted.

"I can hardly wait to get you to my hotel," he said seductively, cupping her cheek. "Tonight, I'll show you how much I love you. Now and forever…"

Looking down, she gasped, "All that's going to have to wait."

He pulled back with a frown. "Why?"

Hana looked up, her expression in shock. "Because my water just broke!"

The cherry trees were newly in bloom when they returned to Tokyo in late March for Ren and Emika's wedding.

It had been a joyful day, full of love and laughter, tradition and cake. As they left the reception, Antonio held his wife's hand as he pushed their baby daughter's stroller. His heart was full of joy. Everywhere he looked, cherry flowers were popping like popcorn on trees, pink-and-white petals trailing in the soft spring breeze like confetti.

"Where are you taking me?" Hana asked him for the tenth time.

"It's a surprise," he told her, also for the tenth.

"Back to the plane, to take us home to Madrid?"

"No."

She blinked, then tilted her head. "To New York, then," she guessed. "So I can help you get a better deal this time."

She never let him forget how he'd gotten hosed in the union deal he'd made without her. A mistake he'd never been stupid enough to make again. From now on, they were partners all the way. At work. And at home. Smiling, he shook his head.

"Where?" she begged.

He grinned. "Come with me."

As he led her down the Tokyo street, Antonio's shoulders became a little straighter. He was filled with pride to have his wife on his arm, and pushing his baby daughter in the stroller. At five months old, Josie was already grabbing her own feet, and clearly a prodigy.

Her birth hadn't been easy. After twenty hours of labor, she'd been born finally by cesarean section in a Tokyo hospital. Every time Antonio remembered that night, he was awed by his wife's power and strength. Afterward, he'd wanted to shower her with jewels, but she'd told him his love was the only gift she ever wanted. "It's yours forever," he'd breathed, his eyes suspiciously wet.

A week later, they'd taken their baby, named Josie after his mother, back to the nursery waiting at their *palacio* in Madrid. Soon afterward, his mother had gotten a chance to meet her namesake. They had photos of their baby being held tenderly in her grandmother's lap, which would always be among their most precious possessions.

Antonio had wanted his mother to come live in the *palacio*, where he could oversee her care. But Josune had refused. "Etxetarri is my home," she'd told him in her softly wheezing voice. "I never want to leave it." But her hand had reached helplessly toward her son.

And so, with Hana's blessing, the Delacruz family had set up housekeeping in the seaside village. They'd rented a cottage just down the cliff from the hospice, and spent time with his mother every day, reading stories aloud, playing cards, just sitting quietly. Antonio had been with her when she'd peacefully died a few weeks later, surrounded by her family, and with a loving smile on her lips.

In one of their last conversations, Josune had told Antonio how proud she was of him, what a good man he was, how much she loved him. He wasn't sure he deserved such praise. But now he was a father, he finally understood.

Because that was exactly how he felt about baby Josie. Every time his daughter did something clever, like lifting her head or making a noise that sounded like "Papa"—something he was absolutely, positively sure she was doing

deliberately, no matter how doubtful Hana was about it—
he felt the need to share it, to praise it, to video record it, to
send it to all their friends. And even—in one particularly
embarrassing incident his wife still teased him about—he
couldn't help mentioning his daughter in a company email
to his eleven thousand employees. His cheeks went hot remembering that one. In his defense, Josie had done something remarkably difficult, sitting up all by herself for a
full thirty seconds.

"She's clearly a prodigy," he'd informed his wife. She'd
laughed, then informed him that his reputation in the business world for cold, ruthless savagery had taken a hit
lately.

"Everyone's starting to think you're a big softy," Hana
had said, then laughed even louder at the horrified look on
his face. Then he caught himself.

"It's all part of my plan to lure them in. I'm ruthless as
ever," Antonio replied smugly. "Trust me."

And he was ruthless. In business, when he wanted to
be. But always, always ruthless about showing his family
how much he loved them.

Now, in the two days they had to spend in Tokyo before they returned home to Madrid, Antonio wanted to do
something for his wife. She didn't care about money. She
didn't care about jewels. But she'd told him once about
something she wanted.

As Antonio pushed their baby's stroller beneath the
warm spring sunshine, he led her to the best park in Shin-
juku for cherry tree viewing. He'd already arranged a blanket to be set up. On top of it, a wicker basket was waiting
for them.

"What's this?" she asked, her forehead furrowed.

"A family picnic," he said. "Beneath the cherry trees."
He spoke the Japanese word, just as his buddy Ren Tanaka
had helped him practice. *"Hanami."*

Her lips parted in shock. "Your accent—it's perfect!"

Stopping beside the blanket, beneath the largest, most beautiful pink cherry tree against the bright blue sky, he parked the stroller. "I want to make all your dreams come true, *querida*. As you have mine."

Hana looked astonished. "I've made your dreams come true?"

Antonio took her in his arms. "You know you have. And you do every day. Especially today."

Hana blushed. She trembled. Then she whispered, "How did you know?"

"You told me last year that…" Then he blinked. "Wait. What are you talking about?"

Blushing, she ducked her head, her long dark hair falling in soft waves over her pale pink trench coat. "You said I made your dreams come true, especially today. So I thought…"

"Thought what?"

Shaking her head shyly, she gave him a slow-rising smile. "I thought you'd somehow found out…" Rising on her tiptoes, she whispered in his ear. He drew back. Now he was the one to look astonished.

"I just confirmed it at the doctor's before the wedding this morning. I heard the heartbeat." Her smile lifted to a saucy grin. "Heart*beats*."

His eyes went wide. "Are you saying—?"

"Twins," she said happily.

With a cry of joy, he pulled her into his arms and kissed her again and again.

She laughed. "If we keep having babies at this rate, Josie will soon be part of a baseball team. You don't mind?"

"Sounds like paradise." Then, remembering how hard labor had been for her, he asked softly, "You're not afraid?"

Hana tilted her head. "I'll have more scars." She put her hand over her dress, over her belly with its cesarean scar.

Then she smiled. "But that's all right. It's *kintsugi*." She looked up at him, her eyes luminous. "Do you remember?"

Antonio's heart was full. "How could I forget? It's the scars that make things truly beautiful." Cupping her cheek, he looked into her face. "Even more beautiful than when they were new."

Hana's eyes widened, and he saw she was surprised he'd remembered. But he'd never heard anything so accurately explain what life should be.

He looked around them. Cherry blossoms were blooming again. Soon, they'd disappear. But every year, they came back. That was the beauty of life, the promise, the renewal. He'd lost so much in his life. But how much more had he gained?

As Antonio curled into the soft blanket beneath the pink flowering tree, with his chortling baby in his lap and his newly pregnant wife resting her head on his shoulder, he knew that everything he'd lost was a tiny fraction, the merest drop of water, compared to the Pacific Ocean of happiness all around him. And as he kissed his wife tenderly on the forehead, he knew broken hearts, mended and made new, were the strongest and most powerful of all.

* * * * *

COMING SOON!

We really hope you enjoyed reading this book. If you're looking for more romance, be sure to head to the shops when new books are available on

Thursday 20th March

To see which titles are coming soon, please visit **millsandboon.co.uk/nextmonth**

MILLS & BOON

Coming next month

A SCANDAL MADE IN LONDON
Lucy King

'Miss Cassidy?' said the concierge a moment later, his voice bouncing off the walls and making her jump. 'Mr Knox will see you now.'

Finally.

'The lift on the right will take you directly to the penthouse.'

'Thank you,' she said, mustering up a quick smile as she got to her feet and headed for said lift on legs that felt like jelly.

The doors closed behind her and she used the smooth ten-second ascent to try and calm her fluttering stomach and slow her heart-rate. It would be fine. She and Theo were both civilised adults. They might be chalk and cheese, but they could handle this. What was the worst that could happen? It wasn't as if she was expecting anything from him. She just had a message to deliver. It would be fine.

But when the lift doors opened and she stepped out, all thoughts of civility and messages shot from her head because all she could focus on was Theo.

He was standing at the far end of the wide hall, with his back to a huge floor to ceiling window, feet apart, arms crossed over his chest. The interminable rain of the morning had stopped and sunshine had broken through the thick cloud. It flooded in through the window, making a silhouette of him, emphasising his imposing height and the powerful breadth of the shoulders. Although clothed in jeans and a white shirt, he looked like some sort of god, in total control, master of all he surveyed, and she couldn't help thinking that if he'd been going for maximum impact, maximum intimidation, he'd nailed it.

Swallowing down the nerves tangling in her throat, Kate started walking towards him, her hand tightening on the strap of her cross-body bag that she wore like a shield. His gaze was on her as she approached, his expression unreadable. He didn't move a muscle. His jaw was set and he exuded chilly distance, which didn't bode well for what was to come, but then nor did the heat suddenly shooting along her veins and the desire surging through her body. That kind of head-scrambling reaction she could do without. She didn't need to remember how he'd made her feel when he'd held her, kissed her, been inside her. She needed to focus.

'Hi,' she said as she drew closer, his irresistible magnetism tugging her forwards even as she wanted to flee.

'What are you doing here?'

The ice cold tone of his voice stopped her in her tracks a couple of feet away, obliterating the heat, and she inwardly flinched. So that was the way this was going to go. No 'how are you, let me take your jacket, would you like a drink'. He wasn't pleased to see her. He wasn't pleased at all.

Okay.

'We need to talk,' she said, beginning to regret her decision to deliver this information in person. With hindsight, maybe an email would have sufficed.

'There's nothing to talk about.'

'I'm afraid there is.'

His dark brows snapped together. 'Your sister?'

'She's fine,' she said. 'Thank you for what you did for her.'

'You're welcome.'

'Did you get my note?' Shortly after he'd fixed her finances she'd sent him a letter of thanks. It had seemed the least she could do. She hadn't had a response.

He gave a brief nod. 'Yes.'

'She loves the flowers.'

'Good.'

'It was thoughtful.'

'It was nothing.'

Right. Beneath the force of his unwavering gaze and impenetrable demeanour Kate quailed for a moment and was summoning up the courage to continue when he spoke.

'Are you in trouble?' he asked sharply.

'That's one way of putting it.'

'What?'

'Sorry, bad joke,' she said with a weak laugh although there was nothing remotely funny about any of this.

'Get to the point, Kate,' he snapped. 'I'm busy.'

Right. Yes. Good plan. She pulled her shoulders back and lifted her chin. 'There's no easy way to say this, Theo,' she said, sounding far calmer than she felt, 'so here goes. There's been a...*consequence*... to our...afternoon together.'

A muscle ticked in his jaw. 'What kind of consequence?'

'The nine-month kind.'

There was a moment of thundering silence, during which Kate's heart hammered while Theo seemed to freeze and pale. 'What exactly are you saying?' he said, his voice tight and low and utterly devoid of expression.

'I'm pregnant.'

Continue reading
A SCANDAL MADE IN LONDON
Lucy King

Available next month
www.millsandboon.co.uk

LET'S TALK
Romance

For exclusive extracts, competitions
and special offers, find us online:

- facebook.com/millsandboon
- @MillsandBoon
- @MillsandBoonUK

Get in touch on 01413 063232

For all the latest titles coming soon, visit
millsandboon.co.uk/nextmonth